To Jan—

DEADLY
SANCTUARY

Sylvia Nobel

the fun starts here!

**Nite Owl
Books**

11-10-01

Phoenix,
Arizona

Phoenix, Arizona

This is a work of fiction. The characters, incidents, and dialogues are products of the author's imagination and are not to be construed as real. Any resemblance to actual events or persons, living or dead is entirely coincidental.

For information, contact Nite Owl Books
4040 E. Camelback Road, #101
Phoenix, Arizona 85018-2736
(602) 840-0132
1-888-927-9600
FAX (602) 957-1671
e-mail: theniteowl@juno.com
www.niteowlbooks.com

ISBN 0-9661105-7-9

Original cover art by Roger Patterson
Digital retouching by Christy A. Moeller
ATG Productions

Library of Congress Catalog Card Number: 97-75426

To
My loving family and
supportive friends

****

The author also wishes to acknowledge the invaluable assistance of the following people:

The Maricopa County Sheriff's Department
The Yavapai County Sheriff's Department
The Yavapai County Medical Examiner
Maricopa County Sheriff's Posse:
James Langston, Search & Rescue
The Courier, Prescott, Arizona
Richard R. Robertson, Investigative Projects Ed.
The Arizona Republic
Phillip Swift, Ed. *The Wickenburg Sun*
Tumbleweed Home for Troubled Children
Harold Perlman, Pharmacist
Steven Bowley, M.D.
Ronald Junck, Attorney at Law

Deadly Sanctuary—Winner 1999
Arizona Book Publishing Association's
Glyph **Award for**
Best Mystery

Also by Sylvia Nobel
The Devil's Cradle—A Kendall O'Dell Mystery

And writing as Natasha Dunne:

A Scent of Jasmine

1

"Oh...my...God. What have I done?" I murmured aloud, staring transfixed at the barren desert valley below the roadside overlook. No way could this be my new home. No way. As I consulted the Arizona road map once again, a hostile brown wind charged up the steep cliff, whirling my hair into a tangle and filling my eyes with grit.

I began to regret my impulsive decision to take the newspaper job in Castle Valley. But, had there been any choice? All through the drive from Pennsylvania I had tortured myself with 'If onlys.' If only I hadn't been forced to a drier climate because of asthma. If only I hadn't lost my job at the *Philadelphia Inquirer*. If only Grant hadn't lost interest in me. If only, if only...

An odd snuffling, snorting sound made me whirl around and I froze in shock at the sight of six weird-looking creatures approximately the size of large dogs standing between me and the safety of my car.

A tentative step forward caused one of the grayish, bristle-coated animals to let out a bark and clatter its long, sharp fangs. What the devil were these things? They looked ferocious, like something out of a science fiction movie. Heart hammering, I shrank back against the stone retaining wall and edged a glance behind me to the sheer drop. There was no escape unless I suddenly developed the ability to fly.

A surge of panic contracted my chest. Stay calm, I urged myself. The last thing I needed right now was an asthma attack and to make matters worse, I realized that I'd left my inhaler in the car. If only a balky fuel pump hadn't detoured me off the freeway to Prescott for repairs, I wouldn't have even been in this godforsaken spot.

For some strange reason the beasts lost interest in me and dipped their heads to root among the dry weeds, flicking only an occasional wary look at me. Well, Kendall, what more can you do to screw up your life?

As I stood baking in the warm April sunlight, I cringed inwardly remembering how my well-meaning father had oversold my abilities to his old newspaper colleague, convincing him I was already a big time investigative reporter.

"Dad!" I'd whispered fiercely, "You know I was only in research."

He'd cupped his hand over the receiver. "It's not like you have a lot of options, Pumpkin. This place isn't far from Phoenix and he's got an opening. You talk to him." He set the phone against my ear.

"Hi," I said in a small voice. Morton Tuggs intimated that not only would my investigative background be a plus, he also needed someone he could trust. Three weeks prior, he stated, one of his reporters had mysteriously vanished without a trace.

That snagged my interest, but I felt a vague sense of foreboding when he seemed reluctant to answer any further questions on the phone.

"If you decide to take the job," he'd added gruffly, "we'll talk more when you arrive."

That would have been the time to confess my amateur status, but I'd said nothing.

The sound of an approaching vehicle pulled my attention to the road and a surge of relief washed over me when a tan pickup pulling a horse trailer roared into view. I waved my hand and the truck eased to a stop on the far side of the road. Two men got out. The driver, a tall lanky man wearing mirrored sunglasses, strolled toward me then stopped in his tracks and stared.

His older companion limped up behind him and gestured to my Volvo. "You got car trouble?"

I shook my head and pointed. Both men peered around the car, looked back at me, at each other, then broke into wide grins.

"Those pigs botherin' you, little lady?" asked the tall one, tipping the hat off his forehead, his mouth working a piece of gum. There was an unmistakable note of sarcasm in his voice.

Pigs? These hairy, sharp-toothed things were pigs? But why should that surprise me? They were like everything else I'd seen so far in this hot, dusty place: wild, prickly, and ugly.

He stepped forward, clapped his hands, and hollered, "Eeeeyaah!" The animals squealed and galloped away.

He turned back to me and swept the wide brimmed western hat from his head, revealing thick, blue-black hair. With exaggerated flair, he executed an elaborate bow, his smile mocking. "Always glad to assist a delicate damsel in distress." Even though I couldn't see his eyes, I could tell by the slow movement of his head that he was eyeing me from head to foot.

Damsel? Was that how I appeared? Delicate? Weak? Helpless? I squared my jaw. Was it just his macho behavior that irritated me, or the fact that I was burnt out on men altogether? A failed marriage and a broken engagement certainly entitled me to that.

The older man explained that the creatures were wild pigs called javelinas. "They look a mite fearsome, but won't usually hurt you unless you go after their young'uns." A friendly smile creased his sun-leathered face. By the look of their clothing, I gathered I'd come across some genuine Arizona cowboys.

"Should have guessed," the tall stranger said scornfully, pointing to my license plate. "She's a bird."

I bristled. "What do you mean?"

"Snowbird," the other man explained. "You know, tourist. Winter visitor. Folks who come here for the warm weather and then skedaddle."

"But," the contentious one cut in, "not before you people pollute our air, clog up our roads, use up our water, and trash the landscape."

"No offense intended, ma'am." The old cowboy shot a questioning glance at his friend.

But I did feel offended. Without stopping to think, the lie leaped to my tongue. "I am not a snowbird. For your information, I happen to be relocating to Castle Valley. I've accepted a very important...managerial position at their newspaper." I regretted my words immediately and wondered why I should even care what this arrogant man thought.

For a long minute they stared at me in silence, and then the tall cowboy grinned. "Well, now, is that a fact?"

A sharp ringing sound like metal striking metal, and a high whinny from the trailer got both men's immediate attention. "Come on, Jake," said the younger man, "we've wasted enough time. Let's get them back to the ranch." He reached the trailer in long strides, and I could hear him speak in a soothing voice to the horses.

I thanked Jake for his help, adding, "How do you stand him? He's the rudest man I've ever met."

His grin was sheepish. "Oh, don't pay any attention to Bradley. He doesn't mean any harm. Just doesn't like newcomers much, and you look a powerful lot like..."

His words faded as the ground suddenly swirled beneath me. I brushed a hand over my forehead as Jake stepped forward. Grabbing one arm, he led me to sit on a nearby rock in the shade of a scraggly tree. "You got water with you, little lady?" A look of concern deepened the creases around his eyes. "It's real dangerous to be out here without some. People dehydrate in a matter of hours. The desert, it ain't nothing to fool with."

I decided I'd rather die than admit I was an ignorant snowbird. "Yes, I have plenty in the car." He didn't need to know I had only a can of pop.

Bradley shouted from the truck. "Come on, Jake. Let's roll!"

I thanked Jake again for his kindness. He touched the brim of his hat murmuring, "Don't mention it," and limped away.

The dizzy spell behind me, I slumped into the ovenlike interior of my car and downed the last of the warm soda, jumping in alarm when a hand reached through the window on the passenger side.

Bradley dropped a thermos on the seat beside me. "You might need this."

I glared at him. "I'm fine. And anyway, I would have no way of returning this to you since it's highly unlikely we'll ever meet again." The haughty tone in my own voice surprised me.

The corner of his mouth lifted slightly. "It's a small world. You never know." Waving a final salute in my direction, he headed back to the truck. I felt like he'd given me the finger as they pulled away. His bumper sticker read, WELCOME TO ARIZONA. NOW GO HOME!

By the time I reached the sign telling me Castle Valley was fifteen miles away, I'd drunk half the water and was feeling rather foolish. The cowboy had been right after all.

As I slowed for a cattle guard, I noticed a girl alongside the road. It wasn't my habit to stop for hitchhikers, but when she frantically waved her hand, I pulled onto the shoulder and waited as she stooped to pick up her pack.

"Hey, thanks for the ride, lady." She plopped onto the seat beside me. "Jesus, it's hot out, ain't it?" I agreed and tried not to notice that she hadn't been within whistling distance of a shower for some time. "You headin' for Phoenix?"

"No. Just to the next town."

"Oh." A look of resignation flickered across her thin face. "No biggie. I'll get another ride. You care if I smoke?" She flipped a limp blond curl behind one ear.

"I'd rather you didn't," I answered, trying not to stare. Not only did she have a multitude of colorful tattoos, her left ear had been pierced eight or nine times. The array of earrings jingled when she moved.

6

"Hey, no problem." There was a hard edge about her. I noted her ragged jeans and faded T-shirt. What in the world was this girl doing out here in the middle of nowhere? Was she a runaway? She couldn't be more than sixteen. As we continued down the road, she spoke little, staring straight ahead with vacant green eyes.

I dragged my thoughts from the girl to examine my new surroundings. Morton Tuggs had told my father that Castle Valley was a beautiful place, and more healthful than Phoenix for me because it had no smog and was higher in elevation. My initial reaction was one of extreme disappointment. What a dinky town. It looked old and dilapidated, not at all what I'd imagined. A sign read: Population 5000. I wondered if that included the wildlife, as a prairie dog skipped across the road in front of me.

At least the sunset was gorgeous. It lit the sky in shades of red and orange, tinting the rock wall to the east a brilliant gold.

I stopped near the Greyhound Bus station, pressed a twenty dollar bill into the girl's hand, and suggested there might be a church or shelter where she could spend the night. She thanked me and got out, saying the money would come in handy since she was headed for Texas. As I watched her walk away, I suddenly felt lucky. Unlike her, I'd be staying at a cozy motel tonight and I had a job waiting.

The following day, I rose early, downed my asthma medication, and prayed the dry weather would cure me swiftly.

As I drove toward town, I wondered how I would survive in this place. The newspaper building looked just like the rest of the downtown area. Old and weatherbeaten.

The receptionist at the *Castle Valley Sun* greeted me with a dimpled smile, and introduced herself as Ginger King. She seemed delighted to hear that I might be joining the staff and took my elbow in a friendly manner while ushering me to Morton Tugg's office which was situated at the end of a short hallway.

I couldn't help but notice the smudged walls and frayed carpet as we reached the open doorway. From inside, a loud voice boomed, "The hell you say?" Hesitating, I turned questioning eyes to Ginger. "Don't fret none, sugar pie," she soothed, patting my hand. "His bark's a mite worse than his bite. Y'all can set yerself right there in front of his desk." Giggling, she gave me a little shove forward.

The bald, red-faced man seated at the incredibly cluttered desk waved me in while continuing to harangue whomever was at the other end of the phone.

The wooden chair wobbled on uneven legs when I sat. Clutching my purse in my lap, I surveyed the room. It was crowded and shabby, relieved only by bright travel posters adorning the walls. Then my gaze fell on Morton Tuggs.

"I wish I'd never let you talk me into this god-damned thing," he shouted, thumping the computer monitor. He didn't have hair one on the crown of his head, but as he listened intently, his fingers absently fluffed, then pressed flat, the tufts of fuzz perched over his ears like gray cotton balls. "I don't give a rat's ass what you say, just get the hell over here and fix it!" The phone dinged when he slammed down the receiver.

After a few breaths to compose himself, he threw me an apologetic smile. "Sorry about that." He reached out a welcoming hand. "So, you're Kendall O'Dell? Good to meet you. I see you got Bill's red hair. Quite a guy your dad. I guess he told you the story?" His brown eyes looked solemn, faraway. I took his hand, knowing he must be remembering the day my dad had saved his life when they'd both been foreign correspondents during the Vietnam War. "It's nice to finally meet you too, Mr. Tuggs." His other hand swiped impatiently at the air. "Tugg. Tugg. Everybody calls me Tugg." A hint of humor lit his face. "Except when they're calling me Tugboat behind my back." I smiled, finally relaxing. We talked for a few minutes about what my routine assignments would be, the fact that his wife Mary had located several houses for me to look at and other general subjects.

During a lull in the conversation, I shifted uncomfortably in my chair. Was I wrong, or was Morton Tuggs deliberately avoiding the subject I most wanted to discuss? I cleared my throat. "You said on the phone you needed someone with my investigative background and someone you could trust. Do you want to tell me about this missing reporter?"

A look of anxiety etched his face. Instead of answering, he rose, shut the door, and returned to his desk where he laced his fingers in front of him. "I have to tell you that I've agonized for several weeks over how to handle this. It was my intent to have you look into it but, under the circumstances...perhaps it would be best not to pursue the matter further."

I eyed him suspiciously. He wasn't behaving very much like the hard-boiled newspaper editor my father had described. "A man doesn't vanish for no reason. What did the police report say?"

"There was a search. It was called off last week. I've pressed, but there doesn't seem much interest in

9

pursuing the case. The official line coming down is that he probably just got bored with our little burg and skipped."

"What do you think?"

Tugg absentmindedly fluffed the patches of hair again. "John Dexter wasn't real well liked. He delighted in digging up dirt on people. Go through some of the back issues and you'll see what I mean. He had a knack for really pissing people off. But," he added, "even though he was sort of flaky at times, I can't believe he'd just up and go with no notice."

"So, I'll talk to the police and see what I can come up with. Perhaps there's a lead they've missed."

"No!"

I jumped as his fist crashed on the desk. Then, noting my obvious shock, he said, "I'm sorry. I didn't mean to startle you…it's just that…I'm not sure giving you this assignment would be the right thing to do."

Butterflies fluttered in my stomach. The major reason for my trip, resurrecting my aborted career, was fading before my eyes. "I'd appreciate a shot at this."

He swiveled in his chair and stared silently at the poster of Greece. After a minute he said quietly, "If you decide to work on this, it'll have to be strictly on the Q.T. Nobody else can know, and I'd caution you to be very, very careful."

His attitude disturbed me. It wasn't what he was saying, it was what he wasn't saying.

"Mr. Tuggs, Tugg…" I tried to keep the irritation from my voice. "You're going to have to level with me on this or I don't see how I can help. If you suspect foul play, which I gather you do, why aren't the police pursuing it, and why aren't you pushing for answers?"

As if struggling mightily with a difficult decision, he dropped his eyes and drummed his fingers on the desk. Abruptly, he pulled open a drawer and extracted a ragged piece of paper. He stared at it, chewing his lower lip. "John called me at home the afternoon before he disappeared. We were having a big get-together for my daughter and it was so noisy I was having trouble hearing him. I wish now I'd paid more attention 'cause I only remember bits and pieces of what he said." He sighed heavily. "Something about meeting a girl later. Her information would tie into what he'd been working on earlier in the week, and if he was right, it would blow the lid off this town." He stopped, rubbed his temples as if in pain, then continued. "He'd been going through some files over at the sheriff's office and told me he'd discovered something weird. I'm not sure if there's any connection, but, I found this in his desk a couple of days ago."

I studied the smudged paper he handed me. In between a profusion of doodling, I read the scattered phrases: Med records gone. Both cases. Dead teens. T prof...Connection? Possible cover up?

Before I could speak he added, "One more thing. And, this is a doozy, the part that's really got me boxed into a corner. The last thing he said before he hung up was, "'Whatever you do, don't mention this to Roy.'"

I looked up. "Who's Roy?"

The pained expression again. "My goddamned brother-in-law."

It was frustrating having to drag every word from him. "So?"

"He owns half this newspaper and...he's the sheriff."

2

I left Morton Tuggs' office, my head still reeling from his disturbing revelations, and trotted after Ginger, who'd been charged with familiarizing me with the layout. For the moment, I pushed the John Dexter puzzle to the back of my mind.

In the paper-littered production room, I shook hands with Harry, a big, burly man with coffee stains on his T-shirt, and then Rick, who peered at me owlishly through thick, horn-rimmed glasses. Lupe and Al, busy on the phones with classifieds, flashed preoccupied smiles. While Ginger prattled on, filling my head with endless personal statistics about each employee, I strained to maintain an expression of interest. The place was much smaller than I had imagined.

"And this here's your office." She gave a grand sweep of her hand.

Inwardly, I cringed in dismay at the sight of the dingy room crammed with several filing cabinets and three scarred desks topped with piles of clutter. Two smeary windows faced east overlooking the parking lot.

"Jim's out on assignment, but I see Tally's still here. He writes all the sports goodies." She nodded toward a man hunched over a desk in the far corner with his back to us, the phone cradled on his shoulder. A playful lilt edged her words as she sang out, "Hey, darlin'! Y'all turn 'round here and say 'howdy' to your new roommate."

Apparently absorbed on the phone, he didn't acknowledge us, so I told Ginger I'd meet him later. No sooner were the words spoken when he swiveled his chair around and stood to face us. Our eyes met, and my mouth sagged open as a jolt of recognition shot through me. It couldn't be! There in front of me clad in boots, jeans, and a checkered shirt, stood the tall, lanky cowboy from yesterday. The pig chaser.

Once again, he bowed deeply. "Bradley Talverson at your service...again, ma'am." His lips twisted in a wry smile as he motioned toward a tiny, metal desk. "I hope you'll find the...ah...accommodations here in the executive office to your liking."

With a chill of embarrassment, I remembered my fabricated tale of an important managerial position. So, that's why he'd acted the way he had. He must have thought I was a complete ass and I had no doubt my face was as red as it felt. The expression in his dark eyes challenged me to react. For what seemed an eternity, I wrestled with disbelief, regret and irritation. There seemed only one right thing to do. I laughed.

A look of surprise flitted over his lean face. "Well," he chuckled, widening his stance and folding his arms across his chest. "I'm glad to see you have a sense of humor."

Ginger regarded the two of us with astonishment. "Y'all know each other?"

"In a manner of speaking," he told her, and I couldn't help but notice his eyes brushing over me again. We parted on a handshake and my promise to return his thermos in the morning.

As I moved to the front door, I could tell by the look on Ginger's face that she was dying to know how we'd met. But I'd have to tell her some other time. Tugg had arranged for me to meet his wife, Mary at her realty office, and I was already late.

En route to the address, I thought about the rest of my conversation with Tugg. The newspaper had been owned by his wife's family for many years and her father had been editor up until four years ago when ill health forced him to retire. Under pressure, Tugg had given up a good position at the *Arizona Republic* in Phoenix and relocated to Castle Valley. He'd found the *Sun* in sorry shape and deeply in debt. A large infusion of cash was needed to keep it afloat, but no lending institutions were interested. Help had finally come from within the family. Roy Hollingsworth, recently married to Mary's twin sister, Faye, had advanced the money.

"You can see why I haven't been able to pursue this myself," Tugg had said glumly. "I'm between that rock and hard place you always hear about. Can you imagine what would happen if the paper accused Roy of dragging his feet on this investigation? If he pulls his financial support, we're sunk, not to mention that Mary would probably divorce me."

I asked him the best way to approach the subject with his brother-in-law.

"With caution," he warned. "Roy's not a man to piss off. He's got a hard head, a short temper, and," Tugg emphasized with a scowl, "he carries a gun. Just remember that." Ushering me toward the door, he'd apologized for placing me in such a delicate spot, but felt with my background I'd be able to dig up something without being discovered. Once again, the opportunity had come for me to declare my amateur status, and, as before, I thought better of it.

"Why don't you just hire a private detective or something? That way there'd be no tie to the newspaper."

He looked weary. "I'm barely collecting a salary now. Where would I get fifty bucks an hour to hire one?"

As I parked the car at the Castle Valley Realty office, I had more than a few misgivings about my decision to accept the position.

Mary Tuggs welcomed me with a beaming smile as I stepped inside her office. "I'm so very glad to meet you."

At five foot eight, I towered over her tiny, round frame. "My goodness, aren't you a sight! You remind me of a young Katharine Hepburn."

That clinched it. I decided I liked Mary Tuggs a lot. Outside again, I wondered if she'd need a leg up as we approached her red Bronco. Somehow she scrambled into the driver's seat without assistance. She showed me several unremarkable dwellings nearby, renting for astronomical prices, and then, noting my dismay, suggested a place located five miles north of town. "Morty thought you might like to at least look at it," she said, swinging onto the main highway. "But I'm not sure you'll want to be so far from town."

She told me that the three-bedroom, two bath house was vacant because the elderly owner, Teresa Delgado, was in a Phoenix nursing home recovering from a fall. Afraid of vandalism, she wanted Mary to find a trustworthy renter to occupy it until she returned. "It's been empty for a month now, so she's lowered the rent to get someone in there," she added.

"Sounds interesting," I replied, watching the cactus -covered landscape fly past. There wasn't another house in sight when we turned east and bounced along a rutted dirt road, leaving a plume of swirling dust in our wake.

"This is Lost Canyon Road," Mary informed me. "You'll be quite close to the Castle."

"Castle?"

She laughed and rolled her eyes. "Silly me. Of course you wouldn't know yet. That's Castle Rock," she said, pointing toward a mammoth, multi-colored rock formation. "It was named 'Castillo del Viento' by Spanish settlers. It means castle of the wind, isn't that pretty?"

I agreed and we'd just dipped into a dry sandy riverbed she called a 'wash' and were rounding a turn on the opposite hill, when she suddenly wrenched the wheel to the right. A black Mercedes with heavily tinted windows roared by leaving us in a choking cloud of dust.

My heart racing madly, I wheezed and reached for my inhaler.

"I'm so sorry!" White-faced, she pressed one hand to her chest. "What a maniac. He didn't even slow down." She shoved the truck into gear, grumbling, "That had to be someone from Serenity House. Except for the Hinkle Ranch a couple miles south of Tess's place, no one else lives out this way."

I took a few deep breaths and let the bitter-tasting medication seep slowly into my lungs. "What's Serenity House?"

16

She slanted me a sidelong glance. "Well...it's a mental hospital."

That captured my attention. "No kidding? What's it doing out here in the middle of the desert?"

"The property was cheap. It's on the site of an old Spanish monastery which was crumbling to ruins. Some developer restored it and tried to make a go of it as a health spa. When that failed, a psychiatrist named Isadore Price bought it about six years ago." She pursed her lips into a thin line. "That was probably his Mercedes."

"I hope he's a better doctor than he is a driver."

Mary frowned. "He's kind of a peculiar old bird. Keeps to himself mostly. I've only seen him a few times in town at a couple of social gatherings."

"Have there ever been any problems at this place?"

"To be honest, there was an incident right after they opened. One of the male patients escaped. He'd chopped up his family or something."

I shivered involuntarily.

"This town's never seen such excitement!" Her face became animated at the memory. "There was a huge manhunt, and everyone was pretty much on pins and needles until they found him. After that, a real high fence was built, and from what I've heard it's very well guarded. Nothing else has ever happened."

"How far is it from the Delgado place?"

"About two miles or so. And, of course, that's the whole idea of having it so secluded." She glanced at me again. "If it bothers you, I can turn around right now."

"No. I'd still like to see it."

"Okay," she said, steering onto another dirt road named Pajaro del Suspiro. Explaining it was Spanish for 'Weeping Bird,' she braked the truck in front of a brick-red ranch-style wooden house surrounded by golden palo verde trees and saguaro cactus.

I got out and took a sniff of the warm, pristine air. Yep. Just what the doctor ordered. I followed Mary up the stone walkway and when she pointed to the giant rock formation, I stopped in amazement. It did resemble a castle and the effect was breathtaking.

While she fiddled with the door key, I listened to the lonesome keening of the wind and wondered if I could stand to live in such isolation. My misgivings faded as she led me through the spacious interior, decorated in bright Southwestern colors and heavy, Spanish-style furniture. It was a gigantic improvement over the cramped apartment I'd just left in Philadelphia, and far cheaper. I expressed surprise that she'd had difficulty keeping it rented.

"The trouble is," Mary said, showing me through the sunny kitchen, "most renters want a signed lease, and Tess won't have it because she wants the freedom to return on short notice. That's the minus, but," she added with a cheery smile, "here's a plus. The last tenants left in such a hurry, I never got a chance to refund their deposit. So, if you decide to take it, the first month would be free."

"I like the free part, but, what does the 'left in a hurry' part mean?"

Mary opened the front door. "They called me out of the blue late one night, and announced they were leaving right then and there."

"Why?"

There was no mistaking her tone of skepticism. "Tess certainly never mentioned it, but...they swore this place was haunted."

3

Fascinated by Mary's intriguing remark, I chose to put aside my misgivings and move in. The proliferation of insects that trooped in and out of the Delgado house the first few days bothered me more than the supposed phantom. I'd always considered myself fairly brave for a woman, having no particular fear of snakes, mice, or bats. But, when it came to insects, spiders especially, I turned into a shivering coward. There seemed to be an abundance of the eight legged creatures about, plus scorpions, centipedes, and humongous roaches. At my request, Mary sent the exterminator.

On his second visit in three days, overall clad, grizzle-faced, Lloyd "Skeeter" Jenkins of the Bugs-Be-Gone Exterminating Company, told me all I needed to know, and more, about the insects and rodents indigenous to the great state of Arizona.

"Now I kin git rid o' them pesky mice fer ya, an' the powder I'll lay down'll keep them centipedes and scorpions on their toes, so to speak. Spiders is something else again.

Them suckers kin walk right over the stuff with them long legs o' theirs."

He left me with the sage advice to "never put yer shoes on in the mornin' till you've whopped 'em good. There's no tellin' what kinda critter mighta moved in an' set up housekeepin' durin' the night."

I wondered if I'd ever get used to the bugs, the dust, and the scalding sun. The calendar said it was still April but I could have sworn spring had been canceled and we'd gone right into summer as it was already in the 90's. My asthma had improved, but I was miserably hot.

"Don't you worry, sugar," Ginger had soothed hearing my complaint, "as soon as your blood thins, y'all will git used to it." I wasn't sure I wanted my blood to thin.

My first week on the job was an exercise in frustration and adaptation. The *Sun*, a sixteen page tabloid, was published only twice weekly, Wednesdays and Saturdays. I sorely missed the daily deadlines, the lively newsroom chatter, and stimulation of the big city. I knew I couldn't go back to damp, cool Pennsylvania and face a life of being incapacitated, yet I didn't want to stay either.

My other co-worker—young, blond, brash and not overly bright Jim Sykes—didn't sympathize with my position. He grabbed all the interesting assignments while I got the leftovers. If I had to cover one more banquet, Ladies Club function, or write one more article about who was visiting whom from out of town, I felt I'd go nuts.

After banging my knee on the narrow desk for the third time that morning, I grumbled, "I hate this damn thing."

Bradley Talverson swiveled around at my remark, and taunted me with a crooked grin. "Welcome to the club. We all started at the rookie desk. Now it's your turn."

"Yeah," young Sykes joined in. "Now that Johnny boy's split, you're low man on the totem pole."

I glanced swiftly from one to the other. Neither man seemed particularly disturbed by his disappearance, and I reminded myself again that even they could not know of my secret assignment. I phrased my question carefully, trying to sound indifferent. "Oh, yeah. What was he like? John Dexter, I mean?"

Bradley's eyes narrowed. "All hat and no cattle."

I raised an eyebrow. "Come again?"

"He was a pain in the ass. Interested only in trash journalism."

"But he was real popular with the ladies. Married or single, right Tally?" Jim's eyes gleamed wickedly.

I knew there was some significance to the remark by the deadly expression on Bradley's face before he turned his back to us. His constant mood swings puzzled me. Sometimes he was cordial and friendly. At other times, withdrawn, angry almost, as if he were struggling with some inner demon. More than once, I'd caught him looking at me with an unreadable expression in his dark eyes.

Anxious to pursue the subject of John Dexter, I had just formulated my next question when Ginger stuck her head in the doorway. "Come on, sugar, let's shake it. Time for lunch."

Damn! If only she had waited five minutes. Bradley and Jim resumed their work; my chance for more questions gone for now.

As we walked the three blocks to the Iron Skillet, I silently thanked God for Ginger King who'd unabashedly inserted herself into the vacant slot in my life marked: friend. Short and round with light brown hair and sparkling ginger-colored eyes, she bubbled over with good humor. She was also a hopeless gossip. Endearing, but hopeless.

Three days earlier, during our first lunch together, she'd shrieked with laughter when I recounted my story of meeting Bradley, whose close friends called him Tally, she informed me. I learned about her family, her life in Texas, and her heartfelt desire to settle down and have children.

"How old are you, sugar?"

"Twenty-eight."

"Well, y'all still have some time. I'm gonna be thirty-three next month, and eligible men in this town are scarcer than hen's teeth."

Mingled between anecdotes about the good citizens of Castle Valley, she skillfully extracted large chunks of my background.

"I got married right after college, but it barely lasted two years."

"Oh, that's a shame." For a few seconds her expression was sympathetic, then it turned impish. "So, what happened? He beat ya? Chase other women? Was he gay?"

I laughed. "I think you've been watching too many talk shows. Sorry to disappoint you, but it was nothing so dramatic. I'd been working at my dad's newspaper since I could read and could do every job there practically in my sleep.

"I was restless, ready to move on and my husband was studying to be a pharmacist. His plans included us staying in Spring Hill, complete with picket fence and a dozen kids. Mine didn't. Neither of us could change, so we parted friends. He got the dog, and I took my maiden name back."

Throughout the remainder of the meal, she'd pressed me for further details, and it was amusing to hear some of the things I'd told her, repeated by other staff members the following day. Some details were embellished almost beyond recognition.

With that in mind now, as we entered the restaurant and slid into the red vinyl booth, I vowed to talk less of myself and concentrate on extracting information from her.

"Oh, lookee here," she cried, eyeing the menu with regret. "Chicken and dumplin's. And me on a stupid diet again."

"Go ahead and have it if you want it."

She drew back in mock horror. "Easy for you to say, being skinny as a rail. Food don't go to my stomach, darlin'. Everything goes right here," she complained, patting her hips.

We were both giggling when a chestnut-haired woman interrupted, asking for our order. "Oh, Lucy," Ginger gushed, a sly expression stealing over her features, "this here's Kendall O'Dell. Kendall, this here's Lucinda Johns. She and her Aunt Polly own this place."

When I told her how much I'd enjoyed the previous lunch, she smiled and thanked me. As she took our orders, I couldn't help but notice her enormous bustline. It made me feel positively flat.

"Kendall's our new gal on the beat over yonder at the paper. Ain't that nice?" The syrupy tone of Ginger's voice surprised me.

Curious, I glanced at her, then back to Lucinda in time to see her smile shrink. "I see. Congratulations." She cast a speculative glance at me before turning away.

A mischievous light gleamed in Ginger's eyes. "Okay," I demanded, "what was that little scene all about?

You might as well have told her I have AIDS by the way she acted."

"I just wanted to see if she'd act jealous."

"Jealous of whom?"

She studied her fingertips. "You."

"Me? Why?"

"'Cause she's had her eye on Tally since grade school. Her knowing y'all are there practically sitting in his lap all day'll keep her on her toes."

"I'm surprised at you. That was downright catty."

"I can't help myself."

"Well, she needn't worry. I'm totally burnt out on the male sex at this moment."

She cocked her head in question, so I told her the barest details about my shattered romance with Grant Jamerson, glossing over most of the painful details. "It was for the best, however. He'd have made a lousy husband."

As the noisy lunch crowd filled the room, I watched Lucinda and another waitress scurry from table to table. Five minutes later, she set the plates down in front of us without a word and managed the barest of smiles before rushing away.

I shook my head sadly. "Shame on you, Ginger. I've only been here nine days, and already I have a mortal enemy."

"Oh, flapdoodle. She'd have found out about y'all eventually any hoot. She keeps pretty close tabs on him."

I dug into my tuna salad. "So, they're an item?"

"If Tally was willing, she'd drag him to the preacher tomorrow. He's quite a catch y'know."

Ignoring her implication, I buttered a roll and yawned my disinterest. "To each his own, I guess."

"A gal could do worse."

I stopped eating. "Forget it, Ginger. I don't mean to sound condescending, but I can do better than a hired ranch hand."

She choked on her sandwich. "Ranch hand! Didn't anybody tell you? He and his family own the Starfire. It's one of the biggest dang cattle ranches in the state."

I felt like my chin was going to hit the table. The sparkle in Ginger's eyes reflected her enjoyment.

"Well, what's he doing working at that two bit...I mean at the paper?"

"He ain't been there but two years. He needed to git his mind off of what happened, I guess." A dreamy look came over her face. "It musta pert near stopped his heart when he laid eyes on you the first time."

"Why?"

"With all that flaming red hair? He's gotta be thinking of his wife, Stephanie."

I'm sure my face looked incredulous. "If he's married, why should Lucinda be jealous of me?"

"He ain't married no more. Stephanie's dead as a doornail. Rode out one stormy night on one of them prize appaloosa horses of his and got throwed off. Died of a broken neck, she did." It was obvious by the satisfied gleam in her eyes that she was relishing every word.

"No kidding?"

"Yep. But that ain't the half of it." She lowered her voice. "Now, I ain't one for carryin' tales, but some folks 'round here didn't think it was no accident, including our very own John Dexter."

"Really? And, what did he think?"

"That Tally killed her."

4

Ginger's remark blew me away. While the disclosure about Bradley was shocking, more intriguing yet was John Dexter's connection.

"Okay, you've got my undivided attention. Why did he suspect Bradley had anything to do with her death?"

She opened her mouth to speak when a loud voice from across the room cut her off. I turned to see Lucinda blocking the exit of a rather disheveled looking teen-ager clad in ragged jeans and tank top.

"This ain't a charity dining room. I'm sick to death of you free loaders jumping off the bus and coming in here to order up a meal you can't pay for!" She hustled the girl out the door. "You want a free meal, get your butt to the shelter three blocks over."

The teen cast a spiteful glance at Lucinda before slinking away, and I couldn't help but think of the pathetic young girl I'd picked up last week.

For a few seconds, the room was bathed in silence, and then one grizzled customer drawled, "Aw, Lucy. Now what'd you go an' do that for? She looked real pitiful, like a starved pup. You're not gonna go broke sharin' a sandwich with the kid." That brought a hoot of laughter from the man's companions.

Lucinda fixed him with a formidable glare. "You mind your own business, Elwood. I wouldn't care if it was just once in a while, but this is getting real old. It seems like every ragamuffin runaway in the country makes a beeline for my place. I can't afford to feed all of them. Let that Phillips woman do her job." With that she dusted her hands together and marched behind the counter.

"Poor little things," Ginger sighed, her expression troubled. "My sister Bonnie was showing me a magazine article just last week. They're called throwaway kids." Her voice got lower, more confidential. "As young as eleven or twelve they're turning tricks for food and money. Ain't that jest shameful?"

"Awful. What shelter is Lucinda talking about?"

In between bites of her sandwich, she told me about the Desert Harbor Shelter located in a "big ol'" house on Tumbleweed, and run by a woman named Claudia Phillips. "I heard tell the place operates on a shoestring. She can't do a whole lot but give them kids some food and clothes and a place to stay a spell." Then, with an ominous tone, she added, "Them are the lucky ones. Some of them little gals just plum vanish. Poof!"

"Vanish?"

"White slave traders."

"What are you talking about?"

"It was in all the papers. This gang was taking blue-eyed blonde gals and selling 'em to them people over yonder for their harems or some such thing."

"Oh, Ginger, get real."

"I swear on my mama's Bible! And then there was that bunch in Mexico snatching 'em up for human sacrifices."

Impatient to return to the previous subject, I steered the conversation back to John Dexter's suspicions about Bradley.

"Oh, yeah. Well, as I was sayin'..." She glanced at her watch and wailed, "Good Lord, it's almost one o'clock. Tugg's gonna have my fanny in a crack if I'm late again! I gotta scoot."

Twice now in two hours I'd let myself get sidetracked. "Wait a minute! You can't just drop a bombshell like that and then leave me hanging."

"Sorry, sugar. Lookee here. Why don't y'all come on over to supper tomorrow night? I'll rustle up a pot of my famous Texas chili, some homemade cornbread, and fill in the rest."

"Okay."

She scribbled her address on a napkin and bolted out the door.

Aware that I had twenty minutes to kill before covering another terminally boring meeting at City Hall, I stepped outside, squinting into the glaring sunlight. I'd walked only a few feet from the door when one of Ginger's remarks struck me. Had I been so busy concentrating on what John Dexter had to do with Bradley's wife that I'd missed something important? Plopping down on the nearby shaded bus bench I pulled out the note Tugg had given me and read it again, zeroing in on the phrase, "dead teens."

I flipped open my notepad. In the center of the page, I drew a circle, wrote John Dexter's name in the middle, and then extended lines outward like bicycle spokes. On each line I placed one of the statements in the note, then leaned back against the hard wooden backrest to study it, only vaguely aware of people and traffic.

Was I way off base or could there be some connection between the dead teens and the runaways Ginger spoke of? Dexter had referred to something odd in some files at the sheriff's office. Were they the same ones he'd mentioned in the note?

I blew out a long breath. Obviously, I had my work cut out for me. On a new page, I made a note to go through past issues of the *Sun* and study the stories Dexter had written on the two cases. Step two would be the doozy; tactfully asking to see the files without agitating Roy Hollingsworth whom I'd finally met for the first time the previous Friday. Tugg had assigned me to cover the police blotter, or log as they called it. That would put me in the sheriff's office at least once a week.

I'd been surprised when I met Roy. From Tugg's description, I had expected to encounter a thoroughly uncooperative, disagreeable, perhaps even dangerous man. He appeared to be none of those, greeting me with a wide smile and a neighborly handshake. Standing well over six feet tall, his substantial stomach protruding over a gigantic turquoise belt buckle, he looked less like an adversary than he did a big, friendly bear. In uniform.

As we chatted, I couldn't help but stare at his curious eyebrows. They were light blonde, very fuzzy, and perched over his silver blue eyes like two giant caterpillars. I hid my surprise when he brought up the subject of John Dexter.

"Morty's been real unhappy with me over our manhunt for John Dexter, but as I tried to tell him, we can't produce the man out of thin air. Me and Deputy Potts, along with members of the sheriff's posse and other law enforcement agencies, combed this area for weeks and couldn't find a trace of him." Shrugging his aggravation, he added, "It's been real frustrating for me, too."

He was very convincing. I began to wonder if Tugg was on the wrong track. "I'm sure we'll hear from him sooner or later. When did you last see him?"

"Julie," he shouted. "Pull the file on John Dexter for me." Moments later, a slender, dark-haired girl appeared from another room and handed him a folder. The sheriff rifled through it as Julie and I exchanged introductions.

"He disappeared on March 29th, and I may have been the last person in town to see him. The reason I know that is because I wrote him a speeding ticket that day."

Tugg hadn't told me that. "Where did you ticket him?"

"Heading south on 89 toward Phoenix. He seemed real nervous when I stopped him. Agitated. He was...well, let's say, verbally abusive, but for John that wasn't out of character." He smiled wryly. "So you see, I don't think anything unusual happened to John. I think he had something else going. Why he didn't give Morty notice, I don't know." When he frowned, the two blond caterpillars fused together into one.

While he shuffled papers into the file, I decided either he was being quite up front with me or he was a remarkably good actor. He'd ushered me to the door, inviting me to come anytime or call him if I had any questions. Because he'd been so damned likable, it would make my job all the harder.

A car backfire jolted me back to the present. I closed the notebook and rose stiffly from the bus bench. The meeting ran for over two hours, and it was late afternoon when I returned to the newspaper office. Ginger greeted me with a smile reminding me again of dinner the following evening. I hauled out three boxes of back issues of the paper to take home with me.

The wind was blowing across the desert floor, whipping up funnels of yellow dust when I reached the house. Before going inside, I paused as I always did to admire the spectacle of Castle Rock. Ever changeable, depending on the angle of the sun, it glowed in shades of peach and burnished copper.

After an early dinner, I phoned my parents. They seemed pleased I was settling in. Dad asked about my job, Morton Tuggs, and my asthma. With forced enthusiasm, I told them about my new life and promised to call them again soon. As I hung up the phone, a sharp pang of homesickness enveloped me. To ward off the blues, I turned up the television and cleaned the kitchen.

Still filled with restless energy, I went outside to sweep the walkway and water the small front garden filled with a bright orange sea of desert poppies. The sound of a vehicle made me look up. The black Mercedes I'd seen the first day purred down Lost Canyon Road followed by a white van. Was that perhaps my nearest neighbor, Dr. Price? I'd been meaning to check out Serenity House for days now, but hadn't had the time. I decided a nice long walk would do me good. Mary Tuggs had said it was about two miles away, so I should be back before dark.

It was so quiet I could hear my tennis shoes crunching on the rocky road. Except for the birds and an occasional gust of wind, nothing disturbed the silence.

When I reached a fork in the road, I chose the left which looked well traveled. The right fork, overgrown with tall grass and tumbleweeds, snaked off into the desert. I slowed my footsteps as I approached a large sign with bold red letters announcing: DANGER! NO UNAUTHORIZED PERSONNEL BEYOND THIS POINT. The high fence topped with jagged coils of razor wire looked ominous, but in a way it made me feel secure to know it was there. For a fleeting second, visions of violent ax-wielding mental patients flashed through my mind like scenes from a cheap horror movie. "Don't be stupid," I muttered under my breath. I'd read that many of the new drugs did an excellent job of subduing patients.

I peered through the chain-link fence. Enclosed inside a second fence I spotted the top of an ancient bell tower. Patches of red tile roofs and white stucco buildings were visible among the groves of palms and cottonwood trees. It looked quite peaceful and not at all threatening.

Then, seemingly from out of nowhere, two enormous Dobermans rushed to the fence, eyes gleaming, teeth snapping, their throaty barks echoing through the stillness. My heart pounded as I jumped back. Without hesitation, I retreated. All during the walk home, the memory of the dogs' snarling faces kept me in a state of watchful anxiety.

Sometime during the night, the wind kicked up again. It whistled around under the eaves and rattled the windows. For hours, I thrashed about restlessly. When I finally did fall into a deep sleep I kept having the same annoying dream over and over. A voice kept calling for me to get out. "Get out. Get out."

The persistent phrase was so irritating, I finally opened my eyes. Then I heard it again. Was I awake or still dreaming?

"Get out!" The voice was quite distinct that time. This was no dream! Pulse racing, I sat bolt upright in bed and stared at the partially open arcadia door. "Who's out there?"

Besides the murmur of the wind rustling through the trees, I thought I heard footsteps disappearing into the distance.

5

Moonlight, bright and harsh, lit the patio area and the vast desert landscape beyond, in cold blue tones. Wind-tossed cottonwoods joined waving fan palms to send lacy shadows dancing across the table and scattered lawn chairs. My heart hammered in my ears as I stood in the doorway searching for the reason I was now awake. I snapped on the back patio light and called out again, "Okay, who's out here?"

Not really expecting an answer, I listened intently, hearing only the branches of the palo verde tree scratching against the side of the house. The effect was definitely eerie, and I was more aware than ever of my total isolation.

After I'd closed and locked the door, I reached for my inhaler. Several deep breaths of the medication loosened the tightness in my chest, bringing a semblance of calm. Perhaps the former tenants believed in ghosts, but I didn't. The first thing that came to mind was perhaps there had been another escape from Serenity House. That thought was definitely unsettling.

The digital clock glowed 2:30. Sleep was now out of the question, so I brewed myself a pot of strong coffee and settled down to read past issues of the *Sun*. Might as well make use of the unexpected time.

Three cups of coffee later, I found what I'd been looking for. The first body, unearthed the previous June, had been so badly decomposed, the medical examiner's report stated that cause of death and positive identification was probably impossible. He'd placed the age of the girl, based on the few skeletal remains, at somewhere between thirteen and eighteen years of age.

The second body, discovered in late September hadn't been positively identified until last month. Fifteen year old Charity Perkins from Tulsa, Oklahoma had been in trouble with the law and was a chronic runaway. Apparently, she'd become lost and fallen into a rocky wash. After two shaken ranch hands had reported the find, the autopsy revealed a sharp blow to the skull, presumably due to her fall. Homicide was not ruled out, but no trace of foul play, nor any link between the two deaths had ever surfaced.

John Dexter's last article insinuated that because of misplaced evidence by someone in the sheriff's office, the data from the second girl had not been entered into the NCIC (National Crime Information Center), therefore hindering positive identification. He'd hinted none too subtly that the job had been bungled. It wasn't hard to see why he'd been disliked. Some of his pieces were malicious and dangerously close to being libelous. I wondered why Tugg hadn't taken him to task.

I rejected the thought of a fourth cup of coffee and pulled out my notebook, adding the name of the one girl onto the spoke for dead teens and a question mark for the other. If both these events were accidental, was I on the right track, or did John's cryptic note refer to different cases?

The melancholy cooing of mourning doves alerted me to the fact that it was dawn. I yawned widely. It was almost time to get ready for work, but as I began to bundle the newspapers back into the box, curiosity concerning one of Ginger's remarks overcame me.

I rifled though the papers in the last box until one headline shrieked up at me: Wife of Local Rancher Killed! The photo underneath made my scalp prickle. It's said that everyone has a twin somewhere in the world and while Stephanie Talverson was not that, there was a definite resemblance between us. Our noses were different, hers more pug, mine more aquiline, and she didn't have my cleft chin. Our eyes were similar, but the hair was the most startling feature. We wore the same loose, curly style, but because the photo was black and white, I couldn't tell if it was the same shade as mine.

I looked up and stared out the window at the glowing horizon, now understanding the startled look Bradley had worn when we'd met. He must think of her whenever he looked at me.

My assignment sheet was full when I arrived at the office. Lack of sleep left me groggy and lightheaded all day, and even during the busiest moments, the previous night's episode bothered me.

By late afternoon I had a throbbing headache. Behind me, I heard Bradley hang up his phone. With Jim gone, the room grew silent. Since hearing Ginger's damning revelation, his presence had made me slightly jumpy, although the idea of him being a murderer seemed preposterous. Even though I didn't know him all that well, he just didn't seem to fit the part. Nevertheless, I'd had difficulty meeting his eyes all day.

I sneaked a sideways glance toward him and froze when he turned in his chair and caught me. I averted my eyes immediately.

"What's going on with you? And don't tell me you haven't been staring at me oddly all day."

"I don't know what you're talking about," I snapped back. I could hardly say, 'Excuse me, but did you murder your wife?'

He rocked back in his chair and grinned. "Don't try to deny it. You're captivated by me and you're dying for me to ask you out." He extended his arms outward. "I'm yours for the taking. Just say the word." His eyes gleamed a wicked challenge.

When he wasn't putting on his macho cowboy act, he could be dangerously attractive. "In your dreams." I was relieved when my phone rang. It was Tugg summoning me to his office. No doubt he'd be expecting some answers, and other than a few hunches, I had zip.

Tugg motioned for me to close the door when I entered. "Well, Kendall, what have you been able to come up with?"

I told him my thoughts concerning the two bodies found in the desert. If they were the ones Dexter had referred to in his note, I would need a little more time for Roy to get comfortable with me, thereby making it easier to ask for the files.

He looked thoughtful. "What you need is a good cover story."

"I have an idea. Ginger told me about some of the problems with homeless girls in this area and a little about the Desert Harbor Shelter. Why don't I do a series on the runaway problem? That would allow me to do some snooping and not tip our hand."

His eyes filled with admiration. "That's a great idea! And what's more, you can tie it into the annual fund raiser coming up weekend after next at Whispering Winds."

"What's that?" He explained that one of the locals, Eric Heisler, had gone on to become a successful Phoenix attorney and had turned the old Rocking Z dude ranch into a first class tennis club visited by the wealthy, the beautiful people from the world of show business, and the tennis circuit. The event had been the brainchild of his divorced, twice widowed mother, socialite Thena Rodenborn. Why not, she'd suggested, tap into this elite clientele to gather funds for some of the local charities including her favorite, the girls' shelter?

"You can get some background information beforehand by talking to Thena and to the woman who runs the place. Phillips I think her name is," Tugg said. "Tell 'em the publicity will alert more people and bring in extra bucks for their pet projects. Then you can cover the fund-raiser itself and you may be able to pick up more tidbits there." He paused and gave me a questioning look. "So, what did you think of Roy when you met him?"

I hesitated, hating to tell him Roy seemed like a hell of a nice guy, and that perhaps he was all wrong in thinking the sheriff was involved in anything questionable.

"Ah...he seemed friendly enough. We'll see how cooperative he is when I ask to see the crime report on those two girls."

"Good work. You're your father's daughter all right." He stood, came around the desk and patted me on the shoulder. "I'm confident you'll find out what happened to John."

As he ushered me from his office, I sincerely hoped he was right. So far, as an investigative reporter, I'd given myself a big fat F.

On the way back to my desk, I collided with Bradley as he rounded the doorway. His hands shot out to steady me, and for the brief time I was pressed against him, the unexpected tingle I experienced left me disconcerted. I sprang back, mumbling my apology.

"So what time shall I pick you up tonight?" He tipped back his hat, his eyes brimming with mischief. "Six? Seven?"

I eyed him with suspicion, wondering if he had planned the accidental encounter. "I can't tonight."

"I could make it eight if that's more convenient."

"If nothing else, you're persistent."

"How about Mexican food? I heard through the grapevine, you've never eaten it."

"Yes, I have."

His expression was scornful. "I don't mean that frozen crap, and I don't mean one of those places like Taco Stop. I mean the authentic stuff."

"Thanks, but I'm due over at Ginger's this evening. Perhaps another time."

"I'll hold you to that," he said firmly. As he walked out I tried not to notice what great buns he had. I was anxious to get to Ginger's house and hear the rest of the story about him. Perhaps it would put my doubts about him to rest.

Fifteen minutes later, I rang the doorbell at Ginger's pink, adobe bungalow. Nature was putting on yet another spectacular sunset performance, lighting the western sky in brilliant shades of gold and crimson. Inside the house a dog yipped, the theme song from a well-known game show blasted, and a shrill voice screeched, "Someone answer that dadblasted phone!"

I heard Ginger call, "It's not the phone, Nona, it's the doorbell. Brian, get it, will ya!"

A tall young man swung the door open. He had sandy hair, hazel eyes, and Ginger's friendly dimples. I jumped as a fluffy gray and white cat sprinted between my feet and vanished behind the house.

"I'm Brian, the baby brother." He extended his hand. "You must be the famous Kendall O'Dell?"

"That's me." I shook his hand, noting that except for the eye color, he looked like a clone of Ginger, right down to the spray of freckles across his nose.

"Hello? Hello!" Behind Brian, an elderly woman in a wheelchair shouted into the phone, "Well, for pity's sake, speak up! I can't hear you." Beside her, a small brown dog danced and yelped in my direction.

Ginger rushed into the room wiping her hands on a red and white gingham apron. "Hang up, Nona!" She threw me an apologetic smile and waved me inside as she shushed the dog.

I tried not to gape at the old lady's outrageous appearance as she wheeled up close to me. Over a brightly printed housedress, she wore a pink feather boa wrapped loosely about her sagging neck. Two bright splotches of rouge on crinkled cheeks, heavy blue eye shadow, and a platinum blonde wig with ringlets perched precariously on her head, completed the bizarre picture.

"Nona," Ginger said in a firm voice, "this is Kendall. Remember I told you she was coming for dinner?"

"Candle?" Nona squinted up at me. "That's a real funny name." Before I could correct her she added, "I'm

Wynona Callaway. I'm sure you've heard of me. Brian, fetch my scrapbooks!"

I arched a brow at Ginger, trying not to look as bewildered as I felt. The dog set up a mournful wailing.

"Shut up, Susie!" Brian pointed a threatening finger at the noisy animal, then turned to me. "You'll have to excuse the pandemonium. Simple things like a doorbell ringing can be known to cause a major crisis around here." He grinned impishly. "If you hurry, you can still escape."

"Oh, hush, Brian." Ginger pretended to smack him. With a devilish laugh, he threaded his way around a collection of mismatched furniture, and disappeared down a hallway.

Grimacing in mock anger, Ginger pushed the old lady to the television. "Kendall will look at the scrapbooks later, darlin'. Right now, why don't you finish watching your show and we'll eat in two shakes of a dog's tail." She touched Nona's gnarled hand tenderly and motioned for me to follow her into a homey, but jumbled kitchen.

Ginger was not a neat cook. The counters were strewn with crusted pots and smeared with tomato sauce. Dishes towered in the sink, but I didn't care. The heavenly aroma made my mouth water and stomach grumble. After declining my offer of help, she poured a glass of lemonade and told me to 'park my butt' at the kitchen table.

"You're probably wonderin' why Nona's wearin' that silly wig, right?"

"Was she wearing a wig?" I said straight-faced. "I hadn't noticed."

She cackled with glee and told me her grandmother had first been a silent screen actress, and then gone on to do theater in New York and London. "She was a real looker in her day," Ginger sighed. "Poor ol' love, she's too vain to admit she's almost bald. You should see her bedroom all chock full of ol' costumes 'n' wigs 'n' stuff. It's practically a museum!"

I told her I'd be delighted and we both giggled hearing Nona shout suggestions to the contestants on the game show. "Ask for an E, you jackass! An E!"

What I really wanted was to get to the subject of Bradley, and especially John Dexter, but I patiently waited as she told me about her new boyfriend, Doug Sauers, who worked at the Whispering Winds Tennis Ranch. I perked up at that, remembering what Tugg had said about attending the fund-raiser. "This one is worth keeping my eye on," she said with a wink. "He's got him a good job, and he ain't never been married before. Like the spider and the fly, I'm gonna have to set my trap real careful like, so's he don't get away like the others."

I sensed she was deliberately making me wait, so I interrupted her. "Come on, Ginger. Out with it."

"Patience, Girl, patience." Her eyes blazing with mischief, she poured herself a glass of lemonade, and scooted a chair up close to me. Then she launched into her tale with gusto.

On his twenty-fourth birthday, Bradley had stunned his family when he told them he'd decided to do something else with his life besides run the ranch. He wanted to get a degree in journalism and write. Overriding the strong protests from his father, Joseph, and tears from his mother, Ruth, he'd packed his things and headed east to stay with an uncle, ignoring his father's threat to disown him.

Following graduation, which his father refused to allow either his mother or sister to attend, Bradley met a dazzling red-haired socialite named Stephanie Tate. A sizzling romance ensued, and they married over the bitter objections of both families.

"Some folks 'round here say she was the cause of his pa's death," Ginger informed me, solemnly stirring the ice cubes in her glass with one finger.

"How so?"

"Old Joe Talverson's temper was legendary. He wasn't easy to take even if you liked him. Anyhow, when Tally finally brought Stephanie home, it was hate at first sight for her and his pa. They squabbled like a pair of fightin' cocks."

"How did she get along with the rest of the family?"

"About the same. Ronda, that's Tally's sister, stayed out of her way most of the time, but, she told me Stephanie deviled the bejesus out of Ruth who's just a tad flighty in the head, ya know."

"What do you mean?"

Ginger made a face and twirled her finger beside her temple. "Kinda teched."

I drew back in surprise. "You mean she's mentally ill?"

"Well, she ain't no candidate for the nut house or nothing. She was always jest a mite fragile. Ronda says it's chronic depression."

"I see. Go on."

Between sips of lemonade, Ginger recounted Bradley's dilemma. His father was leaning on him hard to stay, and Stephanie, claiming she couldn't survive in such a primitive place, was threatening to leave him. He'd finally given in to her tantrums, and the two had returned to the east coast. Shortly afterward, Joseph Talverson had his first stroke. "Tally's ma called and lectured him about duty, roots and all that. So he came back, dragging his reluctant bride with him." Ginger rose to stir the bubbling chili and chop lettuce for the salad.

"What happened then?" I asked, finishing my drink.

"It wasn't too long after that his pa had another stroke. Up and died, he did. Having Tally home made Ruth and Ronda happy as clams, but Stephanie went plum wild, drinking, staying out till all hours, making no secret of her runnin' around on him. Flaunted it in his face, she did. Ronda said they had some hellacious fights."

I gave her a sharp look. "Was John Dexter one of her lovers?"

Ginger wore a look of disdain. "That's what he wanted everybody to believe, and she did come onto him pretty hot 'n' heavy one night over at Buck's Corral. Knowing John, he wouldn't have turned it down."

"So I've heard. But that aside, tell me why he thought Bradley was responsible for her death?"

Half the town, she replied, was gathered at the Starfire Ranch for the annual barbeque dinner. It was the end of the week-long Gold Dust Days celebration held each June. All evening, Stephanie had been drinking heavily and flirting outrageously with all the men, including John.

"Tally stood it as long as he could," Ginger stated, bending to pull a pan of cornbread from the oven, "then he hauled her into the barn. Ronda said everyone could hear her screaming at him. Afterward, she stormed into the house and he went back to his guests. It was pert near dark when she up and rode off into the desert. Hell bent for leather. When Ronda told Tally, he took off after her, saying he was worried about her horse spooking 'cause of all the lightning that night. Anyhow, he found her an hour later face down in a cholla field holdin' a handful of reins."

"Jesus," I whispered trying to absorb all the details. Something still didn't add up. "Ginger, I must be dense, because I still don't get why Dexter suspected Bradley. It sounds like a freak accident to me."

"It was supposed to look like that, sugar, but there's those who didn't believe it then...and still don't."

"And why is that?"

Her eyes sparkled with excitement. "Word around town was them reins might've been cut."

6

Her dramatic exposé sent a little ripple of shock zinging down my back. Ginger quickly added that even though the motive apparently existed, the inquest had cleared Bradley. I wondered. Was he innocent or had he cleverly covered his tracks? But then, she'd also said there'd been hundreds of people there that night. Who else in Castle Valley would have benefited from Stephanie Talverson's death?

Ginger appeared pleased that her news had scored high on my astonishment scale. She shooed me from the kitchen with a request to fetch Brian while she finished preparing dinner. I went reluctantly, still bursting to ask more questions. Could this latest revelation mean Bradley had something to do with Dexter's disappearance? But that didn't add up. Two years was sufficient time for the feud between them to have cooled.

By the time I knocked on Brian's door, I'd convinced myself the two incidents were unrelated. We chatted for a few minutes until we heard Ginger holler 'chow's on!'

Everything tasted delicious. I couldn't remember the last time I'd stuffed myself so much at one sitting. The strawberry shortcake crowned with a mound of whipped cream almost finished me off.

"Don't let me eat another bite," I said pushing away from the table.

"What's that?" Nona inquired with interest. "You've been in a fight?"

Everyone giggled and then jumped when the big cat I'd seen earlier vaulted with a bang onto the front screen. "Let Churchill in will you, Brian?" Ginger asked. Brian got up, opened the door, and the cat sauntered in, tail waving, its mouth clamped onto something most definitely alive.

"Good Lord!" Ginger leaped to her feet. "He's got a scorpion!" Startled by her scream, the cat dropped the creature which lay still for a few seconds, and then barreled across the carpet.

Brian moved swiftly and crunched the thing under his boot. The cat looked displeased.

Ginger sank into her chair, patting her chest. "Them things give me the apoplexy."

Of course, that brought a rash of favorite insect stories. When my turn came, I told of the boy who'd put a spider down my back in the sixth grade. It brought howls of laughter from everyone.

Ginger held her stomach. "Y'all really took off your clothes?"

"Down to my skivvies," I answered dryly. Ginger coaxed a reluctant Brian into helping her wash the dishes. In the meantime, Nona entertained me with photos and articles about her long theater career. Her scrapbooks made me feel

47

a little sad. It was hard to believe that the young, vivacious person in the pictures was now this shriveled old woman.

Brian had rented a movie and we'd just reached the thrilling climax when the doorbell rang.

"Now who could that be?" Ginger's expression was puzzled. "It's past nine o'clock."

"Bonnie," she gasped, swinging the door wide. "What a nice surprise..." Her voice trailed off. "What's the matter? Where's Tom?" She pulled a heavy set woman with streaks of violet mascara staining her cheeks into the room. I remembered Bonnie was Ginger's sister.

"Tom's out of town," the woman sobbed, "but I couldn't wait until tomorrow to tell y'all." Then to my amazement she laughed, blurting out: "Ginger, it's finally happened!"

"What? What's happened?"

"God has answered our prayers. We had a meeting with that lawyer y'all recommended, and guess what? We're getting us a baby!"

Ginger clapped her hands. "Oh my Lord! You finally got in to see Eric Heisler."

That grabbed my attention. I recognized the name as the Phoenix attorney who owned the tennis ranch.

"That's right." Bonnie dabbed her eyes with a tissue. "He is the most wonderful man...no, he's more than that. He's an absolute god."

More shrieking. That was followed by the two of them jumping and hugging. I met Brian's amused glance as he shrugged. Drama seemed commonplace in this household.

When things quieted, I told Ginger I had to go, not wanting to intrude on what was obviously private family business.

"Oh, don't go on my account," Bonnie said after Ginger introduced us. "I wish I could share this news with the whole world. Let's have us a celebration party!"

Not wanting to spoil the festive atmosphere, I agreed. Anyway, I was curious to hear her story. We all filed into the kitchen where Brian pulled out a bottle of sparkling champagne he said had been in the refrigerator since the Carter administration.

Glasses clinked during the noisy toast. Then Bonnie launched into her tale, recounting fifteen years of miscarriages, fertility drugs, blind leads, anguish and waiting. They'd even, she admitted, placed ads in newspapers, hoping to appeal to interested teens.

"The turning point was Ginger talking about my problem to her boyfriend," Bonnie said with a misty-eyed smile while squeezing Ginger's hand. For my benefit she added, "You know, he works in the pro shop at the tennis ranch and, well, I must say, I almost fainted when Eric Heisler's secretary called me."

Ginger was ecstatic. "I just asked Doug if he'd put in a good word for me."

Bonnie chimed in, "We didn't know what to expect because we'd heard his fees were like astronomical, but he was so nice, and so easy to talk to. And even though he told us that he hasn't handled too many adoption cases, he promised he'd do the best he could for us."

Ginger good-naturedly bawled her out for keeping her meeting a secret and I noticed Nona nodding in her chair, the empty glass still clutched in one hand.

Bonnie looked contrite. "I was afraid to say anything. We've had so many failures. But when he called me today to say that he knew of a young woman expecting in June, I tell you I about busted a gut."

Nona started to snore, so Ginger and Brian excused themselves to help her to bed. Bonnie went on to tell me some of her experiences with adoption agencies.

"I appreciate you sharing this with me," I commented to her. "Being a reporter I always want to know everything about a subject and I honestly didn't know adopting was such a ticklish business."

"Please don't take this wrong, because it isn't meant to sound biased, but it isn't as difficult if you don't want a white baby."

"Why is that?"

"Because there's an unbelievable shortage of 'em."

"Why?"

"For one thing, the abortion laws changed everything," she confided, pouring herself another glass of champagne. "People don't have kids they don't want anymore. But the most important reason of all is that over eighty percent of pregnant, unmarried teens keep their babies." She shrugged. "It used to be something to hide, to be ashamed of. Not anymore. The stigma is gone and so are all the adoptable babies."

The wait, she added, through private and state agencies averaged five to seven years if you could pass the rigid restrictions which included income, education and religious affiliation.

"We're great on all that stuff except I up an ruined everything by havin' a nervous breakdown over this a few years ago," she said in an anguished voice. "I miscarried the baby after five months and it just about sent me over the edge. It put a big black mark on my record." Her voice trembled and her brown eyes misted again.

My heart went out to her. This was a woman who'd obviously been to hell and back.

When Ginger returned, she insisted Bonnie stay the night and not make the return drive to Prescott due to the late hour. She happily agreed and I said good-night after congratulating her again on her forthcoming adoption.

Ginger clicked on the porch light and followed me outside to my car. We stood for a moment chatting as a warm desert breeze fluffed our hair. Above us, stars blazed from the inky canopy of night sky.

The more I got to know her, the more my affection grew for this pixie-faced Texas girl. Ginger had welcomed me into the cozy bosom of her family and filled the emotional void I'd been suffering since leaving my own home and relatives so far behind.

"Thanks for dinner," I said smiling. "I thoroughly enjoyed it and meeting your family." I opened the car door. "That was a really nice thing you did, getting your friend Doug to put in a good word for Bonnie. I'm looking forward to meeting him, but then, I guess I'll get that chance when I cover the big charity affair at the tennis ranch."

"I'm going to be there myself." She told me she and some other members of her church congregation had volunteered to help park cars and assist in the kitchen. Doug Sauers would be bartending.

A cunning look crept over her face. "Wear something real sleek and sexy if you want to catch his eye."

"Whose eye?"

"Why Eric Heisler's, of course! This guy is special. Dangerously rich and real...cosmopolitan like." She raised an eyebrow suggestively. "You know, more your cup of tea."

I laughed. "Oh, Ginger, will you stop with the matchmaking. I'm not ready to get involved with anyone."

"Oh piffle. It cain't hurt to have a look see. Tell you what. I'm a fixin' to go into Phoenix on that Saturday morning to see a foot doctor about these pesky corns, so why don't you and me go together? I can show you around town, we can shop, have lunch at one of them fancy restaurants and still be back in plenty of time to get ready for the big shindig at seven."

She had such a pleading look in her eye I couldn't refuse. Anyway, it would be a nice change and I did want to see Phoenix.

Random thoughts tumbled about in my head like clothes in a dryer as I drove home. The sky over Castle Rock glowed faintly, announcing the imminent moonrise.

Bonnie's face, filled with eager desperation as she'd discussed her longing for a child, stuck in my mind. Funny, I'd never given it much thought before tonight. I guess I'd always figured if I ever got married again and decided to have children, *poof*, I'd just have them. Would I feel like Bonnie, if that didn't happen?

I mentally laid out my plans for the following week as I swung the car onto Lost Canyon Road. It would be busy. Besides my regular work, I'd have to squeeze in my undercover assignment.

An extreme sensation of weariness washed over me as I pulled into the driveway. Sorely in need of a good night's sleep, I hoped there would be no disturbance tonight.

Settled into bed, my thoughts involuntarily returned again and again to Bradley Talverson. Even though he'd been insufferably rude at our first meeting, since then, he'd been pleasant, attentive almost. Could Ginger be right? Was he attracted to me because I reminded him of his wife? Had he been so insanely jealous of her that he'd rather have her dead than with another man?

Jesus! Why couldn't I stop thinking about him? The last thing I needed right now was a man to complicate my life. Remember, I reminded myself, they're all trouble.

Exasperated, I turned over, thumped the pillow and tried to make my mind blank. Given his scandalous background, and as illogical as it seemed, right before sleep clutched me, I reluctantly acknowledged what I'd been trying hard to ignore. I was far more attracted to him than I wanted to admit.

7

The second week of May ended with the thermometer outside the front door of the *Sun* pegged at one hundred degrees. Everyone else at the office seemed oblivious to the heat while I wilted like a head of warm lettuce.

Hot as I was, I did feel better. My asthma attacks had decreased to the point of only using my inhaler once a day, if then. And for that I was grateful. Even so, I missed rain. Actually I would have settled for a cloud at that point.

"Hang onto your hat," Ginger said, tossing mail onto my desk. "When them monsoons blow in around July, y'all are gonna think this is downright cold. Come rainy season we're talking about heat and humidity."

I gave her a quizzical look. "You mean it actually does rain here? I swear my skin is so dry, I feel like a lizard."

"Relax, sugar. Besides getting y'all gussied up in some fine new clothes, we'll get us a barrelful of body lotion to boot."

Laughing, I agreed and then went back to work, tapping out a story concerning the upcoming Gold Dust Days celebrations.

Bradley, who'd been out most of the morning, came sauntering in, sailed his hat onto the wall hook, and then rolled his swivel chair up close to mine. I tried not to react to his closeness by pretending to be utterly absorbed in my copy.

"You busy?" His knee was almost touching mine. I looked up at him. For a fraction of a second before answering, I studied the chiseled contours of his lean face. When our eyes met, a jolt shot through me, almost like the time I'd stuck a bobby pin in a wall socket.

"Sort of. What do you need?"

He flashed me that crooked grin. "I heard you're covering the fund-raiser tomorrow night. I'm going to be there too, interviewing some of the tennis bigwigs. You've heard of Ron Holiday, haven't you? Second seeded at Wimbledon? He'll be there."

I wondered what he was getting at. "I'm impressed," I said, keeping my voice casual. "What's your point?"

"I was thinking. Since you're on the way, what say I stop and pick you up?"

Sideglancing, I noticed Jim's gaze glued on us. I ought to refuse him again, but for the life of me, I couldn't think of any reason why I should. Anyway, what harm could there possibly be?

"Well…" I hesitated. "I wouldn't want to inconvenience you…" Why was my heart beating so erratically?

"No inconvenience at all. See you at six-thirty." He touched me lightly on the shoulder and pushed back to his desk.

Jim's bratty face wore an expectant smirk. I hoped he hadn't seen how much the simple encounter had shaken me. Bradley and I were simply two co-workers covering the same story. Period. Right?

With an effort, I pulled my wandering thoughts back to work. After completing the copy, I hauled out my journal and studied the notes from the previous week.

My interview last Monday with town socialite Thena Rodenborn had been quite informative. I'd let out a low whistle of admiration at the sight of her sprawling Santa Fe-style adobe house flanked on both sides by well-kept gardens. Tugg had told me she was a wealthy widow and by the look of the place, plus the sleek gold Lexus parked in the driveway, there was little doubt.

She greeted me with a cheery smile and escorted me into a beautifully furnished sitting room. Had I not known, I would have never guessed by her slender, youthful appearance that this woman was in her early seventies.

"My dear, I certainly cannot take all the credit," she'd said in answer to my question regarding the shelter. "Reverend Gleason, who's the pastor of the Valley Chapel along with a lovely, lovely lady by the name of Violet Mendoza were absolute saints in helping me get it started." She explained that the pastor had donated the space and Violet had managed the daily activities of the shelter. Through further questioning I learned that an anonymous benefactor five years earlier had provided the funds needed to purchase the house which was now the Desert Harbor Shelter. That happy event had been tempered by the sudden death of Violet Mendoza when she'd been struck down one night by a hit-and-run driver.

"Shortly after that terrible tragedy we were blessed, absolutely blessed, to get a woman like Claudia Phillips to take her place, and frankly, I'm surprised she's stayed on so long considering the small amount we're able to pay her." But," she added hastily, wagging a well-manicured finger, "she's very efficient."

She applauded my idea for a series on runaways and suggested I talk to Claudia as soon as possible.

When asked about the upcoming fund-raiser she spoke enthusiastically about her son, Eric, and how successful the gala event had been last year raising money for not just the shelter, but other local charities.

"I'm so glad you'll be attending," she said as she showed me out the door. "My son makes sure everything is first class. It is the social event of the season," she finished, her voice filled with pride.

The interview with Claudia Phillips proved to be more difficult. When she didn't return my third phone call, I'd hopped in the car on Tuesday afternoon and driven to the two-story wooden house on Tumbleweed Trail.

A weather-bleached sign announcing the name swung back and forth, squeaking softly, as I walked under it. I noted the narrow, dead end street had only four houses set back from the curb on large lots. It was quiet and deserted.

I knocked on the ragged screen door, thinking the rather dilapidated house could certainly use some repairs. Nothing happened for a minute, so I knocked again. Finally, a stocky young woman most likely of Mexican descent answered with "You need help? ¿si?"

I said I'd like to see Ms. Phillips. Smiling, head bobbing, she led me into a small office, pointed to a chair and then backed out the door. Apparently, she spoke little English.

Even though the room was sparsely furnished it gave me comfort to know there existed in these harsh surroundings a sanctuary. Had my young blonde hitchhiker made it here for help?

I'd already formed a picture of Claudia in my mind. She'd be plump, fiftyish, benevolent, overflowing with motherly compassion... My thoughts halted as a tall, slim woman dressed in an expensively cut cream-colored suit glided into the room and froze. I wondered if I wore the same look of surprise on my face.

"Yes?" Her voice was low and husky. The glint of suspicion in her eyes remained even after I'd introduced myself.

"I'm sorry to come without an appointment, but I have a four o'clock deadline to get this in tomorrow's edition and since you didn't return my calls...well." I smiled, but she continued to stare at me coldly. When I mentioned I'd spoken to Thena Rodenborn, her attitude thawed a bit. With the grace of a panther, she seated herself behind the desk and needlessly smoothed her dark hair, already pulled tightly into a silky chignon.

"I'm extremely busy today, Miss O'Dell...but since Mrs. Rodenborn requests it, I can speak to you for..." She hesitated, glancing at her thin gold watch. "Ten minutes."

I wanted to say, "Well, whoop-de-do! Don't do me any favors, your ladyship." Instead, I mustered another professional smile and launched into a series of questions concerning runaway girls and what part the shelter played in their lives.

In a voice completely devoid of any emotion she gave me a dry run-down. "The homeless problem in this state is not considered by legislators to be of much social importance, even though the numbers of runaways increase by the month. We exist on a minimal...really pathetic amount of assistance from the Department of Health Services and an occasional Runaway and Homeless Youth Grant from the federal level. Needless to say, we rely heavily on private donations and we still receive some help from the Valley Chapel." While she talked, she rubbed the back of one hand with the other.

The curtain at the window beside her fluttered gently, wafting the scent of her sweet perfume toward me. I was genuinely puzzled by her cool attitude. Was this normal or was she annoyed with me because I'd come without an appointment?

In the short time remaining she explained that most of the girls stayed only a few days, usually moving on to larger metropolitan areas like Los Angeles where welfare budgets were more substantial.

"We can give them a change of clothes, food, some medical assistance and help them out with bus fare," she continued, "but due to our limited funds we're unable to provide much more."

"How do the girls find this place?" I asked.

"Posters at the bus station, some of the churches and the clinic direct them to us."

And Lucinda Johns at the cafe I added ruefully to myself. She rose then, announcing the conclusion of the interview. I thanked her, stating my intention to do a series on the problem after the fundraising event and could I return for more details and perhaps interview some of the girls?

She rubbed her hand harder. "Interview?"

"Yes, you know, to kind of personalize this. And perhaps I could take some photos..." I halted as her eyes narrowed. They were a peculiar shade of violet.

"I think not, Miss O'Dell. I do after all, have an obligation to protect these girls' privacy."

"Please think it over. I can assure you of their anonymity and I would, of course, shadow their faces."

She showed me to the door. "It's really against policy."

"Whose policy?" It couldn't hurt to push a little.

"Mine." Her smoldering gaze challenged me to respond. It was obvious I'd overstepped the line.

"Thank you so much for your time," I said, faking a warm tone. "You've been most helpful. Perhaps we can talk another time when you're not so busy."

"Perhaps." She inclined her head and shut the door.

Inwardly fuming, I turned and strode to my car. It was ego deflating to be so thoroughly skunked on a story. With a touch of defiance, I yanked my camera from the car, snapped a few pictures of the house's exterior and then slumped behind the wheel. I'd gain nothing by alienating Claudia Phillips so I'd have to think of a different approach.

Before leaving, I surveyed the house once more. It was then I noticed the slight movement of the curtain at the office window. If Claudia Phillips was so terribly busy, why was she watching me?

I'd returned to the office and made the afternoon deadline with ease. The rest of the week went smoothly, but now, as I sat studying the notes three days after the interview, I couldn't seem to shake the feeling that something about the woman just didn't click. The more I thought about it, the more I was reminded of drawings in some of my childhood activity books. What's wrong with this picture? What doesn't belong here? I flipped to the back of the notebook and added Claudia Phillip's name to the list.

"Hey, O'Dell, wake up! I'm talking to you." Jim's demand combined with being hit on the head with a paper wad pulled me from my reverie.

"What is it?" I said with a slight touch of irritation in my voice.

"A bunch of us are going over to the bowling alley for happy hour and then," he paused and scooped his right hand forward, "knock down a few pins. You want to come?"

"Bowling? I don't think I can stand the excitement." That brought a laugh from Bradley. Jim muttered for me to 'suit myself' and swaggered out. I felt a little guilty then. Though annoying at times, he was only trying to be friendly.

But then, I couldn't have gone anyway. I had one last stop before heading home. John Dexter's place.

At four o'clock Bradley left with a reminder that he'd pick me up at six-thirty sharp the following evening. I agreed, cleared my desk and headed to my car.

The Ocotillo Village Apartments had obviously seen better days. The peeling pink stucco walls seemed to sag in the late afternoon sun. As I picked my way through the littered courtyard, I suppressed a shiver of revulsion at the sight of a chipped swimming pool filled with murky, oily-looking water.

I counted twelve units before knocking on a door that had one F missing from OFFICE. A small grayish lizard clutching the doorframe turned bulbous black eyes in my direction.

The manager, a greasy looking little man with leering eyes and boozy breath invited me inside the dusty, cluttered room.

"Have a seat." With eager movements, he removed a pile of newspapers from the chair in front of his desk. The way his gaze lingered on my body made my skin crawl. But...perhaps he could be useful. So, I gave him an extra flash of leg as I crossed one over the other.

Practically slobbering, he ran around behind the desk and pulled out a blank rental agreement. "I don't have a unit available right at this minute," he said, fumbling for a pen, "but just as soon as one opens up, you can be sure you'll get it."

It was difficult, but I mustered up what I hoped was a bewitching smile.

"I'm not looking for an apartment, actually."

The gleam of anticipation in his beady eyes faded. "Oh. Well...what do you want?"

"I'm looking for someone. My...ah brother, David, gave me a couple of things that belong to a friend of his who used to live here. David's in the service and he's been transferred to Germany. Before he left, he asked me if I'd return this guy's stuff." I gave him another wide smile. "So...I was hoping you could give me his forwarding address."

He reached for a rolodex file. "What's his name?"

"John Dexter."

A scowl creased his face. "Dexter? That son-of-a-bitch broke his lease and skipped. Sorry, can't help you."

I pouted. "Oh dear. So, you don't have any idea where he might be?" It was hard to maintain the beguiling expression.

He reached for a cigarette, lit it, and blew out a long stream of acrid smoke.

"I don't know if there's anything to it, but I did overhear him having a row with his little wetback girlfriend here when I was working outside number six one night shortly before he took off."

"Really? What about?"

"Something about tickets to Nogales."

"Nogales?"

"Yeah. You know. In Mexico."

"Oh. So he and his girlfriend went to Mexico?"

"Not hardly. She's still here so I figure he must've had him another hot little number down south," he said jerking his thumb to the right. "John was, how shall I say, real popular with the ladies, if you get my drift?" He gave me a suggestive wink.

I got his drift. "His girlfriend is still here?"

"Yeah."

"What's her name?"

At that, his eyes narrowed suspiciously. "Say, you ask an awful lot of questions. Why do you want to know?"

Uh oh. I'd asked one too many. "I...just thought she'd know where he is."

"I might know her name." The wily smile revealed a row of tobacco stained teeth. "How about you and me go have a drink? We can talk some more."

That was it for me. I looked at my watch. "Oops. I'm terribly late for my appointment. Thanks anyway." Before he could move, I jumped up and got the hell out.

Halfway down the street, a thought stopped me. When he said the girlfriend was still here did he mean still here in Castle Valley or still here at Ocotillo Village?

On a hunch, I doubled back to a row of mailboxes I'd seen near the entrance gate. I ran my finger along the names and when I came to number seven I whispered, "Bingo."

Fortunately, it was on the end, out of sight of the office. I knocked softly and when a pretty dark-haired girl of perhaps nineteen or twenty answered I asked, "Yolanda Reyes?"

"Yes?"

"I was wondering if I could talk to you for a few minutes about John Dexter?"

A look of sheer hatred blazed in her eyes. She screamed something in Spanish and for the second time that week I had a door slammed in my face.

8

A brilliant sunrise lit the eastern sky as Ginger and I headed toward Phoenix for our day of shopping. It was sheer delight to see a few thin wisps of clouds stretching outward from the horizon like long, white fingers.

As I drove, I tried to concentrate as Ginger jumped from subject to subject, conferring upon me bits and pieces of information about the residents of Castle Valley.

Every now and then I'd interject a word, but my mind was on something else. I wasn't accustomed to having doors slammed in my face and my first instinct had been to knock again and keep on knocking until the girl answered. Yet I had no desire to attract the attention of the sleazy apartment manager.

I felt discouraged on the one hand and hopeful on the other. She couldn't elude me forever. And her violent reaction convinced me that she might be a valuable link to information concerning John Dexter.

As far as Claudia went, I didn't know what her problem was. She'd seemed more than a little edgy.

Too bad for her, but I was going to show up again like a stray cat on her doorstep. It was curious indeed that my questions appeared to have caused her such agitation.

"Sugar? Did y'all hear what I said?" Ginger's demand interrupted my thoughts.

"Uh...I'm sorry. I was thinking about something else."

"Bet you a dollar to a doughnut you're daydreaming about tonight. Now listen up, if y'all play your cards right, I'd say you got yourself a mighty fine chance of snagging Eric Heisler. Here's some of his vital statistics."

"Ginger, I'm going to smack you in about one minute."

"Oh piddle. You mean to set there and tell me y'all ain't even the teensiest bit curious about him?"

"No."

"You lie!"

"Okay, maybe a little." I learned a lot in the space of two minutes. He was gorgeous, forty-one, and divorced.

"How long has he been single?" I asked braking the car to avoid a jackrabbit streaking across the highway.

"Hmmmm. Five years, six maybe."

"What happened?"

"Well, from what I heard, it was a real messy business. Seems one of the gals working at his office was his mistress, so his wife really stuck it to him in the divorce settlement."

I glanced at her. "This sounds like a good plan. You want me to get involved with a man who cheated on his wife?"

"That was never proved, and besides she wasn't no saint herself. Seems she was real friendly with one of the tennis pros at their country club. So don't be too quick to point a finger. Anyhow," she said with a defensive sniff, "Doug says Eric's a real fine man. Generous to a fault. Bonnie said so too. She told me yesterday he's not even going to charge them his regular fee."

What a pill she was. Bent on matchmaking, Ginger wasn't going to be satisfied until she carried out her plans. It would be useless to argue with her, so I just laughed. Secretly, I was curious to find out if he could live up to all the rave reviews.

As we neared the outskirts of town, I pushed my thoughts aside and concentrated on the swell of traffic and unfamiliar streets.

Phoenix was a kick. Like Philadelphia, it was big and bustling, but all similarity ended there. Instead of soot blackened, ivy covered monuments and crumbling ghettos, this crisp looking desert city boasted wide thoroughfares studded with waving palms. The skyline shimmered with modern glass highrises and the enclosed, air-conditioned shopping malls were simply delicious. Following her appointment with the doctor, Ginger and I had a ball exploring the stores and then lunching at an elegant restaurant.

By late afternoon, we'd visited at least ten different shops and couldn't agree on what type of outfit I should buy.

After some good-natured arguing, I finally settled on a sleek, knee-length emerald green cocktail dress.

"If you ask me," Ginger remarked following the purchase, "I liked that itty-bitty black one better."

"Please. I don't want to look like a hooker. I'm there on assignment, remember? Anyway, the green one is more practical. Boy, I miss my old salary. I can't eat for a month now because of this."

It was time to head home but Ginger insisted we stop at the cosmetics counter before leaving. She purchased a bottle of her favorite cologne and spritzed us with two different scents, exclaiming, "Oh, looky here. A sample of Shalimar." She inhaled the fragrance and blew out a blissful sigh. "What do you think, should we live dangerously and buy some?"

I looked at the price and made a face. "At two hundred an ounce? I don't think so."

Pretending to pout, she sprayed a liberal amount on my wrist and returned the bottle. I sniffed it appreciatively and then started in surprise. I had smelled this sweet scent recently. But where?

It bugged me for a half an hour before the answer came to me. Claudia Phillips had been wearing it. "Tell me," I asked Ginger while maneuvering the car into the flow of freeway traffic, "what do you know about Claudia Phillips?"

She giggled. "You mean other than the fact that she looks like Olive Oyl?"

"Yeah. Other than that."

"Well, let's see." She hesitated while chewing her thumb nail. "I see her here and there around town. I don't know if she's got a boyfriend..." After another short pause she said in a surprised tone, "Come to think of it, I don't really know much about her at all. Why?"

"I can't put my finger on it. There's something about her that strikes me wrong. She supposedly earns a mere pittance at the shelter and yet, when I interviewed her the other day, she had on what looked like a designer suit and she was wearing Shalimar."

"Beats me." Ginger yawned in obvious disinterest.

An accident a few miles from Castle Valley stalled us in traffic almost forty minutes, so I was running way behind schedule by the time I dropped her off and eased the car into the carport. The hall clock chimed six-fifteen as I stepped inside. There was no way I could be ready in fifteen minutes. Bradley would just have to wait.

In the bedroom, I threw off my clothes and then, clad only in bra and panties, padded towards the bathroom where I stopped in confusion. The door was closed. Funny, I didn't remember shutting it when I'd left this morning?

I edged it open and stepped cautiously in. A split second before I pulled the shower curtain aside, I had a premonition something was wrong.

Rational thought deserted me at the sight of what was in my tub. The scream that rose to my throat almost choked me. There must have been a dozen huge spiders crawling and tumbling about, some halfway up the side.

Led by the cold hand of panic, I careened off the doorjamb and bolted, unthinking, into the hall and straight out the front door.

"Jesus Christ!" I shrieked to no one as I stood on the walkway shivering with fear and revulsion. The thought of one of those horrid creatures touching me turned my stomach cold. How the hell had all those spiders gotten into my tub? How was I going to get them out of the house? I thought wildly. A broom? Yes! A broom. No wait. A shovel? Think. Of course! The only logical solution was the vacuum cleaner.

It took me about five minutes to quit shaking as I rationalized the situation. Calm down, I urged myself. You're out here and they're in there, so you're safe.

My breath wheezed in my throat. I needed the inhaler but had no intention of going back inside. A few more shallow breaths had just begun to reinstate a semblance of self-control when the sound of a vehicle approaching sent me into a second fit of panic. I wasn't dressed! Instinctively, I dove behind the fountain in the courtyard as Bradley's truck braked to a halt.

How was I going to explain this? I looked around hastily to find something to cover myself with, but, of course, there was nothing. I could find only one thing to be thankful for at that moment. At least I hadn't stripped naked.

A split-second fantasy had me running down the walkway and into his arms for aid and comfort. But even though I was terribly relieved to see him, I steeled myself against it. What would that do to my self-esteem? Was I to appear once again as the damsel in distress?

Clad in a black western suit and looking taller and leaner than ever, he stopped in his tracks when he saw me crouching beside the fountain. His face registered disbelief.

Stupidly, I said the first thing that popped into my head. "You're early."

Hat in hand, he cocked his head to the side and stared at me. "So it would appear."

Why had I said that? Subconsciously I knew, and I hated it. As he'd done with the javelinas, there was little doubt he was going to have to rescue me again.

"I may be wrong," he said, moving closer, "but don't you think you're slightly underdressed for this dinner party?"

"No. I always go to black tie affairs in my underwear."

He gave me a thin smile. "Well, whatever smokes your shorts." I said nothing and he added, "Okay, so do you want to tell me what the hell you're doing out here? Somehow I find it hard to believe, even though you are a greenhorn, that you'd make it a practice to prance around barefoot among the cactus?"

I groaned and closed my eyes for a moment. Why was I behaving like such a coward? "I need help. I can't go back in the house."

"Why not?"

"Because there's a herd of spiders the size of softballs in my bathtub." Thinking of it gave me the creepy-crawlies all over again.

He looked quizzical. "A herd?"

"Yeah. Go see for yourself." I stood up on one foot and winced as I plucked several cactus thorns from the other.

He started toward the house and then unexpectedly turned in my direction. Startled, I crossed my arms over my chest. It didn't hide much.

In silence, he removed his jacket and draped it gently around my shoulders. A warm, masculine scent wafted from the fabric. He made a great show of trying not to look at my mostly naked body. He failed.

I suppressed a gasp as his touch sent a fiery tingle through me. "Thank you," I mumbled, clutching the coat around me.

He returned in a moment. His inquisitive gaze bored into mine. "Someone's played a rather spectacular joke on you. I don't think I've ever seen that many tarantulas all together in one spot before."

A thought struck me. "How come they haven't crawled out?"

"That's curious. By the smell, I'd say somebody sprayed WD-40 on the porcelain. They can't get enough traction to climb up."

The idea that someone had deliberately planned this sent another chill of horror through me. It had to be someone who knew about my spider phobia. Ginger? But no, Ginger couldn't do something so despicable.

Something else occurred to me. "I wonder how whoever it was got in?"

"I checked already. The arcadia door in your bedroom was unlocked."

"That's impossible. I remember very clearly locking it before I left this morning."

Bradley sighed. "Are you the only one with a key?"

"Well, no. I'm sure Mary Tuggs has one. But she's an unlikely candidate." Who, I wondered, was a good candidate for this prank?

"Then you must have left it unlocked," he concluded with manly logic.

"I didn't." My annoyance increased when I noticed he wasn't really paying attention to what I said but was instead studying my bare thighs. "Could you...could you just get rid of them for me? Please?"

He nodded slowly. "I'll do it, but it's going to cost you," he said with mock seriousness.

God, the man was exasperating. I gave him the evil eye and said, "Taking advantage of a woman in distress certainly would never occur to you. Right?"

"Never."

"So what do you want?"

"Dinner."

"Dinner?"

"That's it."

"Okay. You've got a deal." I gestured toward the house. "Now would you please..."

Smug-faced, he left and I wondered if there was some kind of therapy that would address my phobia? One thing did please me, however. Two months earlier, this much stress would have caused a major asthma attack. This time I'd handled one without the inhaler.

He came out carrying one of my new pink pillowcases. There was a wriggling lump at the bottom. I shivered again and said ungraciously, "Why did you use my new pillowcase?"

"Oh, excuse me. I didn't think you'd care that much about how I disposed of them." Impishly, he shoved the bag toward me. "Do you want to transfer them to a color you do like?"

I jumped back. "Get them away from me! You might as well burn that with them in it, cause I'll never use it again!"

He shook his head at me sadly as if I were mentally deficient. "Calm down. I'm not going to kill them," he said quietly. "Tarantulas are perfectly harmless and they're an important part of the environment."

"Please. I don't need a biology lesson. Just do something with them."

I watched him walk across Lost Canyon and when he returned the pillowcase was neatly folded in his hand.

"Mission accomplished," he said with a grin. It took every bit of will power I possessed to walk back into that house. I made him walk ahead of me into each room as my gaze darted back and forth from every corner and into every nook and cranny. Sunday or not, Mr. Jenkins, the exterminator, would be hearing from me first thing in the morning.

Bradley gallantly offered to clean the tub which I accepted. In a nonchalant manner he handed me the two pairs of panty hose that were hanging over the shower curtain. "Nice texture," he said fanning one eyebrow at me.

When he finished, he folded his arms, leaned against the doorframe. "If you like I'll stay in here with you while you shower. Just to keep a lookout, of course."

He looked wicked and devilishly attractive. Never in my wildest dreams did I think I'd end up sharing such an intimate situation with him.

"You're too kind," I said pushing him out the door. By the time I'd showered and dressed, I was angry.

What kind of a sick mind was at work here? And to what purpose?

There was no time to style my hair as I'd planned, so I brushed it until it lay in soft curls around my bare shoulders.

Satisfied with my appearance, I grabbed my shawl and camera bag. I checked to make sure the arcadia door was secured and then swept into the living room.

"I'm ready," I announced in a breezy voice. "Let's go." Bradley eyed me appreciatively and gave a low whistle. "Wow! Pretty snazzy."

"Thank you," I said with an exaggerated curtsy.

"I must say I liked your other outfit too."

My cheeks flamed. "Because you're a gentleman, I know that particular fact won't go beyond this room."

A fiendish twinkle danced in his eyes. "Who told you I was a gentleman?"

He looked so full of orneriness, I couldn't help but laugh. "You're a hard man to deal with, Bradley Talverson," I remarked as he seated me in his truck after we'd left the house.

"And a hard man is good to find," he quipped.

74

The mood lightened, I settled back in the seat and watched the remains of the sunset glow on the horizon like the scarlet embers of a dying fire. Lost in thought, I said little during the trip to Whispering Winds.

The memory of the tarantulas in my bathtub would probably haunt me for years to come. Someone in Castle Valley knew it would. And that someone was going to extraordinary lengths to frighten me away from the Delgado ranch.

9

It hadn't occurred to me to suspect Lucinda Johns until I entered the main room at the tennis ranch with Bradley. As I admired the lavish surroundings with pleasure, she suddenly separated herself from a group of other women and made a beeline for him. Dressed in a red gown cut so low it gave new meaning to the word cleavage, her eyes burned with naked lust. When she spotted me standing near him, her steps faltered, her expression altered dramatically. For a second she looked so distressed I thought she might burst into tears. Instead, she threw me an indignant glare and flounced from the room.

Bradley, having been cornered by noisy, back-slapping friends, had apparently not noticed. Ginger had told me that she was wildly jealous of Bradley. Was she my tormentor? But how could she know of my phobia? Unless...? It was time to find Ginger.

Thena Rodenborn had said this was the social event of the season and I believed it. The men looked striking in dark suits and tuxedos, while the women glided about in colorful designer gowns. I felt very much at home in the casual elegance of the place. It was every bit as nice as any of the finest hotels I'd visited in New York, Pittsburgh or Philadelphia.

There was to be a silent auction later, so I made note of some of the items laid out on the long tables.

Across the room, working behind the bar, I spied Ginger. It took me a few minutes to weave my way through the noisy throng.

Ginger's voice peeled like a bell. "Hey, girlfriend! Where y'all been?"

"I was detained by a slight problem."

"I'm Doug Sauers," said the smiling, cherub-faced man behind the polished counter. "I've heard all about you."

"And I you." He squeezed my hand in a friendly shake and we chatted for a few minutes. He filled a tray with mixed drinks, handed it to Ginger and before she could get away I said, "I need to talk to you when you have a second."

"I'm kinda tied up for a spell, but I'll hunt you up after dinner's served, okey dokey?"

"Fine. Right now, I guess I'd better earn my keep." With Doug's permission, I stashed my shawl and bulky camera case behind the bar, then set off, camera in hand, to gather information and snap photos of Castle Valley's uppercrust and out-of-town VIPs.

Thena Rodenborn, all aglitter in a blue sequined dress, introduced me to some of the major contributors from the Phoenix and Prescott areas respectively. Most people, when hearing I was a reporter, posed willingly.

I'd gathered quite a bit of material as the dinner hour neared, so I retreated to a quiet spot near an enormous stone fireplace to condense my notes. A large picture window to my left overlooked lighted tennis courts.

A sudden indrawn breath made me whirl to face a set of startled, cobalt-blue eyes. Some emotion I couldn't read flickered across the man's stunningly handsome face and then vanished.

I opened my mouth to say something and then shut it again as he stepped forward. Before I could object, he caught my free hand and pressed his lips to it. His slightly graying blonde hair caught the rainbow reflections from the crystal chandeliers overhead.

Then, in a deep, masculine voice, guaranteed to raise goose bumps on the most frigid of women, he said, "Wait. Don't speak. For one so endowed with such a rare and radiant beauty, I suspect you must be a princess." He tightened his grip on my hand. "Come. We must be away, you and I. My castle awaits."

What was this? A knight in a shining black tuxedo? I couldn't help but smile. Without a doubt, this had to be the most superb hunk of maleness I'd ever laid eyes on in my life. The air between us crackled with sexual electricity.

"Well," I said, keeping my voice light, and gently disengaging my hand, "that's definitely one of the more original opening lines I've ever heard."

He looked stricken. "Dear lady, do you doubt my sincerity? How deeply you wound my vanity."

I laughed aloud. The man was an absolute poet. A real charmer. I decided he must be a television personality from Phoenix.

"Do I get to know your name?"

"Kendall O'Dell. What's yours?"

"Eric Heisler."

I widened my eyes. Ginger and Bonnie had referred to him as a god. That he was.

"Eric! Darling!" Thena Rodenborn bore down on us and grasped his arm. "Naughty boy. Gone for two weeks and you can't take even one little minute to let me know you're back?"

"I'm sorry, mother," he said kissing her lightly on one cheek, "my flight was delayed. I arrived here not fifteen minutes ago."

She beamed up at him, "My dear boy, you work too hard."

Eric flashed her a tender smile before returning his attention to me. "So, mother, have you met Miss O'Dell?"

"Oh, yes indeed. She's here to write a story for the newspaper."

Another one of those inscrutable looks passed swiftly over his face. Had he assumed I was one of the moneyed citizens of Castle Valley? An heiress? Would his interest evaporate now?

Thena responded to someone calling her name and excused herself, saying she'd see us later.

Eric watched her leave and then turned back to me. "So, you're a reporter?"

"I hope you're not disappointed."

"Should I be?"

"Only if you were expecting a sizable donation. Alas, I'm afraid I'm not a princess, just a poor working girl here to cover this event, which I must say is most impressive." I flipped my notepad to a new page. "Coincidentally, you're at the top of my list of people I wanted to meet."

"If that is the case, then my evening is a great success already." He had a radiant smile. "If you don't have a dinner companion, I'd be honored to have you sit at my table."

Flattered, I started to accept when Bradley's voice cut in sharply, "Kendall, my little desert flower, there you are." I flinched with surprise as he hooked his hand possessively through my elbow and pulled me next to him. I flashed him a sizzling look which he ignored. Even though he wore a tight smile, cold dislike was mirrored in his eyes as he stared at Eric Heisler.

"Bradley." Eric acknowledged quietly. And then with just a touch of coolness he said to me, "I'm sorry. I didn't know you were here with someone."

"I'm not." I tried to pry my arm from Bradley's iron grasp.

"Now don't cause a scene, darlin'," Bradley said in a soothing voice. "I have to feed her on time or she gets real cranky," he added, patting my arm.

Eric and Bradley, visually dueling, faced each other like two pawing bucks about to lock antlers. Then Eric, in courteous retreat, smiled graciously at me and excused himself, murmuring perhaps we could talk another time.

Wistfully, I watched the 'god' walk across the room out of sight, and probably out of my life. I turned to Bradley and freed my arm from his grip, then stuck out my chin and repeated through clenched teeth, "My little desert flower? I have to feed her on time?" My voice rose shrilly. "I could strangle you!"

"Calm down," he said under his breath. "I knew you'd want me to intercede."

"Now, why would I want that?"

"Because, you were drooling all over yourself. It isn't ladylike."

"I wasn't drooling. And even if I was, it's none of your business. I'll thank you to butt out of my affairs."

He looked amused. "Did you know your eyes are the same gray color as thunderheads during a summer storm?" He leaned closer. "I can actually see sparks of blue lightning."

I was so angry with him I wanted to cry. Aware, however, that people were now watching us, I said coolly, "Tell me, Bradley, were you born aggravating or do you have to really work at it?"

"With you, it isn't work and please call me Tally." Bastard was what I'd have liked to call him, but I refrained. Why had he acted so hateful toward Eric? I took a couple of calming breaths. "I really am quite hungry now. And I'm also very cranky. If you pull any more stunts like that on me, I can't be responsible for my actions. Got it?"

Without waiting for a reply, I stalked into the dining room. Rather than sit with Bradley, I chose another table nearby. She must have been watching for him because Lucinda pounced on the seat he'd saved for me. She was so close to him, her breasts were practically in his chicken Kiev. He didn't look like he minded and that annoyed me even further.

Why should I let the incident ruin my evening? I turned my attention to the beautifully prepared meal and ate with gusto. I chatted with and enjoyed the company of all my table companions except for the gray-haired, bearded man beside the woman to my left.

He said nothing, just ate and drank. In fact, he mostly drank. Every time a waitress whisked by, he loudly ordered another Scotch.

I almost dropped my fork when one lady addressed him as Dr. Price. Dr. Price? This must be my neighbor from the mental hospital. I watched as he downed a drink in three swallows. He acted like a man under great stress. But then, it had to be a strain working with mentally and emotionally disturbed people every day.

"You know," I began with a friendly smile, "that you and I are neighbors."

He widened bloodshot eyes, hiccuped, and said in a slurred voice, "Neighbors?"

"I rent the house down the road from you and I've been curious about your place." He said nothing, so I continued. "I did a story once concerning some of the new drugs being used to treat the chronically mentally ill. Perhaps we could talk sometime."

I drew back at the expression on his face. He looked like a rabbit caught in the glare of headlights.

"'Scuse me..." he mumbled and rose so quickly his chair fell over. Stunned, I watched him weave from the room. Well! Mary Tuggs had said he was an odd old bird and he certainly was.

Speaking of odd birds, I watched Claudia Phillips slink across the room in a black satin gown so tight it hugged every contour of her lean body. Unkindly, I thought, she looks like a hotdog encased in black satin. How did she do it? The dress looked outrageously expensive.

At that moment Eric Heisler demanded everyone's attention to announce the winners of the silent auction. There was enthusiastic applause when he mentioned the amount of money that had been raised thus far. A quick survey of the room revealed the eyes of every female riveted on him. I smiled ruefully. Apparently I wasn't the only one who found him attractive.

As several other of the town's top dogs droned on about the various charity organizations, Eric stood off to the side of the podium. Was it my imagination or was he deliberately making eye contact with me? He held my gaze for so long, I felt myself flushing. Self-consciously, I looked away. There was no mistaking the bold message that smoldered in his eyes.

Warning bells clanged in my ears. Was I to have two men, who appeared to dislike each other intensely, in hot pursuit? Did I want to open this Pandora's box?

While it was immensely flattering, for the life of me I couldn't figure out why a man of such obvious class and high social standing would be interested in me.

When the dancing started, woman after woman pressed herself eagerly against him. Filled with admiration, I watched him execute a flawless rhumba and then swing the next woman into a graceful waltz. It was probably a good thing I had work to do, or I would have been in line too.

I looked around and noticed Bradley had the tennis pro, Ron Holiday, buttonholed for an interview. Still clinging to his side like Velcro, Lucinda gazed up at him rapaciously. Subtle she was not.

I shook off my irritation and headed toward the bar to get another roll of film. Ginger and I almost collided in the hallway.

"Hey, girl. What did y'all need?"

"You know that story I told you at your house last week? The one about the spider?"

"Yeah."

"Well, did you repeat it to anyone?"

"Why?"

"Just tell me."

"Well, I did mention it to Colleen down at the beauty parlor while she was fixing my hair." Ginger giggled.

"Poor old gal, she laughed so hard, she liked to peed her pants."

"I'm so glad I was able to be the source of everyone's entertainment," I said, slightly annoyed with her. But then, why should I be? I knew Ginger couldn't come anywhere close to keeping a secret. Best learn from this and be wary about what I said to her from now on.

Ginger looked wounded and her hand flew to her mouth. "Oh, fiddlefaddle. I wasn't supposed to tell anyone, was I? Sorry. Sometimes I'm dumber than a box of rocks."

"It's okay," I soothed her. "Just tell me who else was at the salon when you told the story."

She looked toward the ceiling for a moment. "Well...let me see now. There was Coleen of course, Mabel Pritchard, Fran, from down at the bakery, Rita Torres..."

"Is that all?"

"Now don't get your pantyhose in a knot, I'm trying to remember. Saturday's are real busy." She paused again. "I can't remember every single soul..."

"Was Lucinda there?"

Her golden eyes glowed with surprise. "Well, I'll be switched. How'd you know?"

10

So my hunch had been correct. Right now, it appeared that Lucinda was the most likely culprit. Grudgingly, I had to admit that she'd done a pretty good job to date, but she was dead wrong if she thought her little pranks were going to send me scurrying out of town with my tail between my legs.

Back in the ballroom the music from the band blared and I couldn't help but notice Lucinda and Bradley on the dance floor. Why did it distress me to see her pressed so closely against him?

I turned away in disgust and stomped back to the main room. It looked deserted, except for Doug at the bar, and a sandy-haired man, apparently asleep, his head lolling on the back of one of the plush sofas.

My feet hurt from the four inch heels, so I dropped into a nearby chair and kicked off my shoes.

"Are you a pooper too?"

I jumped and turned toward the man on the couch I'd thought was asleep.

"I beg your pardon?"

"A pooper. Party pooper?" He yawned widely.

I laughed. "Is that what you are?"

"God, yes," he groaned, stretching. "At least that's what my wife always calls me. I'm a tennis widower actually."

"Is that like a golf widow reversed?" I asked.

"Yes. My wife, Marcie, drags me to every event within a five hundred mile radius. She hangs around with the pros and talks tennis while I sleep wherever I can find a quiet spot."

I smiled at him. "Don't you like tennis?"

"Oh, sure I do. I even took her to Wimbledon last year. But I get tired of talking about it constantly. Marcie's totally obsessed. Not only does she watch, she plays too. She'd have me on the court day and night, but someone in the family has to work."

"What keeps you busy?" I asked, massaging my aching toes.

"I almost hate to tell you." He sighed, sounding apologetic. "I'm one of those people everyone makes jokes about."

"What? You're in politics?"

"Close. Lawyer. We are the object of great ridicule until we're needed." He reached into his jacket and handed me a card. "Just in case you ever require my services."

I read the firm name. "Well, Mike Scott it's nice to meet you. You're the second attorney I've met this evening."

"We travel in packs at social events," he said with a wry smile. "Like coyotes. Predators, get it?" He bared his teeth and I laughed again. Then he said, "So, who'd you meet, my partner Aaron Hamilton? He's around here somewhere."

"No. His name is Eric Heisler."

"Heisler?" He blew out a sigh. "That guy is one lucky son of a bitch."

Surprised at his tone of resignation, I asked, "Why do you say that?"

"Because, while the rest of us are all fighting over the same rotting carcass he's become a millionaire."

"I thought most lawyers were."

"Hardly. Right now there are more of us than there are clients and we're all sweating receivables. Except him. Five years ago he was just one of fifteen of us at the firm,. Now, he's out buying up property all over the place, he's furnishing a huge place on Camelback Mountain down there in Phoenix, and flying all over the place in his private plane." He shook his head in silent envy. "I tell you there's no justice in the world, pardon the pun."

I cocked my head at him. "So, what makes him so special?"

He shrugged. "Apparently he's picked up some lucrative cases as of late and managed to get some major settlements." He threw me a curious look. "Say, how come you ask so many questions?"

I smiled. "It's my job. My name is Kendall O'Dell. I'm a reporter for the *Castle Valley Sun*."

We both paused in our conversation and looked up as Claudia Phillips swished by. I could smell the sweet scent of her Shalimar perfume. When I called out "Hello," her gaze flickered toward me. For an instant, a look of malice blazed in her eyes, then just as quickly vanished. She nodded, dispensed a tight smile and continued on, disappearing into the ballroom.

"Va va voom!" Mike breathed. "Who was that?" He had an odd expression on his face.

"She runs a girl's shelter here in town."

"What's her name?"

"Claudia Phillips. Why?"

His eyes held a faraway look. "I know I've seen her somewhere before. The name is different...and her hair..." He threw up his hands. "It'll probably come to me at four in the morning."

"Well, if it does, would you give me a call? Here's my number." I tore a sheet of paper from my notepad and handed it to him.

He glanced at it briefly and stuffed the note in his pocket. "Ah, here comes Marcie," he announced brightly, standing to greet a petite, yet athletic-looking blonde. We exchanged introductions, chatted a few more minutes and then they left arm in arm. He'd given me a lot of information and it reminded me that I still needed to get a quote from Eric Heisler. As I squeezed on my shoes, I pondered over Claudia's puzzling behavior.

On the way toward the ballroom, Ginger stopped me to say she was leaving. I told her I had a few more interviews and then I'd corral Bradley for a ride home.

"Wait," Ginger said, grabbing my arm. "I saw you talking to Eric Heisler earlier this evening. Well? What do you think? Is he the yummiest thing you ever laid eyes on, or what?"

Amused, I said, "Yeah. He's yummy all right and if it hadn't been for Bradley butting in when he did, I'd have had dinner with him."

"Good lord! You mean to tell me you got the two of them fighting over you already?"

"I don't think they were fighting over me."

Ginger's eyes widened. "Wait. I remember now why Tally don't like him. I heard tell it's 'cause..." Her voice trailed off and I turned to see Bradley coming toward us. "I'll tell you later," she whispered. She waved good-bye to both of us and left.

"I've saved the last two dances for you," he announced benevolently, flashing me a winning smile.

"Why should I dance with you?"

"Because you want to."

I did want to. I hadn't danced for over a year, but I was still irritated with him for embarrassing me in front of Eric Heisler. "Thanks, but I'm tired."

"No. You're still pouting."

"I'm not pouting," I said evenly and tried to get around him. He blocked my way.

"You certainly have a funny way of showing gratitude."

I glared at him. This wasn't doing either of us any good. "Look, I am grateful for your help tonight, but...what was that little scene with Eric Heisler all about?"

His eyes hardened. "It would take too long to tell you now. Let's dance."

Ignoring my lame protests, he pulled me into the ballroom and onto the dance floor. I'd never danced to country western music before and he patiently walked me though the steps. The second dance was better. It was fairly fast and as he whirled me around I was very aware of his touch. It ignited emotions in me I thought I had well under control.

When he held me tighter, I didn't pull away. Did I dare let my growing attraction surface? There were so many things I still didn't know about him. I wished again that I could just ask him point blank if he had anything to do with his wife's death and get it over with. But I couldn't.

The crowd was thinning as the last song ended. Bradley thanked me for the dances and said he'd bring the truck around front in a few minutes.

When I retrieved my camera bag from Doug, he said, "I'm supposed to give you this note." Puzzled, I accepted the envelope and opened it while I waited outside for Bradley.

It read: Our first encounter was pure enchantment. Will you have dinner with me on Friday? I await your call. It was signed Eric Heisler. His business card was enclosed.

Pure enchantment? Was this guy for real? As Bradley's truck pulled up, I hastily stuffed the note in my camera bag.

On the drive home, I sat quietly while a warm nighttime breeze blew through the open window. Was it just my idyllic mood, or did the desert look particularly beautiful tonight? The moonlight traced soft silver borders on the saguaro cactus and illuminated the distant mountains.

I tried not to think about everything that had happened, but a whole host of unanswered questions lay like a coiled spring at the base of my mind.

"So, why don't you like Eric Heisler?" The question leaped off my tongue before I could stop it.

In the dim light of the cab I saw his features harden. "He's not a man to be trusted."

He can't be trusted? I thought incredulously. And this coming from a man suspected of murdering his wife?

"Oh, come on. In what way? I've heard nothing but glowing reports about him."

"If you must know," he said gravely, "he's one of the men in Castle Valley my dear departed wife chose to sleep with."

11

Scrunched low in the seat, barely able to see over the dashboard, I sipped the last of the lukewarm coffee from the Styrofoam cup. Morton Tuggs would be expecting some answers from me soon, so I had planned the Monday morning stakeout of the Ocotillo Apartments in hopes of cornering Yolanda Reyes. Like it or not, she was going to talk to me today. I'd already been there for over an hour, and now with dawn breaking, I was about to lose the cover of darkness.

A covey of quail scuttled across the dirt road and disappeared underneath one of the dilapidated cars parked along the side of the street. I hoped one of the junkers belonged to Yolanda because it would certainly be easier to follow her on wheels than on foot.

I shifted to a more comfortable position and then mentally sifted through the myriad of unanswered questions that had become my constant companions.

Foremost in my mind was Bradley's bombshell announcement that linked Eric Heisler with his late wife.

When I'd pressed him for further details, he admitted he'd never really had proof of her infidelity, but had strongly suspected it. When confronted, he told me Stephanie hadn't denied seeing Eric, saying she'd consulted him only professionally about divorce proceedings. But she'd been unable to explain why she had stayed overnight in Phoenix several times at Eric's plush home.

While he talked, his eyes had grown cold and distant. I was stunned. After all these weeks of wondering about him, he'd handed me the opening I'd been waiting for. I was all set to plunge ahead with questions when he suddenly clammed up, saying perhaps we'd talk more at the dinner I'd promised him, although no firm date was set.

After he'd left, I wondered if I should have told him that I knew all about how Stephanie had died. But something stopped me. I hated to divulge the fact that I'd been gossiping about him with Ginger.

Waves of revulsion washed over me again as I remembered the spider invasion. I'd been jumpy in the house ever since. My antipathy toward Lucinda, my prime suspect, had grown tenfold. I'd also had time to speculate on the odd behavior of my only neighbor, Dr. Isadore Price. On Sunday, I'd watched from my kitchen window as the black Mercedes, followed again by the white van, sped by. I couldn't understand why the doctor had been so taken aback at my innocent suggestion that we talk sometime. Perhaps I'd best do a little research on Serenity House.

And then there was the problem of what to do about Eric Heisler. He was just about the sexiest man I'd ever met. I wondered if I should let Bradley's accusation that he'd been one of Stephanie's bedmates interfere with the fact that I really wanted to see him again.

A movement at the apartment gates caught my attention. Elated, I watched Yolanda Reyes, clad in blue jeans and a checked shirt, walk toward and unlock the battered Datsun two cars ahead of me.

She wasn't difficult to tail. Her car belched a trail of blue smoke for blocks. I jotted down the license plate for future reference. Two miles later, she swung into an alley adjacent to Sierra Laundry & Dry Cleaning. I pulled up behind her and leapt from the car calling, "Miss Reyes, I need to talk to you."

Her eyes registered blankness first and then recognition, followed by fury. "*¡Puta!*" she spat.

She broke into a run, but I sprinted and grabbed her arm. "Wait! Listen to me. I never knew John Dexter, okay? I'm the reporter who took his place." She paused, looking uncertain, so I quickly added, "All I'm trying to do is find out where he went."

I watched the rage fade from her eyes, and with a feeling of relief, I released her arm.

"So...you were not one of his..."

She didn't need to finish the sentence. "Your apartment manager said John purchased bus tickets to Nogales. Is that correct?"

"*Sí.* He says he does this for her," she said with a thick Spanish accent.

"Her?"

"The girl on the phone. And now...he is gone."

Her deep brown eyes misted. "I know sometimes he will see...the other girls. But he tells me it is nothing how do you say?...so serious." She wiped away the tears on her cheeks and said in a cracked voice, "He says he loves me and we will soon marry."

94

"Yolanda, who called him the night before he van...er...left?"

"I do not know her name. She calls two...three times, maybe."

"How do you know?"

"I was with him."

"You didn't ask who she was?"

"*Sí*. But all he says is, 'I will tell you when the time, it is right.'"

"I see." We were silent for a moment. "Did the police question you about John?"

"Many days later. I can tell them little."

"Did they ever check back with you again?"

"No."

I paused while she yanked a wad of tissue from her pocket. "Listen, John supposedly got a speeding ticket the afternoon he was last seen. If he went to Nogales on the bus, what happened to his vehicle?"

She looked blank. "Vehicle?"

"You know. His car or whatever he was driving."

"I too wondered that. His pickup was new."

"Do you know what make it was?"

She shook her head.

"Color?"

"Red. It has the big, big tires."

"Did he pack his apartment the day he left?"

She shook her head.

"Did he come back for his stuff?"

"No."

I raised a brow. "Who cleaned out his apartment?"

"Days after, two men come driving a big truck. I ask them, 'Are you going to Nogales?' but they do not answer."

"Do you remember the name on the truck?"

She thought for a moment, shifting from one foot to the other while absently pulling on strands of her long, dark hair. "It was one of those...you know...trucks for rent..." She glanced at her watch, looking anxious. "Oh! I am late."

"Just one more thing, Yolanda, and I hate to ask you but...do you have a recent photograph of John?" She hesitated, and I added, "I just need it for a few days." I gave her a reassuring smile. After another moment's hesitation, she hurried to her car and returned clutching a photograph showing the two of them entwined in each other's arms.

"The picture. You promise to give back?" she asked, handing it to me. It was much better than the blurry photo Tugg had shown me. The face of a good looking young man with dark hair and eyes smiled back at me.

"You have my word on it. Here's my number. If you think of anything else, would you please call me?"

She nodded, started to walk away, then turned and gave me an anguished look. "He did not tell me good-bye. Why does he do this when he promises he will come back?"

"I don't know, Yolanda, but I'll sure try to find out." She flashed me a teary smile and ran inside the cleaners. Yolanda's parting statement definitely didn't jibe with what Roy Hollingsworth had said, that John Dexter had simply gotten bored and taken off for parts unknown. And the fact that she had been questioned only once following his disappearance certainly demonstrated Dexter's allegations of sloppy investigating.

While the information was fresh I made copious notes and then headed to the sheriff's office. I had to cross my fingers and hope that Roy would buy my reasons for wanting to look at the files of the dead teens.

As luck would have it, Roy wasn't there. Instead I dealt with Deputy Duane Potts. I smiled to myself. The last few times I had been in to check the police log, his fawning demeanor and thinly-concealed lust had made it rather obvious that Deputy Potts had the hots for me. Perhaps I could use that to my advantage.

"And how are you this fine morning, Miss O'Dell?" he asked with an ingratiating smile as he smoothed what was left of his limp blonde hair with one hand while thumbing his shirt tighter into his trousers with the other.

I forced a dazzling smile. "I'm just great, and you?" As I studied the log, he told me how busy he'd been with Roy out of town the last three days. "I hope he's got some money left when he gets back," he cracked, imparting a knowing look in my direction.

"Why's that?"

"Well, you know how it goes up there in Vegas," he laughed. "Sometimes you win big, sometimes you lose big."

"Does Roy gamble a lot?"

"I guess you might say he's addicted."

"Must be nice to have money to burn."

He was studying his own reflection in the window glass and repeatedly smoothed his pencil thin mustache. Returning his attention to me he said, "Well, I guess we can't all be millionaires like Roy." He laughed heartily at his own joke and I pretended I didn't see him mentally undressing me. The fact that he had a wife and four kids at home sure didn't stop him from gawking.

I rounded my eyes with innocence. "Really? I had no idea Roy had that kind of money. His salary certainly must be a lot better than mine."

"Mine too. But then, we can't all have a rich aunt die and leave us a fortune."

"Oh, I see. Well, Duane, I need a favor. I've been assigned to do a series on runaway teen-agers and in my research of the area, I came across two cases you guys have investigated during the past year."

"Oh, sure. You mean those poor little gals we found in the desert? Yes, siree. We finally got a positive ID on the second girl, but Roy's still workin' on the other one."

He appeared relaxed, talkative, and not the least suspicious. Might as well strike while the iron was hot. "Could I see the files on those cases? I'd like to see if there's anything I could use in my story."

He about fell all over himself. "Sure thing. Be right back."

He was gone for quite a while. When he came out, he said, "Funny you'd want these. John Dexter asked about them too."

I kept my face impassive. "Really? Why?"

"Oh, you would have had to know him. He was always snooping around trying to rustle up trouble. He acted like he was working for the *National Enquirer* sometimes."

"I read in some old editions of the *Sun* that he didn't think ah...you guys were working very hard to solve the second case. The Perkins girl."

He took offense at that. "Well, he was full of shit! Oh, excuse me, I mean...John accused Roy of sitting on his hands, but I'm here to tell you that he worked his butt off on that case. The fact that someone back in Washington screwed up and misplaced the file wasn't his fault. John reported that wrong." He waved a hand vehemently. "It was nothing of the kind. Roy took a real personal interest in that case and this other one too," he said tapping the folders. "Of course, as you'll see, there wasn't much left of the first body.

I read through the reports. "Who did the face sheets on these?"

"Roy."

"His handwriting isn't the best is it?"

"It's awful. I can barely read it myself."

"I'm having trouble with parts of these descriptions as to where the bodies were found. Can you clarify them for me?"

He shrugged. "They were both found on the Talverson ranch."

That jarred me. "That's kind of a strange coincidence, isn't it?"

He shrugged and made a face. "Not really. He's got one hellacious bunch of land. Thousands of acres."

I kept my expression bland even though the information left me feeling non-plussed. I examined every sheet of paper in the files and it didn't take me long to discover John Dexter had been right.

"Um...there's reference made here to toxicology reports yet I don't find them in either of these files. Is there some reason they're not with the autopsy information?"

He blinked and frowned. "Well, no. They should be there." He came over and stood close to me. In fact he was so close, his shoulder touched mine. "Hmmm. Well, they must've been misfiled. He thumbed toward the back and said in a low voice, "Julie's real nice, but a little dense. She's famous for losing things and misfiling." He puffed out his chest. "I'll look into this for you. By the way, is there some special reason they're so important to you?"

I'd been hoping he wouldn't ask. "Having them would really help me out with this article. Make it more complete and round out the series, you understand."

He gave me a knowing nod even though I'm sure he didn't have a clue as to what I was talking about.

I thanked him for taking the time to help me, and asked him to contact me when he found the missing reports. He promised and about broke an ankle getting to the door to open it for me, and then saluted good-bye.

In the car once more, I studied Dexter's note again. The first clue was now confirmed...wait just a minute! I'd misread it. It didn't say 't prof.' It said 'prop'. Obviously 'T prop' stood for Talverson property.

While Deputy Potts had dismissed it as unimportant, John must have thought it significant or he wouldn't have written it down. The implication made me feel a little ill. This might be the connection he'd referred to. Add the two teens plus Stephanie and that meant three people had died on the Talverson property in two years. I interrupted my next thought before it fully materialized.

My last stop before heading into work was the bus station. It was a tiny place located in a crumbling brick building next to a shoe repair shop and across the street from Lucinda's restaurant. The smell of homemade bread filled the air and it was easy to see why the place would act as a beacon to hungry travelers. That thought triggered the memory of the scraggly young girl Lucinda had so roughly ejected.

I savored the cool blast of air-conditioning as I stepped inside and immediately introduced myself to a portly white-haired gentleman named Farley Shupe. After chatting about the warm weather for a few minutes, I told him about my story on the runaways. He verified the fact that Castle Valley appeared to be a dropping off place for teens, girls especially.

"It just churns my gut to see those pathetic little gals. I make it a point to send them over to the shelter for something to eat."

"It must be a great source of pride for the town to have someplace these girls can go for help."

"It sure is. Before they moved into that house over there on Tumbleweed, I used to direct them to the church. But, there got to be so many, there wasn't room." A look of sorrow passed over his face. "It was a real tragedy when Violet was killed. I used to see her in church every Sunday and I'll tell you, a kinder, more generous lady, I've never known. She had...what do you call it? Real empathy."

"I guess Claudia Phillips is the same sort of person?"

He hesitated a second. "I guess she's got a good heart or she wouldn't be doing what she's doing. She provides their bus tickets and makes sure they've got new clothes and stuff but...I don't know, she seems a bit standoffish, if you know what I mean."

It was nice to hear my thoughts about her confirmed. Reaching into my purse, I pulled out the photo of John Dexter. "Mr. Shupe, do you recognize this man?"

He studied the photo. "Oh sure. That's John Dexter. I guess he left before you got here, huh?"

"Yes. He left quite a few personal items behind in his desk, and I'd really like to send his things along to him. It's my understanding he may have relocated to Nogales with a...friend. Did he mention where he might be staying when he bought the tickets. He did buy two didn't he?"

"Well, I think so." He paged through a journal on the counter and his finger stopped at one of the entries. "Nope. I was wrong. It says here he only bought one ticket to Nogales."

12

Morton Tuggs' well-worn chair let out a squeaky groan as he leaned back and laced his fingers behind his neck. He puffed out an extended breath and stared at the ceiling for a while before meeting my eyes again. "So, what do you make of it to this point?" he asked.

I'd just given him a rundown on all the information I'd uncovered regarding John Dexter. "I hate to tell you I don't know, but, to be truthful, all we have right now is a bunch of unrelated clues and your suspicion that Roy is somehow involved in his disappearance. I'm not getting a clear picture on anything," I said, half apologetically.

He studied one of the many colorful travel posters on his wall while chewing the end of his pen. When he turned back to me, he sounded agitated. "Well, let's go over it again. Maybe something will start to make some sense."

I read my notes aloud for the second time. "John disappeared the afternoon or evening of March 29th. The last person to see him was Roy Hollingsworth who claims John was speeding south on highway 89…"

"And today," he said emphatically, stabbing his pen in my direction, "is the first time I've heard that."

"Do you think Roy just forgot to mention it to you? It's possible, isn't it?"

He looked skeptical. "Is it just me? Don't you think this whole thing a bit odd? I know it happens, but from what you've discovered, do you think John would just up and leave town without saying good-bye to a single soul?"

"Well, I didn't know him, but you said yourself he was a flake."

"So you believe Roy?"

"I'm not making excuses for him, I don't even know the man. But to be perfectly honest, until this morning I was beginning to think you were way out in left field. Now I don't feel that way. There are too many strange clues that have been overlooked or poorly handled by the sheriff's department."

"Do you think it's because Roy's an idiot? Or do you think he's hiding something?"

"I don't know yet. But this is what we do know. John had several secretive phone calls from some unknown female. He bought one ticket to Nogales, Mexico. He called you to say he was meeting someone who had information so vital, it would turn the town on its ear, right?"

Tugg nodded, opened a drawer and took several swallows from a blue bottle. "Stomach's acting up again."

"We know his girlfriend Yolanda fully expected him to return, yet he was never seen again after Roy ticketed him." I flipped to the next page in my notebook. "Now, what we don't know is whether Roy is even involved. If we make the assumption that John met with foul play, then it makes sense that someone cleaned out his place to make it

look as though he'd just skipped town. But what if he really
sent for his belongings? Then where is he?"

Like the shadow from a cloud, another weary,
troubled look passed over Tugg's face. "This business about
his truck really bugs me. John thought his Toyota was the
greatest thing since microwave popcorn. If he bought that
ticket to Nogales for himself, what the hell did he do with
his truck? Sell it in Phoenix before he left? And why would
he do that?"

I heaved a sigh. "I don't know. I could understand it
better if he'd bought two tickets, but one…" Hesitating, I
met his eye. "It sounds to me as if he bought that ticket for
someone else, that he never intended to go to Nogales. I
believe Yolanda when she says he told her he was coming
back. Now all I have to do is find out who he bought the
ticket for."

"What about the missing medical records on those
two dead girls?" Tugg asked. "What's the connection
there?"

"I'm not sure there is one. Potts says the records
exist, but they've been misfiled. He didn't seem suspicious
or upset that I'd asked to see them and said he'd cooperate
in trying to locate them as soon as possible. He also said
Roy has worked very hard on the two cases, and that's
contrary to what John was insinuating."

He groaned and buried his face in his hands. "God,
this is exasperating! The more you find out, the less we
know."

I wondered if he was comparing my reporting skills
to my dad, who'd been tops in his field. "Just give me a little
more time. I'm going to have a look at those medical
records as soon as Potts finds them. Maybe I'll find some

shred of evidence that'll tie Roy into this. What's your game plan if I do?"

"It's funny," Tugg mused, staring blankly out the window. "Half of me wants to tell you to just let sleeping dogs lie, yet the other half doesn't. For my wife's sake, I pray Roy isn't involved. But if he is, and he gets wind of this, he'll sue me, call the loan and this paper is history. Remember, this is a small community. Secrets are hard to keep."

I smiled encouragingly at him. "So far, he doesn't know anything and there's nothing to tie my investigation to you. I've been super careful to say only that I'm looking for Dexter in order to return some stuff he left behind. Who knows, maybe we'll get lucky and discover he really did just skip out." It was obvious that neither of us believed that.

I returned to my office to study the assignment sheet. With the first of June fast approaching the town was gearing up for the week long Gold Dust Days celebration. Jim jokingly called it the 'last gasp' before the snowbirds packed up and made tracks for their homes in the east and midwest. After that, he informed me, Castle Valley citizens pulled in the sidewalks to wait out the sizzling summer.

"Sounds charming," I muttered while copying my assignments, then looked up as Al Robertson from classifieds stuck his head in the door.

"Hey, you guys, everybody's getting together after work tonight to chug a few beers and celebrate Lupe's birthday. We're all meeting over at Angelina's around six. You wanna come?"

He gave me a wide smile and a feeling of warmth spread through me. For the first time I felt accepted as 'one of the gang.'

"Count me in," Jim replied with enthusiasm.

"Well, Kendall," Bradley said, leaning back in his chair, "this will be your chance to have some authentic Mexican food." His steady gaze made my pulse skip.

Smiling, I said, "I'm looking forward to it."

"Okay, see you folks later." Al saluted and left. All three of us had assignments centered around Gold Dust Days. Jim grabbed his camera and left. I knew Bradley was on his way to the fairgrounds to talk with rodeo personalities, and my assignment was to interview the head of the Chamber of Commerce and the winner of the Queen of the Gold Dust Parade competition.

When I returned in late afternoon Ginger, on the phone as usual, gave me an excited thumbs up and a dazzling smile as I went by. I didn't know why until I rounded the corner to my office.

My mouth gaped at the sight. There on my desk stood a vase filled with at least two dozen magnificent long-stemmed roses.

Bradley and Jim both eyed me in silence. Puzzled, I inquired brightly, "So. What's the occasion?" For a fleeting second, I wondered if they were from Bradley. But a big, flashy vase of flowers didn't seem his style.

"We were kinda hoping you'd tell us." A wicked twinkle gleamed in Jim's eyes.

"Apparently, you have an admirer," Bradley said quietly and then turned his back to me. The warm companionable mood I'd sensed earlier seemed to have vanished.

I crossed the room and pulled a small white envelope from the bouquet. "Your promised evening of enchantment still awaits. Please say you'll dine with me on Friday." It was signed: Eric Heisler.

I buried my face in the sweet blooms, inhaling deeply. The man definitely had class. I couldn't ever remember receiving such a romantic invitation in my life. How could I turn it down? And why should I?

Jim was insistent. "Come on, let's have it. Who'd send you a hundred bucks worth of posies?"

"My father," I announced sweetly, meeting Bradley's eyes as he glanced over his shoulder. He had to know I was lying. The stony look on his face made me feel as if I'd done something wrong.

Ginger cornered me later in the restroom, squealing with excitement. "Praise the Lord, you've gone and hooked the big one! Now don't tell me them flowers are from your pa." She closed one eye and wagged her finger in my face. "I knew the second Eric Heisler got a peek at you in that dress last Saturday, he'd be a goner for sure." Placing both hands over her heart, she crooned, "I am assumin' y'all will want me to be your maid of honor. And, missy, how many layers will you be needin' on your weddin' cake? I like chocolate."

"Calm down, Ginger. He just asked me to dinner."

"Well that's just the first step, sugar pie."

"I haven't even agreed to go yet. I'm thinking it over."

She gave me a pained look. "You're thinkin' it over? You're thinkin' it over! Good gravy, girl, you know the odds of catching a stud like him? Why they'd have to be a zillion to one, 'specially in this town."

"I don't know, Ginger. I asked Bradley to tell me why he acted so awful toward Eric, and he did."

Her lips rounded into a little O. "Mercy me! He beat me to it. So, what'd he say?"

I moved to the mirror and applied fresh lipstick. Giving her a sidelong glance, I replied, "That his wife Stephanie and Eric Heisler had been having an affair."

She looked puzzled. "Well, so what?"

"So what? Bradley's asked me to dinner and now, so has Eric."

"Well, good lord girl, we should all have such a problem. I'm gonna have to hogtie my fellow to get him to the altar and you're complaining 'cause you've got two of 'em banging down your door."

I sighed wearily. "Oh, Ginger. I'm not sure I want to get into the middle of something like this. I think they still hate each other."

"That was a long time ago. And remember, Eric wasn't the only guy she was fooling with. What're you kicking up such a fuss about? Everyone in town knew she and Tally was gettin' ready to split."

I zipped my purse shut. "Don't have a heart attack. I'm going to give it careful consideration, believe me."

She sniffed. "Well, I should hope so. Men like Eric only come along once in a blue moon, darlin'. When's the last time y'all even seen a blue moon?"

"Ginger, you're incorrigible." I chuckled and headed toward the door.

"Wait just a second," she said grabbing my elbow. "Y'all recollect when we was talking Saturday night about my repeating your spider story down at the beauty parlor?"

"Yes."

"Y'all gonna tell me why you were so upset about that?"

"Probably, but not right at this moment."

"Oh, me and my big mouth. Tell me what's wrong."

"Forget it, Ginger. You told me what I needed to know. I've got to finish my copy. I'll talk to you more this evening. You are going to Lupe's party aren't you?"

"Is a pig's ass pork? I'm bringin' the cake."

I laughed and almost got out the door when she blurted out, "Will y'all just hold yer horses for one minute?"

"Sorry, what is it."

"I happened to recall who else was down at Coleen's but..." she hesitated coyly, looking away. "If y'all ain't interested..."

"I'm interested."

"When I thought about it some more, I remembered there was old Mrs. Hatterly, she's about ninety if she's a day, and then there was Marcie Ordway, she's the cashier down at the moviehouse, and then there was the one we was talking about Saturday afternoon?"

"Who?"

"You know. That skinny old gal from over yonder at the shelter. Claudia Phillips."

13

Ginger's remark really threw me. I thought about it all the way home. Every time I'd come up with a different theory, out the window it would fly. For the life of me, I couldn't connect her with the spider prank. Why would Claudia Phillips give a hang about anything I did? And what reason would she have for trying to scare me away from the Delgado Ranch? No. The fact that she had been at the salon with numerous other people could only be a coincidence. It had to be Lucinda. Her unbridled passion for Bradley provided the only motive.

Following a quick sponge bath, I slid into my turquoise jumpsuit, brushed my hair until it crackled with static electricity, then stopped by the dining room table to take a big whiff of Eric's flowers. The thought of seeing him again intrigued me. He was definitely one hot-looking guy.

On impulse, I grabbed the phone and dialed the number on his card. It was already past five-thirty and chances of catching him at his office were probably slim, but what the heck, I'd give it a shot.

Seven. Eight. Nine rings. Oh, well, I'd call another time. Then, his unexpected hello made my stomach feel fluttery.

"Oh? Hi. This is Kendall O'Dell." There was a short pause and then in a silky voice brimming with self-assurance he remarked, "I knew it would be you."

"You did? How?"

"Because," he replied, "from that very first moment, I've felt certain our meeting was preordained. The tides which were destined to bring us together cannot be altered."

I wasn't sure what he meant but had to admit the man could really turn a phrase. "Well," I laughed, "I guess you could say that. However, I did plan all along to meet with you...strictly for professional reasons of course."

"I see. And does that still stand?"

"For now," I answered.

He chuckled. "I hope you'll give me a chance to change that status." His voice dropped the caressing tone and became more cordial. "I'm going to assume that was a yes for dinner. I'll pick you up at six."

"Oh, that's not really necessary. I can meet you."

"Humor me."

"All right. But, I don't live in town. I'm sort of out in the boondocks."

"Oh? Where do you live?"

"Since you grew up here you probably know where it is. I'm renting the Delgado house on Lost Canyon Road."

"My dear girl, why in the world are you living out there?"

"It's affordable, the air is good for my asthma problem...lots of reasons."

"Along with your attributes of obvious beauty and intelligence, you must also be quite brave. I don't know of many single young women who would want to live in such an isolated spot."

Knowing how to flatter a gal was certainly one of his strong points. "I'm managing, thank you."

"I know quite a lot of people in Castle Valley even though I don't live there full time anymore. If you wish, I could arrange for you to have a very nice place closer to town."

"I'm fine for now, but if Mrs. Delgado returns any time soon, I may take you up on that. Anyway, I'll see you Friday. By the way, thank you for the beautiful roses. That was very thoughtful."

"I'm glad you like them."

I hung up thinking Eric was exactly the kind of guy my mom would be thrilled with; wealthy, educated, cultured and great-looking. I could hear her now. 'He's perfect for you. Grab on with both hands and don't let go.' I would make a point to call her this weekend.

The clock chimed six. Rats! I was already late for Lupe's get-together. I grabbed my purse and hurried to the car.

Angelina's Mexican Restaurant was located in a crumbling adobe building near the industrial section of town. Two Hispanic women were shouting in rapid-fire Spanish as I passed by an open kitchen door. Whatever was cooking smelled heavenly.

Since the outside of the place looked so dilapidated, the spacious interior surprised me. The rough plaster walls were decorated with colorful strings of chili peppers and beaded straw sombreros. Squat candles sputtered in tiny rounded alcoves.

Over the din of the crowd and the lusty Latin tune thumping from nearby speakers, I heard Ginger's distinctive voice. "Hey, sugar, over here!"

She and the rest of the staff were all gathered near the bar. I could feel Bradley's steady gaze on me as I approached so I met his eyes and smiled. He smiled back. Then with casual grace, he hooked the toe of his boot around a vacant chair and pulled it next to his. I was relieved. I'd expected him to still be annoyed about the flower incident.

I congratulated Lupe on her birthday. By her bleary smile and unfocused stare, I gathered she was already half-plowed. Harry and Rick were perched on bar stools gulping beer in a haze of cigarette smoke.

"Where've y'all been?" Ginger demanded as I sat down next to Bradley and Jim. "I pert near sent the sheriff's posse over yonder to fetch you."

"I'm sorry, I got hung up on the phone."

"Anyone we know?" came Jim's innocent question. I hesitated a mere fraction of a second but it was enough to cause Bradley to say with just a touch of scorn, "I'm sure she had to phone her...father to thank him for the flowers, right?"

So he was still sulking. I met the flinty accusation in his eyes and said coolly, "You're so perceptive."

Turning away, I detected the mirth sparkling in Ginger's eyes. I gave an almost imperceptible shake of my head and hoped, for once, she'd keep her mouth shut.

The conflicting jumble of emotions confounded me. Why should I feel disloyal to Bradley just because I'd accepted a simple dinner invitation from Eric Heisler?

When the waitress asked, I ordered white wine and had to endure some good-natured jeering. Someone called me a "dude" and Jim chimed in with, "Get real. This ain't the Ritz. Nobody orders white wine at Angelina's. I suppose this means you're ordering sushi for dinner?"

There was more laughter. "Hey, I'm easy. What do you suggest?"

Jim hoisted a frosty pitcher, poured the remainder of the liquid into a salt rimmed glass and shoved it under my nose. "This is what you drink at Angelina's!"

"What is it?"

"That," Bradley said helpfully, "is a Margarita. The main ingredient is tequila. It can sneak up on you so I'd go easy if I were you."

"I'm a big girl. I think I can handle it," I said taking a swallow. It was a mild, refreshing drink with no taste of alcohol. When tortilla chips and hot sauce were passed around Bradley again warned me about overindulging.

"Mexican food is a little like the heat. You have to become acclimated to it. It's not for delicate damsels nor the faint of heart," he said meaningfully.

Sparks seemed to ignite in the air between us as we exchanged a long look. I could tell he was deliberately goading me just like he'd done last Saturday night. And like then, I found our verbal sparring stimulating. I felt half elated that he was behaving as though he were jealous, and half irritated that he would use that superior, macho tone of voice on me again. But rather than pick a fight, I gave him a beguiling smile. "Since I'm neither delicate nor faint of heart, I believe I'll survive, thank you."

"Suit yourself," he said rocking back on two chair legs, folding his arms behind his neck. His eyes shimmered with mischief.

I sensed everyone at the table watching me as I popped the first sauce laden chip into my mouth. It took me about five seconds to realize I was in trouble. Even the hottest Thai food I'd eaten didn't compare to this. Scalding tears jumped to my eyes and I stifled the gasp forming in my throat. My God! What was in this stuff? Gasoline? I grabbed the Margarita and gulped it down.

Everyone roared with laughter and after I caught my breath, I inclined my head in Bradley's direction. "Okay, you win that one."

A large table in the far corner of the room had been reserved for us, so we picked up our drinks and trooped over. On the way, person after person called 'hello' to Bradley and some of the others. It was like one big family, I thought, so different from the impersonal restaurants in large cities.

As I scanned the crowded room, I noticed Claudia Phillips. She was apparently giving someone the business. Her pale face was intense, angry almost. I craned my neck, but couldn't make out who was sitting opposite her in the booth near the swinging kitchen door. Her edgy behavior toward me during our interview, coupled with Ginger's admission, was still fresh in my mind. It might be interesting to see who was the target of her wrath.

While the rest of my group argued good-naturedly over who would sit where, I pondered several options. A leisurely stroll past Claudia's booth would reveal the identity of her companion, but I was positive the moment she spotted me, her conversation would cease and I would learn nothing. A more sensible plan would be to somehow overhear what she was saying, and that would best be accomplished if she didn't see me.

I faked a cough. "Excuse me for a minute. The smoke in here is pretty thick. I need to ah…go to the ladies room."

"You okay, darlin'?" Ginger inquired. "You want me to come with you?"

I tapped my chest and waved her away. "Not necessary. It's just a little asthma attack. I'll use my inhaler and be right back."

Luckily for me, the restrooms were down a narrow hallway not far from Claudia's booth. I hastily washed my hands and then hurried back out. A telephone located close by would serve as a good prop. I held the receiver to my ear and leaned as far as the cord would allow.

Their voices were all but drowned out by the clatter from the kitchen and the music from a nearby speaker. At first, I got only bits and pieces of conversation. The man's voice was little more than a muffled whine, but all at once I could hear Claudia. Her angry voice carried above the constant din. "We both agreed to do our part. How dare you even think of leaving after all he's done for you!" The man said something I couldn't understand and then Claudia answered, "If she's upsetting the rest of them, you'll have to do whatever is necessary to control her. There's too much at stake. We can't afford to be careless..."

The rest of her sentence was lost when someone nearby dropped a tray. The place was frustratingly noisy. When it quieted I heard her say, "He wants to try it his way. If that doesn't work then you and I will put an end to this once and for all."

Put an end to what? I couldn't stand it anymore. I had to know who she was talking to. I banged the receiver onto the phone and moved to her booth. I stretched on tiptoe and almost got a glimpse of the man when Ginger came up behind me. "Y'all fall in the pot or somethin'?"

Startled, I motioned for her to be quiet, whispering, "I'll be along in just a minute."

"Land sakes, girl," she complained, grabbing me by the arm. "Get your buns in gear. Everybody's waiting on you to order."

It was either go with her or cause a scene. Sighing with frustration, I took a quick glance backward. "Come on, O'Dell," Jim shouted as we approached the table. "You're holding up the party." Harry bawled, "Jesus! My stomach thinks my throat's been cut."

Ginger was blabbering something to me, but I was so preoccupied by what I'd overheard, it was difficult to concentrate. By the time I had an opportunity to turn and look, the booth was empty. Damn. How had she gotten away so fast?

I was mentally kicking myself when I spotted her near the cashier's counter. Craning my neck to look around Harry's ample frame, I froze in surprise to see Claudia headed toward the front door, followed closely by Sheriff Roy Hollingsworth.

Wait a minute, I warned myself. Don't jump to conclusions. So, Claudia and the sheriff left together at the same time. That didn't necessarily mean he'd been the one having dinner with her. Nor did it mean he hadn't.

The party was now in full swing so I had to push the puzzle aside as dinner arrived. While balancing five huge platters, our cheerful waitress solemnly issued a warning that the plates were very hot.

"So, for the full effect," Jim shouted to all. "Grab on to them with both hands." That brought howls of laughter as everyone attacked their dinner with gusto. I stared down at my dish of food, swimming in red sauce and melted cheese.

"Come on," Jim urged, loading up his fork. "Dive right in."

After the first few tentative tastes, I decided that, while savory, this must be akin to swallowing molten lava. The sensation of heat spread from my throat and stomach right down to my toes. I grabbed the water glass hoping no one would notice my teary eyes and dripping nose.

I met Bradley's amused gaze over the rim of the glass. "Don't worry. That's the sure sign of really well-prepared Mexican food."

With a laugh Jim added, "Yeah. If it clears out your sinuses and melts the wax in your ears, you know it's the best."

I dabbed the end of my nose with the napkin. "Interesting side effects."

We'd just finished singing "Happy Birthday" to Lupe when a tall, auburn-haired woman approached the table. She was introduced to me as Bradley's sister Ronda, and I didn't miss the startled expression on her face, nor the meaningful look she exchanged with him. I wondered what each of them was thinking. She was soon joined by Lucinda who'd obviously had way too much to drink. In her desperation to be noticed by Bradley, she laughed too loud and made a fool of herself by trying to sit in his lap. He handled it with grace, but after she and Ronda left, I couldn't help but feel a bit sorry for her.

My pig-headedness got me into trouble as usual. I had ignored Bradley's advice to go easy on the Margaritas and hot tamales. The combined results proved explosive, and I spent a good portion of that night in my bathroom wishing I was dead.

The next day, I was thankful Bradley had gone to Phoenix for three days to cover the Little League finals.

Pale and weak, I'm sure I looked every bit as wretched as I felt. My stomach churned, my head ached, and my tongue felt like it was covered with a thick coat of moss.

"Oh, honey," Ginger soothed as she provided me with alternate doses of aspirin, Kaopectate and sympathy, "it's just a bad case of the trots. Hereabouts, they call it Montezuma's revenge. It happens to a lot of folks when they eat Mexican food."

Positive that my insides were scorched for life, I solemnly vowed I'd never eat the stuff again.

14

By Wednesday afternoon I still hadn't heard back from Deputy Potts about the missing medical records, so I decided to stop by the sheriff's office on my way to cover a city council meeting. It was probably a foolish wish, but I hoped he'd not mentioned my request to Roy. No point in tipping my hand when, at this point, all I had was a growing list of unsubstantiated suspicions.

The weather forecast had called for a record high temperature of 109° and as I left the office and walked to my car in the blinding white sunlight, I felt every stinging degree. Heat waves shimmered from the asphalt and left me feeling slightly dizzy.

"Jesus H. Christ!" I shrieked as I grabbed the door handle. It was so hot I had to use the hem of my skirt to pull it open. Seated in the suffocating interior, I rolled down the windows and blasted the air-conditioner. It puffed out a pathetic stream of warm air that did little to relieve my misery.

At the only stoplight in town, I braked behind a battered pickup. A large golden retriever stood in the truck bed panting furiously in a vain effort to cool himself.

While sweat trickled down the back of my neck and between my breasts, I shifted my weight and muttered sympathetically, "I know how you feel, Buddy."

Overhead, spanning the intersection, a colorful banner announcing the commencement of Gold Dust Days snapped in a brisk afternoon wind so hot I'm sure it must have originated from the gates of hell.

At that moment all I could think of was immersing myself in a cool, blue lake high in the Allegheny Mountains of Pennsylvania.

When I stepped inside the sheriff's office, the effect of cold air against my feverish skin made goose bumps thrive on my arms and the pounding in my head resume.

Roy Hollingsworth looked up from reading material on his desk and said pleasantly, "Afternoon, Miss O'Dell. It's hotter 'n' the strings on a square dance fiddle, out there, ain't it?"

"Terrible," I sighed, patting my damp forehead.

"You'll get used to it."

"I wonder."

"Say, that was a real fine piece you wrote in today's paper about the fund-raiser last Saturday. Now, that's a real worthy cause."

"Well, thank you."

He leaned back in the chair and propped one boot on the desk. "So," he inquired. "I guess you must like your job a lot, huh?"

"Yes, I do."

"Well, now, that's good. Real good." He gave me a broad smile. "I was just wondering something."

"What's that?"

"You coming from Philadelphia and being a big-time reporter and all, I figure you must sort of miss all the big city action. We don't get a whole lot of excitement around here, you know. Oh, we get a few people who want to stir stink, but not often." He paused and cleared his throat. "I'm surprised you've stayed on. I thought maybe our little town would be a mite too slow for the likes of you."

I wondered if there was some hidden meaning behind his words. "I didn't come here for excitement. I came for my health."

"Asthma."

"Word does get around."

"Not too much gets past me." His smile was warm, his eyes weren't. "So, what can I do for you, Miss O'Dell?"

"Actually, I was hoping to talk to Duane for a minute. He promised to find some information I asked for." By the light in his eyes, I knew that he knew.

"Yeah. He said you'd been in here last week asking to see the files on those two little gals. Something about doing a story on these runaway kids?"

"Yes." I gave him an encouraging smile. "By the way, I heard you'd been in Las Vegas. Was your trip successful?"

His face sagged with disappointment. "Naw. I don't know why I waste my time going up there. I've had a hellacious string of bad luck at the blackjack table the last couple of months."

"Sorry to hear that."

He shrugged and said nothing. In the momentary silence that fell, all I could hear was the rhythmic whine of the ceiling fan overhead. So far he'd made no move to get the files. "If it wouldn't be too much trouble, I'd like to look in those folders again."

"Uh-huh." He rose from his chair, took a few steps toward the file room and then turned back to me. "Now, you know these cases are still active so if you come across any new information, you'll report it to me right away."

"Of course."

He returned almost immediately and set the files on his desk. After seating myself in a metal chair nearby, I leafed through the papers. Somehow I wasn't surprised to discover what I wanted wasn't there. I kept my voice casual. "Gosh, I was hoping Duane would find those toxicology reports he said were misfiled."

"Why do you need them?"

"The Perkins case involved a runaway, and since that will be the focus of my series, I hoped I might find something, ah, noteworthy."

"Like what?" He was busy cracking his knuckles.

"Oh, I don't know. Something that might possibly link the two cases together?"

"Reporters! You all think you're so goddamn smart. You think I just fell off a cattle truck yesterday? Don't you think if there had been something to link them I'd have already found it?"

His indignant tone indicated I'd hit a nerve. I thought again of John Dexter's final warning. Roy's blustering would have put me off before, but, since my discussion with Yolanda, Tugg's suspicions about him seemed more and more plausible.

Instead of responding to his question, I decided to venture out on a limb. "Duane said John Dexter had asked to see these same files. Why was that?"

His jaw muscles clenched convulsively and he ran his forefinger across his lips two or three times before answering in a controlled voice. "Understand something, Miss O'Dell. I do my job, and I do it quite well. Dexter was looking for something sensational to sell more papers, so he decided to make me a target."

"So, it's just a coincidence that both toxicology reports are missing."

He snapped the folders shut. "This is a simple case of misfiling. I hope you're not planning to make an issue of this like John did," he said with finality. The closed expression on his face signaled that our meeting was over.

Was that a veiled warning? I tried to imagine this imposing man being raked over the coals by Claudia and failed. "Listen, Sheriff, now that I think about it, I'm sure it's not important." I stood up. "Tell Duane I don't need the reports after all. I'm sure I'll have plenty for my series without them."

A look of relief crossed his face. "I'll be sure to tell him. And if there's ever anything else you need to know, Miss O'Dell, you talk to me personally, okay?" He raised one fuzzy caterpillar eyebrow for emphasis.

I hid my frustration behind a forced smile. "I'll do that."

Elation buoyed me as I drove away. He hadn't answered my question as to why Dexter had also asked for the two files, and he was probably feeling pretty smug right now believing he'd sidestepped me. But, his apprehensive behavior suggested I was on the right track. There had to be other copies of the reports. My next step would be to contact the medical examiner's office.

Darkness had fallen by the time I finished my assignment and got back to the office. Except for Harry, everyone had already left. We exchanged a few words, then he returned to the production area. I went into the small darkroom adjacent to my office and developed the roll of film I'd just taken at the Cowboy Art Exhibit.

Lost in thought, I was sloshing some prints from an earlier assignment in the stop bath when I heard the phone ring. I assumed Harry had gone home as the ringing continued. Whoever it was would just have to wait. By the time I'd eased the prints into the fixer and dried my hands, I calculated it had rung at least thirty times. Someone was certainly persistent.

I ran to my desk and scooped up the receiver. "Hello?" There was no response. I said hello a second time, but all I could hear was the sound of shallow breathing at the other end of the line.

"Jesus," I muttered and hung up. I returned to the dark room and my eyes had just become accustomed to the dull red 'safe' light when I heard the phone again. Probably a wrong number. It rang ten or twenty more times and quit. When it started ringing a third time agitation welled up in me.

"Hold your horses," I shouted, clipping the finished pictures to the drying line. When I grabbed the phone and said 'hello' there was, again, no response. On the verge of hanging up in disgust, I heard a voice murmur, "Is thees the number for John Dexter?"

The fuzz on the back of my neck quivered. "Yes. Who's calling?"

I heard a sob. "Please. I call many nights for many weeks. He will talk now to me, ¿sí?" The female caller spoke barely above a whisper.

"A...he's not available at the moment," I answered quickly. "Can I have him call you back?"

125

My heart hammered with excitement as I snatched up a pen and waited through another long pause filled with ragged breathing. Then, I heard her fierce whisper, *"¡Dios Mio!* They are coming. I cannot talk anymore. Tell heem to bring the money he promise me. He must hurry!"

I yelled, "Wait! Wait! Who is this?" The connection broke and the dial tone buzzed in my ear. In the heavy silence that followed, I stayed glued by the phone, praying the woman would call back. The anticipation of another opportunity to speak with her had my pulse thumping in my ears. There was little doubt this was the mysterious other woman Yolanda Reyes had referred to.

I rose and paced the room. Tugg's suspicions about Dexter's disappearance were becoming stronger than ever. The implications sent a surge of anxiety through me.

The fact that she'd been calling here trying to reach him confirmed that Dexter had never arrived for their meeting. The woman said he had promised her money. Had he also promised her a ticket to Nogales?

The tone of panic in her voice clearly indicated that using the telephone had placed her in a precarious position. Why did she call only at night? I thought of Harry. He worked some nights long after everyone else had gone home. But would he even hear the phone over the racket of the press and the loud music he played? I'd make a point to ask him in the morning.

I sat down to review my notes again, then slumped forward onto the desk. What in the world could be going on in this seemingly sleepy little town that would knock the socks off everyone if it were revealed?

'Don't tell Roy,' John had said to Tugg that last day. Don't tell Roy. It had to be an important clue, but what was the significance?

A sick feeling settled in my stomach. One thing was becoming more certain. It was doubtful that John Dexter was still alive. If that was true, where did it leave me? My watch said 9:30. An hour had passed since her call. I snatched up the phone to call Morton Tuggs. He seemed surprised to hear from me. "You got something?"

It took me about five minutes to fill him in on my suspicions about Roy, coupled with the mysterious phone call.

His anxiety spilled into my ear. "I knew it. I felt in my gut he was up to something. What the hell do you think he's involved in?"

"Beats me. This much we do know. Roy was nervous when I asked for those files again. He didn't threaten me, but it's clear he doesn't want any more bad publicity on those two cases. The phone call tonight confirms that Dexter never reached his destination. And, all we really have is Roy's word that he issued him a ticket. What if he didn't? What if Roy is responsible for Dexter's sudden disappearance?"

"Jesus Christ," he moaned softly. "This is just what I was afraid of. Why the hell am I doing this? If it turns out Roy's done something awful, it's gonna just kill Mary, and I'll be jeopardizing the paper at the same time."

I knew what Tugg meant. There was no concrete proof of any misdeed, only assumptions, and certainly nothing we could print. Judging by Roy's reaction this afternoon, he'd waste no time in pulling the plug if we did. Of course, that meant my job would be down the tubes as well.

"Tugg, do you think perhaps we should contact the county attorney's office about this?"

He was silent for a moment and then echoed my doubts. "And tell them what? We still don't have one goddamn shred of evidence that he's even involved, and you know he'll deny everything."

"You're right, but perhaps our mysterious lady will provide some clue. I can't stay here twenty-four hours a day, so if it's all right with you, I'll get with the phone company tomorrow and have call forwarding activated."

He agreed, told me to be careful, and hung up. I returned to the darkroom, finished my prints and then went home.

Before retiring, I studied the photo of John Dexter again and added several more things to my notebook. The data filled almost one full page. First thing tomorrow, I'd call the medical examiner's office in Prescott and ask for copies of the toxicology reports. I would also return the picture to Yolanda and see if she had remembered anything else about him which might have some significance.

My head was spinning with questions and details as I climbed into bed and lay listening to crickets chirp. Away, in the distance, I heard the distinct yipping of coyotes.

Sleep was a long time coming and when it finally did, it was filled with a series of jumbled, ghoulish nightmares. In one dream Sheriff Hollingsworth, laughing like a maniac, was bearing down on me in his patrol car as I ran and ran, seemingly in slow motion. In another, John Dexter kept appearing over a hill, around a corner, always beckoning for me to follow. He'd always vanish before I could get to him. Then, I was in a room filled with flowers. Hundreds of them. Eric was there. He put out his hand to me and smiled. I reached to take it when Bradley appeared out of the shadows. His face was a mask of fury when he drew out a long knife and plunged it into Eric's stomach.

There was blood everywhere. My sudden indrawn breath wakened me. Bathed in cold sweat, I sat up and hugged my knees until my heartbeat slowed. Rather than risk another set of nightmares, I got up, slid open the arcadia door and stepped outside onto the back patio. A warm breeze met me. I stood there for a long time and allowed the silence to soothe my taut nerves. Eastward, over the massive silhouette of Castle Rock, I watched insistent tendrils of dawn coax the darkness from the night sky. I hugged myself in enjoyment. Sunrises and sunsets in Arizona were so dramatic.

The last few days, wispy dry-looking clouds had begun to appear, adding just a touch more color to these already breathtaking spectacles. I wondered if it meant that the summer rains everyone assured me of were on the way.

Across the yard two kangaroo rats skittered into a hole, and somewhere nearby an owl hooted. I shook my head in awe. Only a short while ago I'd been absolutely positive I didn't belong in this wild, desolate state. But, now I knew with a curious certainty that even with the dread of sizzling summer staring me in the face, if I were ever to leave this place, I would miss it terribly. How could one love and hate something at the same time?

Later, as I left for work, one of the linen trucks I'd seen on several other occasions, drove past headed toward Serenity House. The driver honked his horn and waved. The sight of his truck reminded me that I was to check the truck rental places today.

The Gold Dust Parade was scheduled for Saturday morning and there seemed a frenzy of excitement and anticipation among the townspeople. Kids out of school were bunched on street corners, colorful posters announcing the events were tacked to phone poles, and the sound of hammering from workmen erecting grandstands filled the early morning air as I drove through the downtown area. The last big tourist attraction of the year had the streets choked with out-of-town vehicles by the time I finished my second assignment and drove to the first rental lot.

No, the owner did not recognize the photo of John Dexter and had no record of him renting a truck during the first week of April. No one at the other two places had seen him either.

So, I had the answer to my question and it left me with a sick feeling locked in my stomach. John Dexter had not emptied out his apartment.

By late afternoon, I felt disappointed that I'd not made more progress. Yolanda, I was told, would be out of town visiting relatives until next week, and my call to the medical examiner's office was a wash, too. The doctor was busy and would return my call on Monday.

With a sigh of exasperation, I grabbed my notebook and headed across town to complete my final assignment.

When I returned an hour later, Tugg called me aside and told me he'd spoken with the phone company. Unfortunately, the call forwarding feature would not be functional for another day.

Okay, that meant another evening to hang around the office. Not so bad, I thought, since I had a zillion pictures to develop and print. Although Bradley was frequently out, the office had seemed curiously empty the past three days with him gone.

Before Ginger left she invited me to dinner again the following week, saying that Bonnie and her husband Tom would be there too. I gladly accepted, thinking it would be interesting to see them again and hear how the adoption was proceeding, especially since I'd be having dinner with their attorney, Eric Heisler, tomorrow night.

I had no intention of missing the call from my mysterious lady if it came tonight, so I took the phone from Bradley's desk, pulled the cord as far as it would stretch, and set it on the floor just inside the darkroom.

I had asked Harry earlier if he'd ever received any unusual calls in the evening and he'd said once in a while he'd get a wrong number, but that was all. As I'd suspected, he confirmed when the small press was running, it drowned out the noise of the phone.

The thought of the impending call kept me in a state of high anxiety. I must have checked my watch a hundred times and finally chided myself aloud, "Cut it out. If she's gonna call she'll call, if not, looking at your stupid watch won't change things."

By the time ten o'clock rolled around, I was almost finished with my prints and disappointment had set in. She wasn't going to call. I slipped the last negative into the enlarger plate and heard what sounded like a footstep outside the door.

"Harry?" There was no answer so I said, "Wait just a minute, Harry. I have one more print."

There was a sudden rush of fresh air into the room so I knew the door had been opened. Immediate surprise flooded me and then switched to a stab of alarm. Instead of the expected flash of light from the outer room, there was only darkness. But, I had left the office lights on.

I felt a presence even before a shadowy form appeared in the doorway, silhouetted in the dim glow of the outdoor lights which streamed through the office window beyond.

My heart set up an awful racket in my head and my throat closed as the shadow advanced toward me. "Harry? Is this a joke?" No answer. "This isn't funny!"

Clearly it wasn't Harry. Instinctively, I grabbed for a weapon, anything. My hand curled around a bottle of fixer and I hurled it at the shadow. It crashed against the wall, missing its target.

With a small shriek I turned and made a lunge for the light switch just as something crashed down on the back of my head. Searing pain sent me spinning into oblivion.

15

Someone was shouting my name. I wanted to stay in the peaceful blackness, but a sharp, persistent odor interfered, straining to pull me from it.

"Kendall!" the voice commanded. "Can you hear me?" I labored to raise my eyelids but something heavy pressed them down. Sizzling ropes of green and red lightning flashed before me while a knifelike pain jabbed the back of my head.

With great effort, I opened my eyes. The blurry face above me gradually became recognizable. It was Bradley.

"Are you all right?" he asked.

Was I? I blinked several times and tried to speak without success. When I attempted to raise my head, waves of blackness returned. When I came to again, Bradley was waving a vial underneath my nose.

I took a weak swipe at it. "Will you get that stinkin' stuff away from me?"

"Ahh," he crooned with satisfaction, relief mirrored in his eyes. "You're back."

Bewildered, I realized we were both on the floor of the darkroom, the cabinets, counters and sink far above. The globe that covered the overhead light was full of dead bugs. I'd never seen the room from this perspective before. Interesting.

"What happened?" I groaned.

He tipped his hat back. "I was about to ask you the same question."

Still muddled, I asked, "What are you doing here?"

"I work here."

"I know you work here. I mean what are you doing here now? I thought you were in Phoenix."

He cocked one dark brow. "I drove down to cover a story, I didn't relocate there. I got back a little while ago and stopped in to pick up my messages. Instead, I'm picking you up. What happened here anyway?" he asked, watching my face closely.

I pressed a hand to my forehead. "I'm not sure. I was working...I heard the door open, and then I saw someone standing in the doorway."

"Who was it?" His voice was sharp.

"I don't know. It was too dark to tell. I remember going for the light switch and then *whamo*! I think someone conked me on the head."

"From the look of things, it appears that you bumped the corner of this shelf," he said pointing to the jumble of bottles, paper and the wooden board on the floor.

For a second, I stared in confusion. Could I have imagined the shadow?

I looked up and saw him studying me with searching intensity. "Why would someone hit you on the head?" he asked softly.

How could I explain without giving away my secret assignment? "It was probably my wild imagination."

I made a move to rise, but, he firmly pushed me flat to the floor. "Just a minute. I'm not finished examining you yet."

"Examining me? What are you talking about?"

"It's part of my job."

I gave him an incredulous look. "Oh, wait. Let me guess. Besides being a sports writer and a rancher, you also moonlight as a doctor?"

He grinned. "You must be okay now. Your charming wit has returned in force."

I struggled to get up. "Answer the question. What do you mean it's part of your job?"

"Be still a minute. And be quiet." The tone of authority in his voice surprised me, and an unexpected sensation of vulnerability crept over me as I lay on the floor with him kneeling beside me. The thought of his hands exploring my body spawned a pleasurable tingle. Perhaps it was my weakened state or the fact that he was so close; whatever, I was overwhelmed with the sudden desire to reach up and pull his sensuous mouth against mine. My fingers would trace the contours of his face and move from there to his chest, then around to stroke the taut muscles on his back and from there, eventually trailing down to where I'd finally get my hands on those gorgeous buns. God! What was the matter with me? What would he think if he could read my mind? At that moment, I didn't know what to think of myself.

"Your pupils aren't dilated, so I don't think you have a concussion," he concluded, sitting back on his heels. "But you've got a good sized goose egg on the back of your head."

"This still isn't computing," I whined.

He laughed. "Relax. Of course, I'm not a doctor, but I have had some medical training. I'm a member of the county sheriff's posse. Search and Rescue."

The sheriff's posse! An uncomfortable shiver ran through me. "How well do you know Roy Hollingsworth?"

"Pretty well."

"So...you work closely with him?"

He looked puzzled. "On occasion. Why?"

I had a hundred questions I couldn't ask him so I replied, "Just wondered, that's all."

He helped me to a sitting position while I gingerly touched the lump on my head. I hadn't imagined anything. Someone had meant business. Then it hit me. I'd activated the security system before going into the darkroom. If there had been a break-in, why hadn't I heard the alarm? Why hadn't Harry?

Someone must have disarmed it. I slid a suspicious glance in Bradley's direction. Was it just a coincidence he happened to show up at this particular time? Knowing he worked with Roy left me feeling hollow. Could the shadow have been him? But why would he knock me cold and then revive me? It didn't make sense.

When I stood the room swayed a little and he steadied my shoulders. "Thank you," I murmured and then jumped when he quietly asked, "What are you up to, Kendall?"

"Up to?" I hedged. "What do you mean?"

"Come on. You've been all over town asking questions about John Dexter. Why?"

I gulped. "How do you know that?"

"People talk."

Damn. If he knew, so must Roy. Perhaps my charade about the runaways hadn't fooled him at all.

Just then, Harry appeared at the doorway. He surveyed the confusion and stared at us open-mouthed. "What the hell's going on here?"

I was surprised when Bradley told him I'd fallen.

"Christ," he breathed. "I slip out for a lousy ten minutes to get a pack of cigarettes and miss all the excitement."

I assured him that I was all right and he said goodnight. At least I knew now why the security system hadn't been on. Obviously, Harry had forgotten to re-set it when he left. But that brought forth a frightening scenario. It meant someone had been lurking outside waiting for an opportunity to find me alone. When the next thought struck me, my heart lurched painfully. I'd left the notebook containing all my clues lying right on top of my desk.

It took supreme effort to appear impassive as I hurried to my desk. The sight of the notebook resting beside my purse made me giddy with relief. I clutched it to my chest with a silent vow to never let it out of my sight from now on.

At first, it appeared nothing had been touched, but when I opened the top drawer, it was apparent to me that somebody had sifted through the contents with great care. There were just enough items out of place to tip me off. A feeling of certainty settled over me. This wasn't the sloppy work of a thief. Someone had taken the bait and followed up on my fabricated tale concerning personal items left behind by John Dexter.

Bradley's voice broke into my thoughts. "Did you lose something?"

I turned to meet the suspicion in his eyes. "No. I just thought I'd ah...I was just...a..."

"Thinking about rearranging your desk drawers at midnight?"

I dropped my eyes. "No."

I sensed he was waiting for me to say something, and when I didn't he persisted, "So, you're not going to tell me what's going on?"

"I...I can't."

"You mean you won't."

It would have been so nice to confide in him, but I held back. "What's wrong with me being curious about what happened to my predecessor? A better question is why aren't *you* curious about what happened to John Dexter?"

Anger darkened his eyes. "He was a sleaze bucket and frankly I don't care what happened to him after all the shit that came down on me, not to mention the embarrassment he caused my family. I'm just glad he got the hell out of my life."

This was the opening I'd been waiting for. I'd read all John's articles and, by their tone, it was obvious he'd thought Bradley responsible for his wife's untimely death. He'd never missed an opportunity to fan the fires of suspicion.

"Do you want to talk about this?" I held my breath waiting for his answer.

"We were talking about you."

Positive he planned to stonewall me again, I blurted out, "Bradley, I know what happened to your wife."

An inscrutable look passed over his face. "So that's it. I should have guessed. Well, that explains why you're always so jumpy around me."

"That's not true."

He laughed bitterly. "It'll never end, will it? My screwed up personal life made for sensational headlines and kept tongues wagging for hours on end with tidbits of juicy gossip. Don't tell me you're like some of the stubborn jackasses around town who still believe all that crap about me?"

I hesitated and he growled, "Goddamn it, Kendall! You think I killed her, don't you?"

"I never said that."

"But it's crossed your mind, hasn't it?" His face was positively fierce and it frightened me. But mixed with the fear was a curious elation. At last I'd forced some genuine emotion from this man who always seemed to hold himself carefully in check.

I wanted to deny it, but all at once a wave of dizziness passed over me. I put a hand to my head and he was at my side immediately. "I'm calling Dr. Garcia."

"I'm okay," I assured him. "I just need to go home and lie down." Whoever had attacked me wasn't going to have the satisfaction of knowing I'd been hurt. I knew the rumor mill would grind out it's own version of what happened and the last thing I needed was to be the talk of the town. Plus that, I sensed that Tugg was becoming uneasy about my involvement. I knew down deep that he wanted the mystery solved, but how could he, in good conscience, place his old friend's daughter in danger? The thought was distinctly unsettling, but I'd sunk my teeth into this story and I wasn't letting go,

"I'll drive you out there,' he offered.

"That's not necessary."

"I think it is. I'll stop by in the morning and pick you up." The stubborn look on his face left little room for argument.

I could have put up a fuss, but I didn't. On the way home we sat in awkward silence. I hadn't answered his questions and he hadn't answered mine. When we reached the house, he insisted on checking each room and then urged me to lock up.

I told him again how grateful I was for his help and he nodded soberly. As he strode to the door, I felt a pang of regret. Suddenly I didn't want the evening to end on such a sour note.

"Bradley?"

He turned. "Yes?"

"This really has to stop, you know."

"What?"

"It's very shattering for my ego to have you constantly running around rescuing me. I mean, this is the third time in a matter of weeks."

I was glad to see a glint of humor return to his eyes. "I'm just lucky, I guess. By the way, you still owe me dinner."

"I know that."

"Well, let's see now," he said rubbing his chin. "My fee for this latest rescue operation has upped the ante considerably."

I feigned horror. "Don't tell me I have to go bowling or something?"

His laughter lightened my heart. "No. Your payment will be to spend all of Saturday afternoon and evening with me at my ranch where I shall hold you in captivity until your debts are paid."

Remembering my dinner date with Eric, I was relieved that he hadn't asked me to come tomorrow. I gave an exaggerated salute. "As you wish, sir. I always pay my debts. And in the future, I'll try and stay out of trouble."

He cocked his head sideways and then said with mock seriousness, "I warn you, if for some reason I should have to rescue you again, the price will be much higher."

16

I was half afraid Bradley would grill me with questions again when he picked me up the next morning. Instead, we talked about Saturday's parade, and then he gave me directions to the Starfire Ranch which I scribbled in my notepad.

With gentle good humor, he teased me about my reaction to the Mexican food, saying that I should have listened to him and gone easy on the hot sauce. I grudgingly admitted that he'd been right and told him it would be an extremely chilly day in hell before I ever ate it again. He laughed and assured me that I would grow accustomed to it.

Some of the main streets had been blocked off to prepare for the parade so while he maneuvered the truck through a back alley to the paper I pondered over his mercurial personality. One minute he was dead serious, the next he was full of friendly banter, which probably masked his true feelings about a lot of things. Ginger had said that

Stephanie's death changed him. I wondered what he'd been like before the tragedy.

When we reached the parking lot I thanked him for the ride, but, before I could open the door, he grabbed my left arm and gave me a searching look. "Sure you don't want to talk about your little episode last night?"

I cleared my throat uneasily. "No."

He stared intently at me for another minute then released me. "You remind me of my horse, Summer Rain."

"Really."

"She's almost as stubborn as you are."

"Thanks. I like being compared to a horse." As before, our verbal clashing of swords had me on an emotional seesaw. When I got out of the truck, he moved to block my way to the building entrance.

"Hold on. That was a compliment." Mischief sparkled in his deep brown eyes. "It took me two months. She fought and kicked and bit, but you know what?"

I shook my head. He leaned so close to my ear I could smell his aftershave. "Defiant as she was, as headstrong as she was...in the end, I finally did tame her."

Throughout the remainder of the workday, I tried to analyze how I felt about that encounter along with his carefully camouflaged remarks from the night before. The painful end to my engagement in Philadelphia had left me vulnerable and hesitant about getting involved again, especially with a man like Bradley, who apparently still carried with him a ton of emotional baggage concerning his past. It was strange, but I had the odd sense that he was pulling me to him, yet pushing me away at the same time.

By the time I reached home that evening I was glad for the distraction of dinner with Eric Heisler. It would provide some needed breathing room.

Outside my bedroom window, mourning doves commiserated with each other in low, melancholy flutelike warbles. The brisk wind that had howled all afternoon, kicking up towering dust devils and piling tumbleweeds against the side of the house, slackened as the sun reached for the horizon.

Not having a clue as to where Eric planned to take me for dinner, I had trouble selecting something from my sparse wardrobe. All I knew is that I was hot, and whatever I chose would have to be cool. Finally, I settled on the gauzy white summer dress Ginger had insisted I buy when we'd gone to Phoenix.

The wide cloth belt accentuated my slim waistline and I smiled remembering Ginger's lament that if only she were tall like me, she could have carried off this particular style with the handkerchief hemline.

I leaned into the mirror to apply eye shadow, and noticed with surprise that my skin, normally never exposed to much sunlight, had taken on a bronze appearance. My mother would be amazed when she heard. She'd always told me most redheads didn't tan, they just burned. And what was this? A colony of freckles growing on my nose? Oh well. Nothing I could do now. Baking in the Arizona sun was a trade-off for feeling good again.

The hair on the nape of my neck was still damp from the hasty shower I'd taken when I'd reached home a half hour earlier. As I attempted to pin my wild curls into place, a throb of pain emitted as my fingers touched the tender spot where I'd been struck the night before.

There was no question in my mind now that I was onto something big, and it made my stomach quiver with a combination of excitement and anxious anticipation.

144

After making sure all the doors and windows were locked, I checked my answering machine to make sure everything was working correctly. I'd verified the call-forwarding feature and had my fingers crossed the mysterious woman would phone again.

I slipped on white pumps and couldn't figure out why I had an attack of nerves as Eric swung his white Mercedes into the curved driveway. My palms were sweaty when I opened the front door.

The guy was definitely hot and looked like he'd just stepped off the cover of GQ. Clad in cream slacks, an open necked lemon-colored shirt and a blue blazer, he flashed me a brilliant smile and handed me a single red rose. "This exquisite creation of nature pales in the presence of your divine beauty."

I laughed. "Browning or Keats?" I inquired, accepting the flower and adding it to the already stuffed vase of blooms he'd sent me.

"Neither," he answered lightly, his blue eyes crinkling with humor. "Heisler."

"You write poetry?"

"I dabble," he said, ushering me out the front door.

After assisting me into the lush interior of his car, he swooped the filmy material of my dress, which had touched the dusty driveway, and tucked it next to me. In doing so, his hand lightly brushed my thigh. I watched him stride around the front of the car to the driver's side, and thought he looked almost too perfect to be real.

I don't know why it came to mind just then, but I had a sudden vision of Eric and Stephanie together. If the rumors of their love affair were true, it wasn't hard to imagine how intrigued she must have been with this man. He and Bradley seemed as different as two people could be.

"Where are we going?" I asked as we headed out. "I wasn't sure what to wear. I hope this is all right?"

He took his eyes off the road for a second, surveyed my appearance with apparent appreciation, then returned his concentration to driving. "I planned a very special evening for us and yes, you're fine. As a matter of fact, you look stunning in that dress and I especially like your hair that way."

"Thank you," I murmured. He was certainly front and center with the compliments. Just like the night we met, I was a little awed by his attentions. It was a bit disconcerting since he knew next to nothing about me.

I wasn't too surprised when he turned onto the road leading to the tennis ranch. "I brought my notepad along," I said, patting my purse. "I hope you don't mind if I ask you some questions concerning your involvement with the fund-raiser?"

He shot me a quick look of dismay. "Then this is still to be strictly a professional relationship between us? Reporter and subject?" He braked the car in the circular driveway and the young valet jumped to attention.

"We don't have to talk about business the entire evening."

"Good," he said briskly. "I hadn't planned to."

It must have pleased Eric to see the place jammed with people. It was a strange fashion mixture of resort wear, evening attire, or tennis togs. All seemed equally acceptable with the casually elegant surroundings.

Eric spoke to and shook hands with a lot of people. He introduced me to so many, it was a struggle to remember all the names. While I chatted with a talkative couple from Vermont, I noticed him cross the room and say something to Doug Sauers who then nodded and left.

When Eric returned, he slipped one arm through mine and led me up a wide stairway that opened onto an outdoor terrace overlooking the golf course. In the soft glow of lavender twilight, the scenery took on a rather silken appearance; the sky, the craggy mountains in the distance, even the prickly pear cactus plants lining the path leading out to the manicured greens.

I'd expected to have dinner with him in the main dining area, and was a little taken aback as he seated me at the solitary cloth-draped table adjacent to the wrought iron balcony. Bougainvillea vines sporting bright pink blossoms climbed lattice-work along the wall while a mister from above surrounded us with a fine spray of water, neutralizing the warm outdoor temperature. The sound of soft dance music drifted up from the lounge below. It was an enchanting setting.

"So, it's to be just the two of us. Do you entertain all your guests in such a fashion?" I asked, accepting the chilled glass of champagne he handed me.

"Certainly not. I promised you a special evening, so I intend to do my best to make that happen." He deftly lit the two tall candles on the table, then sat down opposite me.

At that moment, Doug Sauers arrived with a plate laden with smoked salmon, caviar and delicate wedges of thin toast. "I'd say, you've made a good start," I said sipping champagne while he filled his own glass. I could tell by the label on the bottle that it was outrageously expensive.

By the time Doug reappeared again with the main course, we had discussed our mutual interest in music, art and literature. When he skillfully steered the conversation to my personal life, I gave him a quick sketch of my background, then concentrated on my poached salmon with

147

dill sauce while he talked about the history of the tennis ranch. Perhaps it was the romantic atmosphere, or maybe it was the champagne, whichever, I finally had to remind myself that I was here on business.

"I'd better get to this interview while I can still write," I said, waving away his offer of more champagne.

He laughed. "I hope you're enjoying this evening as much as I am." His glance lingered on my face and dropped down to the scooped neckline of my dress.

"It's been lovely."

His eyes had a rather hypnotic glow in the candlelight. "It's not over yet."

As flattering as his attentions were, I felt a bit self-conscious. He'd gone to an awful lot of trouble to impress me. To busy myself, I dug my notepad and pen from my purse. "Let's talk about the Desert Harbor Shelter. What caused you to take such a personal interest in it?"

"My mother called one day to tell me about one of the girls she had befriended. She was fifteen, homeless, scared and pregnant. Up to that point, I'd been involved in mostly civil and personal injury cases, and I'd never handled an adoption before. When the word got out, I was astounded at the number of desperate couples who came forward vying for that one unborn child."

"What's the average cost for an adoption?"

He shrugged. "It depends on the situation. The adoptive couple usually agrees to pay the expenses of the birth mother up to the time of delivery and, in most cases, several months after that."

"What are the expenses?"

"The usual. Maternity clothes, room and board, all medical bills including the attending physician, hospital charges and, of course, my fee."

"And what does your fee involve?"

"Many things. Paperwork, interviews, court appearances if necessary, travel time and so forth and so on. As I said, it depends on how difficult the case is."

Doug arrived again and after giving me a friendly wink, took away the plates and left a pot of espresso coffee beside a dish of delicate pastries. It was completely dark now and the sky shimmered with pinpoints of light. I thought about the tennis ranch, Eric's luxurious car, the sumptuous dinner we'd just eaten, and recalled the words of the talkative attorney I'd spoken with last Saturday. Mike Scott's observation that he was doing well appeared to be quite accurate.

While Eric poured coffee, I reviewed my notes in the wavering shadows cast by the candle's flame. "I guess I've kind of taken a personal interest in the adoption process because of Ginger's sister. I understand she'll be getting her baby very soon. The whole family's ecstatic about it."

A benevolent expression lit his face. "I'm glad of that. Unfortunately, I haven't the time to handle too many of these cases, but, when I do it's very gratifying to tackle two difficult situations and take it to a satisfactory conclusion for everyone. If you need more information, I can give you the names of several other attorneys in Phoenix who do this on a regular basis."

His ardent expression led me to believe that underneath his suave, polished manner, he appeared to have a genuine emotional commitment to his clients.

"What do you say we talk about something else now?" he asked.

"Just a few more questions. What can you tell me about Claudia Phillips?"

"Who?"

"Claudia Phillips. Oh, come now. The woman who runs the shelter."

"Oh, of course. I'm afraid I don't know much about her at all. I don't actually have any direct involvement, you know. I see her at the fund-raiser once a year and from what I've heard from Mother she's very efficient. Other than that, we've barely spoken."

"I see."

"Why?"

"When I asked her for a tour of the shelter and to very discreetly interview a few of the girls for my story, she was...shall we say, less than cooperative. I guess I was hoping you could use your powers of persuasion to perhaps get her to change her mind."

"I'll see what I can do."

"Thank you. I'm afraid I have to get up very early tomorrow, so..."

"Of course." He rose and came around to pull out my chair. The familiar strains of a waltz filtered in the open doorway as we crossed the patio. Without warning, he drew me into his arms. "Surely, you can give me one dance before I take you home," he murmured into my ear.

I didn't protest as he whirled me around the floor. When the music ended he didn't let go. Even though I'd sensed this might happen, the shock of his warm lips on mine jolted me right down to my shoes. The pressure of his muscular body conveyed the message clearly that if I wanted it, there was much more to follow.

17

As expected, Saturday morning dawned clear and bright. I'd arrived downtown by six and was amazed to note the number of people already lining the sidewalks, staking out coveted front row spots, preferably in the shade.

"Hey, there!" I swung around to see Ginger across the street waving madly in my direction. I waved back and she made a beeline for me. Oh no. There was little doubt she was going to quiz me about my date with Eric. If I told her, the whole town would know by nightfall.

"Okay, out with it," she demanded, panting. "What happened?"

"Oh, Ginger, I can't talk now, I'm working." She looked so stricken I had to laugh. Patting her shoulder I said, "Don't have a stroke. I know it's going to be torture for you, but right now I have to interview the grand marshal of the parade." She started to protest, so I raised my hand. "I swear I'll tell you later, okay?" Just how much, I didn't know yet.

She made me promise to call her as soon as I got home, even if it was midnight. Amused by her antics, I watched her run back across the street and Nona waved to me from her wheelchair. Brian, holding a colorful umbrella to shade his grandmother, grinned and waved too.

Turning to go, I gasped in surprise as I ran full speed into Roy Hollingsworth. "Whoa there, little lady. You better slow down or I'll have to give you a speeding ticket." He gave me a wide grin, and touched the brim of his western hat. "You have a great day, Miss O'Dell."

I'd been all ready to suspect that he'd played some part in the darkroom attack, but now, as he waded into the gathering crowd, I wondered again if Tugg and I might be wrong about him.

The parade was a hoot, beginning with the kids marching with their pets and continuing from there to the floats, rodeo riders and school bands. It was small townish and some of it terribly hokey, but everyone applauded enthusiastically as if it rivaled the Macy's Thanksgiving Day Parade in New York. I took some great pictures for the following Wednesday's edition and talked Jim into covering my assignment at the rodeo grounds so I would be free to visit the Starfire Ranch that afternoon.

On a whim, I stopped by Mac's Western Store and bought a bright checkered shirt and a pair of crisp, new Levis. I was about to visit a real honest-to-god cattle ranch so I might as well look the part.

Back home, I dressed with care and then studied my appearance in the full length mirror. Not too bad, I decided, rolling the shirt sleeves to my elbows. My tennis shoes didn't really go, but the traditional Stetson hat and leather boots would have to wait until I got a raise or won the lottery.

Before leaving, I double-checked for messages. Damn. The mystery lady still hadn't called. Maybe I'd get lucky tonight.

I followed Bradley's directions, and as the car bumped down the narrow, dusty road through the sun-drenched landscape of cactus and rock, my thoughts returned to Eric. He certainly had gone out of his way to create an interesting evening.

It had been on the tip of my tongue to confront him and voice my misgivings about Stephanie, but I'd said nothing. What if my suspicions were wrong? I'd have spoiled the magical mood of the most perfect dream date any woman could imagine. And anyway, hadn't Bradley acknowledged that even though he'd suspected it, he'd never verified that the so-called affair between Eric and his late wife had ever existed?

After driving me home and extracting my promise to see him again soon, Eric had planted another one of those expert 'guaranteed to leave you talking to yourself' kisses on me. He left no doubt of his intention to pursue me.

Later, in bed, I had a lot of trouble trying to settle myself down and analyze my feelings. I'd never dated two men at the same time before, and it led to a night of feverish tossing and turning.

A family of quail scooting across the road in front of my car jolted me back to the present. I braked and smiled to myself. The road Quail Crossing was aptly named. It seemed as if I'd been driving forever when I finally spotted a stone arch ahead. It read Starfire Ranch. Criminy! Talk about the middle of nowhere.

After parking in front of a rambling two-story ranch house surrounded by towering tamarisk trees, I took a minute to survey this new place. Off to the right were rows of stables, smaller buildings, and what looked like literally miles of gleaming-white pipe fencing. To the left, beyond several large vegetable gardens, stood three neat cottages. Beside them, groups of small children played while women hung out laundry.

The sound of a screen door banging made me turn back toward the house. Bradley's sister Ronda, flanked by two barking dogs, stood on the wooden porch, her fists planted firmly on blue-jeaned hips. She shouted for the dogs to shut up. "I guess you'd be here to see Tally."

"Yes."

A tall, gaunt woman with salt and pepper hair appeared at the screen and without fanfare Ronda said, "Ma, this is Tally's friend...Kendall is it?"

"Yes. Nice to meet you, Mrs. Talverson."

Wide-eyed, she muttered something and threw a questioning look at her daughter who returned it with one of those "what'd I tell you?" looks.

It didn't take a scholar to see I was being compared once again to the legendary Stephanie Talverson and I was beginning to resent it.

Ronda shooed the dogs into the house and then motioned with her head for me to follow her. Her scuffed boots crunched in the gravel driveway as we made our way toward the stables. She made a point of staying a few paces ahead of me so conversation was difficult. As we entered the largest building, I wrinkled my nose at the strong smell of hay and manure. She called out, "Tally, you got a visitor."

In the room to my left I heard the murmur of voices and then seconds later Bradley walked out carrying a saddle. "Hi." He looked pleased to see me.

The smile on my lips froze when Lucinda appeared close behind him. I could see the disdain in her eyes as she scrutinized me. Suddenly, I felt self-conscious in my new clothes, positive I must look the epitome of the Eastern dude.

As if echoing my thoughts Lucinda said, "Now, Tally, you be real careful with her so's you don't muss up those fine clothes."

He slid her a sidelong glance. "Behave yourself, Lucy." Giggling, she hooked her arm through Ronda's and they left the stable together.

I tried to hide my annoyance and turned back to meet Bradley's amused face. "I'm glad you came," he said softly.

My pulse surged. "Thanks for inviting me, Bradley. I hope I didn't take you away from anything...important."

"Before you jump to conclusions, Lucy and I have known each other since grade school. She and Ronda are best friends and she boards her mare here, okay?"

I remembered Ginger saying that Lucinda had developed a sudden and passionate interest in appaloosa horses after Stephanie had died and used it as an excuse to be at the ranch whenever possible. I wondered how often she came.

"And speaking of friends," he said moving closer, "all my other friends call me Tally. Why don't you?"

"You haven't asked me."

"Actually, I believe I did ask you the night of the fund-raiser, but as I recall, you were slightly ticked-off over something."

Over something? I could tell by his expression that we were both remembering his outrageous behavior towards Eric. Best not to revisit that now. "I'd be honored to call you Tally," I said, keeping my tone light. "And now I'm ready to repay the debts I owe you. What exactly is it you expect of me?"

His smile was downright wicked, and I would have had to be blind to miss the intimate message in his eyes. He took another step closer, his gaze now serious with intent. Was he going to kiss me?

"Hold still," he said, reaching toward me. It must have been the rush of adrenaline that made my ears buzz. A delicious shiver of desire raced through me when his hand touched my shoulder, then moved to my hair. I closed my eyes and waited...and waited...and waited. As the buzzing sound increased I blinked my lids open in confusion just in time to see him pulling something with numerous legs from my hair.

I flinched away screaming, "Jesus Christ! What was that?"

He calmly threw something down and ground it with his boot. "Don't have a cow. It was a barn wasp. No harm done."

My romantic fantasy evaporated in a chill of embarrassment and irritation. "Well, why didn't you just say so?"

"I didn't want you to panic."

"Bees have been mistaking my hair for a flower since I was a kid. I can handle them. It's spiders I can't take."

"I remember." He was still standing very close to me and looked like he wanted to say something else, but then he stiffened and abruptly moved away. "Come outside. I'll show you my horses."

I followed him, feeling slightly deflated, wondering if I would ever be able to break down the protective barrier he'd erected around himself.

Pride lit Tally's face as he showed me his line of appaloosa horses. I'd never seen anything quite like them, and felt awed by their unique beauty. Some sported white coats with black spots, some black with white spots, and with some, only the hind quarter region was colored. Tally explained this was called the 'blanket' and that the breed was famous for being highly intelligent, sure-footed, even-tempered, and gentle. They were used not only for racing and horse shows, but also as reliable saddle horses.

I stroked the mottled muzzle of one stallion he called Geronimo and marveled, "Each one is so different. Do you breed them with just any horse or does it have to be a like kind?"

"We practice selective breeding. When people bring their mares, they have to show proof that it's a registered appaloosa or I don't allow them to be bred with my stallions. It's the only way to keep what's left of the line pure."

"Why do you say what's left? Are they rare?"

"Very. During the war with the Nez Perce back in 1877, the U.S. Army slaughtered them by the hundreds."

"That's terrible."

He nodded his solemn agreement, and then brightened as he showed me around the ranch. When we returned to the stable, he asked if I was hungry.

"I could eat."

"Good. Well, we have a ways to go for dinner, so we'd best saddle up."

"What?"

"Saddle up." He cocked his head. "You do know how to ride, don't you?"

I hadn't ridden a horse for many years, only Eastern style, and not very well at that. "I've done some riding."

"Good." He eyed my clothes and finally said, "You can't ride in those tennis shoes. I don't suppose, Annie Oakley, when you bought your new duds, that you included a pair of boots and a hat?"

"No. You didn't tell me either was a prerequisite for having dinner. By the way, where are we going? Am I to believe that somewhere out there where the buffalo roam, there's a five star restaurant?"

He grinned. "You're here to pay your debt, remember? You'll find out in due time." He looked at my feet again. "Wait here." He ducked into a doorway just inside the barn and returned moments later holding a pair of snakeskin boots. Having just priced them at the western store, I knew they were quite expensive. "Try these on," he said, dropping them at my feet.

I imagined they must be Ronda's as I tugged them on. They were a bit snug, but would do. He plunked a wide-brimmed hat on my head and when I looked up he had an odd expression on his face.

"Go ahead and say it. Lucinda was right. I look like I just stepped out of a Sears catalog."

"On the contrary. You look just right to me." I warned myself not to read more into his remark than I should, but nevertheless, it sent a delicious shiver down my spine.

I watched a ranch hand help him saddle two horses and prayed I wouldn't make a fool of myself.

"Are we going on a picnic?" I asked brightly to cover my uneasiness as he helped me mount.

"Sort of," he murmured, cinching my saddle tight and adjusting the stirrups. He looked up at me. "Comfy?" "I think I'll be fine as long as it doesn't move." He laughed. "Just relax and hold onto the reins. By the way, it's a she and her name is Sheba." "Aren't you going to ride Geronimo?" I asked as he swung onto another horse with easy grace. "No. I'll ride Summer Rain. We don't ride the stallions at breeding time. They're rather unpredictable with the mares in heat."

Perhaps sensing my nervousness, Tally assured me Sheba was gentle and responsive. He patiently instructed me on the art of western neck reining, and then urged me to drink plenty of water from the canteen attached to the saddle.

I'd expected to feel hot and miserable with the afternoon sun beating down, but the strong westerly wind made it bearable. Was my blood finally thinning?

I couldn't help but think as we rode off through the open desert toward low cactus-covered foothills, that this was the stuff postcards are made of. I also couldn't help thinking how different Tally's world was from Eric's.

After half an hour or so of light chatter about the hazards of ranch life, the dry weather, and the upcoming annual barbecue, which he invited me to attend, a companionable silence fell between us. Several times I glanced sideways at him sitting tall and straight in the saddle. He seemed as much a part of this land as the sapphire sky and distant purple mountains. A powerful urge to touch him swept over me and I felt a little lightheaded. Perhaps it was the heat.

As if sensing my feelings, he turned his head. "Why do you keep staring at me?"

"I'm not."

"Yes, you are."

I looked away from him, unable to understand why I couldn't ask him about his wife. It didn't bother me to pester other people for information. But this was different. He hadn't invited me to come to his ranch just to look at the scenery. His body language told me that he was interested in something more than mere friendship. But, how did he expect me to hope for any kind of a relationship with him when the ghost of Stephanie stood firmly between us?

For a few more minutes I waged an inner battle until impatience finally overruled temperance. "Tally...we need to talk about it."

"What?"

I could tell by his tight-jawed expression that he knew and planned to stonewall me again. "You know what. Quit playing games with me. If you really want us to be friends, you can't evade talking about what happened to Stephanie forever."

He reined in his horse with such suddenness, she reared slightly and whinnied. Sheba shied and stopped too. Anger blazed in his eyes. "Why do you have to be so persistent about this? Didn't Ginger already give you all the gory details?"

"I need to hear it from you, not second-hand."

"Leave it lie."

"No."

"Goddamn it, Kendall! It's an ugly part of my life. I don't like to think about it or talk about it!"

I was startled to see grief replace the anger in his eyes. Still waters did appear to run deep with this man. I could have stopped it there, but doggedly I charged ahead.

"Tally, it's not healthy to keep this bottled up inside. I...I know how painful it is to lose someone you love and..." The incredulous expression on his face made me falter and when he spoke his voice shook with emotion.

"Love her? Love her! I never hated anyone so much in my life."

18

His admission stunned me. All these weeks I'd been under the mistaken impression that he'd done something he regretted in a fit of jealous rage. So, the sadness in his eyes wasn't for Stephanie. And, if not for Stephanie, who then?

I felt a twinge of remorse as Tally looked upward blinking and clearing his throat loudly the way men do when they're trying to conceal tears. Would I ever learn to keep my big mouth shut? "Guilt is a heavy mantle to carry," he said in resignation.

My heart contracted. "What do you have to feel guilty about?"

He pressed two fingers to his temple. "This is not easy for me to talk about. I've never discussed this with anyone else except Ronda."

I braced myself for the worst.

"The hardest thing of all to face these past two years is knowing that I'm responsible for my father's death."

His father's death? As the information sank in, my shoulders sagged in relief. "Tally, how can you say that? Ginger told me he had a stroke."

"That's true. But, if it hadn't been for my stupidity he'd be alive today and my mother wouldn't still be blaming me for what happened."

He urged the horses forward and, little by little, poured out the story of how he'd met, been bewitched by, and married the beautiful, but spoiled, Stephanie Tate. With the exception of a few new details, I was amazed that Ginger's version had been so accurate.

"But, Tally, it's not fair to blame yourself. You were gone for four years. Isn't it possible your father might have had a stroke anyway?"

As if he hadn't heard me, he squinted toward the distant horizon. "I failed him in every possible way a son could fail a father. I abandoned the Starfire, which he loved more than life itself, and then brought into his home a vicious, conniving little witch who drove him mad with her constant tantrums and outlandish behavior. She made no effort to conceal her disdain for ranch life and my family. My father held a very important standing in this community and he just couldn't handle the shame she heaped on us all."

"If she hated it here so much why did she stay?"

"That's the rub. One evening at dinner, she grandly announced that even if I chose not to accompany her, she was returning to her parents' house."

"Did you try to talk her out of it?"

"No. None of us did. Something else stopped her."

"What?"

"Her illustrious father, who'd made no secret of his dislike for me, was convicted of income tax evasion and sent to prison. As it turned out, he left her family disgraced, and so heavily in debt that she was too ashamed to go back East and face all her snooty high society friends."

My horse shied when a jackrabbit bolted across the path. I grabbed onto the saddle horn as Tally reined in beside me.

"You okay?"

"Fine. What happened next?"

"She decided to stay here and divorce me. Her plan was to grab half the ranch and sell it off to a bunch of grubby land developers just for spite." He threw an accusing look in my direction. "That's what she and your smooth lawyer friend Eric Heisler were cooking up together right before she died."

It wasn't hard to see how John Dexter had reached his supposition about Tally. I couldn't think of anyone who had a stronger rationale for wanting the woman dead. I wanted to snap back that Eric wasn't my friend, but that wasn't true, was it?

He must have decided he'd said enough because all at once his expression became withdrawn and sullen, inviting no more questions. We rode on, not speaking, while the hot wind parched my lips and threatened to steal my hat. Overhead, hawks coasted on air currents, and a lone jet chalked its way across an endless bowl of blue sky. Looking ahead, as far as I could see, there was no sign of civilization. The sense of isolation was so complete it felt as if we were the only two people on earth.

I was burning to get down to the nitty gritty about the night of Stephanie's death, but decided it might be better if he volunteered it. The agonizing admission had granted me another new insight into this moody man.

I shifted uncomfortably in the hard saddle and wondered again where we were going. What little patience I had was wearing thin. It was time to stop, get off this horse and eat. Thoughts of food conjured up visions of last night's extraordinary meal.

"Okay," I sighed. "You know how cranky I get when I'm hungry. So, what's the plan? Are we going to skin a rabbit for dinner or did you have something more substantial in mind?"

At the change of topic, Tally's stiff shoulders relaxed and the troubled look faded from his eyes. "How about fried chicken, beans and biscuits?"

"Yeah, I could go for that," I said shading my eyes while peering into the distance. "Is there a KFC around here someplace?"

"No. Something far better than that. Let's pick up the pace and we'll be there in a few minutes." He coaxed Summer Rain into a smooth lope and without inducement from me, Sheba followed suit. Even though there was some apprehension that I might fall, I couldn't help but feel a thrill as we galloped across the desert.

Before long our lathered horses labored up a rocky hill sprinkled with prickly pear and spiked with fat green forks of saguaro cactus. As we reached the plateau, I got a whiff of cattle manure. Entranced, I stared down into a wide dust-choked valley filled with an enormous herd of bawling cattle chaperoned by whistling, shouting cowboys on horseback. A narrow tree-lined creek shining like a ribbon of aluminum foil snaked across the valley floor and disappeared into the crinkled brown hills.

"Wow!" I marveled. "This looks like a scene from every western movie ever made."

Pride glittered in his eyes. "Welcome to the world of cattle ranching. What do you think?"

"I think it's probably a lot of work."

"More than you might imagine." His eyes held mine and he said quietly, "Kendall, do you like Arizona?"

I shrugged. "Yes and no."

"Now that your health has improved...do you think you'll stay?"

"I don't know, Tally. Wherever I end up, the climate has to be dry. To be truthful, I'm really not sure I want to spend the rest of my life in Castle Valley."

"Too primitive for you?"

"Don't put words in my mouth. If you love it so much how come you left?"

I could tell by his wounded expression I'd hit home. When he finally spoke, bitterness tinged his voice. "Because I was a brainless idiot, that's why. At twenty-four I was sure the last thing I wanted was to spend my life running cattle. I finally got up enough nerve to tell my father I wanted to try for a career in journalism, and he hit the ceiling. What kind of a son was I? The Talversons had worked this land for three generations. When I didn't back down, he never missed an opportunity to ridicule me. We had some awful fights."

"What happened then?"

"I took the money from the trust fund my grandfather left me and hightailed it out. I never planned to come back." He paused, staring vacantly at the distant mountains. "But, life has a way of sneaking up behind you and grabbing you by the ass, doesn't it?"

"You could still leave and try to find your dream."

He shook his head slowly. "No. I know now what I didn't know then. I'd never be truly happy anywhere else. Plus that, I gave my word to my mother that I'd stay on. She never has really recovered from..."

Suddenly the realization of what he said struck me. "So, that's why you write for this crummy little newspaper. You don't need the job. It's simply a tool to fulfill the creative needs you've denied yourself."

He gave me another of those penetrating looks. "Well, Miss Psychologist, you seem to have all the answers."

"Not all of them."

Before he could respond, Jake, the old cowboy who'd been with Tally at our first meeting, came riding up the hill toward us calling, "Miguel is about to have a fit; he's been waitin' supper for the last half-hour. You people gonna eat or not?"

Tally grinned and lifted his hand in greeting. "Sorry we're late."

Jake and I exchanged friendly hellos, and on the way down into the valley, he explained to me that Miguel was their cook. For a second, I had a romantic vision of an old-fashioned, horsedrawn covered wagon, but had my bubble burst when he informed me that the modern-day frontier cook worked out of a four wheel drive truck fitted with a camper shell.

As we neared the throng of noisy animals, I expressed surprise that cattle drives still took place and he explained that four times a year they were herded to different pasture lands to prevent the severe plant damage caused by overgrazing. It was a relatively new concept called rotational grazing and was contrary to the traditional methods used in the past by most ranchers.

As we approached the camper, the tantalizing odor of food overruled the stench of the cattle grazing nearby. With a sigh of relief, I dismounted and hoped I wasn't walking bow-legged. I wished I could massage my aching behind, but refrained. It wouldn't do for him to still think of me as the delicate damsel.

I'd obviously been expected, as curious ranch hands pressed close for introductions. Miguel, the tiny, almost toothless Mexican cook, greeted me enthusiastically and handed me a tin plate piled high with food along with a cup filled with cold lemonade. After several minutes of talk, the men politely withdrew, leaving Tally and me alone to eat.

He led me to a shady spot beside the shallow creek bed and I sat down on the ground, my back resting against the sturdy trunk of an ancient cottonwood tree.

With the plate balanced in my lap, that feeling of unreality crept over me again. Last night with Eric I'd dined under the stars on caviar and poached salmon, and now, I was with Tally, sitting under a tree in the middle of this vast windswept vista, hunched over a plate of chicken, beans and biscuits. The contrast in lifestyles was mind boggling. Did I belong in either of them?

I thought about how I'd describe the last two days to my parents when I phoned them in the morning. They absolutely would not believe it.

After sopping the last bite of biscuit in savory bean juice, I looked up to see Tally watching me.

"So, I gather you liked the dinner?"

I sighed and set my plate aside. "It was wonderful. How I wish all my debts were this easy to pay."

His eyes crinkled with pleasure. "You know something. You don't look so much like a snowbird dressed like that. The hat and boots were just the right touch. You can keep them if you like."

"Really? Don't you think we should ask Ronda first?"

He looked down and fiddled with a long blade of grass. "I'm sure Ronda won't mind."

Perhaps it was the way he said it, I don't know, but on a hunch I ventured, "These don't belong to Ronda, do they, Tally?"

He rose, combed his fingers through his hair, and without looking at me answered, "No."

It was like pulling teeth, but we were definitely making progress. In his own roundabout way, he'd opened the forbidden subject. Hard as it was, I kept quiet and waited while he paced back and forth, apparently struggling for words.

"Kendall," he began quietly, "I would be less than candid with you if I didn't concede that the relationship between Stephanie and me had deteriorated to the point where I would actually find myself daydreaming about her being dead. I wouldn't have thought I was capable of violence, but at times, she drove me to the edge of reason."

I stood up and dusted off the back of my jeans. "What did happen that night two years ago?"

He hesitated for a fraction of a second. "I don't know for sure. There is one thing I am sure of, however, and that is I didn't kill my wife."

Finally hearing the words I'd been waiting for made me feel giddy with relief. "Then who did?"

"What makes you think it wasn't just an accident?"

"But how is that possible? I read John Dexter's article. Someone deliberately tampered with the reins."

"He was such a cocky son of a bitch, so quick to point the finger. Just remember, John had the hots for my wife. He wasn't writing objectively. He was writing to sell papers and take a jab at me. If you'd done your homework more thoroughly, you'd have seen that a month later, he had to retract his story."

"You mean the reins weren't cut?"

"I don't know. I never saw the bridle in question after that night, but John quoted Duane Potts as saying that the tears looked suspicious to him."

"I remember reading that you were the prime suspect because of the rather...er...public quarrel you'd had before Stephanie died. But you were never charged. Why was the case closed so suddenly?"

He shook his head. "Because someone in Roy's office botched the job. Somehow the bridle disappeared. Without evidence, they had no case. Her death was ruled accidental."

Shocked, I turned away from him and stared blankly out into the desert. Tally's statement probably explained why John had been so hot on Roy Hollingsworth's trail. His personal vendetta against Tally had been squelched, and to even the score, he'd decided to make life miserable for the sheriff when he discovered yet more blundering in the subsequent cases of the two teenagers.

I wondered if this was just another example of Roy's ineptitude, or if the evidence had been deliberately lost. But, why would the sheriff cover up the murder of Stephanie Talverson?

I didn't realize Tally had moved close behind me until his voice scattered my thoughts. "What are you thinking?"

Still facing away from him, I said, "Just that it was certainly lucky for you since you had the motive and the means, that the evidence was conveniently lost."

He put a hand on my shoulder and turned me to face him. "So, you still think I'm guilty."

"No. I believe you, Tally. But...do you really think it was an accident?"

"That was the conclusion."

His answer didn't sound very convincing. "What are you saying? That you think it's possible someone did kill her, but you chose not to pursue it?"

His hands tightened on my arms. "Listen to me, Kendall. Some things are best left alone. This is one of them. It's a terrible thing for a person to die like that, but I'm not sorry she's gone, none of us are. She made all our lives a living hell."

"You're hurting me."

He let go immediately, mumbling, "I'm sorry." By the look of dismay on his face, it was obvious something was still eating him up inside.

I thought back to what Ginger had told me. There had been nearly two hundred people at the ranch that night. Who among them would have gained from Stephanie Talverson's death?

"Who else hated her as much as you did?"

His face hardened. "Can't we drop this now? I know it's part your bloodhound nature to run around and dig things up, but in this case, it's best to let sleeping dogs lie." He glanced at his watch, turned, and started to move away. "It's time for us to go back."

I felt hot with frustration. Just when I thought he'd laid all his cards on the table, it seemed as if he was hiding one up his sleeve. "Don't you want to know?"

"Give it a rest."

"Who are you protecting?"

He stopped in his tracks and whirled around, hands closed into fists. The menacing expression on his face made me shrink inside and I stifled a shriek of surprise when I backed into a gnarled tree. As he advanced toward me, I was amazed at my own volatile emotions, which seesawed somewhere between fright and intense desire for him.

"Jesus Christ! What am I going to do with you?"

"Just tell me the truth."

"I did."

Something behind his eyes told me he was still withholding information. And then it came to me. Holy cow. It had been right in front of me all along. There *was* someone who would have benefited from her death.

"What about Lucinda?"

He looked thunderstruck. "Lucy? That's got to be the dumbest thing I ever heard." He was looking at me as if I'd lost my mind. "Lucy may be a lot of things, but I've known her since she was six years old. She isn't capable of murder."

"Then who else could it have been?"

The look of misery on his face was profound. "It may have been my mother."

19

Jake interrupted us, saying apologetically that he needed to talk with Tally for a few minutes before we rode back. We walked to the horses, and as I watched Tally stride away, back straight, head high, my heart went out to him. I don't think I realized until that moment how much courage it had taken for him to share his terrible secret.

How could I have so thoroughly misjudged this man? I'd forgotten the old adage, *Don't believe everything you hear and only half of what you read.* I felt ashamed of myself for re-opening such a raw wound and could hardly meet his eyes when he returned a few minutes later. He stood with his lips pursed together, just staring at me until I felt my face flushing.

Finally, he said, "I ought to be angry with you..."

"And you have every right to be. You told me to mind my own business and..."

I flinched as he reached out and placed his forefinger against my lips, silencing me. "Shhhhhhh. Will you let me finish?" Withdrawing his hand he said, "Actually, I'm not angry. It's a relief to finally get that off my chest. It's been stewing inside me for two years." In a now familiar gesture, he lifted his hat, combed his fingers through his hair, and then replaced it. His face still looked drawn and pale. "I can't go back and change what happened, but I know I'm going to have to deal with this sooner or later. For right now…I just wanted to say thank you."

"You're thanking me? What for? For ruining your afternoon and putting you through hell?"

His eyes softened as he stepped close to me. Like the downy wings on a butterfly, his lips brushed lightly over mine. The kiss was over so quickly I had no time to react with anything except surprise.

"Thank you for being…you."

We had no chance to talk further, because two of the ranch hands rode along with us back to the ranch. During the drive home, I thought over and over again of his gentle kiss. Bone weary, saddlesore and sunburned, I crawled into bed hoping for instant sleep. Instead I lay listening to the lively chorus of night critters and thinking about the day's events.

Memories of Eric's ardent kisses the night before intruded. I felt hopelessly confused, and finally ordered myself to banish all thoughts of both men. I mustn't allow my personal life to become too much of a distraction. The scene with Tally had left me emotionally drained. The new information plus his incredulous statement regarding his mother left me with more questions than I started with.

I sat up, snapped on the lamp, pulled the notebook containing my notes from underneath the mattress, and studied it until my eyes ached. Somewhere in this jumble of names and leads there had to be a clue to John's disappearance.

Exasperated, I tucked it underneath the mattress and turned out the light. At the edge of sleep, the elusive thought burst from my subconscious. My eyes popped open. Of course! What was the common denominator between Claudia Phillips and the sheriff? "The teenage girls," I whispered aloud.

That thought triggered another memory. During our second lunch together, Ginger had said that teens frequently vanished or turned up dead in Mexico. Could it be...

Fully awake, I slid from bed and paced in the dark, while a monstrous theory took shape. What if...what if Claudia and the sheriff were in league to capture and market runaway girls to some international smuggling ring? Or...I thought feverishly, perhaps Claudia was the head of some weird cult that sacrificed them in bizarre rituals. I'd researched Ginger's statement and discovered that within the last year, Mexican authorities had dug up the remains of twenty people who had been first tortured, and then burned to death. There had been some connection to a Cuban drug lord.

If those two girls had been killed trying to escape the clutches of Claudia and Roy, that would explain why the toxicology reports had been conveniently lost. Was that the secret John Dexter hoped to uncover? And if Hollingsworth was involved that would explain why the hunt for the missing reporter had been called off. He already knew John was dead. Where did that leave me?

I threw myself down on the bed and groaned into my pillow. Somehow I had to find the proof that would link Claudia and Roy to the girls' deaths. Did I dare approach Tugg with my wild theories without him thinking I was certifiable? Unanswered questions circled endlessly in my mind as I fell into an exhausted sleep.

I was still mulling over the disturbing possibilities as I phoned my parents in the morning. I felt less sure of myself now. It had made perfect sense last night, but somehow my suspicions seemed preposterous in the brilliant sunlight.

It was comforting to hear their voices, and I felt a sharp pang of homesickness as they talked about family get-togethers, picnics in the woods, and walks in the rain; all things familiar to me, and much missed. I chose not to worry them with details concerning my assignment, and instead kept to the topics of my improving health and the two men I was seeing. After listening, my mother urged me to go after Eric, explaining that he sounded more my type.

I hung up, lingered in a long bath, and I felt almost human again as I headed into town to do more research at the Castle Valley library. The parking lot was almost empty, but that wasn't surprising. It was Sunday, and most of the townspeople were probably at the fairgrounds for the rodeo.

Clara Whitlow, the elderly, blue-haired librarian, welcomed me with a friendly smile and handed me a stack of recent articles on runaways she had volunteered to pick up for me from the main library during her trip to Phoenix the day before. Not only had she brought everything I had asked for, she also included some pamphlets she'd obtained from her cousin who worked at the Arizona Department of Economic Security.

I thanked her warmly, settled into a chair at one of the scarred wooden tables, and began to leaf through the material. Other than the fly bumping in vain against the nearby windowpane, and the low murmur of voices from the adjoining room, there were no other sounds.

Two hours later I sat back and drew in a deep breath filled with the odor of musty books. The information before me was disturbing. Statistics showed an appalling forty-three hundred homeless or runaway children in Arizona within a one year period. Limited funding available through private foundations, corporations, and federal grants provided a dismal forty beds statewide, and most of them were for children younger than thirteen. No state programs existed to assist homeless teenagers.

"Miss O'Dell, how nice to see you."

I glanced around to see Thena Rodenborn approaching. "Well, hello, Mrs. Rodenborn. Were you in the meeting?" I asked in reference to the gathering of the Castle Valley Historical Society who shared space with the library.

Her blue eyes twinkled with humor. "Since I'm the president I guess I have to be." She went on to say that they were in the process of trying to obtain donations to buy the old Hansen house from the heirs. During the past twenty years they'd been able to save three of the town's oldest structures.

"Well, that's really commendable," I commented. "I'm surprised you didn't try for the old mission out near where I live. The one that's now the mental facility."

"Ooohh!" She clasped her hands together. "I'd absolutely love to get my hands on that place. Are you familiar with its history?"

"No."

That was all the invitation she needed. She sat down in the chair opposite me. "It was built in the late 1700's and served as a monastery for trappist monks until the early 1900's. At that point, it was converted to a mission and remained open until about twenty years ago when the Church suddenly decided it wasn't worth the expense. It was such a shame. The place was falling to ruin and vandals had desecrated some of the buildings. As hard as we tried, we could not convince the Catholic Church to donate the mission to the town. We were all shocked when the property was sold to an out-of-town developer."

"Mary Tuggs told me it operated as some kind of health resort before it was Serenity House."

"That's true," she said smoothing the jacket of her peach silk suit. "It was some sort of New Age retreat where people sit around in a triangle, look at stones and drink carrot juice or something." Distress lines etched her forehead. "I almost wept when we discovered the new owner had demolished most of the old buildings. Let me tell you, it took a lot of persuasion to convince him to leave the rectory standing. Why, the bell in the tower alone is priceless." She paused for a breath and then continued in an animated tone. "Has anyone told you the story of the missing monks?"

"No."

"According to what little we've been able to uncover from historical records, supposedly a whole group of them vanished one day and were never heard of again. One theory is they wandered into some of the box canyons behind Castle Rock and were lost. Another is that the monks supposedly dug a series of tunnels beneath the various buildings leading to safe rooms where they could hide in case of Indian attack. But," she added unhappily, "we've never been able to verify this, because no one can get onto the property now."

"Did you talk to Dr. Price about continuing your research on the place?"

"You know that was a curious situation. The first time I phoned him, he was very pleasant and seemed open to the idea of allowing some excavation on the property.

But, when I spoke to him the second time, he told me he was not well. Something about growths on his vocal cords. He said to call back in a few weeks after his surgery."

"Did you?"

"I did, but that was right around the time that horrid lunatic escaped. The one who murdered, then cut up his family or whatever. Did you hear about that?"

"Yes."

"Well, my dear girl, you should have been here." she said, with a dramatic sweep of her hand. "The entire town was in a state of absolute panic until the man was found. Afterward, Dr. Price had that fence erected and when I spoke to him at the fund-raiser three years ago...well, he seemed different somehow."

"Different? In what way?"

"Well, I don't know exactly. He was very aloof and...well...he didn't...sound the same." She shook her head slightly as if the memory still bothered her. "Anyway," she said with a tone of regret, "now he says he can't have people traipsing in and out. He said some of his patients were too unpredictable. I must say, there just wasn't the same level of enthusiasm from the other members of the society to continue the study after the scare we'd all had."

She paused, looking wistful. "So you see, the same fate awaits the old Hansen house. If we fail to raise the money to buy it, the heirs plan to demolish it and apply for commercial zoning. That would be a frightful shame since it's well over a hundred years old. It's as old as this building, as a matter of fact. Did you know that this was once the territorial jail?"

I told her I didn't and would write up a story for the paper if she'd get me all the details. Pink with delight, she thanked me and before she could leave I said,

"Ah…actually, it's very opportune that we met today because I was going to call you. I'm still researching for my series on runaway girls, and I've misplaced some of the notes from our earlier meeting."

"What can I help you with?" I could tell by her blank expression that Eric had not yet spoken to her about arranging for me to have an interview at the Desert Harbor.

"I believe you had said Claudia Phillips arrived quite soon after the death of Violet Mendoza. Had you advertised for a replacement?"

"Why no. We'd only just had the funeral and I hadn't had time to arrange for that yet."

"So…how did she know you had the opening?"

She stared at me blankly before answering. "Isn't that silly of me. It's been quite some time ago and you know, I really can't remember. She just…showed up one day about a week after the tragedy."

"I see. And where was it she'd worked before?"

"I'll have to check my records on that, if I even have them." She seemed lost in thought for a moment. "She did tell me at the time…but I've forgotten. I was still so very distraught over Violet…that it didn't seem important."

"Didn't you think it rather odd that she would just show up out of the blue?"

"What exactly is your point, Miss O'Dell?" She looked a little perplexed.

"Oh, nothing. Just that it was certainly expedient she happened to arrive at the exact time you needed her to take over the operation."

"I thought so too. She's been such a godsend. So efficient. I can only think it was the answer to my prayers that brought her here."

I was glad she couldn't hear how fast my heart was beating. Her vague answers gave some credence to my midnight musings. A car horn sounded outside. "Oh goodness," she fretted. "I forgot Mary Lou was waiting for me. So nice to see you again, my dear." Turning, she hurried out.

I could hardly contain my excitement. Could it be that poor Violet Mendoza's death had not been accidental? This would bear looking into. I made a note to ask for her file when I checked the log at the sheriff's office on my next visit. But that might tip off Roy. Ideas on how to get the file unnoticed ricocheted in my head. There were times when both the sheriff and Deputy Potts were out. Julie, their secretary, could probably help. Afterward, could she be convinced to keep my inquiry under her hat?

It was past noon. Hastily, I finished my research, thanked Clara Whitlow again, and headed for the fairgrounds to meet Ginger. The place was so swamped with people roaming among the various western art displays and food booths, I didn't think I'd ever find her.

When I did, I was so preoccupied trying to make some sense out of the fragmented clues whirling in my head, it was hard to concentrate on her constant prattle and endless questions about my dates with Eric and Tally.

I told her just enough about my encounter with Eric to send her swooning with delight, but carefully hedged my answers about the visit with Tally.

Witnessing my first rodeo ever was a kick and I enjoyed Ginger's screaming antics as much as the bucking broncos and charging bulls. She insisted I sample Indian fry bread, and between us, we managed to devour five pieces, each smothered in honey and powdered sugar.

I had an assignment to cover the melodrama at the Elk's Lodge following the rodeo, so a thin thumbnail of silvery moon hung over my house when I finally pulled into the carport. It had been a long and exhausting day. A good night's sleep was just the ticket.

The heady scent of roses greeted me as I walked into the dining room and my heart leaped when I saw the red light on my answering machine blinking. Five messages! Had my mystery lady called? I punched the button and held my breath as the tape rewound.

Eric Heisler's husky voice filled the quiet room. "Hi, gorgeous, it's Eric. I can't stop thinking about what a wonderful time I had with you. I have to be out of town a few days, but I hope you'll save Friday evening for me. We'll do something really special."

The machine beeped and I smiled ruefully. He really was quite charming.

The second call was a hang-up and the third was Tally. "Um…yes, Kendall, this is Tally…um…if you get in early, call me. I…I'd like to see you again…if you want to. Thanks. Bye."

My stomach knotted. Common sense warned me again that I should not be dating these two men at the same time.

Another hang-up and a beep. At the sound of heavy breathing on the fifth call my heart rate doubled. I switched the volume higher and listened intently. As the silence stretched on and on I began to wonder if it was an obscene call. My finger was poised to hit the rewind button when I heard the message. It made my breath catch in my throat. "Stay away from him," a voice whispered harshly. "Stay away or you will die!"

20

I played the tape back several more times, but couldn't identify the raspy whisper. After the initial jolt of fear, anger set in. The ghostly shadow, coupled with the spider caper was enough to convince me that this was another rotten trick cooked up by Lucinda to discourage me from seeing Tally.

When I finally settled into bed, I decided after several hours of tossing and turning, that sleep was becoming as scarce as rain. A death threat was not a matter to take lightly, not when I considered the fate of Stephanie Talverson. Tally had quickly dismissed the possibility of Lucinda's involvement, but now, I wasn't so sure.

I thought of a half-dozen scenarios as to how I could confront Lucinda, then just as quickly I dismissed them. What good would it do? She would deny everything.

The next morning, I stopped by the Sierra Cleaners and returned the photo of John Dexter to Yolanda Reyes before heading into work. Immediate tears flooded her eyes when I told her I'd talked to the girl who'd apparently been

183

in contact with him. Her distressed expression brought a lump to my throat.

"So...he did not go away with her?" A slight spark of hope illuminated her face.

"Apparently not. The man at the bus station said he remembered selling John only one ticket to Nogales."

She swallowed hard and her lips quivered when she spoke. "So...what does it mean?"

I shrugged. "I don't know yet. She sounded very upset and claimed he promised her money. I'm still hoping she'll call back and I can get some more information. In the meantime, if you remember anything, anything at all about those phone calls, or whatever else John might have said about this girl, will you please call me?"

She nodded and tucked the photo into her blouse next to her heart. Back in the car once more, I felt depressed for having raised her hopes only to dash them to pieces again.

When I got to work, I was happy to find a message from Dr. Crane, the medical examiner. He was out when I called, and I was out when he returned the call after lunch. We finally connected about five o'clock.

"What can I do for you...ah...Miss...O'Neal?"

"It's O'Dell, and I'm working on a series concerning runaway teens. You've had two recent cases which particularly interest me."

"Which ones would those be?"

I lowered my voice, hoping Jim, who was busy writing copy, wouldn't overhear me. "One is Charity Perkins and the other is a Jane Doe found in the desert near here in June of last year."

For a minute, he said nothing and then replied, "Oh yes. Those two. Hmmmm. I'm sure I can find the files, but if you don't mind my saying so, wouldn't it be easier for you to get them from Sheriff Hollingsworth?"

"No. I mean...he's been awfully busy lately and I really hate to bother him again. Apparently, his secretary misfiled the toxicology reports you issued."

"Really? Well, I'll see if my assistant can find them for you. Do you want to hold, or shall I call you back?"

I didn't feel like playing another round of phone tag and I was bursting to get the information today. "If you don't mind, I'll hold."

"Well...it might take some time."

"Fine." Behind me, I heard Jim shut off his computer. He grabbed up some papers and shouted good-bye to me on his way out the door. Good. As the minutes ticked past, my stomach churned and a nervous sweat dampened my forehead. Drumming my fingers against the edge of the desk, I thought about John Dexter again and wondered for the zillionth time what sensitive information could be in the missing reports.

"Miss O'Dell?" Dr. Crane's rough voice jabbed into my thoughts. Hastily, I scooped up a pen. "I found the files. You know, of course, we were unable to identify the first girl."

"Yes. Do you think there's still a chance?"

He sighed. "At this point, it's unlikely."

"Why?"

"Other cases take priority, and unfortunately situations like this get shoved to the bottom of the barrel, if you know what I mean." I could hear him shuffling papers in the background and his next words surprised me. "Hmmmmm. These toxicology reports are still red tagged."

"What does that mean?"

185

"It means I can't give this information to you while the cases are pending. It's confidential and to release it might hinder the ongoing investigations."

"Confidential? But, I was told the reports had just been misfiled, not that they were unavailable to the public."

"Well, according to my records, this information was ordered sealed until further notice."

I let a note of pleading slip into my voice. "Oh, Dr. Crane, I'm certain that must be in error. Are you sure I can't get a copy of those reports?"

Irritation tinged his voice. "No can do. I guess your paper could try and get a court order, but I think the simplest thing for me to do is call Roy and see if this information can be released."

Jesus! The last thing I needed was to have Hollingsworth know I was going around him. "Dr. Crane, I'd rather you didn't do that."

"Why not?"

Why not, indeed? I couldn't tell him what I suspected; that it appeared the sheriff was hiding something. "Perhaps I was mistaken. I certainly wouldn't want to do anything to hinder Roy's investigation. I have more than enough information for my story, so for the time being, let's just forget this, okay?"

"Well...I'd like to get it cleared up."

"Not a problem. I'm on my way over to Roy's office right now, so there's absolutely no need for you to trouble yourself. But before you hang up, maybe you could tell me just one thing. The toxicology report would indicate if particular substances were found in the bodies such as chemical compounds or drugs?"

"Yes. We had a wet tissue sample on the Perkins case and we were fortunate enough to find ah...a small section of the Jane Doe that the coyotes had missed."

His statement brought forth the horrifying spectacle of the poor girl's body torn and shredded by the desert's wild creatures. I swallowed hard. "Can you tell me what you found?"

"You know I can't."

It was agonizing to be so close and be stonewalled. "Just one more thing, Doctor."

"Yes?"

"I know you can't tell me the name of the substance, but don't you think it's suspicious that both girls had traces of the same drug?"

"Considering the type..." His words halted and when he spoke again, there was an icy edge to his voice. "This conversation is over." Click.

"Ah-ha!" Barely able to contain my elation, I added the incriminating data to my notebook. Mentally, I crossed my fingers in the hope that Dr. Crane's slip would assure me he'd not call Roy, since he could now be guilty of illegally divulging confidential police information to a reporter. At the same time, he'd have to be hoping that I'd keep my mouth shut.

So now what? I nervously paced the room. Maybe my theories about Roy and Claudia running a white slavery ring weren't so crazy after all. Had the same drug been administered to subdue the girls until they'd been transported somewhere else? If true, what had happened to interrupt this process?

I needed to talk to Tugg as soon as possible and had gotten only a few feet from my desk when the phone rang again. I grabbed it. "This is Kendall O'Dell."

There was a slight pause, then the silky voice of Claudia Phillips oozed over the line. "I've consulted with my employer and since we spoke a few weeks ago, I've had a change of heart."

"Good. What did you decide?" When she spoke again her words were stilted. I had the impression she was speaking through clenched teeth and that each word uttered caused her intense pain. "If you'd like...I can arrange for you to...interview a couple of the girls here...tomorrow."

"What time?"

"Eleven o'clock."

"I'll be there." I hung up and clapped my hands in triumph. Things were finally going my way and I had Eric Heisler to thank for it. I owed him one now and I'd have to think of a suitable way to repay him on Friday night.

Anxious to talk to Tugg, I couldn't repress my disappointment when I found his office empty. Concerned, I headed for the reception desk. Ginger pulled a gigantic wad of purple bubble gum from her mouth and responded to my question. "Mary called in for him. She said his ulcer was acting up again something awful."

"I didn't know he had an ulcer."

In the know, as always, Ginger said, "Oh yeah. He's got one of them septic ones...or is it peptic? Well any hoot, it's one of them bleedin' type ulcers, and I heard he pert near up and died one time some years ago when it went and ruptured on him."

That news depressed me. Tugg was my only ally in this thing. What if something happened to him?

The phone rang and Ginger answered. A second later, a sunny smile lit her face. Excitedly, she cupped her hand over the mouthpiece, her eyebrows arched expressively. "It's your lover boy, Eric."

I made a face at her and hurried to my desk. Eric's deep voice boomed, "Hey, beautiful."

"Well, hello. This is a nice surprise."

"Why are you surprised? I promised I'd call. You did get my message, didn't you?"

"Yes, I did. And by the way, I want to thank you for arranging my visit to the shelter. Claudia Phillips just called a few minutes ago. It was very kind of you to act so quickly."

"It was no trouble at all. But, on to more important things. Do you have time in your busy schedule to see me on Friday?"

"I'm in your debt, so yes."

He chuckled. "I hope that's not the only reason. If you're in the mood for some adventure I'll pick you up at the airport around five and we'll take my plane to Phoenix for dinner. It's only a half-hour trip by air."

"That sounds great to me." It also sounded terribly romantic.

"Wonderful. Now listen, it usually takes an act of God to get reservations at this particular place, but I've managed it. So, please don't cancel out on me."

"I don't have any other plans. What should I wear?"

His voice grew husky. "Wear something dressy. Sexy. Like that dynamite green number you wore the night we first met."

He certainly knew the right things to say. "Okay, see you Friday."

"I'll be counting the hours."

We said good-bye and cradling the phone, I let out a deep sigh, remembering his searing kiss. He really was very sweet. All at once I felt a prickling at the back of my neck; the kind of sensation one gets when someone is staring daggers at you. Turning, I saw Tally standing in the doorway with his jaw clenched, his dark eyes glowing with fury.

For a tense moment, neither of us spoke. Then, with accusation tinging his voice, he said, "You don't listen very well, do you?"

"What are you talking about?"

"You know exactly what I'm talking about. You think I haven't heard all about your cutesy evening with Heisler? You had no business seeing him."

I stiffened. After witnessing his sensitive side, watching him resurrect his 'macho, superior, ordering the poor dumb female about' routine, really ticked me off. "Well excuse me. I didn't realize I had to clear my social engagements with you."

Tally slapped his hat against his thigh. "The guy's a lizard in a suit. I told you, he can't be trusted."

"What are you? My keeper? Since when do I have to get permission from you before I go out with someone? For your information, I'll see whomever I choose, and furthermore..."

Tally crossed to my desk with such swiftness, the rest of the sentence hung in my throat.

"Goddamn it to hell, Kendall!" His breathing was ragged. Rage and frustration flashed in his eyes. "I thought...I thought that we...never mind."

My anger dimmed slightly at the anxious note in his voice, and I tried to keep my voice calm. "Tally, if you'll just give me a minute and quit having a total cow, I'll explain. Now, can we talk quietly about this?" He didn't answer, so I continued. "Listen, I honestly meant to tell you Saturday but...it didn't seem like the right time to bring it up."

His eyes were hard pinpoints of black steel. "That was him on the phone just now, wasn't it?"

"Yeah. So?"

"You can't see him on Friday night."

I rose to my full height. We were almost eyeball to eyeball. "The last thing on earth I want to do is hurt your feelings, but Eric did me a big favor, so I owe him one. I'm going to see him on Friday whether you like it or not."

"You can't."

I gave him an incredulous look. "What gives you the right to stand there and tell me what I can and can't do?"

"For some strange reason I thought you were a person who kept your word."

"I am."

"Really? You already promised to see me on Friday."

"I did not!"

"Yes, you did."

"When?"

"Last Saturday."

That stopped me cold. I blinked in confusion and closed my eyes momentarily. "What am I not understanding here?"

"So, it was that unimportant to you."

I threw up my hands. "What? What on earth are you talking about?"

"The annual barbecue at the Starfire. You said you'd come."

"That's Saturday, isn't it?"

"No. It's Friday."

I felt like two cents waiting on change. How could I have double booked myself? "Oh…Tally. I thought it was

Saturday." I flipped the pages of the calendar on my desk. "See. I have it right here." It seemed a feeble excuse. "What time is the barbecue?"

"Seven o'clock."

"Until when?"

"Midnight." His voice was as cold as his eyes.

"Well, can't I come by after dinner?"

"You'll miss the start of the hayride at eight-thirty. I sort of had in mind that we'd, that you and I would..." Abruptly, he stopped speaking and stood there shaking his head with disgust.

"Look," I said, attempting to lighten the mood. "I admit I screwed up. It happens. Can't you give a little on this? I can't imagine we'll be much later than ten. How about I come then?"

"Don't bother."

The phone on Tally's desk rang repeatedly but neither of us moved. We were still silently squared off like two stubborn tomcats when Ginger appeared in the doorway. "Well, for pity's sake, will one of y'all pick up the danged phone?" She blinked in surprise as Tally abruptly broke the spell and strode toward his desk. He whipped up the phone, turning his back to me.

Ginger hurried over to me. "What's going on?

I shook my head sadly and whispered, "It's nothing. A slight disagreement." Her searching gaze told me she didn't believe that for a second, but, thankfully, she didn't pursue it. Squeezing my hand she said softly, "I'll talk to you later."

After she left the room I wanted to go to him, apologize for my stupidity, tell him how sorry I was, but the obstinate set of his shoulders rebuffed any advance.

21

Tuesday morning I awoke late, immediately aware of an odd sensation. My skin was clammy and each breath was an effort. Why an asthma attack now?

A quick glance around the room showed nothing out of order. The strong morning sun slanted through the arcadia door, and outside, the birds were making their usual racket. The evaporative cooler on the roof hummed and rattled, but the air in the room didn't feel as cool as it should. In fact, it lay heavy and close.

After a dose of medication, I got dressed, and called Ginger to tell her I wouldn't be in until after my appointment at the shelter. I ate a leisurely breakfast, feeling no urge to hurry, since it was barely past nine. There should be plenty of time to stop by the sheriff's office and check the log.

As I stepped out the front door I was startled by the unreal scene before me. So that's why the air felt so oppressive. Directly north, enormous thunderheads curled over the distant mountains like foaming white waves. After weeks of empty, blue sky, their sudden appearance changed the landscape dramatically. It looked as though someone had come overnight and painted them on the horizon. Rain couldn't come any too soon for me. But, as I climbed into my car, I remembered that the rainy season did not usually begin until July, still three weeks away. Perhaps the "monsoon" would start early this year.

The car made a deep groaning sound when I turned the key. Uh-oh. After a few more tries, the engine finally caught. Relieved, I made a mental note to take it in for service.

I was so busy gawking at the phenomenon of clouds and was so accustomed to there never being much traffic on Lost Canyon, that I pulled out of Weeping Bird directly into the path of an oncoming car. I screamed and slammed on the brakes. My car fishtailed wildly and slid sideways off the road into the sandy shoulder. Finally stopped and gasping for breath, I watched in amazement as Dr. Price from Serenity House accelerated his Mercedes and flashed past, leaving me in a plume of choking dust. "You idiot!" I shouted at the retreating car.

When I tried to maneuver onto the road, the back tires whirled uselessly in the loose sand. After a half a dozen failed tries, I thumped the steering wheel as tears of frustration stung my eyes. "Oh, no. Not now!" Of all the days for this to happen. I had only an hour and a half until my appointment.

It would take only minutes to get back to the house. For a split second, I toyed with the idea of calling Tally. Could he pull me out with his truck? Then, just as quickly, I dismissed the thought. After yesterday's confrontation, I wouldn't have asked him for help if he'd been the last man on earth.

I scrambled out of the car, locked it, and soon discovered the futility of running on the rutted dirt road in heels. At this rate I'd break an ankle. I slowed my pace. The scalding sun beat down on the top of my now throbbing head, and a cluster of tiny gnats buzzed irritatingly around my nose and mouth.

My shoes were full of sharp little stones when I finally reached the house, sweat-drenched and perturbed. There were only two towing services in town, and I was told the wait would be at least forty-five minutes.

Still bummed about Dr. Price's irresponsible departure from the accident scene, I looked up the number for Serenity House and punched the numbers on the phone.

"Hello," said a soothing feminine voice, "you have reached Serenity House. Staff is occupied at this time. Please leave your name and number and we will return your call as soon as possible."

How weird. I'd never heard of a hospital with a recorded message. I hesitated for a second and then left my name and work number.

Estimating the arrival of my tow, I donned running shoes, and then heels in hand, walked back toward the car. The searing wind tumbled my hair and churned up impressive columns of yellowish dust. I had to dive inside my car to avoid one of the whirling dust devils that whooshed past.

Rescue finally arrived in the form of a dented white truck bearing the name, Bud's Towing Service. Large black letters on the front of the hood announced: HELP'S A COMIN'.

I waited impatiently as a heavy-set man in a checkered shirt eased himself slowly out of the truck.

Touching the bill of his smudged ball cap, he said, "How do, young lady. You need towin'?"

"Yes, and boy am I glad to see you."

He grinned good naturedly. "Most people generally are."

After we exchanged introductions, Bud Stovely remarked appreciatively that I had 'right purty red hair,' and asked me how I liked 'reportin' for the paper.' It seemed everyone in town knew who I was, so we chatted for a few minutes in a friendly manner. Whistling slightly offkey, he clanked and rattled the chain while attaching the hook to my car. I asked him if he'd had any trouble finding me.

"Nope. Knew right where you were." He shifted a wad of chewing tobacco with his tongue. "Before I bought out my brother's towing business, I used to drive one of them linen trucks out here to the loony bin every week."

"Really? What's it like inside that place?"

He turned his head and expertly ejected a stream of brown spit, then dragged his shirt sleeve across his mouth. "I don't know. They don't let you inside. I'd pick up the dirty things, and leave the clean stuff right there at the guard station. Some of them wetbacks would come pick it up."

I raised a brow at his derogatory remark, but he seemed not to notice. "Are most of the people employed there Hispanic?"

"Mostly. Them people will work for practically nothing and end up sending most of it back home to Mexico." He paused and reached inside the cab to turn the key, adding, "You couldn't pay me enough to work in a place like that." He went around behind my car, and then came back shaking his head. "How'd you manage to get yourself in such a fix, little lady?"

I told him the circumstances of the accident and he clicked his tongue sympathetically. "I don't see the doc in town too often, but when I do, he's always driving like a house afire. I've seen him more than once down there at the Rattlesnake and he was always half in the bag."

His remark reminded me of the night I'd tried to talk to Dr. Price at the fund-raiser. He'd obviously been totally plowed, and his behavior fit the alcoholic personality. Maybe he'd been coming home from a bender this morning and that's why he hadn't stopped. It didn't excuse what he'd done, and the implication was ironic. An alcoholic psychiatrist spent his days treating the mentally ill?

Bud's voice broke into my thoughts. "Ruben, he's the fellow who tends bar, says the doc's been so out of it a couple of times, he's had to call the sheriff to drive him back out here."

Well, wasn't that interesting? I started to ask him another question but conversation was drowned out by the roar of the winch. Gratefully, I watched my Volvo pulled from the deep sand. When the engine noise stopped, I asked, "Tell me something. Where do the people live who work at the hospital? I hardly ever see any traffic along this road."

"I guess some of them live on the grounds. A couple of times a weeks they switch shifts. Somebody in one of them white vans drives them into town."

"Yeah, I see those vans all the time."

Bud unhooked the chain and gave me a wry smile. "Most of them stick to their own kind. They got their own little community down there south of the tracks. The driver drops them off and then picks up supplies at one of those warehouses catawampus to the auto parts store."

I smiled to myself. Bud was an absolute treasure trove of information, but, not only was I running out of time, I felt like I was about to melt into my shoes.

"There you go, little lady," he said, slowly wiping his hands on a filthy cloth. "I guess that'll about do it for you." He pulled a clip board from the truck and scribbled out the bill.

While I rummaged in my purse for the checkbook, my mind sorted through a myriad of facts. I remembered the odd feeling I'd had on my first visit to Serenity House; the sight of that sinister fence, and the fright I'd felt when the dogs had rushed at me.

"I don't guess Tess Delgado ever had any trouble," Bud said, "but I'd watch yourself if I was you."

"What do you mean?" I asked, accepting the bill he handed me.

"I don't think I'd feel none too safe living so close to a nut house. Did you hear about that maniac who got loose a few years back?"

I told him I had but he proceeded to repeat the story anyway. By the number of gruesome, preposterous details he relayed, I suspected that the story had been embellished by the townsfolk far beyond the original event.

"I appreciate your concern, but, so far, I've had more problems with gigantic insects than I have with mental patients."

He laughed and said, "I know what you mean. I never did run into any trouble that whole time. Hell, I never worried as much about the loonies as I did them damn vicious dogs they got roaming all over the place."

A glance at my watch told me I had to end the conversation. I thanked him warmly while handing him a check. He waited till I started the engine and we waved good-bye to each other as I drove off. Thank goodness he'd come. I heaved a sigh of relief and noted with satisfaction that, barring any more problems, I'd reach my appointment right on time.

Heading toward town, I thought about what Bud had said about never getting inside Serenity House. What about relatives of the patients? How did they get in? There was something very, very odd about Dr. Price and I intended to find out why he'd left me there in the dust.

22

The weather wasn't the only thing different that day. To my surprise, Claudia Phillips greeted me at the door of the shelter wearing a friendly smile that completely transformed her normally forbidding face. She chatted pleasantly for a few minutes about the humid weather, my outfit, which certainly wasn't anything spectacular, and the continuing Gold Dust Day events.

After inviting me inside, we got down to business. No real names were to be used, and no photos without permission. I agreed.

Each of the five tiny bedrooms contained two sagging twin beds, a battered dresser, and an ancient black and white television set. In one room, two girls lay sleeping, in another, a girl was painting her toenails while her companion stared vacantly at the TV.

The small kitchen looked worn, but tidy. A couple of young women, one sporting a rooster's comb of spiked orange hair and the other, obviously a bleached blonde, sat at the kitchen table smoking and playing cards. I smiled, but they glared at me with street-smart eyes, hard with suspicion. Claudia informed me that each girl was required to cook her own meals and wash the dishes. The girls also did their own laundry which permitted the shelter to keep hired help to a minimum. The young Hispanic girl I'd seen on my first visit was busy dusting. She threw me a shy smile which I returned while Claudia crisply announced that no drugs of any kind were permitted inside the house and male visitors were strictly prohibited.

I made note of all the rules as she led me to a small sitting room and introduced me to a girl called Jenny. What an angelic face! Petite and frail, with wavy shoulder length blonde hair, she looked pretty enough to grace the cover of any teen magazine. To me, she didn't look like a typical runaway. But then what was typical? The steely-eyed girls in the kitchen fit more into the picture I'd conjured up, and so had the hardened girl I'd picked up my first day in Arizona. But this girl...like a small child, she huddled against the armrest of the tattered couch clutching a ragged teddy bear tightly to her chest.

I took a chair directly across from her and nodded to Claudia who then excused herself and slipped from the room. It was a relief to know she wouldn't be monitoring every question I asked.

"Hello, Jenny," I said softly.

She lifted her chin and stared back at me with eyes as blue as the bachelor buttons that used to grow each April under the weeping willow tree in our yard back home. Instead of echoing the joy and beauty of spring, her eyes reflected the harsh, cruel tragedies of life.

"My real name's not Jenny, you know," she said, her voice flat.

I gave her an encouraging grin. "I'll use whatever name you want me to."

She shrugged and looked out the window. "It's as good as any."

"Miss Phillips explained to you why I'm here?"

She hugged the bear tighter. "Yeah. She says you want to know why I'm a runner. That's what they call someone like me you know. A runner."

"How many times have you run away from home?"

"Ten, twelve, I don't know. But I'll tell you something, this time I'm not going back. They'll never find me. Never in a million years.."

Claudia had told me she was only fifteen but judging by her grim expression, it was obvious this girl had experienced more adversity in her short life than most people could even begin to imagine.

At first she refused to talk about her past at all, preferring to prattle on about various movie stars, her eventual destination of Los Angeles, and her hopes and dreams of being rich and famous someday. Apparently this was the fantasy that got her out of bed each morning.

"So, you don't think your parents are concerned about you?" I tried to imagine what my own parents would have thought if I had run away. They would have been frantic with worry.

At that, her eyes glazed over. Nervously, she picked at the teddy bear's ears. "My old lady doesn't give a shit what happens to me."

"Why do you say that?"

"She says I'm bad news, that's why. Since the day I was born, I been nothing but trouble." She hesitated, then said softly, "She'd be happy if I was dead."

That jarred me. "Why would she wish that?"

Her lips curled into a bitter smile. She set the bear aside and extended her wrists toward me. Ugly, jagged scars tracked both. A sick feeling invaded my stomach. "You know what she said to me when she came to my room down at the county hospital?

I shook my head.

"She said, 'You stinking brat. How the hell are we going to come up with the cash to pay these goddamn hospital bills?'" Jenny giggled and a devilish gleam lit those magnificent eyes. "You know what I did then?"

"What?"

"I bit her. I grabbed her hand and bit it so hard, she screamed like one of the ladies in those slasher movies. I can still remember the taste of her blood in my mouth," she said, running her tongue over her lips. "It tasted like...real salty, you know? I almost bit her finger clean off before the nurses came and pulled her away." A far away look entered her eyes and she whispered, "Wish I had."

I suppressed a shiver of revulsion and asked what happened next. "They stuck me in the psycho ward at the state hospital for a month. The shrinks gave me all sorts of tests to see if I was like totally whacko, you know," she said matter-of-factly twirling her finger around her temple. "They pumped me full of all kinds of drugs and stuff. Later I got shipped off again. My foster parents were real assholes. But I showed them. Soon as their backs were turned, I split. I would've got away, you know, but I got grabbed for shoplifting."

"What did you take?"

She shook her head in disbelief. "A box of cupcakes. A stupid little box of cupcakes and I end up in the can. The cops called Ma and she hauled me home. But, no way was I staying there." She gave me a sour smile. "I totally hate her.

I hate her so much I hope she croaks." She uttered the last part through clenched teeth.

"Why do you hate her so much?"

"Because."

"Because, why?"

She looked away from me and I could see her swallowing hard. A small spasm shook her. For several minutes we sat in silence, then she turned back to me. Her eyes were dull and lifeless. "When you were little, did you ever have a pretty yellow dress?"

Puzzled by her question, I thought a moment and then said, "Well, yes, I had one. It had little flowers on it."

A serene smile settled on her face and she said in a dreamy voice, "I had one once. It was so, so beautiful. Lace. It had some lace on the pocket, I remember. I think I was only four, but I remember it real, real well."

Something was happening. She sounded and looked a lot like someone under hypnosis—detached, concise, unemotional.

"Did your mother do something to the dress you loved?"

She looked blank. "Ma? No. But, my stepdad did."

My skin was beginning to crawl. "Your stepdad?"

"He took it, you know. He took it off of me so I could never find it again. There was blood on it. I cried and cried and he promised he'd buy me a bunch more dresses."

"Did he?"

"Yeah. He bought me real pretty panties too and said he'd buy me lots of things if I'd just be nice to him. He said I was the prettiest girl in the whole world, and he took bunches and bunches of pictures of me. He said it was real fun to play with me just like I was his little doll..." Her

SYLVIA NOBEL

voice broke suddenly and her face hardened into a mask of anger.

"He told me never to tell. Never to tell. Never to tell…and I didn't for a long, long time. But then, one day I did tell. I told my grandma. She went and told Ma and you know what? After my grandma left, she started beating on me." She rubbed her arms as if she could still feel the pain. "She said I was a lying little bitch and never did anything about it."

Rage sickened me. No wonder she'd run. All the statistics and reports I'd read hardly prepared me for the horror of this girl's poignant confession.

Dry-eyed, she picked up the fuzzy bear, held it close to her, and slowly rocked back and forth, humming to herself. The scene moved me so much, I blinked back tears, tears this girl no longer had. How could anyone so mistreat another human being? A defenseless child, no less? Disgust and loathing for her parents formed a hard lump in my throat.

"How did you end up here in Castle Valley, Jenny?"

"Hitched a ride. This was as far as he was going."

"I see. And how did you find the Desert Harbor Shelter?"

"The sheriff brought me here."

That made my pulse skip. "Really? What happened?"

"Nothing much. I was sleeping outside the library and I guess someone called him to complain. He wasn't mad or nothin' and he brought me straight here."

"I see. And has Miss Phillips been helpful?"

"Oh yeah. She's real nice. Gave me these clothes, lots of food and she's even giving me bus fare cause I'm leaving for L.A. Thursday, you know."

205

"How long have you been here?"

"I don't know. Five or six days. But I'm not staying." Her eyes brightened. "I gotta go someplace with some action. You know, where I can get a job and make a bunch of money. Maybe I'll be a model or be in a movie. I sure can't stay here. This place is like totally dead."

My heart twinged with pity for the pathetic girl. Her whimsical dreams of becoming a movie actress were so naive. The tough, gang-ridden streets of Los Angeles would probably chew her up and spit out the pieces.

"Thank you for sharing your story with me, Jenny." She gave me a sad smile, declining to be photographed. "I can't take any chances on them ever finding me."

I told her I understood and left. Her heartbreaking story had left me feeling hollow.

Several of the other girls agreed to photos and I made sure they were all backlit or had their faces averted. With my wide angle lens, I was able to capture the essence of the bare rooms, emphasizing their empty lives with little hope for a bright future.

Each girl had her own horror story. As I scribbled copious notes, their appalling tales of violence, including sexual, drug and alcohol abuse, prostitution, attempted suicides, abortions, and time spent in and out of jail and juvenile facilities, shook me to the core. I couldn't wait to get back to the office and begin writing my series. My first installment would come out in tomorrow's edition, and with a feeling of tense anticipation, I knew the article would be powerful, thought provoking, and I hoped, something quite different for readers of the *Castle Valley Sun*.

Five of the eight girls informed me they were leaving on Thursday. Three of them were bound for Los Angeles, one for Las Vegas and one had decided to return home to Phoenix.

"So, Ms. O'Dell," Claudia said smoothly as she ushered me toward the front door. "I trust you got all the information you'll be needing for your article?"

"It was very enlightening. I appreciate the fact that you thought it over and decided to let me come." I waited a second to see if she'd mention the fact that she'd been pressured to grant the interview, but she said nothing.

I flipped my notebook open. "If you have a minute, I wanted to ask you just a few questions, you know a little more about your background and qualifications in this field."

A guarded expression crept into those incredible violet eyes. I knew she was going to look at her watch and she didn't disappoint me. "I don't wish to be rude, but you have taken up a great deal of my day."

"So I guess you and Roy Hollingsworth work pretty closely together regarding these girls, huh?"

"I'm not sure I understand your question."

"I'm told that instead of locking these girls up for loitering or panhandling, or worse, he brings them to you."

"On occasion."

"That's great. Really great. So, where did you work before you came to Castle Valley?"

"If I'm not mistaken, your story will be centered around the lives of these unfortunate young women, not me. I feel I've been more than cooperative, and I'm sure you have more than enough material. Right now I'm very late for an appointment and I really haven't the time to speak with you any further." She swung the front door open.

"Well, perhaps I could call you. I just need a little more background on you, something to add some local flavor if you will. I believe you replaced a woman by the name of Violet Mendoza. She'd been dead less than a week when you came. How did you know the position was open?"

Was that alarm mirrored in her eyes? I stood with my pen poised over my notes while she smoothed her sleek hair. "I already gave you quite a bit of information on our first meeting, did I not?"

"Yes...but...not about you personally."

She seemed to be struggling with herself, and when she finally spoke her voice was flat. "My schooling was at the University of Arizona in Tucson, I worked in a small shelter there and also at one in Phoenix. Unfortunately, they were both closed due to lack of funds." The phone in her office rang. "You'll have to excuse me," she said quickly. "I really must go now."

Summarily dismissed once again, I mentally thanked Eric a second time as I climbed into my car. Not only did I have the makings of a dynamite story, but when Roy Hollingsworth read my piece, it should serve to shadow my activities as far as my investigation concerning John Dexter.

Front and center in my mind was the fact that I still needed to find the toxicology reports on those two girls. With a growing certainty, I felt more convinced than ever that the reports weren't misfiled. They had been deliberately removed from the folders. But had Roy destroyed them? If not, were they still somewhere in his office? A wild, bizarre, and surely dangerous plan was taking shape in the back of my head. Somehow, I had to get into the office and see if I could find them. Just how I was going to accomplish that daunting task, I hadn't figured out yet.

23

Back at the office, Jim was tapping out a story on the winners of the bronco-busting and calf-wrestling competitions. In response to my questions, he informed me that Tally was downtown covering the boot race, and that Tugg had gone home sick again. Tugg's illness was really beginning to worry me. After work, I would drop by his house. We needed to talk.

Oddly enough, Ginger wasn't at her desk either. "Is she still at lunch?" I asked Jim.

"Nope," he said, absently shuffling through his notes. "Lupe and Al are covering the phone. I think she's gone for the day too."

"Why? Is she sick?"

"I don't think so. Lupe said she got a personal call and went barreling out of here around eleven-thirty."

That was strange. Ginger never left before five o'clock. I had no time to dwell on it with two other assignments awaiting me and the deadline for my article staring me in the face.

It was almost six o'clock before I finally finished my copy and headed for Tugg's place. Mary greeted me at the door with a sad smile and filled me in on his condition.

"The doctor in Phoenix did some more tests yesterday," she said, ushering me into the spacious kitchen. "He's on new medication and it's making him a little groggy. But, I'm sure he'll be okay in a few days."

She poured me a glass of iced tea and then led me into the living room where Tugg lay on the sofa, napping. His face looked old and pale. A wave of embarrassment swept over me. I should have called first.

"Perhaps I'd best come another time," I whispered as Mary gently shook his shoulder. She motioned that everything was fine.

Watching Tugg's pallid face made me recall what Ginger had said about his reluctance to take over the *Sun*. After thirty-five years in the business, he had been eagerly looking forward to retirement. He had already laid out plans for a European trip before Mary had collared him to run the newspaper her grandfather had founded. Poor Tugg. It was obvious to me his heart wasn't in the job. Ginger's assessment of Mary wearing the pants in the family appeared to ring true.

Tugg blinked a few times and then focused on me. "Oh, hi, Kendall," he said with a wide yawn, throwing off a light blanket. "What's up?"

Mary gave me a friendly wink and left the room. I pulled a footstool next to the couch. "Are you going to be all right?" I asked, while really thinking, 'Tugg, I think I'm about to step into a hornet's nest and I'm going to need you to be well and alert.'

"I dunno," he groaned. "This goddamned ulcer is acting up again and I can't do a blasted thing about it. 'No stress,' the doctor told me. Ha!"

I studied his bloodshot eyes. "Did something happen to trigger this?"

"Probably everything. My daughter, Louise, called two days ago. She's splitting up with her husband and wants to move in with us for a few months with the three grandkids." His shoulders slumped and the deep sigh puffed out his cheeks. "As if I didn't have enough trouble already.

"We're drowning in red ink at the paper and we need another infusion of capital to get new equipment. We just don't have it." He stopped talking, took a long drink of water and then turned to look toward the kitchen. The sound of Mary humming along with the radio and the clang of pots and utensils announced dinner preparations. He put a finger to his lips, indicating silence, and beckoned me to move closer to him. I scooted the stool forward. In a low voice, he said, "Mary and her sister Faye are bugging me to ask Roy for another loan. By the way," he said, giving me a worried look, "he called here night before last. He sounded edgy about your visit the other day. Said he hoped you weren't thinking of stirring up any more trouble at his expense."

"That says a lot, doesn't it? He wouldn't be upset if he didn't have something to hide. My article about the shelter comes out in tomorrow's edition. That should put his mind at ease. He'll see there was nothing more to my questions than gaining information for my story."

"Look. He's jumpy because it's getting close to election time. He can't afford to have any more derogatory stuff printed about him. Your inferences probably set him off. That got Faye upset and now Mary's in a tizzy."

His defeated tone bothered me. "Tugg, you've got me in a real spot. You're going to have to make up your mind what you want to do. If you want me to pursue this, I'll do it, but if you want to drop it, then just say so."

He looked more miserable than I'd ever seen him. "God knows I've thought of having you just forget about it. If I hadn't gotten that phone call from John, it would have just been one of those things. But, like I said, I feel in my gut there's more to his disappearance than him just getting pissed at me 'cause I told him to lay off Roy unless he had something to back up his allegations. It's the timing. It just doesn't sit right."

"And I agree with you, Tugg. It's pretty obvious that I'm onto something. By the way, there are a few things I haven't told you yet."

Originally, I hadn't planned to tell him about the attack on me in the darkroom, but the time seemed right. I repeated the episode, and after I explained my theory about Claudia and Roy, the expression on his face made my heart sink. He was staring at me as if I'd lost my mind.

"The smuggling part might be plausible, but I can't buy your theory about some kinky cult. How could something as weird as that be going on without someone finding out about it?" He threw his hands in the air, adding, "Those are both pretty wild ideas, Kendall. Without proof, we're nowhere."

His continuing skepticism bothered me. "Don't you think I know that, Tugg? I'm trying to get some evidence, but you've given me a rather tough assignment and then tied one hand behind my back."

He leaned his head back against the sofa and crossed an arm over his eyes. "What if I'm dead wrong about John?

He was such a goddamn flake, maybe it's possible he really did just take off."

"How can you even think that after what happened to me?"

He dropped his hand and gave me an anguished look. "I've had a lot of time to think about everything these the past two days. There are a lot more ramifications to this than I originally thought. So many people will be affected. All the employees, their families..."

I cut in impatiently. "Don't be in such a hurry to discount the smuggling angle. The ring operated in both southern Arizona and Texas a few years ago. Most of the people involved were caught, but the ringleader got away. It could have been restarted right here."

Tugg looked blank for a minute and then his eyes widened in astonishment. "You think Roy is the ringleader? Oh, Jesus. Do you have any idea what will happen when this story breaks? Mary will be devastated. This is my family we're talking about, for chrissake!"

His defensive tone struck a nerve. He seemed to have developed a severe case of cold feet. I wondered if his poor health was affecting his judgment.

I fidgeted uncomfortably on the stool as I watched his face crumple in distress. A pang of pity shot though me. It wasn't difficult to understand how he felt. The outcome of this investigation could have awesome consequences.

"Tugg," I said softly, "I don't think Roy's behind this. He's not smart enough. I think the mastermind is Claudia Phillips. There's something about her that just doesn't jibe. She shows up out of nowhere after Violet Mendoza dies, and suddenly there's a large anonymous donation that allows the church to buy a separate house for runaway girls. Don't you see how easy this is? They don't even have to hunt for the girls, they come right to them.

"Then, within the last year those two girls are found dead in the desert and presto, the toxicology reports on both of them wind up missing. Convenient, huh? I'm positive based on what you've told me, John Dexter's note and his sudden disappearance, that these things all tie together. Roy didn't bungle those cases, the misinformation is deliberate."

Tugg sat very still. His face had taken on a grayish pallor.

"Now, I'm not sure yet how the woman John Dexter was supposed to meet that last day fits in, but I'm going to find out. And to do that, I have to have the freedom to get this thing moving, get Roy or Claudia riled up enough to make a mistake."

Looking grim, Tugg rubbed a hand back and forth across his mouth. I could almost see his stomach twisting. What a quandary he was in.

He cleared his throat uncomfortably. "Listen, Kendall, if you're even half right, I don't feel at all good about the position I've put you in. You should have told me right off about that business at the paper the other night because this is beginning to sound more serious than I ever imagined."

"Well, I..."

He put up a hand to silence me. "Look, I can't help but feel a certain responsibility for you because of what your dad did for me, and being an old newspaper man, I also feel it's as important as hell to find out what really happened to John Dexter, but...if he was deliberately killed, as you suspect, how can I, in good conscience, justify letting you continue with this?"

"Tugg, what do you mean? We can't stop now! All I need is one little piece of concrete evidence for the county attorney and they'll take the investigation from there."

A look of pain crossed his face and his hand flew to his stomach. From the coffee table, he scooped up a bottle of pills and popped two in his mouth.

"Tugg, I'm sorry. It wasn't my intention to upset you."

He waved my remark aside. "You haven't done anything I didn't ask you to do, but...I think now, due to the circumstances, that perhaps it would be better if Tally or Jim took over the assignment."

He may as well have kicked me in the stomach. I stood up so fast, the stool fell over behind me. "Oh, no you don't," I said fiercely. "Don't pull this 'because you're a weak, little female' routine on me. Don't forget, the way I read this, John Dexter is most likely dead, and he was a man. What makes you think either of them could handle the assignment any better than me?" He didn't answer so I charged ahead. "I can appreciate the position you're in, and I know you're not feeling well but, damn it, I need to do this!"

He looked doubtful. "I don't know, Kendall."

I took a couple of deep calming breaths and sat down beside him on the sofa. "Tugg, did I ever tell you how much I appreciate the fact that you even hired me? If I haven't, then I'll say it now. I was really in a dismal state of mind when I arrived here in Castle Valley. I didn't know if my health would ever improve, I'd lost my fiancée, my job, everything. You've given me a chance to prove myself. Don't take this away from me now." I gave him a beseeching look, but he dropped his eyes and stared at his clasped hands.

"Give me two weeks, Tugg. Two weeks and I'll have some tangible proof for us to take to the authorities. What do you say? I swear on a stack of Bibles, I'll be careful." I waited in heart-thumping agony, hardly daring to breathe.

"Oh, lordy," he muttered. "I'm probably going to regret this…but, okay. Two weeks." He shook his finger at me. "But you've got to promise me, you'll keep me informed of everything. You won't go and do something stupid just to prove a point?"

Relief poured through me. "I promise," I said, solemnly raising my right hand.

My emotions were still in a jumble by the time I arrived home. It hadn't occurred to me just how much I wanted to solve this case, until it was almost snatched away from me. At least now, I had a little breathing room.

I was also in a state of anxious anticipation over my article and, tucked away in a small corner of my heart lay the thought I tried to evade all afternoon.

The unresolved argument with Tally bothered me more than I cared to admit. I had hoped to see him and clear the air between us. The fact that he'd made a deliberate effort to avoid me all day had been glaringly obvious. I'd have to explain to Eric that I would have only a few hours for dinner on Friday. Being the sensitive man he was, I felt confident he would understand.

The thunderheads that had towered over the northeastern horizon all day had vanished along with my hopes of rain. Jim had told me it was called a 'false monsoon,' though occasionally it did rain in June. But, because of the intense heat many times the rain evaporated before it even hit the ground. "Dry thunderstorms," he'd added sagely. I had never heard of such a thing in my life, and wondered if he was pulling my leg.

Feeling whipped, I dropped into a chair, kicked off my shoes, and let the tepid air blowing from the evaporative cooler wash over me. Harry and Rick had overheard Jim talking to me about the weather and had given me the disquieting news that swamp coolers didn't perform very well in humid weather. I guessed this was as cool as it was going to get.

I didn't realize I'd fallen asleep until the jangling of the phone awakened me. For a few seconds I couldn't figure out why I was sitting in a chair or what time of day it was. I stumbled across the room and grabbed the receiver.

"Hey, girlfriend," came Ginger's cheerful voice over the line. "Your voice sounds kinda funny, y'all been sleepin'?"

I yawned. "Actually, I was. I've had a rather stressful day. So, how come you cut out so early?"

"We've all had us quite a day too. Drop everything, and get your buns over here, girl. We got ourselves a baby!"

By the time I arrived at Ginger's the sun had set the horizon aflame in scarlet. While music from the stereo filled the room, she bustled about filling glasses with sparkling champagne and Brian passed around pieces of cake. Bonnie and her husband Tom held hands and gazed reverently at their new daughter whom Nona held proudly on her lap.

I was surprised to hear of their last minute troubles. They had ended up in a bidding war with another couple over the baby. Their choice was to match the amount offered to the birth mother, or be forced to back out. Taking out a second mortgage on their house and selling some stock had finally raised the amount needed.

"Eric really came through for us," Bonnie crowed. "He made a special trip to Iowa to convince the birth mother we'd make better parents. I'll never be able to thank him enough."

It turned out that was only part of their problem. Tom went on to say that the birth father had made an eleventh hour appearance and decided against signing the relinquishment papers. But, when offered a substantial amount of money, like magic, the paper was signed.

So far, they hadn't given me any definite figures, but I surmised this little girl had set them back substantially, not to mention the emotional turmoil they had suffered.

By the time Bonnie and Tom had packed their car and left for their home in Prescott, it was well past ten. Bed sounded pretty good to me, but Nona insisted I stay and see more of the momentos from her days on the Broadway stage.

"Humor her, will ya, love," Ginger muttered under her breath as we followed Nona's wheelchair down the hallway. During my first visit, Ginger had described Nona's room as a museum and it certainly was. I didn't have to feign interest and felt genuinely astounded as she directed Ginger to pull carefully preserved costumes from a spacious cedar closet. A strong odor of mothballs permeated the room, making me sneeze several times.

Nona's withered face beamed with pride as she recounted each role she had played. The closet was crammed with boxes of wigs, hats and shoes, jars of theater makeup, photos, and piles of yellowing fan letters.

"This is fantastic," I said to Nona while running my hand over a green velvet gown. "I wish I could have seen you perform."

"I got to admit, I was pretty good," she said tucking the photos away in a shoe box.

I thanked everyone for allowing me to share their special evening and Ginger linked arms with me as we walked outside. The night was muggy and still. Not even a whisper of wind relieved the oppressive air. Greenish heat lightning flashed dimly on the horizon.

I remarked again how fortunate Bonnie and Tom were. Not only had they weathered the emotional storm, they'd also managed to come up with the additional funds needed to complete the adoption. It was then Ginger confided that she and Nona had given them money also, and that the total dollar amount had come to forty-five thousand.

I was aghast. "Forty-five thousand dollars! Are you sure about that?"

"Is a frog's ass water tight? Of course I'm sure."

"I can't believe they paid that much for a baby!"

"It's over and done with, sugar. Let's talk about you and Tally. He looked like he was a fixin' to chew the head off a goat when I walked in on the two of you."

I explained what had happened and she remarked, "Y'all ain't going to the barbecue? Well, no wonder he's mad at you. That's one of the biggest shindigs of the year."

"I know, I know. It was so stupid. But it was an honest mistake. Tally didn't really ask me like it was a date or something. I thought it was a drop by thing, you know? I'll scoot out there after dinner."

"So, how you gonna square that with Eric?"

"I hope he'll understand. Boy, I wish I hadn't gotten myself mixed up with two guys. It has really complicated my life."

"Well, for pity's sake, if you ain't the one. I have never in all my born days seen anybody kick up such a fuss about having two boyfriends."

"It's not just that. I'm caught right in the middle of two people who despise each other. I may throw them both back."

Ginger gaped. "You've slipped over the edge, girl."

I laughed at her remark. "I'm not sure what to do. Eric is coming on like gang busters and Tally acts as though he'd like to lasso me with a rope and put the Starfire brand on me."

The dim glow from the porch light illuminated her face just enough for me to make out the impish gleam in her eyes. "Well, sugar pie, I can think of a lot worse things than being lassoed by a man like Tally. Far as I'm concerned, he can park his boots under my bed any ol' night."

"Ginger," I cried, in mock horror. "I'm shocked! I thought Doug Sauers was the love of your life."

Her infectious giggle filled the night air. "Well, now don't have a hissy fit. There ain't no harm in taking a peek at a good-looking man. And speaking of good-looking, where's Mr. Dreamboat taking you for supper on Friday?"

I told her I wasn't sure, and then she asked me how my interview had gone at the shelter. She listened intently, and said she was looking forward to reading my article. I knew there would be at least two other people in town anxious to read it. I wished I could be there to study Claudia and Roy's faces when they got the morning edition. Ginger and I hugged good-night and I left.

At home again, I checked for messages and found none. It was puzzling why the Mexican woman had never called back. "*¡Dios Mío!*" she'd cried. "They are coming." I went over my notes of the conversation again, but the picture remained as fuzzy as ever.

Curled in bed, I realized that if I was going to get any sleep, I'd have to deliberately push the puzzle from my mind. The two week deadline I'd imposed on myself looked insurmountable.

Two things were clear. In order to prove my theory to Tugg, and not have him knock the slats out from under me, I had no choice but to work smart and work fast.

24

By Thursday morning, I felt like I'd been catapulted to the role of local celebrity. My story on the runaways in the previous day's edition of the *Sun* had barely hit the vending machines and mailboxes when the phone started ringing.

Thena Rodenborn was the first to call and congratulate me, saying she'd never read such a well-written article, that it had moved her to tears.

In the midst of my regular assignments, people stopped me on the street to say it had given them a new perspective on a subject they'd known little or nothing about. Many told me they could hardly wait for the Saturday edition which would carry the second installment.

Even my co-workers seemed surprised at the depth of the article. Tugg, who returned to work looking pale and slightly disheveled, gave me a hearty thumbs up. The only dark spot in an otherwise perfect day was Tally's conspicuous absence from the office. Supposedly, he was having some problem at the ranch, but I suspected he was still avoiding me.

Nevertheless, I was pumped and feeling pretty good about myself as I prepared to cover the pig races at the fairgrounds. It wasn't until I dug to the bottom of my camera bag and searched every compartment that I realized my wide angle lens was missing.

I stared blankly at the bag and tried to remember where I'd used it last. Suddenly, it came to me. I remembered setting it on the mantle above the fireplace at the Desert Harbor Shelter during my photo session with the girls on Tuesday. I hated to think how much it would cost me to replace it.

"I've gotta go early," I told Ginger, running past her desk. "I left one of my lenses over at the shelter and I need it for this story. I'll be back after lunch."

She was on the phone, but her smile brightened, signaling that she'd heard me. Outside, I blinked in the fierce, white sunlight and fished in my purse for the handkerchief I used to grab the blistering metal door handle on the car. After burning myself repeatedly, I'd finally gotten smart.

I threw my purse, notepad and camera bag on the passenger seat and slid onto the towel I used to prevent third degree burns on my thighs. I broke into an immediate sweat and groaned with discomfort as I rolled down the window. It had to be at least two hundred degrees inside the car.

When I turned the key, only a faint clicking sound met my ears. I tried several more times and got the same result. "Damn it!" I thumped my hand furiously against the steering wheel. I'd suspected something was going wrong, and I could have kicked myself for not checking it out.

Sighing, I reached to gather my belongings and then looked up as a vehicle pulled in beside me. I looked away just as quickly. "Oh, please," I moaned under my breath, "anybody but him!" The thought of appearing once again as the weak, ignorant female put my teeth on edge. Why, of all the people in the world, did Tally have to drive in at that precise moment. So far, his timing was flawless. Whenever I was in a pickle, there he was.

Since he'd made such a point of ignoring me the past three days, I wasn't about to ask him for anything. I turned my back to his truck, pretending to be completely absorbed in my notes.

He shut off the engine, but I didn't hear his door open. No way would I turn and look. Normally, he just jumped out and went inside. But of course today he seemed in no hurry. Then I heard the truck door slam and the click of boots as he approached my car. I ignored him and tried not to notice the drops of sweat trailing off the end of my nose, making soft pattering sounds on the notepad below.

The footsteps halted but he said nothing. My neck ached from the awkward position and I could feel my temper rising. How long was he going to stand there in silence staring at me?

"So," he finally said, "I guess there's some reason you're sitting out here. Is everything okay?"

"Everything's fine," I said with a tone of dismissal, still not looking at him. He made no move to leave.

"Do you need help with something?"

"If I did, I wouldn't ask you."

He ignored my rebuff. "Is there a problem with your car?"

"No," I shouted, turning to face him. "I happen to like sitting in a car that's a thousand degrees inside, okay?"

"I see." His face was impassive as he continued to stare at me. I was doing quite well in the staring contest until a big drop of perspiration slid into one of my eyes, causing me to blink. With a catch in my voice I cried, "Would you please go away?" The suffocating heat was so unbearable, it was an effort to keep from screaming.

"Pull the hood release," he commanded.

"I said, there's nothing wrong. I do not need your help. I do not need to be rescued. I will take care of this myself, thank you very much."

"Why are you being so unreasonable?"

"I am not being unreasonable!" I'm being...I'm being..."

"Unreasonable," he repeated, quietly finishing the sentence for me. Before I could stop him, he opened my door, took a quick glance under the dashboard and pulled the hood release.

I could have gotten out at that point, the air outside the car, ironically, was much cooler. But, stubbornly, I stayed put.

After a minute or two he strolled back around the raised hood, stopped, and tipped his hat back. "When was the last time you put water in your battery?"

"My battery?" I replied haughtily. "I've never had to put water in my battery. You must be mistaken. There must be something else wrong." Why was I acting so stupid? I couldn't seem to stop myself.

"Well, Miss Ace Car Mechanic," he said, widening his stance, "then maybe you can explain why your battery is as dry as an old buzzard bone." A hint of a smile hovered around his lips and that made me even angrier. I knew myself pretty well and realized I was near the boiling point. With a ragged breath, I bolted from the car. It was a relief to feel the hot wind blowing through my matted hair. Without looking, I knew the wet blouse was molded to my breasts. I threw him what I hoped was a malevolent glare and then recoiled in surprise when he dangled his car keys a few inches from my face. "Here. You were obviously on your way out. Take my truck. While you're gone I'll see about getting you a new battery."

"Please don't bother yourself, and I will not take your truck."

"Why?"

"Because...because...Just because, that's all."

He threw his head back and laughed so loudly, the pigeons roosting on the drain gutter squawked and flapped away. I started toward the entryway, but he reached out, grabbed one shoulder, and spun me to face him. "Look," he began, as I tried to pull from his grasp, "I don't mean to offend your feminist sensibilities, okay? Just relax. This is one friend helping out another, and nothing more."

"Oh, now you're my friend? Well, that's a surprise."

He pulled his hands away so swiftly, I almost reeled. "This isn't about the car at all, is it?"

Well, this was the confrontation I'd been waiting for. Might as well get it over with. "All right. It isn't about the car. For three days now, you've made a deliberate point to ignore me and—"

"Wait just a minute," he said sharply, "Why are you mad at me? You're the one who stood me up."

"I did not stand you up!" I shouted. Then lowering my voice a bit, I added, "At least it wasn't deliberate. I made a mistake. I'm sorry as I can be, but I can't undo it. You, on the other hand, have been acting like a...like a..."

"A horse's ass?"

"Yes! Exactly."

I expected him to respond but, instead, he averted his gaze and stood silently staring at the distant horizon. The wind moaned around the side of the building and sent papers skittering wildly across the parking lot. I said nothing, feeling it was important to wait for his response. Finally, he settled the hat firmly on his head and turned to meet my eyes. "So, then," he said in a controlled voice, "you will be coming out to the Starfire after all."

He hadn't said he was sorry, so I guessed his admission was as close as he was going to get. "I said I'd come, and I meant it."

His expression lightened and so did my heart. "Okay," he said easily, "apology accepted. I'll have Jake hold my wagon for the hayride until you get there."

"Sounds like a plan," I quipped. We exchanged sets of car keys and I fought the sudden weakness that came over me. I decided it was either a result of too much time in the sun, or the aftermath of the adrenaline rush due to my temper tantrum. Perhaps it was both.

Inside the building again, he gave me a friendly salute and disappeared into his office. I downed five or six cups of cold water, explained the situation to Ginger, and then, headed for the shelter in Tally's truck.

The air conditioning unit in the cab of his pickup was downright frigid compared to the one in my car. The blast of icy air against my damp clothing gave me a slight chill.

The confrontation with Tally had served to clear the air between us. I hated to admit it, but I had been troubled since our quarrel last Monday. Depressed even. The more I thought about it the more the implication rattled me.

And, I wondered, braking to avoid a dog running into the street, what about my feelings for Eric? At times, I felt he was more of a curiosity to me than a love interest. He was exciting, innovative, certainly sexually stimulating, and actually more the type of man I'd always been attracted to in the past.

Tally, on the other hand, projected an air of keen intelligence, mixed with a large dose of the same arrogant pig-headedness that I'd always been accused of possessing. That was probably why we always seemed to bring out the worst in each other.

There were several cars parked along the street in front of the Desert Harbor, so I made a U-turn and pulled up to the curb opposite the house. I shut off the engine and gathered my things together. I'd just placed my hand on the door handle when a car appeared in the driveway of the shelter.

Claudia Phillips smoothly maneuvered a dark, late model sedan to the street entrance. The car was packed with passengers, and I realized she must be on her way to the bus station with the girls I'd interviewed two days ago. Before moving into the street, she stopped and looked with care in all directions. She glanced directly at Tally's truck and then away. Apparently satisfied no one was watching her, she turned onto the street.

Instead of going inside to retrieve my lens, I quickly re-started the engine and followed her down the street. Her furtive movements were curious. Why would she care if someone saw her taking the girls to meet the bus? What a blessing I'd taken Tally's truck.

Downtown, I picked a hamburger stand adjacent to the bus depot. I drove in, hastily parked, screwed the telephoto lens onto the camera and trained it on the faces of the girls as they stepped from the car.

There was no look of anticipation or hope, only morose, downcast eyes and sullen expressions. Claudia ushered the girls inside the building, and it was only then I realized something important.

There were only four girls, not five. The girl I'd focused the first part of my series on, the pretty one named Jenny, was not among them.

25

For a few seconds, I stared blankly at the backs of the retreating girls as they trooped inside the bus station. Where was Jenny?

All at once, I knew exactly what I had to do. I ground Tally's truck into gear and tore out of the parking lot so fast I practically mowed down a pedestrian crossing in front of me.

Armed with the knowledge that Claudia would be away from the shelter for a while, I was presented with the tantalizing opportunity to get inside and do a little detective work. All I needed was just one tiny shred of evidence that would connect Claudia and Sheriff Hollingsworth to my macabre theories. I pressed the accelerator harder. Two weeks was an awfully short time to find the smoking gun.

Within two minutes, I screeched to a halt, leaped out, bounded up the front steps and tried the knob on the front door. It was locked. I knocked loudly and waited. No one answered. After a quick glance at the street, I headed around the house, noticing with a surge of elation the back door propped open with a scrub bucket. I stuck my head in the door and called, "Hello?" There was no response. I called again. Nothing but deathly quiet. I wondered where the little Mexican maid was.

I tiptoed tentatively into the dim hallway. A few steps to my right, the kitchen stood empty, and so was the first bedroom to my left. The door to the second bedroom was closed. Ever so gently, I eased it open, wincing at the loud squeak from the hinges. Inside, on one of the beds, a girl lay sleeping. Her face was turned away from me, so I softly called, "Jenny, is that you?" The girl stirred and peered glassy-eyed over one shoulder. It wasn't Jenny. "Sorry," I mumbled, backing away. I didn't recognize her, so she was obviously a new arrival.

I shut the door and checked the other bedrooms. The two girls I'd seen playing cards in the kitchen, lay sleeping in one. It seemed odd to see them all sleeping at this time of day.

I moved toward the living room. The ancient floorboards creaked under my weight and little shivers of apprehension prickled my spine. The silence of the house was so complete it was downright spooky. I paused at the doorway and noted with satisfaction that my wide-angle lens lay atop the mantelpiece just where I'd left it.

Claudia had said her living quarters were on the second floor, so I took the stairs two at a time. There were four closed doors. I tried the first. It was a bathroom. The second opened to reveal a set of dusty stairs that probably led to the attic. The other two doors, boasting shiny new locks, were tightly secured. I knocked lightly on each, whispering, "Jenny? Jenny, are you in there?" When I heard no reply, I felt a stab of alarm. If she wasn't here then where was she?

Filled with a sense of growing dread, I hot-footed it downstairs and, after a hurried glance down the dark hallway, headed for Claudia's office.

The sign on the closed door read: Private. Keep Out. I expected it would be locked and felt relief when the knob turned easily. Without hesitation, I edged the door open and stepped inside. The faint scent of Claudia's cloying perfume hung in the air.

It didn't surprise me that all the drawers in her desk were locked. A check of the filing cabinet netted the same results. Crap. Flooded with disappointment, I started for the door, but stopped when I spotted a Rolodex file on the far corner of her desk.

Yes! I rushed over and quickly leafed through the cards, taking note of the names I recognized. Roy Hollingsworth, Thena Rodenborn, Dr. Garcia, the numbers of several shelters in Phoenix and...what was this? There was one card with only the name Charles written on it. Claudia had doodled something, and then, with bold strokes of her pen, slashed it out. I pulled the card from the file and angled it back and forth in the light from the window. I couldn't be certain, but it looked like she'd crossed out the words: "May you rot in hell." There were hideous little figures of Satan drawn beside the name. How curious. The telephone number to the right had been erased, but I was able to make out the faint remains of the last two digits.

My whole body went rigid at the sound of soft footsteps approaching the doorway. Claudia was going to catch me red-handed in her office and my undercover days would be finished for good.

Numbly, I shoved the card back into the file and waited in breathless agony to be discovered. The startled look etched on the little Mexican girl's face when she rounded the corner probably matched my own.

I exhaled slowly and swallowed hard with relief. There was no point trying to explain what I was doing since it was unlikely she'd understand me anyway. I mustered a weak smile. "Hello there."

"Miss Claudia ees not here. You go! You go!" she said urgently, pointing to the front door.

The fear reflected in her black eyes said it all. Wordlessly, she sprinted to my side, grabbed my hand, and pulled me into the hall, shutting the door behind us.

Then she snapped the lock on the door and frantically motioned for me to leave. When I didn't move, she said, "Very much ah...bad for me if she come. You go *pronto*." The look of sheer terror on her face disturbed me. What was this girl so afraid of?

I stood my ground for a moment and then we both jumped as Claudia's car roared into the driveway. Without another word passing between us, I stepped out onto the front porch. The door closed behind me.

Halfway back to the truck, I remembered my lens. I hesitated for a moment, uncertain, and then did an about face, returning to the shelter. As far as Claudia knew, I'd only just arrived. My reason should not alert her suspicions and would no longer put the young Mexican girl in jeopardy. This was a golden opportunity to trap the very careful, very crafty Miss Phillips and I couldn't pass it up.

As usual, she looked less than happy to see me. I explained why I was there and some of the coolness left her eyes. "And, as long as I'm here," I said, retracing my steps toward the living room, "it would really be great if I could talk to Jenny one more time. I just need a couple more quotes." I swept the lens from the mantelpiece and turned to face her. "Would that be a problem?"

Claudia slowly laced her fingers together and gave me an apologetic smile. "I'm afraid so, since she's no longer here."

"Oh, that's right. This is Thursday. So, of course, you've already put them all on the bus?" I watched her closely to see if there were any signs of discomfort. She appeared cool, confident, in control.

"Yes. Too bad you didn't arrive earlier. You just missed her." Her eyes glittered with triumph, like she was privy to some private joke.

My pulse hammered in my temples. It was an effort for me to conceal how much I disliked this woman.

The housegirl moved past the doorway, flashed me a furtive look, and then froze as Claudia turned and spoke sharply to her in Spanish.

I shook my head in amazement. If I hadn't already known she was lying, I would have had no reason to suspect that she was. The falsehood had slipped off her tongue as easily as raw oysters from a china plate. I tucked the lens into my purse. Could I crack her icy facade if I confronted her? It would have given me intense satisfaction to do so, but I decided against it. I still didn't have one shred of evidence that she was lying. It would be my word against hers.

Instinctively, I knew that she would most likely have a glib explanation for Jenny's absence. This was a woman accustomed to subterfuge.

The Mexican girl answered Claudia in a soft, quavering voice, then bowed her head and hurried away. I wondered what Claudia had said to her.

"And now, Miss O'Dell," Claudia said, returning her attention to me. "Since you now have what you came for, I'm afraid I must ask you to leave. I have work to do." She accompanied me to the door and ended the conversation by remarking that my article had been commendable. I forced a smile and thanked her as I left.

As I drove to the fairgrounds, I felt a tremor of uneasiness. What had she done with Jenny? Was she being held captive behind one of those locked doors? Drugged, perhaps? Or, was she already safely transported beyond the border into Mexico where she'd be shipped off to the Mid-East where wealthy Arabs paid handsomely for blonde, blue-eyed girls?

Somehow, I had to get the goods on Claudia. Nobody was perfect. Somewhere along the way, she and Roy Hollingsworth had failed to cover their tracks. All I had to do was find out where.

There was a sizable crowd at the fairgrounds, and I took the necessary pictures of the brown Alaskan pigs as they raced around the oval track. I copied a few cute quotes from bystanders and hurriedly drove off to the sheriff's office.

The past few days, I had entertained several grandiose ideas about how I was going to get to the files of the two dead girls and those of Violet Mendoza and John Dexter, without Roy's knowledge. One of them involved my breaking into the office in the dead of night and making off with the folders. That seemed ridiculous to me now as I parked in front of the building.

There was only one patrol car in the lot, and I felt a rush of relief when I stepped inside and saw Deputy Potts at the sheriff's desk. He jumped up like a jack-in-the-box when he saw me come in. The loud crack I heard was probably his knee meeting the desk drawer. It was difficult to keep from laughing at his masterful attempt to cover his pain.

"Miss O'Dell!" he gasped. "What a fine sight you are this morning. I missed seeing you this week." As always, his gaze swept over me with deliberate care. I experienced the discomforting sensation that he was mentally removing my clothing piece by piece.

It was tempting to say, "Well, I didn't miss seeing you," but instead I smiled and asked for the daily logs.

"Got them right here." He swept a large black binder from the desk and handed it to me, making sure his fingers touched mine. "Thanks," I said, moving away to the counter. I studied the material and then, keeping my voice casual, I asked, "Say, where's Roy? I haven't seen him around for a few days."

"Oh, he's off to Laughlin. He'll be back tomorrow."

"Again?"

"He's got the bug. Sometimes I think he'd rather be at the blackjack table than be here, if you know what I mean?"

"No, I don't really. Enlighten me."

"Well, it's right there as plain as the nose on your face," he said with an air of importance. "I've seen a bunch of talk shows about people like Roy."

He reacted to my look of puzzlement by saying in a low voice, "You know, he's like an alcoholic, only with him, it's gambling. If he's not in Vegas or Laughlin, he's out on the reservation."

"Is that so?" That was interesting information. If Roy did have a gambling addiction, he might be willing to do just about anything for money. Anything.

Just then their secretary, Julie, entered the room. Her face looked drawn and pale. "Hi," she said in a faint voice.

After she vanished into her office, I asked Duane, "What's wrong with her? She looks sick."

"She's feeling kind of puny today. Probably got a touch of the stomach flu or something. She's been barfing her socks off all morning."

"Well, why don't you send her home?"

He looked wounded. "Hey, I would, but there'd be nobody to cover the phones when I'm not here. As a matter of fact, I was just on my way out. We got a fire going down at Grubber's Feed Lot and I've got to go make sure things are okay." As he gathered up keys and his hat, I had to stifle a gasp when it dawned on me what an incredibly lucky break this was for me. Neither he nor Roy would be in the office. Could I trust Julie not to tell either of them I'd asked to see the files?

It was an effort to keep my voice calm. "Don't let me stop you. I know duty calls and you don't have time to waste talking with me."

He stepped so close I could smell garlic on his breath. "It's my extreme pleasure to talk to you any time, Miss O'Dell. In fact, maybe you'd like to have a cup of coffee with me sometime."

"Sure," I said sweetly. "Will your wife and kids be there too?"

His face flushed several shades of red and he let out a nervous laugh. He winked and shook his finger at me. "That's real good. You have a real good sense of humor. Yes, sirree, Bob. A great sense of humor."

"I do, don't I?" I said, wondering how much longer I could maintain the phony smile. He backed out the door and threw me one last lecherous wink before exiting.

The man had no shame, I thought wryly, watching his car leave the parking lot. When I turned from the window Julie was headed to the back office when she whirled around and retraced her steps. "Could you listen for the phone for a few minutes?"

"You bet." I watched her disappear down the hall, and seconds later heard her retching. I felt badly for her, but also exhilarated as a sudden thought struck me.

I raced to her office and made a beeline for the filing cabinet. It took me only a few tense minutes to locate the Dexter and Mendoza files. With the folders clutched in my shaking hands, I paused for a second to reflect on my impulsive decision. What was I doing? I, Kendall O'Dell, who had never stolen anything in my life, was about to make off with property belonging to the sheriffs' department!

The squeak of the bathroom door opening made my heart drop. There was no time to find the files of the teenage girls, but I wasn't about to lose these two. I closed the file drawer, thinking that Claudia had managed to deter me once today. It wasn't going to happen again.

I sprinted to the lobby and slipped my hot properties underneath the log just as Julie rounded the corner. I hoped I didn't look as guilty as I felt.

"Are you all right?"

"I feel like I'm gonna die," she moaned. "I must've eaten something that didn't agree with me."

"It wasn't Mexican food, was it?" I asked with a sympathetic smile, remembering the miserable night I had spent after too much salsa and too many hot tamales.

"No," she answered.

Half-heartedly, I asked if she wanted me to stay until Duane returned, but she waved me away, saying she'd be all right. With the stolen contraband burning my hands, I rushed to the truck. My throat was tight with excitement. It was tempting to go through the folders now, but the parking lot of the sheriff's office was probably not a wise place for that.

The engine started with a roar and I headed back to the office, wondering if Tally had made good on his word to replace my battery. I kept glancing at the folders, absolutely dying to read them. With a groan of impatience, I realized that I had several more assignments to complete and dinner at Ginger's looming before me. It would be hours until I would have time to study the files. After that, I'd have to figure out how in the world I was going to return them without Roy's knowledge.

26

Tally had my battery charged by the time I got back to the office. I thanked him profusely, and by the warm expression in his eyes, I felt optimistic that the feelings of friendship between us had been rekindled. He expressed again how anxious he was for me to accompany him on the hayride since he was scheduled to be gone on a business trip for the following two weeks. I gave him my word I would be there.

I thought about calling Eric about my request for a shortened evening, but then remembered that he was out of town until Friday.

Dinner at Ginger's was great, as always, but I was so preoccupied by what I might find in the folders I'd taken, it was difficult to concentrate on anything she said. Pleading a headache, I left early and rushed home. After changing into shorts and a T-shirt, I sat down crosslegged on the living room floor to study the data. The feeling of anxious anticipation raised goose bumps on my arms as I flipped open the first file.

A half-hour later, a cloud of disappointment settled over me. John Dexter's file was so clean, it squeaked. In fact, it was absolutely flawless. And that's what bothered me. I couldn't quite put my finger on any one item, but I felt instinctively something was wrong. It appeared as though everything Roy related to me had actually occurred. There was, in addition to his write-up, the reports of the various sheriff's posses that had been involved. The two week search appeared to have been extensive and thorough.

I pulled Roy's copy of the traffic ticket out and studied it. At exactly 4:02 p.m., he had clocked John Dexter speeding south on highway 89 at seventy-eight miles per hour, just as he'd said. With a deep sigh of disgust, I slapped the folder shut.

If this was indeed a cover-up, Roy had done an admirable job. To an objective observer, it was a clear case of a man in a hurry who had planned to carefully disappear from sight. There was no hint of foul play, no sign of his vehicle, and no body ever found.

Violet Mendoza's accident was another matter. After I read her folder from cover to cover, two things stood out in my mind. Number one, what had a woman of sixty-eight been doing at a run-down bar in one of the shabbiest sections of town at eleven o'clock on a Monday night? Secondly, it seemed suspicious to me that the original description of the vehicle given by the witness had been whited out. The report had been filled out in Duane's handwriting, but the insertion was in Roy's sloppy scrawl.

Supposedly, Violet had been struck by a dented green pickup with Sonoran plates. The report had been forwarded to the Mexican authorities, but Duane had added a note stating that he expected little cooperation from them.

It was a simple case of hit and run. Case closed. One week later, enter Claudia.

At that point, my inner antenna was vibrating full tilt. Was it my imagination, or did the whole thing read like a Hollywood script? Everything appeared to be too damned perfect. I remembered Tugg's request to report back to him, so even though it was close to ten, I was anxious to share my thoughts. I dialed his number. After I had gone over all the details I was just a tad annoyed that he seemed somewhat unimpressed with my findings.

"How are you going to get those files back?" he asked, as if that was the most important detail of our conversation.

"Let me worry about that. Now, what do you make of Violet Mendoza's case?"

"I think you might be reading more into this than you should."

It was difficult to keep the sarcasm from my voice. "You don't think it was odd that she was mowed down outside a bar at eleven o'clock at night? Miles from where she lived? A woman of her age?"

Tugg's voice sounded weary. "Listen. Everybody in town knew about Violet's drunken brother Gilbert. He used to hang around several of the bars in town, including the Rattlesnake. It wasn't unusual for the bartender to call Violet to come and get him now and then when he'd tied one on. That's probably what happened. As far as the whiteout—well, maybe the witness changed his mind and Roy had to alter the description of the vehicle. It happens all the time."

I was so nonplussed by his ready explanations, I couldn't speak.

"Look, Kendall," Tugg continued, his voice sympathetic, "I hate to throw cold water on your theory, especially after all the trouble you went through to get those files, but there's just not enough here to print anything. I still need some physical evidence, a witness, a body, something. You know that."

"Does Gilbert Mendoza still live here?"

"Nope. He disappeared a couple of months after Violet died. I heard he went back to Mexico."

"I see." Every direction I tried to move, a door slammed in my face.

I heard him yawn, so I said good-night. My gut feeling that all was not as it seemed stayed intact, even though Tugg's explanation sounded quite plausible. By the time I settled into bed, I felt like I'd been whipped.

The next morning at work, it suddenly dawned on me that Dr. Price had never returned my phone call from last Tuesday. I looked up the number for Serenity House again. As before, I got the recording. I slammed the phone down so hard both Tally and Jim turned to stare at me.

"What's eating you today?" Jim asked.

"I can't believe this. Who ever heard of a mental institution with a recorded message?" I told both of them briefly about my near accident, then added, "I think his behavior is weird, to say the least."

Jim quipped, "Hey, you'd probably act strange too if all you did was work around psychos all day. Maybe he's too busy pumping 'em full of tranquilizers and doing lobotomies to answer the phone. Ever think of that?"

I glared at him and turned to Tally. "You've lived here a long time. What do you know about Serenity House? I think it's peculiar that no one in town seems to know much about it."

He looked amused. "They don't bother us, we don't bother them."

"Well, perhaps the rest of you don't think there's something odd about the place, but I do."

"So what are you going to do? Scale the fence and sneak inside?" He had that challenging gleam in his eyes again.

"Maybe I'll just do that."

They both cracked up laughing and the conversation came to an abrupt end when Tugg called Tally to his office.

By the time Friday afternoon rolled around, I was tired and irritated. In a dusty room at the courthouse, I listened to the clock chime three and, yawning widely, arched away from the ancient wooden table, slamming the property tax records book shut. This was leading nowhere. So far, I had spent no less than five hours, either on the phone or talking to everyone I could think of, and, standing in line at the post office only to reach a big, fat zero.

I could find nothing to give me any clues to Claudia Phillips' background. Either I was a rotten reporter, or she had no past. She owned no property and had no checking account at any of the local banks. That fact seemed very odd indeed. The car she drove was leased in the name of the shelter and no one in town seemed to know anything about her. She apparently had no relatives, boyfriends, or even lady friends. It was as if she had landed from Mars.

The only smidgen of information I gleaned, was that she had rented a post-office box when she had first arrived in Castle Valley five years ago. She had closed the box after one year. That might or might not be significant. But, I did know one thing—that was one of the best ways to keep your previous address a secret.

The student records administrator at the University of Arizona in Tucson, where Claudia had supposedly attended school, told me it would take days, perhaps weeks, to establish if she had been a student there. There was nothing listed under Claudia Phillips. Had she perhaps registered under another name? Did I know what years she attended? Could Phillips be her married name?

My spirits plummeted. For the second time in one day, I questioned my abilities. Why hadn't I asked her those questions during our last interview? If I went back now it would seem extremely suspicious and I doubted she would sit still for such probing.

I got up, stretched, and headed outside into the blinding afternoon sunlight. During the short drive to the office, the conversation I'd had with attorney Mike Scott popped into my head. Perhaps he'd remembered something about her. A phone call was definitely in order.

No one had their minds on work when I returned to work. Jim, Lupe, Al and Rick were all gathered around Ginger's desk, chattering about the barbecue at the Starfire Ranch. The air fairly crackled with excitement. They sounded like a bunch of kids waiting for the circus to come to town. "Hey there," Ginger called when she noticed me. "Tugg said we could all skedaddle early if everything was done. He left about twenty minutes ago and Tally's gone out yonder to the ranch to help set up."

"I'm out of here," Jim announced breezing past me.

"Right behind you," Al yelled after him.

I smiled to myself. A Broadway show was exciting. An evening at Radio City Music Hall was exciting. To me, the much awaited cookout, probably complete with bugs and snakes, didn't strike me as such a big deal. Then I had a sobering thought. Would the day come for me when the most stimulating event of my life would be a small-town barbecue?

Ginger used her hip to close her desk drawer then shut off the computer screen while reaching for her purse with the other hand. "Y'all coming?"

"No can do. I've got to finish up my article first. I guess the sooner I get it to Harry, the sooner he can leave too."

"I guess we'll see y'all later at the hayride."

"That's the plan."

She gave me an impish wink. "Have fun with Eric tonight. Don't do anything I wouldn't do."

"Well, unless it's going to take place in the middle of a crowded restaurant, I don't think you have to worry."

Her musical laughter was still echoing in my ears as I moved to my desk. It took me a half-hour to put the finishing touches on my article and when I got it to the production room, Harry was pacing in obvious impatience. I apologized for being late as he anxiously grabbed the copy.

At my desk once more, I dug Mike Scott's business card from the bottom of my purse and dialed his Phoenix number. His secretary kept me on hold for about five minutes before he came on the line. He remembered me immediately and asked if I was watching any of the French Open Tennis Tournament. I told him that I had been too busy. Had he, I asked, had an opportunity to think about where he had seen Claudia Phillips before?

"Gee, I'm sorry," he said. "I've thought about it a couple of times since then and it bugs me that I haven't been able to place where I've seen her before. I guess I'll think of it eventually, but, if you don't mind my asking, why are you so interested in her?"

I told him a little about my articles on the runaways and her involvement in the shelter. "That reminds me," I said to him. "Does the name 'Charles' mean anything to you?"

"Charles who?"

"I don't know the last name. All I know is that whoever this man is, I have the feeling she doesn't like him very much."

"Hmmmmm. Charles. Nope, I can't tell you right now, but maybe that name will shake something loose."

I thanked him and was about to hang up when he added, "I'm sorry I haven't been much help in answering your questions, but I do have some other information you might find interesting."

"What's that?"

"Did you ever get that interview with Eric Heisler?"

"Yes, I did. Why?"

When he spoke again, a note of caution had entered his voice. "I don't want to be accused of talking out of school, so what I have to say is strictly off the record. Agreed?"

"Agreed."

"All those things I said about how lucky he is? Well, I might have to take that back."

"You have my full attention."

"A buddy of mine who's pretty thick with some of the commercial brokers around town, heard that Heisler is in pretty deep guano with some of his real estate investments here in the valley, and up there where you are, too."

I sat up straighter. "Is that so?"

"Yeah. Listen to this. You know the name of that tennis ranch where we met there in Castle Valley?"

"Sure. The Whispering Winds. What about it?"

"Rumor has it that he's got to come up with a quarter of a million bucks by the end of the month or it goes into foreclosure."

I was astounded. Before I could respond, he apologized, saying he had to take an important call. I thanked him for taking the time to talk with me and he promised to let me know if he remembered anything about Claudia Phillips.

The disquieting news about Eric left me numb for a few minutes. Mike Scott must be mistaken. Eric did not appear to be a man worried by financial problems. To the contrary, he seemed cool, confident, and totally in charge of his life. Perhaps at dinner tonight, I might find out more. That thought galvanized me into action. I had only a little over an hour to get ready.

Once home, it was a rush to shower, dress, and get to the tiny airport by five. The young man behind the counter in the small terminal pointed me in the direction of a snazzy looking red and white Beechcraft King Air.

As I approached the aircraft, Eric appeared in the doorway. "Ah, there you are." He put out a hand and helped me into the plane's plush interior. "You look super," he said, seating me in the cockpit.

I thanked him and watched while he flipped switches, thinking again what a handsome man he was.

He asked if I'd ever flown in a small plane before and when I told him no, he carefully explained everything that he was doing. We sailed down the runway and rose smoothly into the air. Below, the desert floor receded, and out ahead scores of mountain ranges rose in jagged majesty against an orchid sky.

We'd been airborn about fifteen minutes when I said, "I hope this won't be a problem, but I have to be back home by nine."

He threw me an incredulous look. "I hope you're joking."

I explained the mixup to him and for a minute he said nothing, just stared out the windshield. He turned back to me shaking his head. "It was going to be a surprise. I made reservations for dinner in Las Vegas instead and..." he fished in his breast pocket and brought out tickets. "These are for Wayne Newton's show tonight."

I sat in stunned silence and pondered my predicament. I'd given Tally my word and it didn't take a genius to figure out what he would think of me for breaking my promise a second time. "Eric, I don't know what to say."

"Look, Kendall, I don't relish the idea of going back so you can spend the evening with Bradley Talverson, but if that's what you want, I'll do it." The disappointment in his voice was evident and I felt like an idiot. He'd obviously gone to a great deal of trouble. It seemed supremely selfish on my part to ask him to make such a sacrifice.

"I appreciate that, but no. I can't ask you to do that. Let's go on." Once we arrived, I would call Tally, explain the situation, and pray he would understand.

Eric gave me a searching look. "You're sure?"

"I'm sure."

27

After we landed, Eric escorted me to the luxurious white limousine he'd ordered and asked me to wait a few minutes while he spoke to the mechanic. Relaxing in the cool interior, sipping a glass of Dom Perignon, I thought of what Mike Scott had told me about his precarious financial situation and tried to reconcile it with his lavish lifestyle. If he was in trouble, he showed no signs of it.

I'd been surprised to hear that he'd spoken with his mother on Wednesday and she'd read him my article over the telephone. He'd raved about it and said that someone with my talent shouldn't be wasting time at the *Sun*.

When Eric returned, he spoke briefly to the driver and within minutes, we were cruising along traffic-clogged streets aglitter with neon lights and pulsing with throngs of pedestrians. The pervasive air of action and excitement was somewhat tempered when we entered Madame Loussard's French Restaurant and were seated in a cozy, candle-lit alcove.

"I need to make a phone call. Do you know what time we'll be back?" I asked, after the waiter had handed us leather-bound menus.

He hesitated. "I don't know. I didn't want to alarm you, but I was having a bit of a problem on the way in. The mechanic said it may take several hours to locate it."

"I see." I fidgeted with my napkin while I thought of what to tell Tally.

"I'm sorry," he said softly. "My little surprise has caused you to be unhappy. That certainly wasn't my intent."

I smiled. "It isn't your fault."

The flash of jealousy in his eyes disturbed me. "I won't pretend to be happy that you're seeing him, Kendall."

Firmly, I repeated, "I have to make this call."

At that, he looked contrite, "Of course you do. Shall I order for you?"

After agreeing, I located a phone near the restrooms and got the number for the Starfire from information. While the number rang repeatedly, I rehearsed what I would say. Every sentence I formed sounded lame and stupid. Why didn't someone pick the damned thing up?

A woman with a thick Spanish accent finally answered and I knew right away I was in trouble. When I asked for Tally she said, "You call back. ¿Sí?"

"No! I can't call back! I have to talk to him right now. Can you get him?"

The woman said nothing.

"Can you take a message?"

"Message?"

"Do you understand me? I need to leave a message for Mr. Talverson."

"¡Sí! You call tomorrow?"

251

I bit back my irritation. "Get me someone who speaks English. *Pronto.* English. *¿Comprende?*"

I heard her lay the receiver down. More than five minutes had gone by and I was almost out of coins when I heard a husky female voice. "Hi, there. Who are you trying to get hold of?"

"My name is Kendall O'Dell. I'm trying to reach Bradley Talverson. It's terribly important that I talk to him tonight."

There was a pause, then I heard a chuckle, "Well, now, fancy that."

A lump formed in my stomach. I recognized Lucinda's voice.

"Let me talk to Tally," I said, straining to keep my voice calm.

"I'll try to find him, but we're just swamped right now."

We're just swamped? She was talking as though she was the lady of the house. "I want to leave a message for him."

"Why, sure," she answered sweetly. "You just tell me every little thing."

"Tell him, I've been unavoidably detained and won't be able to make it for the hayride..."

"That's too bad."

My fist curled in anger. I could see where this was heading. "Tell him I'll explain in the morning."

"I'll rush out right this very minute and give him the message."

"Yeah, right." I slammed the phone onto the hook, cursing under my breath. Tally would never get the message.

When I returned to the table, Eric jumped up to seat me again and poured more champagne. Determined to make the most of the evening, I shoved the incident to the back of my mind.

As we dined on salad and chicken smothered in a creamy wine sauce, he seemed in exceptionally high spirits. His voice was animated as we discussed politics, world events, the weather, and eventually I pulled the subject around to Bonnie's baby. "They are ecstatic." I told him. "No, wait, more than that. They're floating on cloud nine. The whole family is. I think Bonnie would gladly be your slave, if you asked her."

Eric laughed heartily. "Don't take it too seriously. It's not uncommon for some women to transfer feelings of love in situations like this. It's similar to cases where new mothers develop crushes on their doctors. It's temporary and fades with time."

"I was very impressed to hear how you handled it. It seems like a tremendous amount of work. Since you've been out of town so much, I gather business is good?"

"I can't complain, but having a successful practice is not without its shortcomings. It doesn't leave me much time to devote to worthy cases like theirs." Time, he lamented, was something he'd like to have more of. He showed no evidence of stress, so I decided Mike Scott was guilty of spreading a false rumor.

"And, speaking of time, Kendall," he said, locking my gaze with his mesmerizing eyes. "What I'd really like to do is spend more of it with you."

My heart fluttered uncomfortably. I tried not to, but part of my brain kept returning to the fact that right now I should be bouncing through the desert on a hay wagon with

Tally beside me. The other part, found it hard to resist the attentions of this extraordinary man.

"You're so quiet," he murmured. "Did I say something wrong?"

I gently disengaged my hand from his. "Eric, before we get into this any deeper, there's something that's been bothering me. May I be direct?"

"Aren't you always?"

I chose my words carefully. "I hope I'm completely wrong about this, but...ever since that first night we met, I've had the oddest sense that you're only attracted to me because I resemble Stephanie Talverson."

He stared at me in surprise, then composed his face when the waiter appeared to remove the plates. After ordering espresso coffee, he asked woodenly, "What makes you say a thing like that?"

"Because you looked like you'd seen a ghost, and I'm aware that you and she were...lovers."

He looked taken aback. "Don't tell me you've bought into all those vicious lies invented by the Talversons? Can't you see what Bradley is trying to do? He's trying to poison our relationship." He shook his head sadly. "Kendall, I'm disappointed in you. I gave you credit for having better judgment than to believe unsubstantiated rumors."

"People saw the two of you together, Eric. I'm not accusing you of anything. I just need to know the truth."

For a moment, I was sorry I'd brought it up. He looked so miserable. "I'm not going to lie to you," he said quietly. "I was very fond of Stephanie and, to be frank, it did give me a start that night. Yes, there is a physical resemblance between you, but believe me, that's where it ends."

"I saw her picture in an old edition of the paper. She was gorgeous."

Eric took my hand again. "Kendall, I won't deny that Stephanie was a devilishly attractive woman, but our relationship was strictly attorney and client. You have to believe that."

"I heard she spent the night at your house in Phoenix. Is that true?"

"Yes. She was so overwrought that particular day, I thought it unwise for her to drive all the way back home. She slept in the guest room. It was as simple as that."

Apparently sensing my skepticism, he pressed on. "When she first came to me about the divorce, she was in a terrible state of mind. She told me how desperately unhappy she was at the Starfire. I believed her when she said they all hated her. She seemed genuinely frightened."

"Of what?"

"Bradley. She told me that on more than one occasion he'd been physically abusive." His jaw muscle twitched at the memory. "She said he had threatened to kill her."

His remark startled me and while the waiter fussed about pouring the coffee I remembered the anger in Tally's eyes the day he'd told me of his true feelings for her. It made me feel ill to think she had been a victim of such treatment. In Tally's defense, I said, "People do things and say things in anger that they sometimes don't mean. Isn't that possible?"

"Sure. But, you didn't see how terrified she was. I advised her to get separate quarters immediately, but she insisted on staying through the Gold Dust festivities. If only she'd taken my advice she'd be alive today."

"What do you think happened that night?"

He stirred cream into his cup with deliberate care and arched a brow at me. "What do I think? I think Bradley Talverson tampered with the reins. I think he deliberately goaded her into taking that wild horse of his. And," he added, "I think he used his money and influence to persuade a small town sheriff to conveniently lose the evidence needed to convict him."

I swallowed hard. His hypothesis was very convincing, very believable. But, then, so was Tally's. "I'm sorry I had to bring it up."

Eric's eyes softened. "It's all right. I'm glad it happened. The last time we were together, I sensed you were holding something back. Now that it's all out in the open we can just put it behind us." He glanced at his watch and signaled the waiter. "We've got a show to see. Let's go have some fun."

And we did. The show was a glitzy and spectacular musical experience. Wayne Newton, backed by a first class band and singers, performed for three solid hours, taking turns at playing thirteen separate instruments.

Afterward, Eric took me to the blackjack tables and we made the rounds of other clubs, dropping coins in almost every slot machine we passed. He generously provided all the money, refusing to let me spend a dime. He gambled away nearly a thousand dollars without so much as a wince. The suspicions I'd harbored about his affair with Stephanie, and his financial woes vanished in the wind.

At one point, he phoned his mechanic at the airport and reported back that the problem would take several more hours to rectify. That was okay by me. Las Vegas was enormously stimulating and as we raced hand in hand along the Strip, from one crowded club to another, I was so caught up in the excitement, and so absorbed in his company, I completely lost track of time.

It wasn't until my feet began to ache that I realized with a shock that it was four in the morning. "Summon the carriage," I said, yawning. "I can't drink another drop and I can't take another step."

"Your every wish is my command," Eric said, draping an arm around me.

On the ride back to the airport, he drew me close to him. I'd been rather surprised that he hadn't kissed me all evening. The next ten minutes made up for it. The heat generated by our passionate embrace, combined with the substantial amounts of champagne I'd consumed, made my head spin. I pulled away from him, breathing hard. Self-consciously, I wondered if the driver was watching us in the rear-view mirror.

"Let me catch my breath," I whispered, adjusting my skirt which had climbed more than half way up my thigh.

"I hate for this night to end." His lips closed over mine again. With one hand firmly around my shoulder, he used the other to caress my neck and back. At a snail's pace, he trailed it down to my waist, back up to cup one breast, and then he dropped it lower to massage my thighs. The pleasurable warmth of desire that tingled my skin, made me realize how long it had been since I'd been with a man. As enjoyable as it was, I decided that was as far as I intended to go in the back of a limousine.

"I think I need an ice cube," I panted as the car pulled up and stopped next to the hangar.

"What for?" he asked with surprise.

"To sit on."

He looked delighted and squeezed me harder. "Don't try to fight it, it's bigger than both of us."

"Please. That sounds like a line from a 1940's movie."

He chuckled and kissed the top of my head. "I think it is."

The flight home was a delicious blur. I was thankful he was sober, because we'd have been in Canada had I been piloting the plane. I fell asleep, and when I awoke, the first blush of dawn tinted the eastern sky. I felt more lucid, but terribly exhausted.

It still seemed impossible that we had been out all night. Eric asked me to drop him at the tennis ranch, and before I left, he gave me another torrid kiss.

When he released his hold, he said with emotion, "Kendall, I don't want to have to wait until I come to Castle Valley to see you."

I drew back. "What are you saying?"

"I want you to think seriously about what I said earlier. The managing editor of the Phoenix paper owes me a favor. I say the word, you've got a job. You don't belong here. I mean it. You belong in the city with me."

"Eric, I'm so tired right now, I can't think."

He looked crushed, so I said hurriedly, "I promise I'll consider it. But there are several reasons I can't go just yet. I'm working on...well, a rather sensitive assignment for Tugg and I just can't leave until I've solved...er...finished it."

"How long will it take?"

I thought about the deadline I'd given myself. "I can probably let you know in about two weeks."

"Two weeks! My schedule is so tight, I probably won't even be back here until then. Let me go with you right now," he offered recklessly. "I'll help you pack and you can come to Phoenix now."

"And live where?"

"With me, of course."

"Eric, this is moving much too fast. Are you serious?"

"I've never been more serious in my life," he replied fiercely, pulling me into his arms again.

I pushed away and met his eyes. "I...I can't give you an answer right now. I have to have time to think this over. There's notice on the house, my job. Lots of reasons."

"Now that's something that bothers me," he said, frowning. "I hate the thought of you living out there alone. I don't think it's safe."

"I'm fine. Hardly anyone ever comes out there. I think people are afraid they'll run into an escaped lunatic."

"That's nothing to joke about," he said, a sharp note entering his voice. "All the more reason for you to be away from there as soon as possible."

"I really appreciate your concern, Eric. I'm flattered that you think I'm wasting my life here and you're probably right. But, can't you be patient a few weeks?"

"I guess I'll have to be."

I thanked him again for the wonderful night and drove toward home. Ahead of me the sky beyond Castle Rock glowed in radiant peach.

As I eased into the carport, the events of last night had already taken on a magical quality. Eric's suggestion would require serious thought, but right now all I could think of was a hot shower and crawling between cool sheets.

Shoes in hand, I hurried my steps along the walkway, while pulling the sharp-toothed, decorative combs from my hair. I blew out a sigh of relief. Now to get these pantyhose off.

My loose hair tumbling around my face, I stood at the door struggling to find the house key buried somewhere at the bottom of my purse, and listened to the sleepy buzz of bees in the dark tangle of honeysuckle vines that climbed the latticework along the patio.

I sensed a presence behind me at about the same time I heard a soft footstep. I stiffened as the memory of the darkroom attack zigzaged through my mind. A strangled scream lodged in my throat as I whirled around in time to see a figure step from the shadows.

28

"Where the hell have you been all night?" the shadow growled, moving closer.

The shock of surprise, added to my state of terror, left me speechless for a few seconds. "Tally! What's the big idea sneaking up on me like that? You scared me to death."

"I said, where have you been?" he repeated louder, a note of angry persistence ringing in his voice.

"Don't shout at me. What are you doing skulking around outside my door, anyway?"

"I wasn't skulking and you haven't answered me," he shot back.

The sudden rush of adrenaline subsided and I drew in a sharp breath of air to counter the waves of blackness.

He jumped forward, grabbing my upper arms to steady me. Irrationally, I felt a rush of delight at the pressure of his hands. And it made my heart twist with a kind of insane joy to see the look of distress in his dark eyes. "I didn't mean to scare you," he said in a gentler tone. "But, I didn't know what to think when you didn't show up last night. I was close to calling Roy when you drove in just now."

What a fool I was making myself miserable for nothing. He'd listen to my explanation and everything would be fine. "How long have you been waiting for me?"

"Since around five." He released my arms, but didn't move away.

"I'm sorry you were upset, Tally." I peered around him. "Where's your truck?"

"Jake and the boys are over across the road repairing a fence. I couldn't sleep wondering what happened, so I had them drop me off here. And then, when I didn't see your car..."

"Across the road," I repeated blankly. "What do you mean they're across the road? You mean Lost Canyon? That's your property over there?"

He gave me an odd look. "Yes. I thought you knew that. What about it?"

"Well...I thought...I don't know what I thought. I figured your property ended over there at the highway," I finished lamely, pointing west.

"No. My father bought all but fifty acres from the Delgados years ago. The Starfire land runs east to the hospital, and we border state land to the north."

I stared at him open-mouthed. My mind was trying to tell me something important, but the thought would not materialize. "Tally, I'm really sorry about standing you up last night."

He let out a long sigh. "So, what did happen, Kendall? Did you have car trouble again? Where were you?" It was hard to miss the tinge of accusation edging his words. I felt a tremor of doubt.

"I was in Las Vegas."

His mood of concern evaporated. I watched with alarm, the expression of disbelief taking its place. "What were you doing in Las Vegas?"

"I was with Eric, and before you jump..."

"What?" He grabbed my arms again and I cringed at his expression of fury. This time his fingers bit painfully into my flesh as he backed me up against the side of the house. His face, livid with emotion, was only inches from mine. I couldn't help but remember what Eric had said about his physical abuse of Stephanie, and it made me shudder with fear. "I spent the whole goddamned night worrying about you," he snarled, "and now you're telling me you spent the night with Eric Heisler?"

"I didn't spend the night with him," I shouted back. "Well, I did but...I mean...I was with him, but we didn't...Will you please let me explain?"

"Oh, spare me the details," he said in disgust, releasing his iron hold as if it sickened him to touch me. "This is turning out just the way I knew it would. From the very first day I saw you standing on Yarnell Hill...What an ass I was letting myself in for this. You're just like..." His voice caught and my stomach knotted as his words sank in.

"Go ahead and say it," I dared him, my own anger re-ignited. "You think I'm just like Stephanie. That's what's been in the back of your mind all along. Everything I say, every move I make, you compare me with her."

"She was a whore," he said icily. "Your actions speak for themselves. Don't try to turn this around. I'm not the one who was out all night." He turned his back on me and stomped away. I willed my legs into action, bolted past him, and planted myself on the walkway in front of him.

"Oh, no you don't. I'm not going to stand here and let myself be branded a whore by you. If you'll just quit being so pig-headed and listen to me, you'll see that nothing happened."

We stared daggers at each other for a minute and then he relaxed his stance. "This better be good."

His manner infuriated me so much I could have shot him. "First of all, it really isn't any of your business what happened last night, but since you've elected yourself judge and jury, you might as well hear the facts. I didn't have a clue that Eric was flying to Las Vegas until we were in the air. When we landed, I called immediately and left a message for you."

He looked slightly disconcerted. "I never got a message from you."

"I'm not surprised. Lucinda took it." I watched his jaw tighten and untighten. Gruffly, he said, "Why would she keep that to herself?"

"Oh, come on, Tally. Wake up. It's to her advantage for you to think I'm lying."

He looked down at his boots and twirled his hat in a circle. "All right. Let's say I accept that you called. That doesn't explain why you were gone all night."

"I did not sleep with him, Tally. We had a marvelous dinner, he took me to a fantastic show, and then we gambled till all hours. I simply lost track of the time. We came back. I dropped him at Whispering Winds and I came here. Period. End. *Fini.*"

"Kendall," he said quietly. "I don't think I can go through this again."

"Through what?"

"The misery I put myself through with Stephanie."

"What are you talking about?"

"I'm not going to try and change myself again to oblige the fickle whims of some woman. I am who I am—a cattle rancher. Not some…some slick attorney, like Heisler. If that's the type of man you want, I don't know what else I can say."

"Who's asking you to change? You make me sound so…so shallow. I'm not comparing resumes or bank accounts. And I never said I preferred his lifestyle over yours." Even as I said the words, I was thinking of Eric's enticing offer. "Tally, I can only judge people on how they act."

He narrowed his eyes. "The guy is a first class weasel."

"As opposed to a second-class weasel?" The stony look on his face told me my feeble attempt at humor had failed.

"Frankly, I'd sooner trust a hungry coyote with my cattle than I'd trust him."

I threw up my hands. "Okay, Tally. This is getting us nowhere. I have a monster headache and I don't feel like going any further with this right now. You know, if you'd just back up and look at this objectively, I think you'd see that you've misjudged him."

He threw me an incredulous look. "After everything I've told you about him, I don't know how you can get within ten feet of this guy."

"You want to know why I went out with him? I'll tell you why. Because he's fun, Tally— he's *fun*." I could hear my own voice rising. "He's not morbid. He doesn't keep constantly rehashing his past. He had a bad marriage too, but he's gone on with his life, and so should you."

"You think I'm morbid?" The plaintive note in his voice made my anger melt, and I had a sudden, overwhelming desire to hold him, to tell him that I cared very much for him. But I didn't. Instead, I said, "In a word, yes. Every memory I have of Eric is filled with fun and laughter. Every time I think of you and me together, it involves some sort of heated conflict, or me trying to deal with whatever dark mood you happen to be in."

At that, his face hardened. "Well. I'm sorry you feel that way," he said stiffly, shoving his hat on. "I guess there's nothing more to say." He looked out across the desert. A plume of dust announced that his ride was approaching.

As I watched him stride away, I felt an acute sense of loss, remembering he would be away on business for two weeks. Did I want this to end on such a sour note? "Tally," I called. "Have a good trip."

At first he didn't respond, then halfway down the walk he suddenly wheeled around and marched back to me. The firm set of his jaw and the determined gleam in his eyes made me involuntarily step back.

"Wh...what is it?" I stammered.

"I want you to promise me you'll be careful while I'm gone," he demanded.

"Please, Tally. I'm really not in the mood for another lecture about Eric."

"I'm not talking about him."

I stared in surprise.

"Promise me," he said sharply.

"Okay, okay, I promise, but what..."

"And, the next time you think of me," he interrupted, "think of this." He reached out and yanked me into his arms, bending me so far backward, all I could see was blue sky behind his face.

"Tally, what are you..." The deadly look in his eyes stopped my next words. I let out a little shriek of pain when he grabbed a handful of my hair. His lips came down on mine with such bruising force, our teeth clattered together.

The sun seemed to explode inside my head. This was no gentlemanly kiss. It was raw with anger and desire.

Crushed against his lean body, I struggled with my own emotions of fear and yearning for this rough man. The kiss seemed to go on forever, and I didn't care.

When he finally pulled away, we were both gasping for breath. The blaze of passion he ignited left me shaking and more bewildered than ever.

He gave me a curt nod, turned, and strode away. As if on cue, the blue pickup rounded the bend and braked to a stop. He climbed into the truck and in seconds it roared from view. As if in a trance, I just stood there staring dumbly at the trail of dust hanging above the deserted road.

Slowly, very slowly, rational thought began to return. Somehow, I forced my rubbery legs to transport me into the house. In a half daze I checked the answering machine. There were six hangups, all probably from Tally. And, there was a message from Ginger demanding to know why I hadn't come to the barbecue. No way was I going to deal with her this early. I slipped out of my clothes and headed for the shower. All the while, something kept hammering inside my brain like the annoying *rat-a-tat* of a woodpecker. Tally had said something significant right before that scorching kiss had blotted it out.

As always, I automatically checked the tub and walls for spiders before stepping in. It wasn't until the first blast of water hit me that his words came back to me. "Promise me you'll be careful," drummed in my head. "Promise me you'll be careful." The phrase ricocheted around a few more times, and then I stiffened in shock.

"Damn it!" I screamed. "He told him!" I shut the water off, threw the shower curtain aside, and bounded to the bedroom phone. Dripping wet, I punched Tugg's number so hard, my fingernail broke.

"Hello?" It was Mary Tugg.

I drew in a deep breath, and hoped my voice wouldn't shake with anger. "Mary. This is Kendall. I'm sorry to call so early, but I need to talk to Tugg right away."

"Kendall? It's barely seven o'clock. Can he call you later?" She sounded puzzled.

"No. I need to talk to him now. It's important."

"Well, I'm sorry, Kendall, he had a really bad night. He's on a lot of medication and I'm not going to disturb him. Whatever it is will just have to wait."

I could tell by the firmness in her voice that I wasn't going to get through. "Have him call me at home the minute he's awake," I said shortly and hung up.

With a groan I fell onto the bed, face down. The cool air blowing through the vents onto my damp skin made me shiver. I pulled the covers over me. My life was getting way too complicated. The sinking sensation in my stomach intensified and I punched the pillow. Tugg must have told Tally about my assignment. Why else would he have said such a thing? I pulled the pillow over my head to blot out the brilliant sunlight and lay still listening to the drone of the cooler until I fell into a deep sleep.

The shrill ring of the phone woke me. I fumbled for the receiver and noticed the clock read 11:30. I tried to speak, but no words came out.

"Hello? Is someone there?"

It was Tugg. I cleared my throat noisily. "Sorry about that. I was out all night. Guess I fell asleep."

"You sound as bad as I feel. Listen, Kendall, I've got something important to tell you and..."

"Just a minute," I interrupted. "I've got something to discuss with you first. Why did you do it, Tugg?"

"Do what?"

"Tell Tally," I said heatedly. "And don't try to deny it. You told him what we've been working on, didn't you?"

"If you'll just calm down and listen—"

"You promised me two weeks! I've turned cartwheels to keep this thing under wraps. This is supposed to be my story. What if he lets something slip to Roy? You know the two of them sometimes work together."

"Kendall," he shouted, "be quiet and listen to me. It doesn't matter anymore if Tally knows, or anybody else knows, because it looks like I've been wrong about this whole thing from the start."

I tensed. "What do you mean?"

"I got a letter in the mail this morning. It's from John Dexter."

29

If Tugg had told me California just dropped into the Pacific Ocean and Arizona now had beachfront property, I couldn't have been more astonished. "What did you say?"

"I said I'm holding a letter from John Dexter. Talk about being wrong headed. Pretty pathetic stuff coming from an old newspaper man, huh?" he grumbled. "And to think I've had you on a wild goose chase all this time."

"How can you be sure it's from him?"

The sound of paper crackled in my ear. "I'll read it to you." He cleared his throat and began, 'Dear Tugg— Thought I'd drop you a line to let you know everything is cool with me. Sometimes I feel like shit leaving the way I did with no notice, but, I got an offer I could hardly refuse. I got me the hottest babe down here and her folks have got some kind of bucks! I spend most of my days hanging out at the beach or sailing. Bet you wish you were me. That was a real dead end job for me. Why bust my buns when I can live like a king here? Sorry about our disagreement, but this is best for both of us. Keep smiling!' "It's signed, John Dexter."

Stunned into uncommon silence, it took me a few seconds to find my voice. "Tugg, is this letter typed or hand written?"

"It's typed."

"How convenient. What about his signature? Is it typed?"

"No."

"Well, before we jump the gun, we'd better make sure this letter is authentic. Have you got something at work with his signature on it?

"Yeah, I can check it. But, it sure looks like his."

"What about the postmark?"

"It's kind of smeary. But it looks like Cabo San Lucas. It was mailed last week."

Why did I feel so cold all of a sudden? I sat back, and pulled the covers up around my neck. "I smell a rat. I think someone's fabricated it to get me off the track. The timing is just too perfect. Don't you see? Someone thinks I'm getting too close. Don't tell me you're going to be fooled by this?"

"It does explain his whole disappearing act. You said yourself his girlfriend knew he was on his way to meet with some other woman. They probably cooked this whole thing up so's he could get out of his relationship with the first gal, what's her name?"

"Yolanda Reyes. But, Tugg, what about that phone call two weeks ago? This other woman is still waiting for him. And, what about the ticket to Nogales? Why would he buy only one, and then take his truck?"

"I dunno, Kendall," came the weary sigh. "All I know is, John was not a happy camper when he worked here. He was pissed at Tally, pissed at Roy, and pissed at me for killing his article. You had to know John for this to all make sense. He had a real flair for the dramatic. I think his letter is pretty clear. He saw a golden opportunity to latch onto some wealthy dame and grabbed it."

I sputtered, "But...but...what about his note? What about his phone call that day? If he was planning to leave, why even bother? And what was with all that nonsense about a story that would stand this town on its ear?"

"He was a great one for exaggeration. Most of the time he was full of shit up to his eyeballs and we did have several heated arguments when I asked him to lay off of Roy until he could prove his allegations. The way I'm reading this is he couldn't come up with anything concrete any more than you have, so instead of sticking around and looking like a jackass, he took the coward's way out."

My skin no longer felt cold, but my teeth were chattering. I reached under the mattress, pulled out my notebook, and stared at it numbly. It wasn't difficult to detect the tone of acceptance in Tugg's voice. If he dropped the whole investigation, it would let him off the hook with Mary, her whining sister, and Roy. My fears that his illness was getting in the way of clear thinking, surfaced again and a sense of defeat enveloped me like a shroud. I could see everything I'd worked on the past two months going down the tubes.

His voice broke into my thoughts. "Jesus, Kendall, I know how you must be feeling, but you can't feel any more foolish than I do. I've had you spinning your wheels looking for something that was never there." I could hear Mary's demanding voice in the background urging him to lie down and he muttered, "Yes, yes, in a minute."

"Listen, Tugg. I'm not ready to throw in the towel yet. I think the first thing we need to do is verify the signature. Can we meet at the office right away?"

"I'd never get past Mary," he confided, his tone gloomy. "The doc's got me on another new medication and I'm supposed to take it easy the rest of the weekend. But you can come get the letter. I'll give you the key to the filing cabinet in my office. You can pull John's personnel folder and compare the handwriting."

"Okay, but one more thing before you hang up."

"Yes?"

"Why did you tell Tally?"

"At the time, I had my reasons."

"What are they?" I persisted.

"Look, I haven't mentioned this to anyone at work, but there's a possibility I may have to have surgery. In good conscience, I don't feel I can take a chance on checking into the hospital without someone else knowing what you're working on. Especially after that episode in the darkroom."

"I appreciate your concern, but you did promise me two weeks, remember? Plus that, what help can Tally be to me when he's going to be out of town for two weeks?"

"To tell you the truth, I completely forgot about that until yesterday. These drugs make me feel like I'm walking around in a fog all the time." He lowered his voice. "I don't want Mary to overhear this, but you do realize if the handwriting matches, that…well…we have to tell Roy. And, of course, you'll get the story."

My spine stiffened. Writing an article about John Dexter vegging out in Mexico seemed a poor substitute for the dramatic scoop I had in mind. And the idea of telling Roy set my teeth on edge. "Thanks," I said dryly, and then a thought struck me. "Wait a minute, Tugg. You can't tell Roy yet even if the signatures do happen to match."

"Come on, Kendall," he said, his voice soothing, "I know this has been your baby, but he has to be told. John's case is still open."

"I know that. But I have his files, remember?"

I heard a sharp intake of breath, and then, "Oh, shit! That's right."

"You'll have to give me a few days to figure out how to get them back. That is, unless you just want to march in there and confess what we've been up to the past two months."

He laughed nervously. "Ah...no. I don't think so. How are you going manage that without him knowing?"

"Actually, I haven't had time to formulate a plan yet. But, I will. Let's say Wednesday or Thursday at the latest, okay?"

"All right. I guess a few more days won't make that much difference after all this time."

"No, it won't. And speaking of time, why do you suppose Dexter waited so long to write to you?"

"Who knows? And to think—all this time we've been building up a case against Roy and that Phillips woman based solely on John's disappearing act," he replied, a note of wonderment entering his voice. "Funny how things that looked suspicious at first don't anymore."

"I'll be over to get the letter and key in half an hour," I said, hanging up.

Damn! It would sound irrational to anyone else, but I didn't want the signatures to match. Deep down inside, I was still convinced that Roy and Claudia were involved in something sinister. She seemed devious enough to cook up a fake letter.

I set the answering machine and hadn't gotten two steps from the phone before it rang. I let the machine do its job while I grabbed my purse and car keys. "Sugar pie! Y'all there?"

Ginger's voice filled the room, demanding to know why I hadn't called her back. The flash of guilt made me hesitate. Knowing Ginger, she'd try to pry every last detail from me. No. I'd call her later.

Outside, the searing desert wind blew my freshly brushed hair into a tangled mop. I jammed on sunglasses, and prayed the thunderheads building over the mountains would finally produce the rain I so desperately craved.

The furious pace of events during the last twenty-four hours, coupled with a lack of sleep, left me feeling muddled. I was conscious of the fact that this was probably not the time to be introspective, but, throughout the drive to town, I tried to focus on my feelings for Eric. While his attentions were pleasurable, and I was more than flattered by his kind offer, Tally's kiss had fired intense feelings I hadn't felt for a long time—if ever.

At Tugg's house, I dodged rolling tumbleweeds and flinched at the sting of sand on my face. Mary answered the door and handed me an envelope. I thanked her, expressed my concern for Tugg and hurried to the car. I read the letter over twice and studied the postmark on the crumpled envelope. It looked awfully convincing.

Filled with anxious anticipation, I drove downtown to the newspaper. The building seemed unnaturally quiet with only Harry at work in the production room.

"Man," he said to me with a shake of his head, "you sure missed one hell of a party last night. I thought you were coming?"

It felt like the letter was burning a hole in my hand, so I made up a quick excuse and then slipped into Tugg's office.

I spread the paper flat on his desk and pulled John Dexter's employment application from the file. My hands were sweaty and the headache throbbed at my temples again. "Please don't let it be true," I whispered, positioning the papers side by side.

After a careful comparison of the two signatures, I groaned aloud. Acute disappointment formed a bitter taste in my mouth. Unless this was an excellent forgery, he was indeed alive and well, and living in Mexico.

The next week passed slowly. Without the stimulation of my secret assignment, I felt at loose ends and finally fell into a deep blue funk. Nothing sparked my interest, and the future loomed before me like a black hole of boredom.

Each day, the merciless sun bore down from the white hot sky with such ferocious intensity, it seemed as if my very bones would melt. The complexion of the town changed perceptibly with the onslaught of the Arizona summer.

At high noon, the streets were almost deserted. The few remaining winter visitors had high-tailed it out. The fortunate residents with money had headed for the coast, or escaped to their mountain homes up north. Those who remained toughed it out, some stoically accepting their fate, and others, like me, vocally complaining about the weather we could do nothing about.

On Tuesday, I returned the files to the sheriff's office with such ease it was almost laughable. When I was sure Roy was gone, Duane and Julie had been readily distracted by the cake I brought in to supposedly commemorate my birthday. While their backs were turned, it was a simple matter to slip the folders under some others on Duane's desk. Each would think the other had pulled them out.

Tugg gave John Dexter's letter to Roy and the story broke in Wednesday's edition. I managed to convince Tugg that even though the signatures appeared identical, we should at least have them analyzed by an expert. He agreed, and I mailed the letter and application to Phoenix. We were told not to expect the results for several weeks.

I got the discomforting task of delivering the news to Yolanda Reyes. The stricken look on her face as she read a copy of Dexter's letter made my throat tighten with sympathy.

"This cannot be true," she finally whispered, tears brimming in her eyes. "He loved me! He would not do this thing."

A spasm of emotion shook her. "It is…more bad than if he is dead," she cried, burying her face in her hands. I understood what she meant. If John had died loving her, that was one thing, but to abandon her for another woman was unforgivable. I pressed a tissue into her shaking hands and waited until she regained her composure.

"Look, Yolanda, I'm having as much trouble believing this as you are. My boss seems convinced the letter is from him…but, I'm not so sure."

A ray of hope gleamed from her swollen eyes. "Why do you say this? You think maybe he did not run away with that…that…"

"Listen to me carefully." I went over everything in John Dexter's file with her. "Now, is there anything you can think of that is different than what Roy Hollingsworth has in that report?"

Yolanda blew her nose. "I think it is the same, but I have trouble remembering. If I know that day is the last time I will see him, I would...what is the word...give more attention?"

"I understand and I know it's painful, but if you recall anything different from what I just told you, call me right away."

Back at the office, the revelation about John Dexter caused quite a stir and gave everyone something to talk about besides the heat. Harry used a few words I never heard before and Ginger snorted, "Why that little piss-ant. And to think he had us worried to death, and had all them men out there gallivanting all over God's creation day after day looking for him...well, I'd like to tan his skinny hide."

"I knew he was a flake," Jim remarked in disgust. "What a chicken-shit thing to do."

When I stopped by to get the weekly information from the sheriff's log later that day, it was hard to ignore the look of smug triumph pasted on Roy's chubby face. He wasted no time bringing up the subject.

"Well, well, well, how do you like them apples?" he crowed. "Seems like I was right all along about Dexter. He never was missing. He was just doing what he always did, only this time, he chased some woman's skirt all the way down to Mexico. Guess he's been having a fine old time yankin' our chains."

"Yeah, I guess so." It was hard for me to look at him and even harder to carry on normal conversation. It irked me no end to know that he and Claudia had outsmarted me. They must have laughed themselves sick when Tugg revealed the contents of the letter.

My problems didn't end there. Wednesday evening, Ginger called, breathless with excitement. "Y'all sittin' down, sugar?"

"Should I be?" I asked in a weary voice.

"It might not be a bad idea."

"Jesus, what is it?"

"Lucinda went with Tally to Colorado."

My heart seemed to disengage from my chest and crash land in my stomach. "Who told you that?" I asked hoarsely.

"I got it straight from the horse's mouth. Lucy's Aunt Polly told me."

I grabbed the table for support. All week, the memory of Tally's kiss had kept me in a state of anxious turmoil. It was the one thing that lifted my fractured spirits. Since he'd left, time had crawled to a standstill and I found myself eagerly counting the days until his return. And now this.

Even though Eric had called me twice to tell me how much he missed me, and sent me another expensive bouquet of flowers, some inner knowledge told me that what I felt for him was not the real thing.

In spite of the fact that Tally and I seemed to have almost nothing in common, and he had a host of emotional problems to unravel, I finally admitted to myself that I was in love with him. He had not verbalized his thoughts to me that last day, but I'd felt certain his feelings for me were just as powerful. Ginger's news left me in a state of utter desolation.

The next two days I went through my routine in a stupor. The daily assignments were dull, conversation tedious, food tasteless, and nothing relieved the sensation that my heart had been ripped out and fed through a shredder.

I did a good deal of soul searching. It had been less than six months since my heart-aching breakup in Philadelphia and, against my own advice, I was right back where I started. With age thirty staring me in the face, so far love had provided me with more torment than joy.

When I arrived home Friday afternoon, bad news was waiting for me on the answering machine. "Kendall, dear, this is Mary Tuggs. I hate to tell you this but, Tess Delgado called me today. She's being released from the nursing home the first of July. I'm really sorry, but you'll have to be out of the house by then. Give me a call and we'll talk about finding you a place in town." It was a fitting end to an altogether lousy week.

After pouring myself a glass of wine, I stepped outside onto the patio. As twilight shadows blanketed the distant hills in purple, I breathed in the clear, sweet-smelling air. What would it be like, I wondered, to live somewhere else, perhaps in another cramped apartment. I had to admit that living in such splendid isolation these past months had spoiled me.

How I would miss the song of the wind and the way the stars shimmered at night in the dark canopy of sky. Or the way the moon looked as it rose majestically over Castle Rock. I would miss the sugary scent of honeysuckle and even the prickly cactus garden I had once so detested.

I didn't even realize I was crying until I felt a tear slip off my chin. Hastily, I swiped it away and stepped into the house. It was time to call Eric and tell him I would go for the job interview in Phoenix.

30

The interview on Tuesday afternoon with Barney Wexler, managing editor of the *Arizona Republic*, was a great success. He spoke in glowing terms of Eric and seemed impressed by my credentials and copies of the recent series of articles I'd written for the *Sun*. Yes, there would be an opening on the investigative staff, but it wasn't available until the first of August. If I cared to wait, the job was mine.

My mood was somber after I left his office and started home. This was what I wanted, wasn't it? Career advancement and higher pay?

When I finally broke free of the snarled rush-hour traffic, I couldn't help but notice the massive thunderheads piled high like frothy whipped-cream over the mountains ahead. Every now and then, flickering tongues of violet lightning illuminated their steel-gray bellies. The effect was mesmerizing. A quick run through the local radio stations finally produced a weather report.

A warm air mass was pushing moisture up from the Gulf of California, producing a weather pattern more common during the summer monsoons and, the announcer explained, even though it was too early in the season for such storms, a flash flood alert was in effect for the mountains north and west of the Phoenix metropolitan area. Flash flood? After so many weeks without rain, it sounded impossible.

I couldn't help it. As I drove into Castle Valley I perceived everything with new eyes. The town, snugly tucked beneath the mass of Castle Rock, didn't look as shabby to me as it had that first evening back in April. Since then, this wild, rugged land had become my home.

It was close to six o'clock when I arrived at the paper and walked past Tugg's office. I paused in the doorway, mildly surprised to see him still at his desk.

"Back to twelve hour days?" I inquired.

He looked up and gave me a wry smile. His normally pink face had a sallow cast. "Comes with the territory, as the saying goes. So, how are you doing? What did the specialist say?"

I had told everyone that I'd gone to Phoenix for a doctor's appointment. "I'm much better," I said truthfully.

Tugg smiled. "How about that? I told your dad the dry, desert air would clear you up in no time. Plus that, I got to do him a favor. Of course, it's paid off for me. You're heads above John Dexter. You know, that series was just great. I've had more comments on that piece than anything since I took over this place."

Guilt welled up in me. "Thanks, Tugg. Um...could we talk for a few minutes? In private?"

He threw me a curious glance. "Sure. Shut the door behind you."

I sat down and fidgeted with the material on my slacks while trying to figure the best way to word my resignation.

"So, what's up," he asked, lacing his fingers together.

I reluctantly met his eyes. "Barney Wexler at the *Republic* sends his best."

A thoughtful look crossed his face. "I see."

"Tugg, honest to God, I hate to do this to you, but...well...I've accepted a position on their investigative team. It doesn't start until the first of August, but I wanted you to have plenty of notice."

He blew out an extended breath and studied one of the travel posters. "I know it's because of the way this Dexter thing turned out. I guess it kind of knocked the slats out from under you."

"It's not just that—"

He put up a hand to silence me. "It's okay, Kendall. I can't blame you. It really looked like we were onto something there for a while, and I know this little town doesn't offer much excitement."

I didn't disagree with him.

"Look," he said, brightening. "I worked at the *Republic* for eighteen years and it's a fine organization. I hope you'll be real happy there."

"I'm sorry it didn't work out, Tugg. And I'll never be able to thank you enough for giving me this job when I really needed it. All in all, it's been very good experience." And a very heart-aching one, I thought.

"Don't worry about it. I am glad you're not leaving until August though, because it looks like I'm going to have that surgery."

"Oh, no, Tugg. That's too bad. I thought maybe your stress level would taper off now that the pressure's been reduced."

He shrugged. "The damage is already done. Here's the situation. I'm going to be out of commission about three weeks, and hopefully, I'll be able to find someone to fill your spot when I get back in July. In the meantime, can I depend on you to take on some of my responsibilities?"

"You bet." I swallowed back sudden tears. Why should I miss this shabby little place? Things were clicking into place faster than I could absorb them. I felt oddly detached as if I were viewing myself from a distance. Tugg's lips were moving, but I didn't hear the words. It was an effort to focus on what he was saying. "...so I figure if I divide the work up among you and Jim and Rick, we ought to have all the bases covered."

"Yeah," I mumbled. "That sounds fine."

When I rose to leave, he gave me a friendly hug and I felt even worse. After checking the assignment sheet, I hurried out the door towards my car. At least having the resignation off my chest offered some measure of relief, but even that didn't last long. The notion of spending the long evening at home alone sent me sliding back down the depression chute. I needed something to pick me up, something to take my mind off of Tally and Lucinda, my botched investigation, and the fact that in six weeks, I'd be gone.

Company was what I needed. As I gazed out the windshield at the darkening clouds, an idea blossomed. On impulse, I pulled into a nearby service station and called Ginger from a pay phone.

"Hey, sugar, what's shakin'?"

SYLVIA NOBEL

"To be truthful, I'm feeling kind of down and don't feel like being alone tonight. How would you all like to come over to my place? I'm throwing a rain party."

"A what?"

"You know, to celebrate my first rainstorm."

She giggled. "That's a new one on me."

"Bring Brian and Nona along. We'll have dinner and play cards afterward."

"Well, bless your little heart, but lookee here, darlin', I've already got me a tuna casserole in the oven. Brian's out visiting a friend and Doug's coming over."

"Put the casserole in the fridge and bring Doug with you. The steaks and champagne are on me."

"Steaks and champagne! Well, why didn't you say so, girl? I'll bring pie and ice cream and we'll scoot over yonder in two shakes."

Temporarily pulled from my doldrums, I stopped at the store and happily shopped for dinner. At home, a short time later, I turned on loud rock music and danced around the kitchen.

The potatoes were in the oven and the steaks marinating when everyone arrived. After Nona was comfortably situated in her wheelchair, I filled the champagne glasses and listened to them all chatter. I hadn't planned to tell them my news, but after we had toasted everyone's health and the impending rain, I let it slip out.

Following a stunned silence, Doug smiled broadly and congratulated me while Ginger's eyes filled with tears.

I tried to comfort her by convincing her I'd only be a short distance away, but she said it wouldn't be the same.

And it wouldn't. I knew it and she knew it.

I set out a tray of appetizers and turned on the television for Nona and Doug. Ginger followed me outside

285

and stood in unusual silence while I fiddled with the gas grill. Thunder rumbled ominously in the distance and a sudden rush of moist air, laden with the heavy scent of creosote and manzanita bushes, snuffed out the flame.

"Damn," I muttered, striking another match.

"Looks like we might be in for a gullywasher," Ginger commented, squinting up at the fast moving clouds.

"That's what I'm hoping for."

"Y'all fixin' to leave so sudden like wouldn't have nothing to do with Tally being up yonder with Lucy, now would it?"

I avoided eye contact. "What makes you say that?"

"Well, darlin', unless I'm dumber than owl shit, I'd say you're hightailing it out of town 'cause your little ol' heart's broke."

I squared my shoulders. The vision of Tally making love to Lucinda brought bitter bile to my throat. "I'm going because this offers me career opportunities I'll never have here. And besides that, Eric made me an offer too."

Her eyebrows shot up. "What kind of offer?"

I hesitated. Did I want this to get around town? Then I almost laughed. What difference did it make now? I forked the steaks onto the grill and said casually, "To move in with him."

Her mouth gaped. "Y'all ought to at least give Tally a chance to explain."

I threw her an irritated glance. "You're the one who was pushing the romance with Eric in the first place, and now you're heading up the Bradley Talverson Fan Club? I don't get it."

She looked a bit sheepish. "Seems like, I might've been just a little off kilter. When you first came here, it seemed like you were more suited to Eric. But, things are different now. And what's more, a girl couldn't do much better than a fine and honorable man like Tally…"

"A fine and honorable man?" I interrupted. "This is a person who swore he and Lucinda were just friends, and the next thing I know he's slithered off with her to Colorado. I just can't reconcile that."

"I know it looks bad, but remember Lucy's got a bunch of money sunk into that mare of hers. Maybe it's just a business trip and nothing more?"

"Nice try, Ginger, but it won't wash."

"All the same, I wouldn't be a fixin' to rush into anything with Eric and…"

"I know you don't want me to go," I said gently. "Relax, will you? I'm taking the job but I'm not ready to move in with him. I'm not ready to move in with anybody."

She looked relieved. "Well now, that's more like it."

The roar of a car engine stopped my next words. We both stared in surprise as a jeep, blaring music and overflowing with teenagers, sped past us heading toward the base of Castle Rock.

"This is an odd time for a picnic," I murmured.

"They ain't picnicking. Those kids are headed out for one of them boondockers."

I flipped the steaks over. "What's that?"

"They'll build a fire someplace an' drink beer till they puke."

"That sounds like a load of fun."

The approaching storm lowered the temperature abruptly, and before sitting down to eat, I shut off the cooler and opened the windows. I didn't want to miss one minute of the dramatic spectacle.

Nona entertained us with stories of her theater days and Doug kept us in stitches with one corny joke after another. I noticed the look of adoration in Ginger's eyes and the thought of them being together made me feel warm with happiness.

A blinding bolt of lightning flashed nearby followed by an earsplitting crack of thunder. As if on cue, we heard the splatter of raindrops. We all jumped up and Doug pushed Nona to the screen door.

"It's raining," I shouted, running outside. Laughing with joy, I held my arms out and whirled around and around until I was breathless.

As fast as it began, the rain stopped and sunlight slanted through the clouds. Within minutes, all evidence of the storm had vanished. "What happened?" I cried in disappointment. "That wasn't enough rain to do anything."

"It's kinda like someone grabbing your ice cream cone away after two bites," Nona lamented with a shake of her head.

"Just so you know, that was a typical Arizona rainstorm," Doug commented with a grin. "I'd say it rained about two inches."

I stared at him in surprise. "Two inches?"

"Yeah. The drops were at least two inches apart." We all laughed, but stopped suddenly as the sharp crack of rifle reports split the air.

"What was that popping sound?" Nona exclaimed, looking puzzled.

"It sounded like gunshots," said Doug. We all stood silently waiting for more, but none came.

"It seems like an odd time to be target shooting," I said, peering into the distance.

"It's probably them dumb kids," Ginger announced.

"Or somebody out hunting for rabbits," Doug suggested.

"Let's finish dinner and get to the cards," Nona stated impatiently from the doorway.

It didn't stay cool long. With the clouds blown away to the south, the temperature climbed and it was muggier than before. Reluctantly, I closed the windows and turned on the cooler.

Darkness had fallen and Nona was in the process of dealing the second hand in poker when the incessant blare of a car horn broke into our conversation. We all looked up in surprise as headlights filled the front window. Everyone tensed with fright when the car didn't stop in the driveway.

"Jesus! They're coming right through the glass!" Doug yelled, jumping up.

We all watched spellbound as the vehicle careened wildly and came to a complete stop after ramming the stone fountain. Doug, Ginger and I were all out the door in a matter of seconds. The engine of the jeep was still roaring and Doug shouted for the driver to turn the ignition off.

"What's going on?" I demanded striding toward the jeep filled with teenagers. "Are you guys so totally blitzed, you can't see the road, or this fountain?"

The driver, a tall, skinny boy clad in oversize shorts and a T-shirt, slipped from the jeep and fell to his knees.

"Are you hurt, sugar pie?" Ginger asked, kneeling down beside him. He tried to speak but nothing came out of his mouth. I turned my attention to the passengers and felt a stab of alarm at the expressions of fear on their faces.

The boy on the ground looked up at me and stammered, "Call the sh-heriff. There's a girl out there, and she's d-dead! I've never seen anybody dead before!" He bowed his head and vomited on the ground.

We all stood by helplessly as another teen, this one a girl, leaned out of the jeep and followed suit. A second girl began sobbing, so I approached one of the other boys.

"Can you tell me what happened?"

"We weren't doing anything wrong. Just having a few beers and kicking back, y'know?"

"Go on."

"Jay and Lindsay went off to be alone for a while and all of a sudden we hear Lindsay screaming her head off. We all ran out, and there's...there's this girl laying there. She's all shot up, there's all this blood and..." His voice trailed off.

Doug turned to me. "I've had some medical training, and I've got a flashlight and a first aid kit in my car. I think I'd better check this out right away. What's your name?" he said addressing the boy in the jeep.

"Lester Bosworth."

"Well, Lester, how about you come along and show me where the body...er...this girl is. Kendall, you and Ginger can stay here with the rest of these kids, and you better call the sheriff right away."

"Not on your life," I said firmly. "And miss a scoop like this?" I looked at Ginger and she nodded.

"I'll take charge here." She raised her voice. "Y'all get your butts in the house and wait there till we get hold've your folks. Go on now!"

"Bless you," I whispered in her ear as I ran to get my camera and notepad. I dug my flashlight from the kitchen drawer and on my way out, paused beside Ginger. "I need about ten minutes to look things over before you call Roy, okay?"

"Gotcha," she answered, giving me a thumbs up. I raced outside and jumped into Doug's car. We sprayed gravel as he gunned it down the dark road. We'd traveled less than a mile when Lester yelled, "Turn! Turn here."

Doug veered the car off to the left and bumped along a cattle track. As we drove through a section of broken barbed wire fence, I wondered fleetingly if we were on Tally's land, and then my thoughts stopped cold. Tally's land! Another teenage girl found dead on Talverson property.

"Stop here," Lester shouted, pointing. Doug brought the car to a halt. Illuminated by the bright beams of the headlights, and backdropped by the pitch black sky, the desert foliage ahead looked rather surrealistic.

"She's back under that bunch of trees," he said, pointing to a cluster of palo verdes. "I don't want to see her again," he choked.

"Fine," I said. "You wait here." Armed with my camera, I trudged beside Doug. We passed a poorly extinguished camp fire and picked our way through beer cans and food wrappers. At the edge of the clearing, we snapped on our flashlights. Then, both of us froze at what sounded like someone or something rustling through nearby bushes.

Doug and I exchanged a startled glance. "Who's there?" His voice quavered just a bit as he shined the light back and forth.

We waited, but heard nothing but the usual mixture of night noises.

"You think that was some kind of animal?" he asked.

"I don't know."

He cleared his throat nervously. "Jesus, maybe we'd better wait by the car until the sheriff gets here."

"We can't wait," I urged. "What if the girl isn't dead? These kids aren't doctors. She may need our help." Silently I added, If there is something here, I'm going to see it before Roy has a chance to screw it up.

We walked cautiously, alert for any strange sounds. A few more steps took us to the grove of trees. The earth and bushes all smelled rain freshened. I swung the flashlight from side to side and then we both halted.

Directly ahead, next to a jagged rock outcropping, lay a still figure. We moved closer. Clad in jeans and a pink shirt, she lay on her side, knees drawn up, her head turned away from us. The fingers of her left hand were buried in the sand. A cold sweat enveloped me. I wondered if Doug could hear the frantic hammering of my heart. Trying to swallow was impossible. I couldn't muster a drop of saliva.

"Holy Mother of God," Doug whispered.

There was a considerable amount of blood on her shirt and clotted in her long hair. It was pretty obvious that she'd been shot not only in the back, but also in the back of the head. My skin prickled. This didn't look like the work of a careless hunter.

"I don't think your first aid kit will be of any use," I said quietly.

Obviously distraught, Doug ran a hand through his hair and then knelt to feel for a pulse in her neck. "Her skin is cool. There's no sign of respiration."

I felt sick. "What time did we hear those rifle shots?"

"I don't know. Seven? Seven-thirty?"

"So she's probably been dead about two hours."

"I guess." He stood, absently wiping his hand on his trousers. "I wonder who she is?"

Silently, I shook my head, feeling certain that this third victim was somehow tied into the deaths of the other two teens. It was going to be pretty hard for Roy to pawn this one off as an accident. I snapped the lens cap off my camera and stepped closer. As soon as Roy and Duane arrived, the area would be sealed off, the body quickly covered, and I'd have to rely on them for details.

"We shouldn't touch anything," Doug cautioned me.

"Yes, I know." Doug was a sensitive, law-abiding young man and I had a feeling he would strongly disapprove of my plan to hunt for clues before Roy arrived.

We both jumped at the blast of the car horn. "Why do you suppose he's doing that?" he mused anxiously.

"Doug, why don't you go back to the car and check on Lester. I'll be along in a second."

"You sure? What about the noises we heard earlier? What if it wasn't an animal?"

"If it was the killer, he'd be long gone by now. And anyway, you'll only be a few hundred feet away, and Roy will be here any minute. Go on now. I'll be fine."

He didn't need any more urging. When I heard his steps fade away, I turned back to the body. Steeling myself, I knelt down and shined my flashlight directly on her face. Blank eyes, wide and green, stared back at me. Blonde hair, matted with blood, surrounded her oval face. My heart contracted with pity. Who would do such a cowardly thing?

I played the light around the immediate area and saw a series of footprints in the sand. They could, of course, belong to the kids who'd found her.

Returning the light to the girl, I noted the make of tennis shoes she wore, the exact color of her shirt and the type of jeans. Now that was curious. One pant leg was torn and there was blood on her sock.

The faint wail of a siren in the distance made me stiffen. Gripped by a sense of urgency, I quickly snapped several close-ups of her, knowing full well Tugg would never print them.

The girl's earrings, caught in the flash from the camera, winked back at me. I bent down and looked closer. One, two, three, four, five, six, seven, eight. Eight dangling earrings. I sat back on my heels. That struck a familiar chord. Careful scrutiny of the girl's face brought a sense of dawning horror. Could I be mistaken, or was this the hitchhiker I'd picked up my first day in Arizona?

31

Roy looked more agitated to see me than distressed at the sight of the dead girl.

"You'd best get yourself away from there, Ms. O'Dell," he said tersely, aiming the powerful beam of his flashlight in my direction. "This area's off limits as of right now."

"Of course," I said, moving past him.

"Wait a minute. What's that you got there?" he demanded, pointing to my hand.

"It's a camera," I answered coolly.

"I can see that," he snapped. "What were you doing before we got here?"

His accusing tone of voice disturbed me. I'm gonna nail you this time I thought scornfully. Ignoring his question, I said, "This is a very curious situation, Sheriff. I've seen this girl before."

His eyes widened and he plucked nervously at his downy eyebrows. "You go wait over by Doug Sauers' car.

I'm gonna take a statement from you after I've questioned him and the Bosworth boy."

In the clearing, I noticed Duane cordoning off the site with bands of yellow police tape. When he was finished, he gave me a grim salute and disappeared into the trees to join Roy. The headlights from both police cars coupled with the pulsing glare of their red and blue emergency lights, lit up the desert like a garish stage setting.

I joined Doug and Lester and we all expressed our shared shock, then fell silent. The hiss and crackle from Roy's car radio filled the void.

I was still trying to make sense of what I'd seen. I'd only seen her once, and it had been two months ago, but I felt positive this was the same girl who'd hitched a ride with me.. Hadn't she said she was headed for Texas? So, why had she returned to Castle Valley?

My stomach felt numb. Something was terribly wrong. Roy and Duane returned, looking grim. Roy got on his radio and called Dr. Garcia. Duane summoned Dr. Crane, the medical examiner.

Lester was questioned first, and then Doug. When Roy finished, he announced, "You fellows can go now. Duane, you better follow them back to the Delgado place and get statements from the others." He turned to me, his lips lifting in a crooked smile. "In the meantime, Ms. O'Dell and I will have a little talk."

A shiver of apprehension ran through me as the car lights faded in the distance.

"Get in," Roy ordered, holding the car door open. I hesitated for a fraction of a second before obeying. Roy sauntered around and got in on the driver's side, leaving his door open and the dome light on.

For a time, he said nothing, just sat drumming the steering wheel and then turned to me. "You and Doug Sauers should have known better than to tramp around back there," he said in a harsh voice. "Your careless snooping might have destroyed important evidence."

His critical behavior rankled me. It was probably my high emotional state, but I suddenly felt reckless, defiant, confrontational.

"That seems to be more your department."

"What's that supposed to mean?" he asked sharply.

"I'm not the one who makes a habit of misplacing important evidence, Sheriff. It's my job to obtain facts, not lose them."

His eyes were pinpoints of fury. "I don't think I like your inference, Ms. O'Dell."

"It's obvious to me there is a connection between this murder and the previous two. This will be treated as a homicide, right?"

"A statement will be issued to the press when I'm good and ready."

"Since this is the third murder, will you be calling for assistance from the county attorney's office?"

"No, I won't, and if you don't mind, I will ask the questions. If you had done your homework, you'd have seen that the first death was ruled accidental, and that appears to be the case with the second girl too. There isn't one shred of evidence to indicate either of them met with foul play."

"You can't say that about this one. It's pretty clear this girl was murdered."

"I'm not going to make that determination until the autopsy's been performed and all the evidence has been collected."

"Oh, give me a break, Sheriff. You think she shot herself in the back?"

That hit home. As his face took on the consistency of granite, I suddenly realized the vulnerable position I was in. Whatever happened, it would be his word against mine.

"You'd be wise to just let me do my job," he said softly.

"And I'll do mine."

We glared at each other and then he said, "Let me see your camera."

My pulse leaped. "Why?"

"Let me see it!" He held out one hand.

I craned my head around hoping to see a sign of anyone coming, but saw only the gloom of the desert. I hesitated, fingering the case, and decided that in a physical confrontation, I would be the loser. Reluctantly, I handed him the camera.

With deliberate care, he removed the film, fanned it open, then pocketed it.

"Hey! What are you doing?"

He tossed the camera back and I read the triumph in his eyes. "Looks like the catch is broken. The film just fell right out."

"You may not get away with it this time, Sheriff."

"Get away with what?" he asked with an air of innocence. "I'm simply collecting critical evidence from an uncooperative witness. It wouldn't be wise for you to say anything to the contrary. I hope we understand each other?"

"Better than you think." I could have kicked myself a dozen times for not having my tape recorder with me.

I felt a distinct sense of relief when Duane's car skidded up beside us. Dr. Garcia emerged from a second car and disappeared into the clump of trees.

Then, with Duane taking notes, Roy grilled me repeatedly for details. Were we sure we heard gunfire, or could it have been a car backfiring? What kind of noise had Doug and I heard coming from the bushes on our approach to the site? Had it been an animal, or was it something else? Was I positive I hadn't seen anything? He repeated the last question three times in different ways. The great rings of sweat under Roy's armpits and the sheen on his forehead, alerted me to the fact that he was worried that perhaps I had seen someone. He also questioned me endlessly about the girl's identification. How could I be sure it was the same girl?

Duane drove me home. I felt tense and exhausted. Sleep was nearly impossible and, once again, I had a series of fitful dreams.

I was in a dark, resentful state of mind when I left for work the next morning. In town, I stopped behind one of the white vans that traveled daily to and from Serenity House. The sight of it gave birth to instant irritation. To me, it was a physical reminder of the unapproachable Dr. Price, and his decision to ignore me.

Instead of taking my usual route to work, I followed the van to a rundown warehouse in the seedy section of town south of the railroad tracks. I concealed my car behind a flatbed truck piled with melons. The driver of the van honked twice. Double doors to the warehouse swung open and another man came out.

They exchanged greetings in Spanish and when the driver opened the back of the van, four young Hispanic women climbed out. They headed across the road to what looked like a Mexican shanty town consisting of dilapidated shacks and sagging rusted mobile homes.

So, that's where the hired help lived, I thought, remembering what Bud, the tow truck driver, had told me. I returned my attention to the two men. They loaded what appeared to be boxes of supplies into the rear of the van. Ten minutes later, three different Hispanic women appeared from the cluster of shacks and climbed into the back of the van. Then, with a friendly wave to the warehouse employee, the driver jumped in and left.

There appeared to be nothing sinister afoot. It was a simple procedure to pick up supplies and collect the next shift of workers. What had I expected?

I decided my imagination was working overtime, and dismissed it from my mind as soon as I got into work. Tugg needed to be told about Roy's threatening behavior, so I headed straight for his office. It was empty.

"Where's Tugg?" I asked Ginger.

"He said he'd be in about twelve. Something about taking care of some personal things."

"I see." Discussions of the dead girl in the desert dominated all conversations that day and the story spread quickly throughout the town. Ginger must have been on the phone all night, because the news that I had resigned was mentioned almost in the same breath.

I felt certain that Roy would somehow sabotage the investigation of the girl. For a minute, I entertained the idea of marching over to the shelter and confronting Claudia. I had a pretty good idea how the conversation would go, so why waste the time?

When Tugg finally came in, he called a meeting with Rick, Jim and me to explain the distribution of responsibilities during his absence. His surgery had been scheduled for Monday.

"Tugg, I need to talk to you about last night," I said as Rick and Jim departed.

"You got your copy ready for me to read?"

"That's what I want to talk to you about." I told him of my confrontation with Roy and watched his face harden with anger.

"Goddamn him," he grumbled. "So what do you want me to do?"

"Tugg, I want to run with this. I'm more convinced than ever that John Dexter was on to something. The fact that he left town doesn't erase that. This girl's death simply can't be dismissed as coincidence."

Tugg looked troubled. I could almost see the battle raging inside him. "I agree with you, but, what do you have to link Roy or Claudia with her death?"

"Nothing yet, but I still think our editorial stance should be that Roy is deliberately suppressing evidence involving not only this case but the previous two. I think we should call for Roy's resignation and demand that the county attorney be brought in. All hell's going to break loose when my article comes out on Saturday. Are you prepared for the consequences?"

He grimaced. "Am I prepared for the repercussions this will have on my family? Am I prepared to hold myself responsible for having this paper fold after a hundred years in business? Am I willing to go out on a limb and print our accusations about Roy when we still don't have a leg to stand on? Sure. Sure I am. Go for it. But," he added, narrowing his eyes. "are you prepared? I'm going to be in the hospital for a week. If we do this, you're going to be hanging out on your own."

"I'm willing to take the risk. This article is bound to shake things up enough so that either one might make a mistake. I'm going to be watching both of them like a hawk."

"Jesus, I hope you're right about this. Okay. You've got my blessing."

Energized by Tugg's decision, I raced to my desk to begin the story. Several messages were waiting for me; one from Eric, and one from Yolanda Reyes.

I called Yolanda first. She was out to lunch, so I dialed Eric's number.

"Kendall! Are you all right? I just heard the news from Mother. Why didn't you call me?"

"I thought you were out of town."

"I just got back. I've been worried as hell about you. Even if what happened to that poor girl turns out to be an accident, I feel uneasy with you out there alone."

"It wasn't an accident."

"All the more reason to get into town immediately. I can arrange for you to stay in one of the casitas at the tennis ranch."

At that point I told him about my interview in Phoenix and that I had accepted the job. He sounded thrilled. I also told him that I had to vacate the house by July anyway. The fact that I had no intention of moving in with him, I left out. That news I would deliver in person.

"Listen, I'm going to have to make one more short trip to Dallas, but I will be back Saturday afternoon. Will you hold that evening open for me?"

I hesitated. There was no telling what would happen when my story broke. "Give me a buzz when you get to town, I don't know yet."

"All right. I can call Doug Sauers right now and have him help you move your things."

"Eric, that's very sweet of you, and I will probably take you up on staying at the tennis ranch until I can find another place, but I'm not prepared to move today. I'll let you know when I'm ready."

He was silent, and then said with a sigh, "You are one stubborn woman. But, just to humor me, can't you get someone to stay with you? I'd feel better."

"I'll work on it."

"And lock yourself in at night. It wouldn't be wise for you to be out tramping around in that area until they find the people responsible."

I didn't answer, so he said softly, "I think you know how strongly I feel about you, Kendall. Please be careful."

"I will." I hung up feeling troubled that I couldn't return his affections. I, the stupid fool, was hung up on Bradley Talverson. For a minute, I tormented myself with lurid thoughts about him and Lucinda, then shook them away as I dialed Yolanda's number again. She came on the line immediately. "What's up?" I asked expectantly.

"I have done much thinking, and there is something...ah...not the same as the sheriff writes."

My senses leaped. "What?"

"It is the time of the...what do you call it? The paper he writes?"

"The speeding ticket?"

"Sí. When John goes, he tells me he must go first to the tire place. He cannot travel far on the...extra one."

"The spare?"

"He says it will be ready at four o'clock."

Bingo! My mind raced. If John was picking up his tire at four, how could he have been ticketed by Roy at two minutes after?

I grabbed my pen. "Where was he going?"

"To the place of Pinky Bodeen. It is north of here."

My hand started to shake. North. Not south!

"Thank you, Yolanda. I'll follow up on this right away."

"You will call me back?"

"You bet." I scooped up the phone book and paged to service stations. The second call netted results.

"Where you off to, sugar?" Ginger called as I sprinted past her desk.

"Take messages," I shouted.

Casper "Pinky" Bodeen was an American Indian weighing in the neighborhood of two hundred and fifty pounds and had several front teeth missing. When he smiled, he looked like a friendly Halloween pumpkin.

"How are you doing today?" I asked after I'd filled my tank with gas.

"Trying to make a dollar out of fifteen cents."

I laughed and told him who I was. "Have you got a few minutes?"

"Uh-huh. What can I do you for?"

After a series of questions, he remembered John Dexter. "Oh sure," he said. "I remember him. He had one of those new red Toyota pickups. Man, that sucker was sizzling. Yep. He was as proud as a pup at a fire hydrant and scared silly we might put a scratch on it when we mounted the tire."

"Do you have any kind of records to show what date and time he was here."

"Someplace," he said waving to a grungy office. "He was here kind of late."

"How late?"

A far away look entered his eyes. "Well, I remember he was pretty mad that we didn't have his tire fixed on time."

"His girlfriend said he was supposed to pick it up at four."

"Right. Well, I think it was more like five when we got done."

"How can you be sure?"

"Jeeter!" he yelled. "Come over here a minute." A tall, thin man in grease-soaked overalls joined us.

Pinky explained the situation and he nodded solemnly. "Yeah, I remember that day real clear. I remember 'cause I read in the paper the next week that was the last day anybody ever saw him."

"I'm trying to verify that he was here at four o'clock."

"Yeah, he was here all right. He spent the whole time ragging on me saying he had some kind of important meeting he had to get to. I think we were done a hair before five."

"This is probably a long shot, but do you recall which direction he was headed when he left?"

"North."

"You're sure he didn't go south?"

Pinky looked annoyed. "We were both standing right where you're standing when he left here. I think we both know north from south, and he went north."

"Would you guys be willing to swear to what you just told me?"

They exchanged a glance and nodded. Things were coming together for me at last, I thought jubilantly. Roy was lying through his teeth. I could hardly wait to confront him and watch him squirm. Better yet, maybe I'd keep this to myself and spring it on him in Saturday's column.

Back at the office, Ginger was motioning to me as I stepped into the lobby.

"Mike Scott is on the phone, and he says it's real important."

I charged to my desk. "Mike, I'm glad you called. I hope you have some news for me."

"I'm not sure it's going to help you, but remember that name you gave me when we talked last?"

I flipped open my notebook. "Charles?"

"Yes, well, it clicked something in my brain, and I finally remembered where I've seen the woman you call Claudia. It's been about ten years ago. Our paths crossed when I was working on a case for the prosecutor's office. She didn't look like that and her name was different. I can't remember what it was, but I'm sure it wasn't Claudia."

My heart hammered hard against my chest. "I'm listening."

"We prosecuted a case against a doctor, a gynecologist by the name of Charles Sheffield. It was an important case and caused quite a scandal. He was accused of molesting some of his patients. A lot of the finer details I've forgotten, but you could look up the news clippings at the library. But, I do remember one weird thing."

"What's that?"

"All the victims were young. I'd say ranging in age from thirteen to, oh, maybe eighteen years old."

"Really?"

"Yeah. Pretty disgusting, huh? Well, anyway, we won the case and the guy had his medical license revoked. He got ten years at Florence, and a hefty fine. I seem to recall though that he was released after serving only five years and to my knowledge no one ever heard of him again."

"Did he leave the state? Do you think he's still practicing medicine somewhere else?"

306

"Possibly."

"But, where does Claudia come into all this?"

His voice became animated. "During the trial, she was there in the courtroom almost every day and she testified for the defense in his behalf. She had kind of light brown hair then. Short and fluffy."

"I'm not following. What's the connection?"

"She's Charles Sheffield's sister."

"His sister?"

"Yep."

I had a flash of the Rolodex card in her office with the horrid little devil figures and the words, May you rot in hell! I said, "Hmmmm. Well, I'm not sure what to make of this just yet, but I certainly appreciate your call."

"Glad to be of help. Perhaps we'll see you at another tennis match?"

"Could be." I hung up and sat tapping my pencil and staring at my notes. So, now that I knew who she was, what did I really know? Having been involved in such a nasty scandal would certainly explain why she would have chosen to remain anonymous.

Later that night, I sat propped up in bed with all the information spread out around me. The answer had to be here somewhere. When I closed my eyes, the words swirled and buzzed in my head like a swarm of angry bees.

I forced my mind to relax and all at once, the fragmented clues began to fall neatly into place. Dr. Charles Sheffield had disappeared five years ago. Violet Mendoza had died mysteriously five years ago. Claudia had arrived in Castle Valley to manage the shelter five years ago!

A chill prickled my scalp. An obviously frightened woman with a heavy Mexican accent had called John Dexter with information for sale. Someone else knew where John

Dexter was headed that last day. If I was right, I knew where Jenny had gone and where the young girl we'd found in the desert had been all this time.

A wild scheme began to form in my mind. Armed with nothing more than my hunch and a batch of circumstantial evidence, I knew now what I had to do. There was only one way to accomplish it, and Yolanda Reyes and Nona were going to help me.

32

Yolanda Reyes stared at me as if I'd lost my mind. "You want me to help for you to go inside the house of the crazy ones?"

I kept my explanation brief, anchoring it mostly on John Dexter.

"But, why did he go away?" she asked frowning. "Why did he not meet with the girl who calls him?"

"I think he did."

Her face paled. "So...the letter. It was not from John?"

"I doubt it."

Her hand flew to her mouth. "If John was there, then he is—"

I cut off her next words. "That's what I want to find out. But, I can't get the proof I need unless I can get inside the place. If I'm wrong, I may find that it's just what it's supposed to be—a mental hospital run by an eccentric old psychiatrist, and that will be that. But, if I'm right..."

She dabbed a tear from her eye. "What do you need for me to do?"

"These people have got it cleverly fixed with the fence, the dogs, and the guards, so it's impossible to get in. How those girls got out, we may never know, but I think I know a way I can get past the guards, and that's where you come in."

At first, Yolanda looked doubtful about my plan to masquerade as one of the Hispanic girls from the Mexican shanty town. I convinced her it could be done, and that I would pay whoever arranged it two hundred dollars. The girl would have to speak some English and I needed to have an answer immediately. Yolanda looked worried when we parted.

I, however, was elated, and put the next step in motion. Nona seemed delighted by my sudden visit and surprised at my request for the wig and theater makeup. "It's a bit off season for Halloween parties, ain't it?" she inquired, giving me a quizzical look.

"I've been invited to a costume party. In Phoenix," I added quickly.

"Really? Well, sure, I'll be tickled pink to help you out," she said, digging jars from a drawer. "This color ought to do. It stays on real good, and this stuff'll help you get it off when you're done," she said, pressing the containers into my outstretched hands. "You sure you want to go as a Spanish dancer? I got costumes here for Cleopatra, all manner of royalty, or I could even dress you up like Mae West. I had a bit part in one of her movies once, did I tell you?"

As a precaution, I asked her not to mention my visit to Ginger. It was a surprise, I convinced her. She still looked skeptical, but I had no time to explain further.

Yolanda phoned me at the paper around four o'clock. "I have found a girl named Rosa who can help you. She is not very happy to do this. She says strangers are not welcome there."

"Was she able to tell you anything about the people running the place?"

"No. She says they have warnings never to talk of such matters."

My heart beat a little faster. Her voice grew plaintive. "Señorita O'Dell. Perhaps you should not do this. You do not understand my language. When they hear you talk, they will know!"

"I've already thought of that. You can explain to Rosa that I don't plan to speak at all. She can introduce me as her cousin from Mexico and tell them that I am mute, cannot speak or hear. Tell her I intend to have a quick look around, and then she can tell them I am sick and need to leave when the van goes for supplies the next day. But, I'm still going to need your help tonight."

Yolanda drilled me in Spanish until the wee hours, and later, after I'd donned the makeup and wig, she arranged the meeting at Rosa's trailer. When I arrived, she was openly amazed at my transformation.

Rosa Soto was almost as wide as she was tall, and she looked uncertain as I pressed the twenty dollar bills into her hand. All the while, Yolanda was explaining the setup to her in Spanish. Rosa's gaze kept flickering over me suspiciously and she babbled something back to Yolanda who let out a sigh of exasperation. "She says it is too much risk for only two hundred dollars."

I said, "Tell her I'll pay another three hundred when it's all over."

That did the trick. Rosa gave me a yellow-toothed grin and waved us outside. Before the van arrived, I had given Yolanda an envelope and instructed her to deliver it to Tugg if she had not heard from me by four o'clock Saturday afternoon.

Clustered with the other women outside, I stood silently as Rosa explained to the driver that I was a new employee. While I endured his careful scrutiny, my heart beat erratically. By the time he finally motioned me inside, my knees felt wobbly. I collapsed on the seat and sent a silent prayer of thanks to Nona. So far, the wig, skin makeup, and dark glasses had served their purpose.

I prayed Yolanda was right when she had assured me that of all the people in town, the Mexican community was the one close knit group of people who knew how to keep secrets. Since Yolanda herself was probably here illegally, I knew what she meant.

The interior of the van was suffocating. The combination of smells; warm fruit, strong body odor and gas fumes, mixed with the swaying motion of the vehicle, had me struggling for breath. Pressed closely between Rosa and another woman, I fought the nausea rising in my throat and tried to focus my thoughts on something else.

The key to the mystery had been there in front of me all along. John's crumpled note had made reference to the fact that the first two girls had been found on Talverson property. The third death, coupled with Mike Scott's information regarding Claudia's brother, provided the link I'd been missing. The common denominator had to be Serenity House. Tucked safely away in the desert, hidden from all prying eyes except mine, it provided Roy and Claudia a perfect spot to carry out their nasty smuggling operation. It hadn't been Lucinda trying to scare me away. It had to be the sly Claudia. The driver hit a pothole and I grabbed the edge of the seat to keep from bouncing off.

"It will not be long," Rosa whispered beside me. I nodded and positioned one hand on the ceiling to steady myself. There was no question in my mind that Tugg would brand me as certifiable if he knew what I was doing.

We'd traveled about a half an hour when the van braked to a halt so suddenly, I was almost thrown to the floor. I heard the driver chattering to another man in Spanish and knew instinctively I was now on the grounds of Serenity House, probably at the guard station. My heart was pounding with excitement when the van accelerated and then came to a stop a second time. I made eye contact with Rosa and she squeezed my hand and put one finger to her lips.

The driver opened the doors, letting fresh air flow inside. I drew in a thankful breath and squinted into the blinding sunlight. Carefully, I fingered the pencil flashlight underneath my blouse and felt the bulge of the Swiss army knife in the back pocket of my jeans as I followed the rest of the girls outside.

We were met by a rather severe looking Hispanic woman with iron-gray hair and a terribly wrinkled face. She greeted the girls in Spanish and Rosa motioned for me to follow them. Ahead of us, across a grassy courtyard graced with towering cottonwood trees, loomed an impressive two-story building of white stucco topped with a red-tiled roof. Several smaller wings flanked each end. The one to the right contained the kitchen, Rosa explained in a low voice, and the stone structure next to it was the monastery.

The ancient bell tower, backdropped by Castle Rock, spired upward toward puffy white clouds.

To my right, glossy, sable Dobermans paced restlessly along the inner fence. Set back to my left, nestled in groves of palm and eucalyptus trees, were several wooden structures. The large one looked like a garage, the smaller ones were probably used for storage.

I followed Rosa inside the building through a dark, narrow hallway until it opened into an enormous flagstoned kitchen. The heat emanating from three ovens almost took my breath away. Face averted, I waited beside a long butcher block table while Rosa crossed to talk to a heavy-set Hispanic cook. I knew she was explaining that I could not speak or hear, and that only she could communicate with me through sign language. The cook shook her head in disgust and pointed me to a mound of potatoes. Rosa set to work washing dishes nearby.

So far so good. I was so wired, I could hardly hold onto the potato peeler. Praying that the theater makeup wouldn't wash off my hands as I rinsed the potatoes, I wondered again at my rash decision. My mother had always warned me that my impulsive behavior would one day get me into serious trouble. I hoped she was wrong this time. There should be no danger if I did nothing to attract attention to myself. All I needed was enough time to prove my theory.

The kitchen buzzed with activity, and the dour cook, assisted by Rosa and two others, turned out an amazing amount of delicious-smelling food. The young women shouldered heavy trays back and forth through the swinging kitchen door.

I signaled to Rosa when she returned with her empty tray. While the cook's back was turned I told her I needed some time to check the outside area, and after that the interior. She said she'd figure out a way as soon as the dinner shift ended.

Dusk had fallen by the time I finished three hours of peeling potatoes. I massaged my numb fingers. If I never saw another potato again, I wouldn't care. Rosa jabbered something to the cook and then motioned for me to follow. She handed me a bucket and rags and showed me to a pantry area. "You clean the shelves." She reacted to my look of distaste with an amused grin. "There is a window behind you. How long will you take?"

"Give me at least an hour, and then meet me here." After closing the door firmly behind her, I turned and ran to the window. It was open, so all I had to do was remove the screen. I slipped outside and ducked behind some oleander bushes while I got my bearings. As far as I could tell I was now behind the kitchen building. That meant the garage and other buildings I'd seen on my way in would be to my left. Keeping my back to the wall, I edged around the corner to the right. The courtyard area before me was brightly lit. Beyond that, a few hundred feet from the gate, a silhouette filled the window of the guard tower. Quietly retracing my steps, I anxiously wondered if the grounds were patrolled at regular intervals by guards accompanied by the vicious-looking dogs. It was a chance I had to take.

The bright moon presented a problem. I had to wait until it vanished behind a cloud before making my move. Drawing in a deep breath, I sprinted across the open space into the shadows beneath a grove of trees, then dashed across a driveway to what I guessed was the garage. Exhilarated and gasping for air, I made my way behind the building and peered through a small, grimy window into the dark interior.

The clouds were drifting away from the moon when I discovered a nearby door. I pushed it open and slipped inside. The narrow beam of my pencil flashlight did little to break the gloom, but between that and the moonlight streaming in some larger windows on the south side, I could make out two of the white vans and Dr. Price's black Mercedes.

My hand was on the door handle when the sudden sound of approaching footsteps from outside broke the silence and almost stopped my heart. I ducked behind the Mercedes and held my breath. Lights flashed on above me and I saw two dark-haired men enter from a door in the front.

Frantically, I looked for a place to hide. Laughing loudly while conversing in Spanish, the men seemed to be headed right for me. In a panic, I dropped to the floor and scrambled underneath the car, almost losing my wig in the process.

Flat to the floor, my cheek pressed against the cool concrete, I was eye level with their shoes. Inexplicably, the desire to giggle was almost overwhelming. I bit the inside of my lip and shut my eyes. When one of them opened the car door on the driver's side, I almost lost it. Oh, shit! Don't let him start it.

I could hear one of the men rummaging around inside and then to my relief, saw his feet reappear and heard the car door slam. Only after they'd shut out the lights and left did I move. And then it was a tremendous effort to get my rubbery legs to support me.

"You are definitely insane, O'Dell," I muttered as my racing pulse gradually slowed. I finished searching the garage, being careful to use my flashlight as little as possible.

Disappointed to find nothing of interest, I stepped outside again. I was about to lose the moonlight behind the mass of dark clouds now gathering over the top of Castle Rock. Beyond the garage, I saw the outline of another structure about a hundred yards away. Crouching low, I hurried noiselessly along a sandy path.

When I reached the building, I felt comparatively safe, situated well behind the main house and out of sight of the guard station. I circled the structure. There were no windows and in the dim glow of my light I read the large sign on the door. POOL CHEMICALS DANGER! KEEP OUT. Underneath, it warned in Spanish: ¡PELIGRO! ENTRADA PROHIBIDA.

I started to move away and then stopped in my tracks. Wait a minute. What was so dangerous about pool chemicals? I turned back, playing the light over the padlock which I tugged to no avail.

The lock was solid, but I noticed the strip of metal behind it was anchored to the splintery wood with rusted screws. After a few minutes of frustration, I was finally able to pry it loose with my knife.

After a quick look behind me, I pushed against the door. It was stuck. I pressed harder. The wood was probably swollen due to the humidity, I thought. One more firm shove and the door loosened. I winced at the protesting squeak of hinges as I edged it open.

When I stepped forward something soft brushed my face. Involuntarily, I jumped back and shined the light into the opening, shuddering. A web that seemed the size of a trapeze net covered the doorway. An enormous spider scuttled from the middle of it and disappeared above the doorframe.

317

I considered going no further until the faint beam of my flashlight picked up a shape in the gloom. Whatever it was, it was big.

I grabbed a stick and stifled the urge to scream as I cleared away the web. Not daring to even think about where the spider was, I bolted inside and approached the mass which was covered with a tarpaulin. I lifted the canvas back and gasped. Bright red paint glittered back at me. I had found John Dexter's truck.

33

Even though I had been half expecting it, the discovery left me in shock. The burning question of what had happened to John Dexter's truck was now answered. And what of John? The sense of immediate danger was strong as I stood rigidly contemplating my next move. Better proceed with extreme caution, or risk the possibility of becoming instant dog food.

I couldn't very well bring back the whole truck as proof, but I needed something tangible to show the county attorney. It took only a minute to locate the truck's registration. It read: John J. Dexter.

Outside again, I pulled the door shut while stuffing the small paper in my pocket. A sudden flash of lightning made me jump. The wind had picked up, and the smell of rain was in the air. Rumbles of thunder accompanied me as I alternately sprinted and crept back to the pantry where Rosa waited.

She threw me a worried look. "You are very late!"

"I'm sorry," I said, brushing the remains of leaves and dirt from my clothing and hair. "I got delayed."

"I must take coffee to Dr. Price. Where do you want to go?"

"With you." To substantiate the second part of my theory, getting a good look at Dr. Price was next on the list.

Again, she gave me a troubled look and shrugged. She explained to the cook that I needed to accompany her so she could put me to work scrubbing floors. That seemed to satisfy her.

Rosa led me from the kitchen through a maze of wood-paneled hallways to a wide staircase. Dr. Price and the head nurse lived in a suite of rooms in the main structure and the patients were in the building beyond, she explained, gesturing towards arcadia doors. In the low light, I could just make out a palm draped breezeway that connected the two buildings.

At the top of the stairs, she motioned for me to put down the bucket and take the heavy tray from her. The aroma of coffee and the sight of the fresh cookies made me wish I'd eaten earlier.

"*Oficina del doctor,*" Rosa whispered, knocking lightly on the door before pushing it open.

I followed her into the room, my heart hammering in my ears like a kettle drum. My feet sank into plush ruby-colored carpeting as I surveyed the room, taking in a series of tall bookcases and stylish overstuffed furniture. A glance to my left revealed a connecting bedroom and to my right, at the furthest corner of the rectangular shaped room, I spotted Dr. Price seated at an impressive mahogany desk.

"Who's that with you, Rosa?" he asked in a guarded tone. His gaze swept over me, lingering for long seconds. I tensed. What an idiot I was. It hadn't occurred to me to give myself a name.

I met the panic in Rosa's eyes. "Her name is...Angelica. I am...I will be...away next week. So...I am having to train her for me," she finished lamely. For being put on the spot, her story was quite good. I felt a rush of gratitude.

Dr. Price rose and took several faltering steps. The light from the chandelier caught the reflection from the cut glass liquor decanter perched on the corner of his desk. He pointed to a small table nestled between two upholstered chairs. "Set the tray over there," he directed me, his voice slurring.

Careful not to react, I kept my face bland and looked at the floor as I passed him, suddenly doubting myself. He looked so damned authentic; tall, gray haired, distinguished. But not old, I thought setting the tray down. Not old. And not sick, as Thena Rodenborn had described. As far as I was concerned my question was answered, but my elation was tempered by apprehension.

It would be best to get out of here now, continue my exploration of the place, gathering evidence, and then lay low until tomorrow.

"Angelica," Dr. Price purred. "You have beautiful hair. I'd like it very much if you'd bring a cup of coffee to my desk."

Pretending not to hear, I busied myself arranging the dishes on the little table.

"What's the matter? Are you deaf?" he challenged. It was an effort not to turn around while Rosa hastily explained my condition. "But, she is a good worker. And, she can read instructions," she added helpfully. I had to stop myself from throwing an admiring glance at her. She was really getting into the part and earning her five hundred dollars.

"So she can't speak or hear," he muttered. I heard his approach and my skin tingled knowing he was close behind me. Casually, he reached around my hand and tapped the cream pitcher. The white liquid poured onto the rug.

"How careless of me." His voice was smooth as velvet. What the hell was he up to? I thought, kneeling to sop the cream with one of the cloth napkins.

"I will get the bucket to clean it," Rosa said quickly.

"No. Let her do it. You go and get me some more cream. And have Señora Morales go to the cellar and get me more brandy."

I turned my head ever so slightly in Rosa's direction. The look of fear in her eyes made me even more uneasy.

"Please, Dr. Price," she implored. "I will clean it. Angelica can get what you need."

"Do as you're told! And close the door behind you." It was hard to breathe normally as I returned my concentration to the spill.

"Angelica, you're a very pretty girl," he said softly. I felt his hand on my shoulder. "And you look so very, very young." Every muscle in my body strained as I fought for control.

When his hand started to trail down my back, remnants of Mike Scott's conversation filtered through my mind. All the patients molested by Charles Sheffield were adolescents.

I warned myself to stay calm, or my sleuthing would end right here. Trying to keep my face hidden behind the long black hair, I pushed his hands away, got up and headed for the door.

My hopes of escape vanished when I felt his arms close around my waist. I wouldn't have thought a man as apparently drunk as he seemed could move that fast. He clapped a hand over my mouth and dragged me across the room toward his bedroom. I struggled against him as he kicked the door shut and shoved me toward the bed. The look of unbridled lust in his glazed eyes conveyed his wretched plans for me. His arms locked around me and I shook my head violently, fighting to keep his lips away from mine. "Oh, now, don't be that way," he said, fumbling for the zipper on my jeans.

"Take your hands off me, you filthy bastard!" The words exploded from my lips before I could stop them. He released his hold slightly, drawing back with disbelief.

"What's going on here? I thought you couldn't talk? Why you little fake!" A crazed smile crossed his face and he lunged for me again.

I screamed, "You're the fake, you stinking child molester!" He grabbed my wrists, so I tried to knee him in the groin. If he hadn't been so drunk he'd have realized at that point I wasn't who I claimed to be, but his actions seemed driven by a demonic hunger.

I ducked out of his grasp and almost made it to the door when he grabbed my hair. The wig slipped off and he shouted, "What the hell is this?" His arms closed around me again as I grappled for the doorknob.

He yanked me backward and wrestled me to the floor. Straddling me, he pinned my arms firmly and stared, his eyes widening with recognition. "Well, I'll be..."

The door opened behind him. I prayed it was Rosa, but before I could call out for help, the words locked in my throat. Claudia Phillips stood in the doorway, a look of rage on her face.

"Charles! You make me sick," she seethed. "Must you diddle the hired help? I would think you'd get enough to quench your obscene appetites."

"My dear sister, this one, I think you'll agree, is a little different." He rose to his feet, grabbed a handful of my hair and jerked me to a sitting position.

The look on her face when she saw me was worth remembering. "You!" Her violet eyes flashed fire. "How did she get here?" she demanded, crossing to where I sat.

"I'm not positive, but I think she came in with Rosa," came his reply.

Concern for Rosa almost overruled my own fear. As calmly as possible, I said, "She had nothing to do with this. You two might as well pack it in, because I know what you've been up to out here. My editor knows too."

Claudia's face blanched. She turned to her brother and cuffed his head. "You idiot! If you hadn't let that mangy girl escape she wouldn't be here. I'm sick to death of cleaning up after you."

"But, Sissy..." Charles Sheffield whimpered like a whipped dog. "What are we going to do now?"

Her mouth twisted and she returned her deadly stare to me. "Rosa will be dealt with just as the other little snitch was. As for this one..." she landed several vicious and painful kicks in my side. "I should have never let him talk me out of my original plan for you. And, I should have had Roy finish you off that night in the darkroom." The toe of her pointed shoe connected with my forehead and sent me reeling backward. Through a mist of pain, I heard their frantic whispering.

They had moved a few feet away from me, so I eyed the door with hope. A groan escaped my lips as I struggled to my knees. It felt like she'd broken some ribs and a few drops of blood spattered on the carpet from my head wound.

"Get Raoul up here," she snarled. "Then lock her in the storage room until I figure out exactly what I'm going to do with her."

"We have to be careful," Charles said in a strained voice. "You remember what he told us. A second dead reporter's gonna tip everybody off for sure."

I wondered who *he* was as I was roughly hauled to my feet. Were they talking about Roy? Held tightly from behind by Charles, I faced Claudia's deadly-cold eyes. "I've worked too hard to let you destroy everything," she seethed. "So now, you're going to have to vanish, Ms. O'Dell. Vanish into thin air, just like our nosy friend Dexter." Her maniacal laugher sent an icy chill down my spine.

She marched into the study. "Bring her in here." Charles gave me a hard shove across the room, then threw me into a chair. "Don't move!" he commanded, then crossed to the desk and grabbed the phone.

The pain in my ribs was so intense it was difficult to keep from crying out. I heard Charles speaking in Spanish and my heart seemed to stop beating when I heard him say Rosa. I cried, "If you touch one hair on her head..."

"Shut up!" Claudia smacked my face with such force, my ears rang. For someone so thin and wiry, she had incredible strength. Eyes watering, I lunged for her, but only succeeded in tearing the sleeve from her blouse.

"You bitch!" she screamed just as the office door banged open. A brawny man bearing a rifle rushed in, seized my arm and jammed the barrel into my face. "You come with me, ¿sí?" he said with a fiendish grin.

Charles grabbed my other arm. "You'd better come along quietly," he warned ominously, "or you may not even make it downstairs." He flashed a smile over his shoulder to Claudia. "We can't have her upsetting the patients, now can we?"

"Get her out of here!" Claudia spat, punching numbers on the phone. My legs felt like rubber bands. I half walked and was half carried down the stairs, through the maze of hallways back to the kitchen area, and then guided down a set of worn stone steps into a musty, damp smelling room.

They led me across a cobweb-infested basement, down another short flight of steps, and stopped before a formidable-looking wooden door. "Let me go!" I fought with every ounce of strength I could muster. At the clatter of a key in a lock, I screamed, "Rosa! Where ever you are, get the hell out of here!"

"Shut her up!" Charles wailed. Raoul shouldered the door open and gave me a ferocious shove that sent me sprawling into darkness.

34

I landed with a thud on a dirt floor. The room was every bit as black as a darkroom. Not a speck of light filtered in from anywhere, even under the door. It was surprisingly cool too. Wincing from the pain in my ribs and head, I cautiously pushed to my knees.

My hand flew to my back pocket. Thank heavens, they hadn't discovered the knife. And double thanks, they hadn't found the flashlight tied to the ribbon around my neck hidden in my bra. I fished it out and directed the narrow beam of light around my prison.

Claudia had referred to it as a storage room, but it more resembled a dungeon. An ancient refrigerator leaned against the far wall, along with a few cardboard boxes and a pile of lumber. The rock walls were smooth as cobblestones.

There was absolutely no doubt that Claudia planned to kill me. She had probably been calling Roy as I was being dragged from the study. I didn't even want to imagine what they would do to me.

I rose to my feet and turned my light toward the door. There wasn't much time. I had to find a way out before the batteries ran down.

The last thing I remembered was the sound of a bolt scraping into place. A careful examination of the thick wooden door made my spirits plummet. There appeared to be neither latch nor knob, nothing to grab onto. It didn't take a genius to figure out that this room wasn't really used for storage. Had John Dexter been imprisoned here before he'd been murdered?

I clicked off the flashlight. Try as I could, I couldn't remember how far we'd come from the steps that led to the kitchen. If I shouted and pounded and kicked the door, would someone hear me? It was worth a shot.

"Help! Can anybody hear me? Help!"

Sometime later, I turned my back and slid into a weary heap, my voice hoarse, my palms raw and full of splinters. How much time had passed? What were they waiting for? A flash of light on my watch produced another disappointment. During one of my violent encounters, the hour hand had broken off. Great. Now I couldn't even count the last hours of my life. For awhile, I just sat and cried. The sounds of my own sobs finally stopped me. What good would this do? I needed to think. Giving into panic was no solution.

Summoning new-found courage, I snapped the light back on and rubbed the sleeve of my shirt across my eyes. Perhaps there was something in here I could use as a weapon against them when they returned.

The inside of the dented refrigerator produced a musty smell. Nothing of interest there. Next, I examined the contents of the cardboard boxes. They were full of empty mason jars, old newspapers, broken dishes and roaches! The biggest, blackest one I'd ever seen scurried up my sleeve. Lunging backward, I screamed and swiped at it with the flashlight until I heard it drop to the floor.

The frantic movements made me dizzy with pain. Would it crawl up my leg now? I clutched my rib cage, and backed up against the wall, giving in to a fit of hysterical laughter. At least I wasn't alone, I thought incoherently, sliding to the floor. There were probably oodles of roaches and spiders to keep me company.

Hours must have passed in the total blackness as I sat huddled in a corner trying to figure out how I was going to escape. Why, oh, why hadn't I confided in Tugg? By the time Yolanda delivered my letter, it would be too late. The memory of Charles Sheffield's hands roaming over my body made me shiver in disgust. By Claudia's remark, I gathered he had the freedom to do whatever he wished with the girls before their final destination. How sick! How revolting. What would happen to me when Roy finally got here? Would Charles be allowed to complete his gruesome plan for me?

Morbid thoughts whirled in my head like dust devils, carrying me to sleep. When I awoke I was lying flat on the floor. Everything came flooding back. Oddly, I felt clear-headed and calm. I switched on my precious little flashlight and played it over the ceiling. People never look up, I thought incongruously.

With no feeling of fear, I watched one of the shiny black roaches crawl across the ceiling and disappear into a hole above the refrigerator. A moment later it reappeared, and then a second one. Idly, I followed their progress down the far wall. The roaches were the lucky ones. They could get in and out of this place at will.

Wait a minute! I sat up and shot the beam back toward the ceiling. Where were they coming from?

From the woodpile, I pulled out a two by four and then used my knife to dig a small hole in the floor where I inserted the flashlight. I pounded the wood against the ceiling, listening closely. There was a definite hollow sound in a small area above the refrigerator.

My tennis shoes squeaked against the smooth metal as I scrambled on top of it. Desperately, I tried to remember the details of what Thena Rodenborn had told me about the old monastery. There were a series of "safe rooms," she'd said, for the monks to hide. Also, she had mentioned a series of escape tunnels. Had I discovered the entrance to one of them? It was almost too much to hope for.

"Oh, please, please," I whispered, using the knife blade to scrape away layers of dirt. A crevice appeared, and the more I scraped, the clearer the outline became. There was a trapdoor directly above my head. I pushed hard, straining every muscle.

After several minutes, I sat down, gasping for breath. It wouldn't budge. How long had it been since someone opened it? A hundred years?

There had to be a way. I needed something as a lever, something I could slip into the crack and jack the door open far enough for me to insert one of the two by fours. The five slender pieces of wood I chose, cracked instantly.

"Damn!" Something much more solid was needed. I jumped down and searched through the boxes. Nothing. Even in the cool temperature, I could feel the nervous sweat beading on my forehead. Tears of frustration blurred my eyes. I was doomed. There was nothing here.

I sat down on the floor beside the flashlight. The beam was definitely getting weaker. This was not a job I could do in darkness. Think. Think of something!

My head ached again. Mingled with thoughts of escape were strong sensations of hunger and thirst. Visions of the freshly-baked cookies on the tray in Charles Sheffield's study tortured me.

With a weary sigh, I rose and began my hunt again. When I got to the refrigerator, I tugged open the door and stared dully at empty shelves. A sudden thought emerged from my foggy brain. The shelves!

"Good old steel." I laughed aloud, resuming my perch on top of the old icebox. The shelf slipped easily into the crevice. Pushing down, I heard the welcome creak of protest from the old timber. Debris rained on my head as I strained against the wood. My God, the thing was heavy. I pushed again with all my strength, and finally, it moved upward enough for me to grab the board I'd balanced against the wall. I shoved it into the space, safely propping the door open. There was a rush of cool, damp air.

Calling on strength I didn't think I possessed, I shoved the trapdoor up and back, my sense of triumph mingling with the knifelike pain in my ribs.

After retrieving the flashlight and using my shirt sleeve to dust the debris from the top of the refrigerator, I hauled myself up through the hole and lay on my back until the pain subsided. Smart guys, those monks. I would bet money that Claudia and Company didn't know about the trapdoor. And they must not find out. I'd have to lower it again.

I thought it was strange that there was no handle or latch attached to the top to pull it up, so I rested it on the metal shelf. It left just enough room for me to pry it open with my fingers.

Turning, I shined the light around. Just as I thought. Openings high enough to crawl through yawned from opposite directions. For a few seconds, I toyed with the wild notion of venturing into one of the tunnels and just as quickly dismissed it. The ever-weakening beam of my flashlight rendered that sheer folly. I clicked it off to save what little energy was left and lay in the dark, so hungry, thirsty and exhausted, I couldn't even muster up a feeling of panic about my seemingly hopeless situation.

I finally decided that I'd rather die peacefully in the dark than face the horror of what lay ahead of me in the room below. On that dismal thought I fell into a deep sleep.

35

I'm not sure how long I'd been asleep when I heard the screaming. I jerked awake. A slit of gray light seeped through the crack.

"You bungling fool!" Claudia's shrill voice turned my spine into a column of ice. "How could you do something so stupid? Do you have any idea what is going to happen to us if she has escaped? I could kill you!"

"She has to be here someplace," came Charles' anxious voice. I heard boxes being moved, frantic scraping. Don't look up, I prayed fervently.

"You pathetic son of a bitch, you didn't lock the door properly," accused Claudia.

"I did! I swear I did. Ask Raoul."

"Oh, Jesus Christ," she shrieked. "I don't have time to argue about this. Get on the phone to Roy. Tell him to get his ass back here right away."

"But, he just left an hour ago. He's going to be real mad about this," Charles whimpered.

"Never mind. I'll call him. In the meantime, we have to find her."

"What shall I do, Sissy?"

"Just get out of my sight. Get Raoul and Carlos to help you search the grounds. Do you think you can handle that?"

There was a thick silence for a few seconds and then Charles complained, "I still think it's impossible. No one's ever gotten out of here before. Let's look again."

"What do you think she did?" snapped Claudia. "Climb through the ceiling?"

Her words turned my stomach over. I held my breath waiting for the worst, but then I heard their voices moving away.

After several silent minutes passed, an amazing realization cut through my fear. I hadn't heard the door close. I scrambled to my feet, pried open the trap door, and cautiously peeked down. Faint light from distant windows streamed through the open doorway. I sent a prayer of thanks to God, then lowered myself down. Alert for any sound, I moved with deliberate care across the basement to the head of the stairway.

I hesitated. Deliverance from my prison presented a new set of problems and might only serve to plunge me into further danger. I had no idea which direction would lead to freedom. Others held here against their will had escaped, I reminded myself. The question was, how?

When I eased the kitchen door open a few inches, I got two shocks. First, it was pouring rain, and second, the clock above the stove where the cook stood with her back to me read four o'clock! A tantalizing whiff of whatever she was cooking made my stomach rumble. Yesterday's lunch seemed light-years away.

When she suddenly turned in my direction, I ducked away, shut the door, and ran back down the steps. Expecting to hear her behind me, I frantically searched for a place to hide, finally wedging myself behind a pile of boxes. In breathless silence, I waited and then it hit me. Without my wig, how was I going to move about unnoticed? By now, the entire staff would no doubt be on the alert.

When the cook didn't appear, I collapsed in relief. For a while I just laid on the floor, my knees drawn up to my chin. Then I thought of something. I still had the makeup on and I fingered for the dark glasses in my shirt pocket. All I had to do now was figure out how to conceal my red hair.

Quietly, I rummaged through boxes and shelves. My search ended in one of the scrub buckets piled against the far wall. With a surge of elation, I pulled out a pile of stiff rags and chose a worn bandanna which I tied tightly around my head. Then I picked up the bucket, grabbed a mop, and headed up the steps. One thing I knew for certain. Risk or no, I had to have a look into the area where the supposed patients were kept. After that, I didn't know.

I cracked the door once again and waited patiently until the cook had her back to me, then swiftly opened the door, crossed the few feet to the doorway and out into the hall. It was mercifully empty so I hurried to the double doors Rosa had shown me the night before and slipped into the open breezeway that she'd indicated connected the main building to the patient wing.

The overhanging palm fronds thrashing in the wind protected me somewhat, but my head scarf and clothes were damp before I reached the arched doorway and crept inside.

The long hallway, adorned with colorful posters of rock stars, was painted a delicate pink and lined with large potted plants. I'd only gone a few feet when I heard footsteps. My heart lurched painfully as a heavy-set Hispanic woman rounded a corner and began speaking to me in rapid Spanish. By her tone, I could tell that she was issuing an order, but not one word did I understand. Squelching the knot of panic that coiled in my stomach, I fought to keep my presence of mind. It was only her gesture toward the muddy footprints on the white tile floor that saved me.

"*Sí*," I answered, pushing the damp string mop across the floor. Apparently that was the right thing to do, for she turned and continued out the door behind me.

I let out a shuddery breath. That had been way too close. Self-preservation told me I needed to stay out of sight and I sent up a hopeful prayer that Yolanda would get the note to Tugg by five.

I mopped my way down the hall, noting that each closed door was painted in a muted pastel. It was strangely quiet. Rounding a corner, I collided head on with a girl probably in her early teens. "Jesus!" I whispered, reaching out my hands to steady both of us.

"I'm sorry," she mumbled, barely glancing at me. Puzzled, I watched her shuffle away. She moved like someone in a trance. How odd.

A door opened to my right, so I dipped my chin and pushed the mop again. Out of the corner of my eye I saw a pretty blonde girl walked past me, her expression calm, almost dreamy. I stifled a gasp of surprise. It was Jenny from the shelter. Unreal. My theory was coming eerily to life.

I followed her, pausing as she stepped out onto a spacious glass enclosed patio. Raindrops pounded the roof and rivers of water cascaded down the tall windows. Through the mist, Castle Rock loomed large.

Secreted behind an enormous potted rubber plant, I surveyed what must be the recreation room. Jenny called a greeting to several girls sprawled comfortably on sofas in front of a big screen television. Four other teens played ping-pong at the other end of the room.

I stared in fascination as one of the girls rose from the couch and waddled by, her belly swollen in pregnancy. In fact, with the exception of Jenny, each of the girls appeared to be in some stage of impending motherhood.

It took a few seconds for the awful truth of the matter to sink into my tired brain. What in heaven's name was going on here? My mind whirled in confusion and then my neck prickled when I sensed someone behind me.

I spun around and stared directly into Eric Heisler's chilly blue eyes. The gun in his hand was pointed directly at my chest. "My dear Kendall. What a pity you didn't listen to me and get out of town while you had the chance."

36

The body can only handle so much distress, I decided, as a feeling of numbness radiated over me. I stood unmoving when Eric stepped close and fastened talon-like fingers around my upper arm. A waft of his expensive aftershave tickled my nose. He looked wonderful in his well-cut, charcoal gray suit and as out of place as a snowman in the desert.

.   "Mr. Richardson," said a soft voice behind me. "I need to talk to you about the baby, about the money."

Several other voices chorused the name. Mr. Richardson? I glanced up. The expression on his handsome face was tranquil, but his eyes reflected a glimmer of apprehension. He swallowed convulsively and strengthened his grip, pulling me to his side. I felt the warning jab of the revolver in my sore ribs. "I can't speak with you right now, my dear," he said, his tone smooth as velvet. "I have an important meeting with my...honored guest here. But, I'll return shortly and we'll talk."

Instinctively, I stiffened as he urged me into a turn. "Don't do anything to upset the girls," he ordered in a harsh whisper. "Come along quietly, and you won't be hurt."

As we moved along the deserted hallway, I fought to make sense of what I'd witnessed. All the girls were pregnant. One of them asked about money. Money for what? What was Eric's connection? I mentally sifted through the data in my notebook and suddenly the misty curtain of confusion began to lift. Wait a minute! My hypothesis about Claudia and Roy was all wrong. The new theory emerging was so monstrous, so outrageous, it was an effort to contain my rising panic.

When we reached the study, he closed the door behind us and sat me firmly in a chair. "Stay there." He moved to the window, looked out, and then began to pace back and forth. Beads of sweat glistened on his forehead.

I began, "Eric, what in the hell..."

He brandished the gun in my direction. "Shut up! I'm trying to think."

I cringed inwardly. It was different, oh, so different, to see him shaken, his cool facade cracked and peeled away.

"Damn it! Why couldn't you mind your own business? All I needed was a little more time."

My mind worked feverishly. I felt it was crucial to keep him talking, but it was an effort to keep the tremor from my voice. "So, that's why you killed John Dexter. He found out about your baby-selling scheme, didn't he?"

He looked stricken. "I didn't! It was an accident."

"And those three girls? You're going to tell me they were accidents too?"

His tongue flicked over his lips. "That was unfortunate. But, I couldn't have them talking to anyone. It would have ruined everything." As his pacing continued, I could see his mind racing behind his eyes.

Unexpectedly, he moved close beside me and stood without speaking. Was he going to shoot me now? I closed my eyes and then recoiled with surprise when I felt his fingers caress my hair.

"We could be so good for each other, Kendall." I suppressed a shudder. To think I had been alone with this maniac. And I'd let him kiss me. "It was never my intent to see anyone harmed," he continued, "but, sometimes to achieve something truly great, sacrifices have to be made. Do you understand what I'm saying?" His breathing was sharp, uneven.

Keep him calm, I warned myself, a wary eye on the gun hanging limply in his right hand. "I'm not sure I do," I said in a soothing voice. "Why don't you explain it to me."

"It's so very simple. You see, I figured out a way to perform a very important service for society. Everyone involved benefits." His tone of voice worried me. It had an almost singsong quality. "Think about it. I rescue these poor homeless waifs, who no doubt would end up on drugs or in jail, or most likely dead, and provide for them a stable, comfortable environment. The best of everything. Food, clothing, medical care. And in return, they supply a valuable and rare commodity. I've made so many people happy. There are countless couples in this country crying out for healthy white children." He shrugged. "I provide them."

The ring of sincerity in his voice made my throat tighten. This man was definitely on the edge. Why hadn't I seen it? With great effort, I kept my face bland. "Let's see if I have this right. Your friend Claudia lures these already troubled girls to the shelter, chooses the ones she feels will be good candidates, brings them here, they are..." I almost retched on the words. "They are impregnated by Charles Sheffield alias Dr. Price. He provides maternity care, delivers his own babies, and then you auction them off to the highest bidder, is that about it?"

He tipped my face toward his. "I hate the tone of accusation in your voice. Please say you understand the importance of what I'm doing here."

"Of course. Of course, I understand." To myself, I added, I understand all right. You prey on innocent people. You're playing God, selectively breeding people the same way Tally breeds his prize appaloosa horses.

He smiled with satisfaction. "See, I knew you would once I explained it. Rochelle was so wrong about you."

"Rochelle?"

"Claudia to you. She's so impetuous. She wanted to kill you right away, but I told her no. Another dead reporter would arouse too much suspicion." He knelt in front of me and laid the gun on the floor. "I need your silence and your cooperation. I don't want to have to kill you, Kendall."

"That sounds like a good plan to me."

A frown wrinkled his forehead. "I suppose we could keep you here for a while. Just until things die down about poor Tanya."

"Tanya?"

"The girl you and Doug found." He sighed. "Why she would want to leave the paradise I've created here, I'll never know. But," he added, brightening, "Roy will take care of things, and then you and I can go away for a while." He searched my eyes for a response. "Maybe to Europe. What do you think of that?"

I didn't know whether to laugh or cry. Go away with him, or die? Some choice. Acutely aware of the gun only a few inches from my grasp, I managed a stiff smile. To my horror, he gathered me in his arms. I tried not to wince as his lips touched mine.

It was a struggle to keep from shoving him away. Carefully, I edged my hand downward toward the floor. Just then, the door behind him flew open. Eric jerked away, and we both gaped at the vision in the doorway. Claudia's face was at first a white mask of shock, and then realization colored her sharp features. Her lips pinched together like a drawstring bag and a look of cold hatred glittered in her eyes. "You miserable, lying bastard!"

Before I could grab it, Eric scooped the gun into his pocket and scrambled to his feet. "Rochelle!" His distracted gaze darted quickly between the two of us. "I...I didn't hear you come in."

"Obviously." She fingered a small caliber handgun that matched her deadly expression. She raised it toward him. "I heard what you said to her. You never did love me, did you? You've been using me all these years just like you use every one else. I'm not going to do it this time. I refuse to stand by and let you make a fool of me twice."

"Now, darling," he said, starting to move toward her. "Calm down. I can explain everything."

"Stay where you are!" Her hands shook and Eric froze in his tracks. "I don't want to hear any more of your lies. Five years I sacrificed for you," she continued, her chest heaving. "Five long years. I do all the dirty work, I take all the risk, and what do I get? Shit! Just wait one more year, my love," she grimaced, mimicking his voice. "And then we'll be married. Yeah, right. You son of a bitch, I'll kill this red-headed whore just like I killed your precious Stephanie!" She let out a peal of hysterical laughter and then a thick silence settled over the room. They stood as still as two mannequins, staring at each other.

I was stunned. Claudia had killed Stephanie Talverson? While they evil-eyed each other, I slid to the floor beside the chair. The look on Eric's face was murderous. "You killed her? You?" "Did you think I'd just stand by and do nothing while you screwed your new little playmate right in front of my nose? Did you?" He hadn't needed much to send him over the edge, but that did it. Shouting, "You vicious bitch!" he lunged for her. There was a momentary scuffle and the gun went off. I ducked behind the chair and heard her scream in terror. "Eric! I'm sorry. Forgive me. Darling, please forgive me." There was a second shot, a thump, and then stillness.

"Jesus H. Christ!" I whispered. Hardly daring to breathe, I poked my head around the chair. Gun in hand, Eric stood over her unmoving form. He turned slowly toward me. I stared at the growing red stain on his left shoulder then met his panic-glazed eyes.

"My God. I've killed her! I didn't mean to do it," he choked, looking wildly around the room. "It was self defense. She was crazy! You could see that, couldn't you?"

I needed to do something, say something, but I was speechless.

"I have to get out of here," Eric said suddenly, moving to the desk. He laid his gun down and swore as he touched the bullet wound in his shoulder. "No evidence," he mumbled, frantically pulling folders from a drawer and tucking them under his arm. "Mustn't leave any evidence behind. Nothing to implicate me. They'll think Charles did it." He chuckled, and then a sob caught in his throat. I almost felt sorry for him. He was pathetic and appeared to be losing touch with reality.

Slowly, I rose to my feet and pictured myself dashing across the room to get Claudia's gun. Even if I did, I had no experience with firearms. Only in the movies did the heroine pick up a loaded gun for the first time in her life and shoot the villain squarely in the heart. "Eric, you might as well give it up. You can't kill everybody," I said, a sudden calm stealing over me. "Charles knows, the girls know, I know, and by now Morton Tuggs knows."

He looked at me blankly. "Morton Tuggs?"

"I left him a note. He knows about all of you. Even Roy."

Dismay clouded his face and he leaned heavily against the desk. I started to move toward the door when he looked up at me. The malevolence in his eyes punctured my fleeting sense of triumph. "Well then, you will have to be my ticket out of here."

My mouth went dry. "What do you mean?"

He looked smug as he picked up his revolver and aimed it at me. "Very simple. You're going to act as my shield. If anyone tries to stop me, I'll kill you."

"It won't work."

"Of course it will," he said, his voice brimming with superiority. "Mexico is less than an hour from here by air. Turn around," he growled, shoving me against the wall. He dug his knee painfully into the small of my back, wrenched my arms behind me, whipped off his necktie and bound my wrists. "There," he grunted, pulling the knot tight, "you may think you're smarter than I am, but you're not. Move!"

Eric's wild mood swings terrified me. Woodenly, I moved down the stairs. He stayed close behind. The rain had stopped and the air felt warm and clammy. The sky to the north looked ominously dark. When we reached his Mercedes, he shoved me in the driver's side and roughly

SYLVIA NOBEL

pushed me to the passenger seat. Then, he climbed in, still pointing the gun at me. I wondered why. Did he expect me to grab the gun with my teeth?

He backed out and then jerked to a halt as Charles ran up and banged on his window. Eric's jaw muscles worked furiously. "Goddamned pervert," he whispered under his breath, pushing the button to lower the window a few inches.

"Hey, Eric, don't worry," Charles panted, "we're going to find her. She has to be here..." His words died as he stared dumbfounded at me, then looked anxiously at Eric. "Does Rochelle know you have her? Where are you going?"

"I have my own plans for Ms. O'Dell, Charles. Rochelle knows all about it."

"I thought we agreed to take care of the problem here."

"Why don't you run upstairs and talk to her. She'll explain things to you."

"So, everything goes on just as always?"

"Yes."

I had the notion, by the whiteness of Eric's knuckles as he clutched the steering wheel, that if the gun hadn't been pointed at me, he'd have shot Charles with no qualms.

He ran the window back up, terminating the conversation. Charles backed away from the car, looking uncertain, and then bolted for the main building.

Eric saluted the guard, and once the gates and snarling dogs were behind us, I felt a slight sense of relief. Perhaps I could convince him to set me free.

I couldn't believe the transformation of Lost Canyon Road. There must have been an extraordinary amount of rain to cause the wide crevices and deep puddles. No sooner

345

had the thought crossed my mind than Eric slammed on the brakes. In front of us, the normally dry wash was running like a river. I stared, fascinated, at the churning water and sensed his hesitation as he read the DO NOT CROSS WHEN FLOODED sign. "We can make it," he stated firmly. "I've done it before."

My heart skipped. "Eric! Don't be crazy. You'll drown us both!"

Ignoring me, he lowered both front windows, and then arched over me to study the water level. "I just crossed this a few hours ago. It isn't that high."

"It looks too dangerous." He gave me a disdainful look. "I've lived in Arizona all my life. I know what I'm doing." He eased the car into the swollen wash. Stiff with fright, I watched the water climb, and then a movement ahead caught my attention. Was that a car coming this way?

I tucked my knees under me and sprang for the open window, screaming, "Help! Help me!"

Eric reached out, hooked his fingers into my belt, and dragged me back beside him. He grabbed a handful of my hair and twisted it painfully. "Sit still."

I struggled against him and then our movements froze as we both became aware of the strange noise at the same time. It sounded like the roar of a freight train.

The look of puzzlement in Eric's eyes switched to horror. I turned and saw a wall of water at least three feet high, headed right for us. Eric's screams mingled with my own as the churning brown tide struck the car.

37

A wave of cold water slapped me, the force of it jamming me between the dashboard and steering wheel. With my nose almost touching the windshield, I watched in horror as we rocketed down the wash. When the car ricocheted off the embankment, I was thrown painfully against the passenger door. After choking on the third mouthful of muddy water, I decided to quit screaming and concentrate on my next breath. Caught in the swirling, churning current, the car bounced and bucked liked a wild bronco.

"Eric!" I shouted. "Untie me!" He paid no attention. When the top of a jagged rock loomed ahead I screamed, "Look out!" We hit head on. The sudden stop punched the air from my lungs. Fumbling madly with my bonds, I watched with despair as Eric began to scramble out the window.

"Wait, I can't swim like this! Help me!"

Ignoring my plea, he clawed for a hold on the rock, still half in and half out of the car when another surge of water sent us spinning away. Eric cried out and pitched forward, flailing his arms wildly. To my amazement, he ended up clinging to the hood ornament. For a brief second, our eyes met. I read death in them. His face looked almost serene as he yelled, "Tell Mother...I'm sorry."

Then, the force of the water tore him away. In a matter of seconds, he disappeared into the rain swollen wash. "Jesus!" I screamed, struggling desperately to get loose. The car was twisting in a circle now, adding disorientation to my waking nightmare.

The water-soaked cloth around my wrists finally loosened, and I jerked my hands free as the car jolted to a stop once again, lodged on something below the surface. In fascinated horror, I stared at the swiftly running water only a few inches below the windows.

Stranded in the middle of the wash, the banks on either side probably less than fifteen feet away, I had no doubt I'd meet the same fate as Eric if I tried to make it to shore. It would be best for now to stay put and wait for help. That idea was short lived as the car settled further and water began to pour in.

There was nothing to do but climb onto the roof. I scrambled out and up, spread-eagling myself face down on the slippery surface. I clamped my fingers around the window frames and hung on, alternately praying and shouting for help. Whoever had been in that vehicle on the road must have seen what happened.

Overhead, thunder rumbled in the storm-darkened sky. "Oh, no," I groaned. The quickening wind blew against my wet clothes, sending me into shivery spasms. When the first big drops of rain splattered on my back, I closed my eyes and waited for the worst. Thoughts of my childhood and all those I loved, played out before me.

The steady blasts of a horn jerked me to reality. I squinted through the driving rain and felt a jolt of disbelief. It didn't seem possible, but Tally stood on the muddy embankment waving his hat and shouting something I couldn't hear as he held up a coil of rope.

Gesturing with his hands, he began to run upstream. I was saved! A sensation of overwhelming relief swept over me. I'd never been so glad to see anyone before in my life. How had he found me? That must have been him on the road. I craned my neck in his direction and willed my stiff, aching fingers to continue their hold. He strapped on an orange lifejacket, secured the rope around a tree, tied the other end under his arms, and then waded into the water.

Forever. It seemed like forever, but suddenly, as if in a dream, he was there beside me. The rushing water brought him against the car with a resounding thump.

"Kendall! Are you all right?"

"I think so," I gasped.

He pulled in the slack and wound the rope around the side-view mirror, anchoring him closer to me. "I've already radioed the sheriff's posse for help. Whose car is this?" he shouted, uncoiling another piece of rope.

"Eric Heisler's."

"Heisler? Where is he?"

"Dead."

"What happened?"

"Tally," I panted. "It's a terribly long story. Can we talk later? I just want to get out of here."

"I'm working on it," he said grimly, and then added with a glint of humor in his eyes, "you said you wanted rain. Well, you got it."

"Very funny."

"Here." He extended a section of the shorter rope to me. "Can you tie this around your chest?"

The thought of cinching it tightly around my sore ribs wasn't pleasant, but there was no choice. "I guess so." Tentatively, I let go with one hand and grasped the cord. He reached up and grabbed my thigh, steadying me as I let go of the other side and rolled onto my back. The effort to tie the knot left me breathless. "What do we do now?"

He tied the other end of the short rope onto his knot. "You come into the water with me. The current will carry us to shore."

I hesitated, staring at the muddy, foaming water, and then met his eyes. They reflected concern, confidence, and something else. He held out one hand to me. "Tally, you promised not to rescue me again."

"Request permission to break my promise."

"Permission granted." I edged toward him, then stiffened in fright at the sight of a massive log rushing at him. "Tally! Look out!" Before he could react the log struck him from behind, smashing him into the side of the car. He fell face forward into the choppy water. Still connected together at the chest by the short rope, I felt the sharp tug against me. The longer length of rope, still attached to the tree trunk on shore, strained, and finally snapped under the weight of the tree trunk.

"Tally!" Without another thought for myself, I jumped into the raging current and pulled his head above water. His head lolled to the side, resting atop the life vest. Thank heaven for that.

But as I watched the end of the rope trail uselessly away in the torrent, it was difficult to quell the surge of hysteria. Just keep his head above water, I urged myself, taking up the slack between us. I wound the middle of the rope around the mirror and that helped hold me upright while my legs were pounded with rocks, sticks, and unknown debris sweeping by.

The storm seemed never-ending and my spirits sagged as darkness settled. Where was the back up he'd ordered? Someone had to find us soon. "Tally! Wake up. Please wake up." All around us, extraordinary forks of magenta lightning slashed the sky, followed by deafening cracks of thunder.

I hugged his body close to mine, surprised at the depth of feeling I had for this man. The lump on the center of his forehead expanded and I ran my fingers over it, trailed them down to his cheeks, which I patted gently, then traced his lips, thinking it was an extremely odd time to want to kiss him.

"A little mouth to mouth might not be a bad idea," he said with a weak grin, his eyes opening slowly.

"Tally! Thank God. How long have you been conscious?"

"Long enough."

"Are you all right?"

He grimaced and let out a groan. "Except for the fact that I think my arm is broken, yeah."

"It's all my fault. What now?"

"We wait."

"For what?"

"DPS will be on their way by now," he said, squinting upward. "The worst of the storm seems to be over."

No sooner had he spoken than we heard the unmistakable clatter of helicopter blades. The chopper swung over the nearby trees, shining its cold blue light down on us. Then it was directly overhead, the sound earsplitting, the blast of air from the blades whipping my hair across my face.

I insisted the paramedic take Tally first because of his arm. He protested, but I won out. It seemed like another hour spent in the cold water before the basket came back down for me. It was a dizzying ride up, swinging back and forth in the wind.

It felt wonderful to have the blanket wrapped around me, a steaming drink cupped in both hands. Tally didn't make a sound as the paramedic fussed and fiddled with his arm. He kept his jaw locked, his eyes fixed on me. Despite the warmth of the blanket, my teeth continued to chatter uncontrollably.

"Is there something I can get for you, miss?" the young man asked, turning his attention to me.

I kept eye contact with Tally. "Yeah. Right now, a big plate of hot tamales sounds pretty good to me."

38

A week had gone by and Castle Valley was still abuzz, rocked to the core by the revelation of Eric's sordid "baby mill" operation—just as John Dexter had predicted.

Claudia, (I could never think of her as Rochelle) survived her gunshot wounds. After the discovery of Eric's body the following day, she and Charles confessed their part in the scheme, and Roy was picked up by the U.S. marshall's office. To my immense relief, Rosa had been discovered hiding in the shed where Dexter's truck had been concealed. The door had always been locked prior to my break in, so the guards didn't think to look there. Charles admitted he'd had orders to destroy the truck, but had let greed get the better of him. He'd planned to use it later after interest in Dexter's disappearance had died down.

I thought about these things and others, as I hunched over Tugg's desk proof-reading the day's copy. He had asked me to take charge during his recuperation from surgery. Everyone at the office had gladly pitched in, and there was a lot of excitement when my first-person story was picked up by the wire service.

Amid all the praise, I had to humbly remind myself how foolish and how lucky I'd been. My injuries were mild, a couple of cracked ribs, compared to Tally's concussion and shattered arm, which had required two surgeries. We had talked briefly two or three times on the phone, but because of my long working hours I'd only had a chance to visit him a short time at the hospital in Phoenix and even then, he'd been too groggy to talk much.

The investigation at Serenity House had unearthed more gruesome details. Not only had sheriff's deputies discovered the body of Dexter buried in the ancient cemetery, also found were the remains of eight teenage girls. Autopsies revealed they had either died in childbirth or been shot as Dexter had. Traces of the same drug were found in each girl's body.

Charles Sheffield acknowledged his use of Thorazine, a drug commonly used to subdue mental patients. It had kept the girls calm, yet not harmed the fetuses. Claudia had also dispensed it at the shelter to make the girls easy to handle. It made sense now why Roy had gone to such lengths to keep the toxicology reports from both Dexter and myself.

It still bothered me greatly that I'd almost fallen prey to Eric's evil charms. The job offer and declarations of love had all been part of a masterful ploy to lure me away from the house. Claudia had confessed her role in playing the "ghost" outside my bedroom that had easily frightened away the former tenants. When that and the spider episode failed, she had arranged for Roy to ambush me in the darkroom. Eric had ordered her to stop, but because of her obsession for him, she hadn't been able to resist leaving the threatening message on my recorder.

Her confession also contained other fascinating information that filled in some of the gaps. Eric's affair with Claudia had brought him into contact with Charles after he'd been released from prison. Broke and minus his medical license, Charles had fallen deeply into debt. It was during that period that Thena asked for Eric's help, and the real Dr. Price, who'd been little known in the community, had died in a Phoenix hospital. Because Eric was executor of his estate, and Dr. Price had no relatives, he was the only one aware of his passing. The realization of just how lucrative the adoption business could be, and the idea to increase the supply of babies, led to the demise of poor Violet Mendoza, who'd been coldbloodedly run down by Claudia. Roy had altered the eyewitness report and a week later Claudia slipped into the dead woman's position at the shelter.

Meanwhile, Eric was secretly funneling the real mental patients to other institutions, and then Charles, in full disguise, was installed as the new Dr. Price. That certainly explained why Thena Rodenborn hadn't recognized his voice the second time she spoke to him about exploring the old monastery. And it was also crystal clear why he'd left the table so suddenly the night of the fund-raiser and hadn't stopped the day he'd run me off the road.

The sharp ringing of Tugg's phone interrupted my thoughts. He announced he'd just arrived home from the hospital and wanted to know how things were going. It had been a zoo without him and Tally, but we'd all worked long hours to get the paper out. "I'm proofing my article for Wednesday's edition, now," I informed him.

"I feel like I've been on the moon for two weeks," he complained. "What other evidence has turned up?"

"Deputy Potts called me a while ago. They found another body yesterday. Charles has confirmed that it's the Hispanic girl who first contacted Dexter."

"No kidding? The one who wanted to exchange information for money and the ticket to Nogales?"

"Right. That's why I never heard from her again."

"Jee-zuss! What else?"

"This is hard to believe, but Caesarean sections were performed on several of the girls before their due dates. Eric apparently needed the extra cash to cover land payments."

"Un-friggin'-believable."

"He would have collected almost two hundred thousand by the end of the month with the births of four babies, enough to pay the note due on the tennis ranch."

Tugg groaned. "This is the sickest thing I have ever heard."

We talked a while longer about work and then Tugg told me the real reason for his call. As I listened to his intriguing proposal, a delicious surge of anticipation warmed my cheeks. His news, coupled with the call from his wife earlier in the week, added another dimension to my growing list of options.

By the time I reached home, the evening sky was a celebration of color, the bright amber rays transforming the spires of Castle Rock into a golden crown.

I was fishing for the keys to the front door when I heard a vehicle approaching. My skin tingled with delight as Tally's truck rolled into the driveway.

Jake waved at me from the driver's seat and I saw Tally's warm smile. I got a memory flash of the first time I'd seen the two of them at the top of Yarnell Hill last

spring, how frightened I'd been of the javelinas, how much
Tally's surly attitude had enraged me. Time had changed a
lot of things.

I crossed to the truck and opened Tally's door. The
white sling around his arm contrasted with his brick-red
shirt.

"He's not supposed to be up and out yet, is he,
Jake?" I chided. Tally had a look of pained concentration as
he stepped from the truck.

"I tried to stop him, miss, but, he'd have none of it."
His tanned face wrinkled in a cheery smile.

"Aren't you glad to see me?" Tally's eyes reflected
mock indignation and the hint of a question.

"Of course I am." The mere sight of him had my
pulse racing, and I wished I could forget that he'd gone to
Colorado with Lucinda.

Jake pulled a brown paper bag from the truck, thrust
it into Tally's hand, and then waved good-bye, saying he'd
return after running errands in town.

We stood close together, facing each other, our eyes
locked. I hoped I wasn't reading too much into his intent
expression. The silence stretched between us until he finally
said, "Do me a favor, would you? The next time you decide
to do white-water rafting, I suggest you get something a
little more seaworthy than a Mercedes."

"I was up for something different that day. But, I
will take your advice."

He paused again. I knew that wasn't what he'd
planned to say, but it was an easy conversation opener.

"How's your arm?" I asked.

"I won't be doing any roping for a while."

"I feel awful about that. Would you like to come in
and sit down?"

"In a minute. Right now I'm enjoying being up and outside again. I'm not a very good hospital patient, I'm afraid."

I grinned. "Why doesn't that surprise me?"

He returned my smile. "When I wasn't drugged on pain killers, I read your articles. I guess I'm going to have to eat my words." His eyes glinted with humor. "Not only are you anything but a delicate damsel, you're also quite a cunning detective."

"Thank you."

His expression grew serious. "What's going to happen to those girls?" He nodded toward Serenity House.

"It's going to be an awful mess to untangle, if that's even possible. Some couples paid for babies they'll never get, and a few of the girls want their babies back. The problem is, the adoption records were lost in the flooded wash."

"I told you Heisler was a slime."

"He was more than that. He was a psychopath."

He cleared his throat and shifted his weight. His discomfort was obvious. Clearly, he had something more to say.

I broke the silence. "So, how was Colorado?"

He faced me squarely. "Just so you'll know, Lucy came along to buy another mare. She shared a room with Ronda, not me."

It was hard to hide my elation.

He extended the package to me. "This is for you."

Puzzled, I opened the bag and pulled out a cream-colored western hat. Running my hand over the smooth felt, I marveled, "It's beautiful. But, you already gave me one the day..."

He placed one finger gently against my lips, silencing me. "Shhhh. This one didn't belong to someone else. It's a small thing for saving my life."

I blurted out, "But, you saved mine first."

"I think we're even now in the rescue department, but it's more than that. I feel like you saved me twice over." His finger slid from my lips to caress my cheek. "I've been among the walking wounded for two years, carrying that load of guilt, thinking my mother was responsible for Stephanie's death. You'll never know what a relief it was to find out it was Claudia."

"I think I have a pretty good idea."

"Let me help you," he said, positioning the hat on my head. "It looks good on you. Natural."

"Thank you."

"Kendall..."

My heartbeat quickened with wild anticipation. "Yes?"

"I heard about your job offer in Phoenix, and Ginger told me a national magazine is interested in you as well...so, I guess that means you'll be leaving soon?"

I glanced at the full moon pushing its way over the mountain and took a deep breath of clear, desert air. "Well, it just so happens that a third option has presented itself."

"And, what would that be?"

"Tugg just informed me that Thena Rodenborn has acquired the *Sun* and he's decided to resign and do the traveling he's always dreamed about. That leaves the position of editor open."

"Interesting."

"The other thing is that Tess Delgado has decided to move into one of those retirement properties, so...I'm thinking about making an offer on this place."

"Is that so?"

"Uh-huh."

"Does this mean you might consider staying on?"

"I'm giving it careful thought."

He leaned closer, slipping his free arm around my waist. When his lips pressed against mine, gently this time, the stars seemed to explode and shower down from the sky.

Breathless, we pulled apart. He tipped the brim of his hat back from his face in that familiar, endearing gesture.

"Well, now, ma'am," he said in his best western drawl, "you reckon there's any way I could convince you to think about putting the O'Dell Ranch under the Starfire brand?"

I looked up at him, pushing back the brim of my hat. "Well, sir, I reckon you could try."

Sylvia Nobel currently resides in Phoenix, Arizona with her husband and eight cats. She is a member of Sisters in Crime and Mystery Writers of America

We hope you enjoyed **_DEADLY SANCTUARY!!_** If you did, would you take a few minutes to share your thoughts with us? _____

_____

I purchased the book at _____

Also, if you would like to receive a postcard informing you when the next Kendall O'Dell mystery is published, we will place you on our mailing list or you can e-mail us at: <u>theniteowl@juno.com</u>   Web address: <u>www.niteowlbooks.com</u>

Name _____

Address _____ City _____ State ____ Zip ____

Mail to: Nite Owl Books, 4040 E. Camelback Road, Suite 101
          Phoenix, Arizona 85018 Ph: 602-840-0132 or 1-888-927-9600